"Johansen has consistently taken huge narrative risks with this series. . . . With richly developed characters who are never boring black-and-white, and villains who are as fascinating as the heroes, the finale of this outstanding series will be talked about by readers."
—*Library Journal*, Pick of the Month

"Find out the result of Queen Kelsea's bejeweled sacrifice in the finale of our favorite fantasy trilogy."
—*Entertainment Weekly*

"A heart-pounding, epic conclusion . . . one that's been eagerly anticipated, so if you haven't read the prior two books, you'll definitely want to get on top of that."
—*BuzzFeed*

The
Fate
OF THE
Tearling

Also by Erika Johansen

The Queen of the Tearling

The Invasion of the Tearling

VOLUME III

The
Fate
OF THE
Tearling

A Novel

Erika Johansen

HARPER

NEW YORK • LONDON • TORONTO • SYDNEY

First U.S. hardcover edition published 2016 by HarperCollins Publishers.

HarperCollins books may be purchased for educational, business, or sales promotional use. For information, please email the Special Markets Department at SPsales@harpercollins.com.

FIRST HARPER PAPERBACKS EDITION PUBLISHED 2017.

Designed by Leah Carlson-Stanisic

Map by Nick Springer Cartographics, LLC.

Image by Naturemania/Shutterstock, Inc.

Library of Congress Cataloging-in-Publication Data

Names: Johansen, Erika, author.
Title: The fate of the Tearling : a novel / Erika Johansen.
Description: First edition. | New York : Harper, [2016] | Series: Queen of the tearling ; 3
Identifiers: LCCN 2016032312| ISBN 9780062290427 (hardback) | ISBN 9780062290434 (ebook)
Subjects: LCSH: Queens–Fiction. | Alliances–Fiction. | Imaginary wars and battles–Fiction. | BISAC: FICTION / Literary. | FICTION / Fantasy / Epic. | GSAFD: Fantasy fiction.
Classification: LCC PS3610.O2546 F38 2016 | DDC 813/.6–dc23 LC record available at https://lccn.loc.gov/2016032312

ISBN 978-0-06-229044-1 (pbk.)

17 18 19 20 21 LSC 10 9 8 7 6 5 4 3 2 1

For Shane, who never asks me to be anyone else.

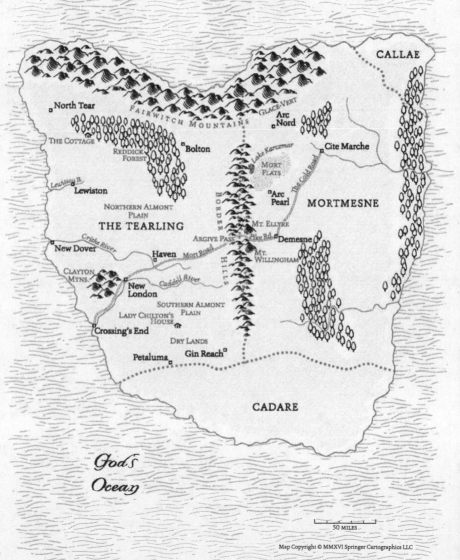

Fairwitch
Sea

CALLAE

North Tear

FAIRWITCH MOUNTAINS

GLACE-VERT

Arc
Nord

THE COTTAGE

Bolton

REDDICK
FOREST

Lake Karczmar

Cite Marche

Levieux R.

Lewiston

BORDER HILLS

MORT
FLATS

Arc
Pearl

The Cold Road

MORTMESNE

NORTHERN ALMONT
PLAIN

THE TEARLING

Crithe River

ARGIVE PASS

Mt. Ellyre

Pike Rd.

Demesne

New Dover

Haven

Mort Road

Mt.
Willingham

CLAYTON
MTNS.

New
London

Cuddell River

LADY CHILTON'S
HOUSE

SOUTHERN ALMONT
PLAIN

Crossing's End

DRY LANDS

Petaluma

Gin Reach

CADARE

God's
Ocean

50 MILES

Map Copyright © MMXVI Springer Cartographics LLC

The
Fate
OF THE
Tearling

The Orphan

Long before the Red Queen of Mortmesne came to power, the Glace-Vert was already a lost cause. It was a forgotten taiga in the shadow of the Fairwitch, its hardened plains revealing only the barest hint of grass, its few villages mere huddles of huts and mires. Few chose to venture north of Cite Marche, unless no other option presented itself, for life on these plains was harsh. Each summer the villagers of the Glace-Vert sweltered; each winter they froze and starved.

This year, however, they had something new to fear. The frozen hamlets were sealed tight, surrounded by newly built fences, and behind these fences men sat sleepless, hunting knives across their knees, little more than shadow sentinels. Clouds covered the moon, though these clouds did not yet signify the snows of Fairwitch winter. On the foothills above, wolves howled in their strange language, mourning the scarcity of food. Soon desperation would drive the packs south into the forests to hunt for squirrels and stoats, or the rare small child foolish enough to venture alone into the winter woods. But now, all at once, at ten minutes past two, the wolves fell silent. The only sound heard over the Glace-Vert was the lonely moan of the wind.

In the shadow of the foothills, something moved: the black figure of a man, climbing the steep slope. He was sure of foot, but he moved carefully, as though anticipating hazards. Except for his quick, light breathing, he was invisible, nothing more than a shade among the rocks. He had come through Ethan's Copse, stopping there for two days before continuing northward. During his time in the village, he had heard all manner of tales about the plague that beset its inhabitants: a creature who walked in the night, taking the young. This creature had an old name in the upper Fairwitch: the Orphan. The Glace-Vert had never had to worry about such things before, but now the disappearances were spreading south. After two days, the man had heard enough. Villagers might call it the Orphan, but the man knew the creature's real name, and though the man ran like a gazelle, he could not escape his own sense of responsibility.

He's free, the Fetch thought bleakly, wending his way through the thorns on the slope. *I didn't end him when I had the chance, and now he's free.*

The idea tormented him. He had ignored the presence of Row Finn in the Fairwitch for many years because the man was contained. Every few years a child would disappear; unfortunate, but there were greater evils to contend with. The Tearling, for starters, where nearly fifty children disappeared every month under a state seal of approval. Even before the vast evil of the shipment, the Tear had always been like a wayward child, needing constant care. The Raleighs alternated between indifference and predation, and the nobles fought for each scrap while the people starved. For three long centuries, the Fetch had watched William Tear's dream sink further and further into the mire. No one in the Tearling could even see Tear's better world any longer, let alone muster the courage to dig for it. Only the Fetch and his people knew, only they remembered. They did not age, did not die. The Fetch stole to entertain himself. He took a petty enjoyment in tormenting the worst of the Raleighs. He kept his eye on the Tear bloodline, almost idly, trying to convince himself that it might matter. Tear blood was easy to track, for certain qualities always presented eventually: integrity, intellectualism and iron resolve. A few Tears had been hanged as traitors over the years, but even under the noose, they never lost the subtle air of nobility that seemed to distinguish the family. The Fetch recognized this nobility: it was the aura of William Tear, the magnetism that had convinced nearly two thousand people to follow him across an ocean into a vast unknown. Even the Mort bitch, flawed as she was, carried a tiny hint of that glamour. But the Red Queen did not breed. For a long time, the Fetch had been convinced that the line was lost.

And then, the girl.

The Fetch hissed as a thorn dug into his hand. It did not puncture the skin; he had not bled in lifetimes. Many times he had tried to end himself, before giving it up as a lost cause. He and Row, both of them had been punished, but he saw now that he had been blind. Rowland Finn had never stopped plotting for one moment in his life. He, too, had been waiting for the girl.

She was the first Raleigh heir who did not grow up in the Keep. The Fetch observed her often, visiting the cottage in secret when he was idle, and sometimes even when he was not. Initially, he could not make out much. Kelsea Raleigh was a quiet child, introspective. Most of her education seemed to be in the hands of that eternal battleaxe Lady Glynn, but the Fetch sensed that the girl's personality was being quietly and surely shaped by the old Queen's Guard, Bartholemew. As she grew older, the girl surrounded herself with books, and this, more than anything, convinced the Fetch that she merited special attention. His memories of the Tears were constantly fading, losing their bright shine and becoming dim. But this he remembered: the Tears had always loved their books. One day he had watched the girl sit under a tree in front of the cottage and read a thick book all the way through in four or five hours. The Fetch had been hidden in the trees more than thirty feet away, but he knew absorption when he saw it; he could have crept up and sat down across from her and she would not have noticed. She *was* like the Tears, he saw now. She lived inside her head as much as out.

From that day on, one of his people had been on the cottage at all times. If a traveler showed a bit too much interest in the occupants—men had followed Bartholemew home from the country market several times—the interested party was never heard from again. The Fetch wasn't even sure why he exerted so much effort. It was a gut feeling, and one thing William Tear had drilled into them from the beginning was that instinct was a real thing, a thing to be trusted. The Fetch sensed that the girl was different. Important.

She could be a Tear, he told his crew one night over the fire. *She could be.*

It was always possible. There were several men in Elyssa's Guard whose origins he did not know. Tear or not, the girl demanded close scrutiny, and as the years passed, he subtly shifted his course. Whenever Thomas Raleigh showed signs of forging an actual alliance with one of the powerful nobles of the Tear, the Fetch would turn all of his attention toward that noble, robbing caravans and storehouses, stealing crops and then vanishing into the night. Enough theft on Thomas's watch, and any potential alliance was quickly soured. At the same time, the Fetch began to lay his own groundwork in Mortmesne, just beneath the Red Queen's feet. Should the girl make it to the throne, the Fetch knew, her first test would come in dealing with the shipment. Mortmesne was wide open to anyone who knew how to exploit unrest, and after years of patient work, there was a healthy rebellion under way. So many things to attend to over the years, and so he had naturally let Row Finn slide.

A shape rose suddenly from the rocks ahead, halting his climb. To anyone else, it would appear to be merely a dark silhouette, but the Fetch, who had a great gift of night vision, saw that it was a child: a young boy, five or six years old. His clothes were little more than rags, his skin pallid with the cold. His eyes were dark and impenetrable. His feet were bare.

The Fetch stared at the child for a moment, chilled to his marrow.

I didn't end him when I could have.

The boy darted forward, and the Fetch hissed at him, like a cat. The boy's eyes, which had brightened in anticipation, abruptly dimmed, and he stared at the Fetch, bewildered.

"I am not meat for you," the Fetch snapped. "Go and get your master."

The boy stared at him for a moment longer, then vanished into the rocks. The Fetch covered his eyes, feeling the world tip crazily inside him, a dark vortex. When the girl had cracked the New London Bridge, certainty had crystallized inside him, but all moments since then seemed like a parade of doubt. She was in Mort custody, and Howell's last message made clear that they were preparing to transport her to Demesne. The True Queen had arrived at last, but she had come too late.

Something was descending the slope. Just a wisp in the darkness, but it had been a long time since anyone could sneak up on the Fetch. He stood his ground, waiting. The last time they had sat down for a conversation had been . . . when? More than two centuries earlier, James Raleigh still on the throne. The Fetch had wanted to see if Row could kill him. The meeting had turned into a cutting party, all right, but neither of them had shed a drop of blood.

We were friends, the Fetch remembered suddenly. *Good friends.*

But those days had vanished into the distant past, several lifetimes gone. As the black shape before him resolved into a man, the Fetch steeled himself. The settlers of the Fairwitch had created a great deal of apocrypha around the Orphan, but at least one piece was true: they said that the creature had two faces, one light and one dark. Which one would he see today?

Light. The face that turned toward him was the same one the Fetch had always known: pale and autocratic. And sly. Row had always been able to talk circles around anyone; long ago, he had talked the Fetch into the worst decision of his life. They regarded each other in silence, standing on the windy slope, all of Mortmesne laid out behind them.

"What do you want?" Row asked.

"I want to talk you out of this." The Fetch swept a hand at the mountainside below them. "This course you're on. No good will come of it, not even for you."

"How do you know my course?"

"You're moving south, Row. I've seen your things stalking at night in the villages below the Glace-Vert. I don't know your endgame, but surely poor Mort villagers can have no part of it. Why not leave them alone?"

"My children are hungry."

The Fetch sensed movement on his right: another of them, a little girl of perhaps ten, perched on top of the rock, watching him, her eyes fixed and unblinking.

"How many children do you have now, Row?"

"Soon they will be a legion."

The Fetch stilled, feeling the dark hole inside him open a bit wider. "And then what?"

Row said nothing, only smiled wide. There was no humanity in that smile, and the Fetch fought the urge to back away.

"You already wrecked Tear's kingdom once, Row. You really need to do it again?"

"I had help in wrecking Tear's Land, my friend. Has it been so long that you've forgotten, or do you absolve yourself?"

"I feel responsible for my sins. I try to repair them."

"How are you faring with that?" Row spread an arm to encompass the land below them. "Mortmesne is an open sewer. The Tear continues to sink."

"No, it doesn't. It's been propped up."

"The girl?" Row laughed, a hollow, dismal sound. "Come now, Gav. The girl has nothing but a loyal retainer and a gift for public relations."

"You don't fool me, Row. You fear her as well."

Row remained silent for a long moment, then asked, "What are you doing here, Gav?"

"Serving the girl."

"Ah! So you've swapped loyalties yet again."

That stung, but the Fetch refused to be baited. "She has your sapphire, Row. She has Tear's sapphire, Tear's blood. She's been there."

Row hesitated, his dark eyes unreadable. "Been where?"

"To the past. She's seen Lily, she's seen Tear."

"How do you know?"

"She told me, and she's no liar. It's only a matter of time before she gets to Jonathan. To us."

Row didn't answer. His eyes darted from rock to rock. The Fetch, sensing that he had finally broken through the wall of indifference, swallowed his anger and pressed forward. "Do you not see, Row, how this changes things?"

"It changes nothing."

The Fetch sighed. He had held back a last bit of information, tucked it away, to be used only in case of direst need. This was a desperate gambit, one that would put Row on the hunt. But these were desperate times. The Queen was in Mort custody, and without her, the Fetch feared that the Tearling would tear itself to pieces, Row or not.

"The crown's been spotted."

Row's head snapped up, like the head of a dog scenting something on the wind.

"The crown?"

"Yes."

"Where?"

The Fetch did not answer.

"How do you know it's not the Raleigh crown?"

"Because I destroyed the Raleigh crown, years ago, to make sure Thomas could never wear it. This is the real crown, Row."

"My crown."

The Fetch's heart sank. Once upon a time he had helped this man, not just willingly but eagerly. They had both committed terrible crimes, but only the Fetch had repented. Row grabbed and took and never looked back. For a moment the Fetch wondered why he had even bothered to come up here, but he pushed the thought aside and plowed onward.

"If we got hold of the crown, Row, we could give it to the girl, fix things. We could make up for the past."

"You spend all of your years tortured by guilt and assume that others do the same. Don't imbue me with a conscience. If my crown is out there, I will take it back."

"And then what? All the kingdoms in the world won't change what's happened to us."

"I see your idea now. You think the girl can end you."

"It's possible."

"Will she do it, though?" Row's mouth crimped in a malicious grin. "She's an easy child to read, and she's besotted with you."

"She sees only a handsome young man."

"Why did you come up here, really?" Row asked, and the Fetch caught a gleam of red in his eyes as he moved closer. "What did you hope to accomplish?"

"I hoped to come to an agreement. Help me find the crown. Help me repair the Tearling. It's never too late, Row, even now."

"Too late for what?"

"To atone for our crimes."

"I have committed no crime!" Row hissed, and the Fetch was pleased to see that he had touched a nerve. "I wished for better, that was all."

"And Katie?"

"You should leave." Row's eyes were burning brightly now, the flesh of his face turning pale.

At least he still feels, the Fetch told himself, then realized how little that meant. There was no emotion in the world that would ever outweigh Row's hunger.

"And if I don't leave?"

"Then I will let my children have you."

The Fetch glanced at the girl who perched on the nearby rock. Her eyes shone almost feverishly, and against his will he found himself uneasy. The child's bare feet, her toes clenched on the frozen rock, bothered him deeply, for no reason he could ever articulate.

"What are they, Row?"

"You were never a reader, Gav. This is old magic, older than the Crossing, even older than Christ. Ancient creatures, these, but they serve my will."

"And you let them loose in the Glace-Vert?"

"They have just as much right as the next animal."

This statement was so much in character that the Fetch nearly laughed. He and Row might have been right back on the banks of the Caddell, fourteen and fifteen years old, each holding a fishing pole.

"Go, now." Row's voice was low and venomous, his skin so white now that it seemed bleached. "Do not get in my way."

"Or what, Row? I long for death."

"Do you long for the deaths of others? The girl?"

The Fetch hesitated, and Row smiled.

"She has freed me, Gav, broken my curse. I have no use for her anymore. If you get in my way, if *she* gets in my way, I will finish her. It will be the easiest thing I've ever done."

"Row." He found himself suddenly pleading. "Don't do this. Think of Jonathan."

"Jonathan's dead, Gav. You helped me kill him."

The Fetch hauled back and swung. Row went flying, crashing into a nearby rock, but the Fetch knew that when Row got up, there would be nothing, not even a mark.

"Ah, Gav," Row whispered. "Have we not done this enough already?"

"Not enough."

"You make your new world, and I make mine. We'll see who comes out on top."

"And the crown?"

"*My* crown. If it's out there, I will have it."

The Fetch turned and stumbled away, nearly losing his footing on the slope. Ten steps downward, he found that his eyes were blurred with moisture. The wind bit through him. He could not think of Tear without crying, so he turned his mind to what came next.

The priest had been missing for more than a month, and the trail had gone cold. The Fetch's people were spread out over northern and central Mortmesne, but he would need to get some of them back. Lear and Morgan, perhaps Howell. The Fetch had spent a long time crafting the rebellion that now raged across Mortmesne, but the crown was paramount. They would all need to hunt for it. And then there was the girl—

He sensed eyes on his back, turned, and felt the chill of the wind penetrate more deeply into his bones. The slope behind him was covered with small children, white faces and dark eyes. Bare feet.

"God," he murmured. The night seemed filled with phantoms, and he heard Jonathan Tear's voice, centuries away but very close. *We won't fail, Gav. How can we fail?*

"We did fail," the Fetch whispered. "Great God, we failed so badly."

He turned and continued down the slope, too fast for caution, almost running now. Several times he nearly lost his balance, but he could not get down soon enough. As he reached the bottom of the slope, he broke into a sprint, tearing across the foothills toward the copse where he had tethered his horse.

On the hillside far above, the children waited silently, a still comber that covered the wide slope. They breathed steadily, a hoarse rattle that echoed against the rocks, but no plume of air was visible between their lips. Row Finn stood at their forefront, watching the tiny figure below. Once upon a time, Gavin had been the easiest man in the world to manipulate. Those days were long gone, as was Gavin himself, his real identity subsumed and steeped in the mythology of the man they called the Fetch. That man would be real trouble, but Row remained sanguine as he surveyed the pale ocean of children around him. They always did as they were told, and they were eternally, unrelentingly hungry. They waited only for his command.

"The crown," he whispered, feeling a great excitement course through him, excitement he recognized from long ago: the hunt was beginning, and at the end there lay the promise of blood. He had waited almost three hundred years.

"Go."

Book I

Chapter 1

The Regent

Examined in hindsight, the Glynn Regency was not really a regency at all. The role of a royal regent is simple: guard the throne and provide a barrier to usurpers in the rightful ruler's absence. As a natural warrior, the Mace was uniquely suited for such a task, but the warrior's exterior also concealed a shrewd political mind and, perhaps more surprisingly, a devoted belief in the Glynn Queen's vision. In the wake of the abortive second Mort invasion, the Regent did not sit quietly, waiting for his mistress to return; rather, he bent all of his considerable talents toward her vision, her Tearling.

—*The Early History of the Tearling,* AS TOLD BY MERWINIAN

For a brief period, Kelsea had made a practice of opening her eyes whenever the wagon hit a bump. It seemed as good a way as any to mark the passage of time, to watch the landscape change in small flashes. But now the rain had stopped, and the bright sunlight made her head ache. When the wagon jolted her awake again, from what seemed an endless nap, she worked to keep her eyes tightly closed, listening to the movement of horses all around her, the jingle of bridles and the clop of hooves.

"Not so much as a piece of silver," a man on her left grumbled in Mort.

"We get a salary," another man replied.

"Our salary's tiny."

"That's true enough," a third voice broke in. "My house needs a new roof. Our pittance won't cover that."

"Stop griping!"

"Well, what of you? Do you know why we're going home empty-handed?"

"I'm a soldier. It's not my job to know things."

"I heard something," the first voice muttered darkly. "I heard that all of the generals and their pet colonels, Ducarte on down, are getting *their* share."

"What share? There's no plunder!"

"They don't need plunder. She's going to pay them directly, from the treasury, and leave the rest of us hanging out here in the wind!"

"That can't be true. Why would she pay them for nothing?"

"Who knows why the Crimson Lady does anything?"

"That's enough of that! Do you want the lieutenant to hear?"

"But—"

"Shut *up!*"

Kelsea listened for another minute, but heard nothing more, and so she tipped her head back into the sun. Despite her persistent headache, the light felt good on her bruises, as though it were permeating her skin to heal the tissue beneath. She hadn't been near a mirror in quite some time, but her nose and cheeks were still swollen to the touch, and she had a fairly good idea of how she looked.

We've come full circle, she thought, stifling a dark chuckle as the wagon hit another bump. *I see Lily, I become Lily, and now I have her bruises to match.*

Kelsea had been captive for ten days: six spent tied to a pole in a Mort tent, and then the last four chained in this wagon. Armor-clad men on horseback surrounded her, precluding any thought of escape, but the horsemen weren't Kelsea's real problem right now. The problem sat on the far side of the wagon, staring at her, his eyes narrow slits against the sun.

Kelsea had no idea where the Mort had found this man. He was not old, no more than Pen's age perhaps, with a meticulously groomed beard that wrapped like a strap beneath his chin. He didn't have the bearing of a head jailor; in fact, Kelsea was beginning to wonder whether he had any official capacity at all. Was it possible that someone had simply tossed him the keys to Kelsea's bonds and put him in charge? The more she considered it, the more she was sure that this was exactly what had happened. She had not had even a glimpse of the Red Queen since that morning in the tent. The entire operation had a distinctly improvised feeling.

"How are you, pretty?" the jailor asked.

She ignored him, though something seemed to shudder in her stomach. He called her "pretty," but Kelsea didn't know whether it was a personal comment or not. She *was* pretty now, Lily in duplicate, but she would have given anything to have her old face back, though she didn't know if being plain would have allowed her to escape this man's attentions. After their third day in the tent, he had administered a thorough, careful beating to her face and upper body. Kelsea didn't know what had set him off, or even whether he was angry; his face remained empty, void of expression, the entire time.

If I had my sapphires, she thought, staring back at him, refusing to drop her eyes lest he view such behavior as weakness. Weakness encouraged him. Kelsea had spent many hours of this journey fantasizing about what she would do if she ever got her sapphires back. Her short life as queen had comprised many forms of violence, but the threat presented by the jailor was entirely new: violence that seemed to come from nowhere, to accomplish nothing. The very senselessness of it made her despair, and this, too, reminded her of Lily. One night, perhaps a week ago, she had dreamed of Lily, of the Crossing, a bright and gaudy nightmare of fire and raging ocean and pink dawn. But Lily's life was encapsulated somehow in the sapphires, and they were lost to Kelsea, and now she wondered, almost viciously, why in hell she'd had to go through that, to see so much. She had Lily's face now, Lily's hair, Lily's memories. But what purpose did it all serve, if she couldn't see the end of the story? Row Finn had told her that she was a Tear, but she didn't know what that was worth without the jewels. Even Lady Andrews's tiara was gone now, lost in the camp. Everything of her old life had been left behind.

For good reason.

True. It was important to keep the Tear before her now. Her death must lie somewhere at the end of this journey—she wasn't even sure why she was alive now—but she left behind a free kingdom, headed by a good man. Her mind conjured an image of Mace, grim and unsmiling, and for a moment she missed him so badly that tears threatened to spill from beneath her closed lids. She fought the impulse, knowing that the man who sat across the wagon would take pleasure in her distress. She was sure that one of the reasons he had beaten her so badly was that she had refused to cry.

Lazarus, she thought, trying to alleviate her dismal mood. Mace sat on her throne now, and although he did not see the world precisely as Kelsea did, he would be a good ruler, fair and decent. But still Kelsea felt a subtle agony, growing with each mile traveled. She had never been outside her kingdom, not once in her life. She didn't know why she was still alive, but she was almost certainly going to Mortmesne to die.

Something slid along her calf, making her jump. Her jailor had reached across the floor of the wagon and was stroking her leg with one finger. Kelsea could not be more revolted if she had found a tick burrowing into her skin. The jailor was grinning again, his eyebrows lifted as he waited for a response.

I am already dead, Kelsea reminded herself. On paper, she had been a dead woman walking for months. There was great freedom in the thought, and that freedom allowed her to draw her legs inward, as if to curl up in the corner of the wagon, and then, at the last moment, to arch her back and kick her jailor in the face.

Down he went, landing sideways with a thump. The riders around them exploded in laughter, most of it unkind; Kelsea sensed that her jailor was not very popular with the infantry, but that fact would not help her here. She tucked her legs beneath her and brought her chained hands forward, ready to fight as best she was able. The jailor sat up, blood trickling from one of his nostrils, but he seemed not to notice it, didn't even bother to wipe it away as it worked its way down toward his upper lip.

"I was only playing," he said, his voice petulant. "Doesn't pretty like games?"

Kelsea didn't reply. The rapid changes in mood had been her earliest indication that he wasn't right in the head. There were no patterns of behavior that she could anticipate. Anger, confusion, amusement . . . each time, he reacted differently. The man had noticed his nosebleed now, and he wiped the blood away with one hand, smearing it on the wagon floor.

"Pretty should behave herself," he scolded, his tone that of a tutor with a wayward pupil. "I'm the man who cares for her now."

Kelsea curled up in the corner of the wagon. Again she thought, ruefully, of her sapphires, and with a blink of surprise, she realized that she actually meant to survive this journey somehow. The jailor was only one in a series of obstacles to be overcome. In the end, she meant to go home.

The Red Queen will never allow that to happen.

Then why is she taking me back to Demesne?

To kill you. She probably means to put your head in the place of honor on the Pike Road.

But this seemed too easy to Kelsea. The Red Queen was a direct woman. If she wanted Kelsea dead, Kelsea's body would be rotting on the banks of Caddell. There must be something the Red Queen wanted from her, and if so, she might yet go home.

Home. This time it was not the land she thought of, but people. Lazarus. Pen. The Fetch. Andalie. Arliss. Elston. Kibb. Coryn. Dyer. Galen. Wellmer. Father Tyler. For a moment Kelsea could see them all, as though they were gathered around her. Then the image was gone, and there was only glaring sunlight in her eyes, making her head ache. Not a vision, only her mind, trying to free itself. There would be no more magic, not anymore; the reality was this dusty wagon, rolling inexorably onward, taking her away from her home.

T he Mace never sat on the throne.

Sometimes Aisa thought he might. It had already become a joke among the Guard: the way the Mace would climb the dais with his purposeful stride . . . and then seat himself on the top step, hulking arms resting on his knees. If it had been a long day, he might condescend to use the battered armchair nearby, but the throne itself remained vacant, an empty monolith of gleaming silver at the apex of the room, reminding them all of the Queen's absence. Aisa was sure that this was exactly what the Mace intended.

Today, the Mace had ignored the dais altogether, electing instead to sit at the head of the Queen's dining table. Aisa stood just behind his chair. Several people were standing; even the enormous table would not hold them all. Aisa judged little threat of violence here, but she had a hand on her knife, all the same. She rarely let go of it, even when she slept. On the first night after the bridge—Aisa's mental life now seemed to be divided into Before and After the Bridge—the Mace had given her her own room, right on the periphery of the Guard quarters. Though Aisa was fond of her siblings, she was relieved to be free of them. That part of her life, the old part, the family part, seemed to cleave away when she worked with the Guard. There was no space for it. Aisa felt safe in her new room, safer than she had ever felt, but sometimes she would still wake in the mornings and find her knife in her hand.

Arliss sat beside the Mace, one of his foul cigarettes jutting from his teeth, shuffling the stack of papers in front of him. Arliss lived by facts and figures, but Aisa didn't know what good his records would do him here. The problem of the Queen could not be solved on paper.

Next to Arliss was General Hall, accompanied by his aide, Colonel Blaser. Both men were still dressed in full armor, for they had just come in from the front. For the past week, the last remnants of the Tear army had trailed the vast Mort war train as it crossed the Caddell and began a slow but steady progress eastward, across the Almont. As impossible as it seemed, the Mort were withdrawing, packing up their siege equipment and heading home.

But why?

No one knew. The Tear army had been decimated, and New London's defenses were paper-thin; Elston said that the Mort could have torn right through them. The army was keeping a close eye on the invaders, in case of a trick, but by now even the Mace seemed convinced that the withdrawal was real. The Mort were leaving. There was no sense in it, but it was happening, all the same. General Hall said that the Mort soldiers weren't even looting on their way home.

All of this was good news, but the mood at this table was anything but ebullient. There had still been no word on the Queen. Her body had not been left behind when the Mort moved out. Maman said she was a prisoner, and the thought made Aisa's blood boil. The first duty of a Queen's Guard was to protect the ruler from harm, and even if the Queen wasn't dead, she was still at the mercy of the Mort. Even Maman could not say what was happening to her in their camp.

On the other side of the Mace sat Pen, his face pale and drawn. Whatever agonies Aisa and the other guards endured over the Queen's welfare, no one was suffering like Pen, who had been the Queen's close guard . . . *and more*, Aisa thought. He was little use these days, for he seemed able to do nothing but mope and drink, and when someone called his name he would only look up in a slightly confused manner. Some part of Pen had been lost on the day the Queen broke the bridge, and although he sat next to the Mace, in the place of a close guard, his gaze remained fixed on the table, lost. Coryn, who sat beside him, was his usual alert self, so Aisa didn't worry, but she wondered how much more slack Elston was going to extend to Pen. What would it take for someone to voice the truth: that Pen was no longer fit for the job?

"Let's begin," the Mace announced. "What news?"

General Hall cleared his throat. "I should give my report first, sir. There's good reason."

"Let's have it, then. Where are the Mort?"

"They're in the central Almont now, sir, nearing the end of the Crithe. They make at least five miles a day, closer to ten since the rain stopped."

"Nothing left behind?"

Hall shook his head. "We have looked for traps. I believe the withdrawal is genuine."

"Well, that's something, at least."

"Yes, but sir—"

"What about the displaced?" Arliss demanded. "Can we start sending them home?"

"I'm not sure it's safe, certainly not right on the heels of the Mort war train."

"Snow has already fallen in the northern Reddick, General. If we don't harvest the crops soon, there'll be nothing to reap." Arliss paused to emit a plume of smoke. "We also have every problem an overcrowded city ever faced: sewage, water treatment, disease. The sooner we empty it out, the better. Maybe if you—"

"We've sighted the Queen."

The entire table came to attention. Even Pen seemed to wake up.

"What are you waiting for?" the Mace barked. "Report!"

"We spotted her yesterday morning, out in the Crithe delta. She's alive, but manacled, chained to a wagon. There's no opportunity for her to run."

"She broke the fucking New London Bridge in half!" Arliss snapped. "What chains could hold her to a wagon?"

Hall's tone was cool. "We couldn't get a perfectly clear look at her; the Mort cavalry is too thick. But I have a man named Llew who has the vision of a hawk. He's fairly confident that the Queen no longer wears either of the Tear sapphires."

"What is her condition?" Pen broke in.

Spots of color darkened Hall's cheeks, and he turned to the Mace. "Maybe we should discuss—"

"You discuss it right now." Pen's voice had sunk very low. "Is she wounded?"

Hall looked helplessly at the Mace, who nodded.

"Yes. Her face is bruised up; even I could see it through the spyglass. She's been beaten."

Pen sank back into his chair. Aisa couldn't see his face, but she didn't need to. The slump of his shoulders said everything. The entire table sat in silence for a moment.

"She was upright in the wagon, at least," Hall finally ventured. "Healthy enough to stand. I don't think she has any broken bones."

"Where is this wagon?" the Mace asked.

"Right in the center of the Mort cavalry."

"No chance of a direct attack?"

"None. Even if my army weren't reduced to a fraction, the Mort are taking no chances. At least a hundred feet of heavy horse surround her on all sides. They're hustling her along the Mort Road, outdistancing the infantry. I can only assume they're making straight for Demesne."

"The Palais dungeons." Pen rested his forehead on one hand. "How the hell do we get her out of there?"

"The Mort rebellion is poised to move down to Demesne," the Mace reminded him. "Levieux's people will be useful."

"How do you know you can trust him?"

"I know."

Aisa raised her eyebrows. She hadn't thought much of Levieux, who had left the Keep more than a week earlier. He was handsome, but good looks meant nothing in a scrap. His man Alain did know good card tricks, but they weren't a patch on Bradshaw's. A magician might be able to get into the dungeons of the Mort Palais, but the Mace didn't trust magicians.

"The Red Queen will surely face a problem on her right flank now," Arliss mused. "There's no plunder . . . no gold, no women. I don't know how she got her army to walk away, but they won't be happy."

"So much Levieux has surmised. Unpaid soldiers make wonderful rebels. He expects to be able to recruit heavily when the army gets home."

"And what is that to us," Pen demanded, "if we don't have the Queen?"

"We'll discuss it later, Pen," the Mace admonished. "Be soft now."

Aisa frowned. The Mace kept coddling Pen, trying to talk him out of his foul moods, ignoring it when Pen was insubordinate. Aisa would have given Pen a long stretch of suspension and, failing that, a sharp slap to the face.

"Continue to send me reports about the withdrawal," Mace

told Hall, "but your focus is the Queen. Pick two of your best to follow her into Mortmesne. Make sure we don't lose sight of her. Dismissed."

Hall and Blaser stood and bowed, then headed for the doors.

"We need to talk about the Arvath," said Arliss.

"What about it?"

Arliss gathered his papers and put them aside. "A mob did some damage in the city this morning. They seem to have gathered in the Circus and gone from there, all the way to Bethyn's Close."

"There are always mobs."

"This one was special. Their main point of contention seemed to be the lack of morality in the Queen's government."

The Mace frowned, and so did Aisa. Even as the problem of the Mort rapidly receded, another had sprung up to take its place: the Holy Father. The very day the Queen left the city, the Arvath had publicly announced its refusal to pay property tax, as well as intent to absolve any layman who refused to do the same.

"What connects this mob to the Arvath?" Coryn asked.

"Nothing," Arliss replied. "The mob disbanded long before the city constables could get near, and there's no army to deal with civil unrest anymore. But they broke into a house on the edge of the close and brutalized the two women who lived there. Immoral lifestyle."

A muscle had begun to twitch in the Mace's cheek. "The Holy Father thinks if he pushes me hard enough, I won't collect the Queen's taxes. He's wrong."

"The nobles still refuse to pay their taxes, except for Meadows and Gillon. The Creche will take the bulk of the Treasury. We've lost the income from the toll gates on the bridge. In a few months, we're going to be in real trouble."

"They'll pay." The Mace grinned, such a cheerful, murderous grin that Aisa recoiled, but a moment later his face sobered. "Any word on the two priests?"

"Not a peep. They've vanished. But the Arvath has heard that we're keeping up with their bounty." Arliss dug through his stack of papers again. "Yesterday's message from the Holy Father demands that we retract our own reward for Father Tyler, in hope of heaven."

"In hope of heaven," the Mace repeated. "One day, I'm going to send that man to meet Jesus myself."

"One more troubling report. Two days ago, one of my runners spotted several priests leaving New London, taking the back road around the city."

"Where did they go?"

"Demesne, most likely. My man tracked them well down the Mort Road."

The Mace's face darkened.

"Should we pursue it?" Elston asked.

"No," the Mace replied after a few moments' thought. "If he's dealing with the Red Queen, my source in the Palais will tell us what passes. What else?"

Arliss looked down at his list. "We have to bring in the harvest before the snow comes. The entire kingdom is starving for fresh fruit and vegetables. I would think the first farmers to get back out there and cut a crop could command their own price."

"That's no incentive to those who farm a noble's patch."

"Yes, but all the nobles are still in New London." Arliss smiled, a smile of such mischief that Aisa could not help liking him in that moment, foul-smelling cigarettes and all. "If Lord Such-and-Such fails to mind his own land while the Mort cross it, who's to say where the produce went?"

"And what if the Mort do their own looting on the way home?" Elston demanded.

"They're not. I asked Hall's second. They're leaving the land untouched, God knows why." Arliss shrugged. "Let the farmers go and cherry-pick. Even a few days' crops would help them cover their winter, if they managed to be the first to market. And their success would beckon the rest."

The Mace nodded slowly. "You handle it."

"Merritt is still outside, sir," Elston reminded him.

"How many Caden with him?"

"Three."

"That's all?"

"Yes, sir. But not just any three. The Miller brothers."

"Oho." The Mace considered this information for a moment. Aisa didn't know who the Miller brothers were, but there had been a bitter debate about letting any Caden into the Queen's Wing. Elston didn't like it, and neither did most of the Guard, but the Mace was determined to have them, and Aisa hoped he would have his way. She longed to see real Caden up close.

"Well, bring them in."

The Mace ascended the dais, and Aisa held her breath, waiting. But he ignored the throne entirely, merely settled himself on the top step as Devin let the Caden through the doors.

The leader, Merritt, was well over six feet tall, but he moved like the Mace, with the easy lope of a big man who could summon great speed if needed. An ugly scar marred his forehead. Aisa, who had taken several knife wounds to her hands and arms over the course of her training, didn't think the scar was clean enough to have been made by a blade. If she had to guess, she thought it came from human fingernails. She had heard of Merritt; everyone had, for even among Caden, he was elite. But the three men behind him were a puzzle.

They entered the room in a triangle, one in the front and two at the back, a defensive formation that Aisa recognized from her own training. Their blood-colored cloaks were incongruously bright against the grey stone of the Keep walls. Physically, the three men were unlike: one tall, one medium height, one short, and they displayed varying shades of brown hair, from sandy to dark. Yet they shared a curious similarity, not physical, that Aisa could not pinpoint. When one moved, so did the other two; they oriented themselves as a triad without speech or other overt signals, and Aisa sensed that they had worked together for a very long time. Elston, in his capacity as provisional captain, had decreed that none of the Caden were to come within ten feet of the Mace, and now Aisa was glad for his caution. These three looked like trouble.

Merritt pointed to his three companions in turn. "Millers. Christopher, Daniel, James."

The Mace considered them for a moment and then said, "I heard you three were cast out of the guild."

"The guild thought better of it," Christopher, the tallest, replied mildly.

"Why?"

"We are useful, Lord Regent."

"You were useful six years ago. I've heard nothing of you since."

"Yet we haven't been idle," said James.

"Of course not." The Mace's voice sharpened. "You were hunting the Queen."

The three men remained silent, staring truculently back at him, and finally the Mace relented.

"Past is past. I have a job for you, and for as many members of your guild as wish to come."

"Our guild is very busy," James replied, but the response sounded automatic to Aisa. She wondered if they always said no the first time.

"Yes, you are busy," the Mace replied, a thread of mockery entering his voice. "We've heard the stories. Caden as highwaymen, Caden as rent boys, Caden running dogfights and worse."

"We do what we have to. What of it?"

"These things are beneath you, not what you signed up for. They damage your guild's prestige. I have a better job. Difficult and dangerous work. Some finesse required, as well. Even if I still commanded an intact army, I would not trust soldiers with such work."

The third Caden, Daniel, spoke up for the first time. "What job is this?"

"Cleaning out the Creche."

James chuckled. "That's easy. All you need is a cistern."

"Not easy at all," the Mace replied, unsmiling. "Close quarters down there, women and children in conditions of considerable danger. Men, too, the Queen would want me to note. I want the innocent out safely, the pimps and promoters alive and in custody."

"What's the price for this job?"

"Flat fee. Ten thousand pounds per month for three months full. If your guild can't do it by then, I doubt it can be done."

"Bonus for early completion?"

The Mace looked to Arliss, who nodded grudgingly and said, "Get it done—and mind you, I mean *done*—in two months, and we'll pay you for three."

The Millers turned inward, muttering to each other while the room waited. Merritt did not join the huddle, merely stood by, impassive. He had already agreed to help them for free; Mace said the man owed the Queen a debt. But Aisa had her doubts. What sort of debt would make a Caden work for nothing?

Above her, the Mace watched the three brothers with an indifferent expression, but this no longer fooled Aisa. Something was driving him. She had never heard of the Creche before the bridge, and no one would tell her of it directly, but by now she had overheard enough to have the measure of the place: a warren beneath the city where the worst vices were tolerated, where children younger than Aisa were sold for profit and entertainment. The idea of the place haunted her. Da had been bad, but he was only one man. The thought that there were many such people, all of them doing terrible things, that there was an entire underground world of children going through the same nightmare . . . it ate at Aisa, kept her awake at night. It seemed to eat at the Mace, too, for he and Arliss were focusing much of their energy on the Creche, though Arliss grudged the money. No one argued with the Mace on this matter, but nothing could move quickly enough for him, and now Aisa was almost certain that she saw the Queen's shadow over his shoulder, goading him. Driving him.

The Caden came to some sort of agreement and turned back to the Mace. Christopher spoke for them.

"We will present your proposal at the next full meeting of the guild. In the meantime, the three of us will look into the job, without price or commitment."

"Fair," the Mace replied. "Since you're working without price, I will not give you deadlines. But time is of the essence. I wish to have this business sewn up before the Queen comes home."

The three Caden looked up sharply.

"What makes you think she's coming home?" James asked.

"She is," the Mace replied, in a tone that closed all discussion.

"If you accept the job, you will deal with me for payment," Arliss told them. "There will be no advances or other rubbish of that kind, so don't even try."

"But I will ask for a small advance, all the same," Daniel replied. "The girl, there."

He pointed at Aisa.

"We've heard about this one," Daniel continued. "They say she has a knife hand, but we've never seen such a thing. Before we go, may I beg a demonstration?"

The Mace frowned. "You wish to fight a child?"

Aisa scowled. She hated it when they remembered her age.

"Not a real fight, Lord Regent," Daniel replied. "Only a demonstration."

The Mace tipped a questioning look toward Aisa, and she nodded eagerly. To spar with one of the Caden! Even a draw would be an extraordinary thing.

"If you take a wound, hellcat," the Mace murmured, leaning closer, "*you* will be the one to explain it to your mother."

Aisa was already tugging at the straps on her armor, shedding it and pulling her knife from its sheath. Fell had commissioned this knife especially for Aisa, of the same shape and make as the knives carried by the rest of the Guard: fashioned on the old Belland model, both a flat and a curved cutting edge. But Aisa's hands were small, and Venner thought she needed less circumference in the hilt, as well as a thinner blade. Fell had given the job to a weapons forger he favored, and the result was a solid knife that was a joy for Aisa to wield. Venner always said that a good knifeman made the weapon part of his hand, but Aisa sometimes felt that she had gone beyond even that, the knife not only part of her hand but part of herself, keeping her demons at bay. Even Da would fade into the distance when she was armed.

The Caden, Daniel, had dropped the rest of his weapons, but his knife glimmered, half hidden, in his hand, a longer blade than her own. Venner had seen it too, for he pointed at Daniel's weapon and called out, "Not a fair fight!"

"Disadvantage is a natural part of battle," Daniel replied, addressing the Mace. "I have more than a foot of height on her as well. However, since she's a child, I will hold my blade farther up the hilt than I would normally do. Fair?"

The Mace looked to Aisa, and she nodded. She would have fought the man with even steeper disadvantages; more glory in it that way.

"Watch yourself, girl!" Venner called. "Remember your gifts!"

Aisa took a good grip on her knife, holding it edge-down. Venner had told her many times that her size would always be a disadvantage in a fight, but that she could make up for it with speed and trickery. The rest of the Guard had gathered to give them a sparring floor perhaps twenty feet in the round, and a distant part of Aisa's mind heard bets being laid all around her.

"I do not aim to wound you," Daniel told her, positioning himself ten feet away. "I only want to test what you've got."

This statement meant less than nothing. Venner and Fell did not aim to wound her either, but Aisa already had several healed slashes on her hands and arms. The fight was the fight.

"Take a swipe at me," Daniel ordered, but she did not. Venner had taught her that early aggression was a mistake. Attacking when she had no advantage would cost her the protection of her ribs and throat.

"Cautious, eh?" Daniel asked.

Aisa did not respond; she was too busy sizing him up. He kept his arms tucked in close to his ribs, conserving energy. His reach would be longer than hers. If she was going to get close to him, she would have to take at least one blow off her forearm. She began with a series of controlled lunges, each of them slower than she could move, none as far as her actual range. Her blood was singing now; Venner would say it was adrenaline, but Aisa knew that it was really the song of the fight, of being all alone in a corner with nothing to rely on but herself and her blade. She tasted metal in her mouth.

The Caden suddenly leapt forward, waving one arm to distract her while stabbing with the other. But Aisa had learned to keep her attention on the knife hand, and she ducked it easily, rolling beneath the thrust and ending up on her feet.

"Quick," Daniel remarked.

Aisa did not reply, for she had spotted something as the Caden turned to follow her: his left leg was weak. Either a limp, or, more likely, a recent wound. He was protecting the leg, subtly keeping it out of the zone of contact. Aisa feinted, making a halfhearted lunge for his throat, and hissed as his knife slashed across her forearm. But at the same time, she released a sharp kick toward his left kneecap, pointing her toe as the Mace had taught her. The Caden gave a muffled grunt of pain as he stumbled and went down to the floor.

"Ha! That's the stuff!" Venner shouted. "Close, girl! Close while he's down!"

She jumped on the Caden's back, aiming her knife for his throat, but he had already moved to block, and she could not get a good grip. He gave a tremendous heave, throwing her over his shoulders, and now it was Aisa's turn to groan as she landed on her back, thumping her head against the stones.

"All right, Aisa?" the Mace called.

She ignored him and scrambled to her feet, keeping her eyes on the Caden, who circled her. She had hurt him when she went for his knee, but he had hurt her as well; the cut on her forearm was deep and her free hand was slippery with blood. Venner had been training her to increase her endurance, but she already felt herself tiring, her muscles slowing down. She adjusted her grip, seeking a new opening. The Caden would never let her near his weak leg again, but her earlier clumsy feints might have worked; he was not protecting his ribs so well as he had before. She would have a shot with one good lunge, but it would cost her.

"Watch your footing," Daniel advised her. "Blood on the floor."

"You'd like me to look down, wouldn't you?"

Grinning, he swapped the knife to his right hand. The guards around them grumbled a bit at this, but Aisa wasn't bothered; Venner was switch-handed as well. She kept her eyes away from the spot she wanted, the poke of his ribs behind his left forearm, just outside the protection of his armor. She was facing a superior opponent, taller and faster and better skilled, and in a fight to the death she would have been finished. But here all she needed to do was score a touch.

She knew the moment he meant to come for her, for he took a

deeper breath just before he lunged, sweeping his knife in a broad arc, going for her shoulder. Aisa ducked and raked her knife across his ribs. The jab was not clean; it nearly jerked her knife from her hand, and at the same time she felt a stabbing tear in her bicep. But she heard him hiss in pain, just before he grabbed her and whirled her around. Aisa lost her balance and a moment later stood helpless in his grip, his knife at her throat. She forced herself to hold still, panting. The Caden wasn't even out of breath.

"Let her go," the Mace commanded.

Daniel released her, and Aisa turned to face him. For a moment they merely stood there, staring at each other, as the guards around them began to argue and hand over coin.

"How are you with a sword?" Daniel asked.

"Only fair," Aisa admitted. Her slow progress at mastering a sword was a sore point.

"I went easy on you, girl, but not that easy, and I'm one of the best knifemen in the guild." He considered her for a long moment. "Gifted with a blade, mediocre with a sword . . . you're no Queen's Guard, child. You're an assassin. When you reach your full growth, you should quit this mausoleum and come talk to us."

He touched the wound at his ribs, then raised a hand to the Mace, his fingers dabbled with blood.

"Thank you, Lord Regent. A good show."

Aisa grabbed her armor and returned to her spot below the dais. Kibb winked as she went. Rebuckling her breastplate, she wiped blood across her front. After the meeting was done, the Mace would likely allow her to go and have Coryn doctor her arm, but not now, for she had asked for this fight. That was fair, but she was losing blood, and after a moment's thought she looped the ripped lower half of her sleeve around her arm and cinched it tight.

"Our business here is done," Christopher told the Mace. "We'll return when the guild has an answer."

"If the guild says aye, I can give you at least twenty Queen's Guards to assist."

"Refused. We want no amateurs involved."

A murmur of displeasure went through the Guard, but the Millers had already turned and walked away.

Merritt chuckled. "I have no particular love for those three, Lord Regent, but they are good for your purpose. As for me, I stand ready to serve the Queen."

He followed the other Caden toward the doors, and Aisa felt her muscles relax. Though she would not have admitted it to anyone, she was turning Daniel's words over in her mind.

"That leaves Queenie, doesn't it?" Arliss asked. He had remained at the table during the fight, which surprised Aisa; she would have thought that Arliss would be the first to collect bets. "What's to be done?"

"We're going to get her," the Mace replied. "But she would kill me if I left the kingdom to fall apart behind us. Some triage is needed."

Aisa felt a light touch on her arm, turned, and found Coryn examining her knife wounds.

"Ugly, m'girl, but not too deep. Get your sleeve out of the way and I'll stitch these up."

She tore the remaining fabric from her sleeve.

"That was a good fight you made of it, hellcat," the Mace remarked. "But you allowed him to put you off balance."

"I know it," Aisa replied, gritting her teeth as Coryn began to disinfect her wounds. "He was faster than me."

"The awkwardness of youth. It won't last forever."

Even another day seemed too long to Aisa. She felt herself caught in a terrible middle ground: too old to be a child, too young to be an adult. She longed to work as a grown-up, to perform a job and earn money, to be responsible for herself. She was learning to fight, but many of the Guard's lessons were not taught but absorbed: how to conduct herself in public, how to think of the Guard before herself, and the Queen above all. These were lessons in maturity, and Aisa took them as such. Yet there were still times when she wanted to run to Maman, to lay her head against Maman's shoulder and have Maman comfort her, just as she had when Aisa was a hunted child.

I can't have it both ways.

Coryn's needle pierced the flesh of her forearm, and she took a deep breath. No one in the Guard talked about these things, but she knew, somehow, that how one dealt with injury was just as important as how one performed in a fight. Looking for distraction, she asked, "What does cast out mean?"

"What?"

"Those Caden. You said they were cast out."

"So they were, six years ago. They cost the guild a great profit and got thrown out as a result."

"Ai!" Aisa yelped. Coryn's needle had touched a nerve of some kind. "What did they do wrong?"

"There was a young noblewoman, Lady Cross. Lord Tare had an eye for her—and for her family lands as well—but Lady Cross had a secret engagement with a young man in the Almont, a poor tenant farmer, and she refused Lord Tare at every turn. So Lord Tare abducted her, took her to his castle on the southern end of the Reddick, and locked her in the tower. He swore that she would stay there until she agreed to marry him."

"Marriage is stupid," Aisa snapped, gritting her teeth as Coryn pulled the thread tight. "You'll never catch me getting married."

"Of course not," the Mace replied with a chuckle. "But Lady Cross, not being a warrior, did want to marry, and she wanted to marry her young man. She sat in Lord Tare's castle for two months and wouldn't budge an inch. So then Lord Tare had the excellent idea of cutting off her food."

"He *starved* her to get her to marry him?" Aisa grimaced. "Why didn't she just marry him and run away?"

"There's no divorce in God's Church, child. A husband always has the right to drag his wife back home."

Da had done that, Aisa remembered. Several times during her childhood, Maman had made them pack their few belongings and steal away, but the journey always ended up back at home with Da.

"Then what?"

"Well, Lady Cross was wasting away, still refusing to budge. It became quite a matter of contention in the kingdom."

"Didn't her fiancé do anything?"

"There wasn't much he could do. He had offered Tare the few pounds he had. Lady Cross's family tried to ransom her as well, with no luck. Lord Tare was in the grip of something by then, you see; his pride had become wrapped up in making the woman submit. Many nobles applied to the Regent on Lady Cross's behalf, but the Regent refused to send in the Tear army for what he deemed a domestic matter. Finally, when it was clear that Lady Cross would die in that tower before anything changed, the Crosses pooled their money and hired the Caden to get her out."

"And did they?" Aisa asked. She found herself enchanted; it was like listening to one of Maman's fairy tales.

"Yes, and a slick piece of business it was too," Elston chimed in. "James posed as the lady's cousin, come to beg her to relent, and Christopher and Daniel his two retainers. They met with the lady for an hour, and when they came out, she agreed to marry Lord Tare. He was overjoyed, and arranged the wedding for the very next week."

A feint, Aisa thought. Sometimes she thought that all of life could be reduced to the fight.

"In the week before the wedding, Lord Tare kept Lady Cross under heavy guard, but the entire kingdom thought she had truly given in. The Captain, here, insisted that she had not"—Elston saluted the Mace with two of his fingers—"but the rest of us were fooled, and we thought no less of Lady Cross for it. Starvation is a terrible death."

"Then what?" Aisa asked. Coryn had gone to work on her bicep now, but she barely noticed.

"The day of the wedding, and Lady Cross was dressed and in her best. The Arvath sent the local bishop to perform the ceremony. Lord Tare invited half the kingdom to witness his triumph, and the church was stuffed with his guards and guests. The Crosses refused to attend, but the rest of the nobility were there, even the Regent himself. Lady Cross went up to the altar and followed the bishop through the ceremony, every word, two hours of it, until they were married."

"What?"

"The wedding concluded peacefully, and I tell you, the minute it was over, Lord Tare's worries were done. He had her lands and title, and that's all he wanted. He stayed downstairs to get drunk with his house guard while Lady Cross went upstairs to take off her wedding gown. An hour later Tare went looking for his wife, and she was gone, snatched easily. By the time he had mustered a recovery party, she was already halfway across the Reddick."

"But she was married."

"Seems so, doesn't it? Lord Tare pitched a fit, went after the Caden with bloodhounds and such, and when he couldn't find them, he appealed to the Regent. It took two days for anyone to even think of consulting the bishop, but when they did, they found him bound in his palace, along with his guards. The bishop was starving and furious, and certainly a very different man from the one who'd performed the wedding."

"This is the clever bit, hellcat," the Mace cut back in. "I don't speak Latin, but I know several people who do, and they told me that the marriage ceremony was gibberish. There was a long sermon on the virtues of garlic, another on the rules of rugby, God knows what else. Lady Cross promised to love and serve beer all of her life. She spoke Latin, you see, and Lord Tare did not."

Aisa considered this for a moment. "What about the people in the audience?"

"Plenty of people at the ceremony spoke Latin, and a few of them were even Lord Tare's friends. But none of them said a word, not until later, when they bore witness that the marriage had been a sham. Those three Caden took a gamble, but a good one. By the end, the entire kingdom sympathized with Lady Cross. The only people who truly wanted her brought to bay were the sadists and woman-haters, and the Caden bet high that none of them spoke Latin."

"A good gamble," Arliss grumbled. "I lost a fortune on that wedding."

"What did Lord Tare do when he found out?"

"Oh, he swore up and down the Tear that he would have his revenge on all of them: Lady Cross, the Caden, the false bishop—who was never found. But he had no legal claim on the lady, and by the time the matter was sorted out, she was already with her farmer."

"Did she marry him?"

"Yes, and was disowned by her family as a result. That's where the Millers got into trouble; they were supposed to return the lady to her family, but they took her to the farmer instead. The Crosses only paid half the price on the job. The Caden were furious, and kicked the brothers out of the guild. They were also excommunicated by God's Church, though I doubt they cared about that."

"But they did it," Aisa mused. "They saved her."

"Yes, for a good return."

"What about Lord Tare? What happened to him?"

"Oh, he still sits up there in his castle, bitter as winter beer," the

Mace replied. "He's taken to plotting away at the Queen's downfall, and if I could prove he was in the Argive in the spring, his neck would already be stretched. But for now, I leave him be."

That was disappointing. In a real fairy tale, the villain would have been punished.

"Do they always work together?" she asked. "Those three brothers?"

"Yes. Many Caden work in such small groups, particularly when they have complementary skills. But they can also work in concert. All Caden working toward a combined goal would be quite a sight to see."

"But why the Creche, sir?" Coryn asked. "I thought the Queen was the priority."

"She is, but she'd never forgive me if I made her the only priority. She charged me, you see." The Mace blinked, and for a moment Aisa thought she saw the sparkle of tears in his eyes. "I didn't know what she meant at the time, but she charged me to fix this place. She charged me to look after the defenseless as well as the great, and that task can't wait until she comes home."

A fist thudded against the great double doors of the Queen's Wing, making Aisa jump. The Guard drew in to surround the Mace. Devin and Cae opened the doors a fraction, but the only person who entered was a Keep servant, dressed entirely in white. Aisa could not make out her words, but their babbling, hysterical tenor was clear from across the room.

"What's that, Cae?" the Mace called.

"There's a problem downstairs, sir. With Thorne's witch."

"What problem?"

The Keep servant stared at the Mace, her eyes wide. She was not a young woman, and her face was cast in white.

"Speak up!"

"She's gone," the woman croaked.

"What of Will? Her guard?"

But the woman could not answer. Cursing, the Mace jumped down the stairs and strode out of the Queen's Wing. Aisa followed him, down the corridor and three flights of stairs that led to Brenna's makeshift prison. She feared Brenna; they all feared her, even the bravest of the Guard. A visit to Brenna's rooms was a dangerous thing, but Aisa was unable to stop thinking of the Caden's words.

When you reach your full growth, you should come and see us.

They rounded the final corner and the Mace came to a dead halt, ten feet from Brenna's chamber. The door was wide open, but it was guarded by a puddle of blood. The smell hit Aisa like a slap. Flies had already gathered around the puddle in a swarm, and one of them buzzed around Aisa's head until she waved it away.

The Mace began to move forward, but Elston placed a restraining hand on his chest. "Sir. Let us go first."

The Mace nodded, though Aisa could feel him chafing at the restriction. Elston and Kibb went into the chamber and Aisa trailed a few feet behind them, wanting to see but not wanting to. She peered around Elston, then recoiled as she spotted a bright red mass in the corner.

"Is it safe?"

"Yes, sir," Elston replied, but his voice was strange, and he backed away as the Mace approached, giving Aisa a full view that she regretted. Will was lying on the floor, his throat mangled, as though an animal had been at him. Aisa had never seen a dead body before; she expected to feel sick, but her stomach took the unpleasant sight in stride. The Mace had never allowed Aisa to be alone with Brenna; for the two occasions she had come down here on rotation, she had been paired with Coryn or Kibb. Will had been a decent guard, but the witch had clearly been too much for him. Perhaps they should have been working in pairs all along.

Kibb had squatted down next to Will, and now he lifted one of the dead man's arms, examining his hands, which were covered with blood.

"Tissue under his fingernails, sir." Kibb looked up. "I think he did it to himself."

Aisa returned her gaze—not without some dark fascination—to the ruin of Will's neck. Why would a man claw out his own throat?

I am stronger now than I used to be, she realized, staring at the corpse. *I can bear it. One day, maybe, I'll be able to bear anything.*

"Get some servants with strong stomachs to clean this up," the Mace commanded. "And make sure Ewen doesn't come down here."

"Should we send a party after the witch?"

"No. Put out a reward, sure; she's a distinctive woman. But it's unlikely to accomplish anything. Coryn only snatched her by purest luck last time."

"But I'll bank my sword we know where she's going," Coryn murmured. "Jesus, look at that."

Aisa shook herself from the bloody wreck on the floor. Brenna's room was clean and comfortable, not luxurious, but with plenty of space and several decent pieces of furniture. The remains of a meal, some hours old, sat on the table, drawing its own share of flies. But it was the far wall that Coryn meant, and the sight of it made Aisa draw a deep, pained breath. The wall was covered with strange symbols that seemed to dance over the stone, a constellation in sickly orbit around a single word, all of it drawn in blood.

GLYNN

Chapter 2

The Town

The group of committed utopians who made the original Cross-ing with William Tear shared a grand dream of a great society, peaceful and egalitarian. Numbering nearly two thousand, they settled in the shadow of the Clayton Mountains, on the bank of high foothills that would become modern-day New London. They learned to farm, voted by town meeting, and took care of each other. In this idyllic setting, the town grew by leaps and bounds; the population exploded, nearly doubling in the generation after the Crossing. Religion was a strictly private matter, and violence was forbidden. To the outward eye, William Tear had brought his grand vision to life.

—*The Early History of the Tearling,* as told by Merwinian

The trip up the hill was a slog.

Katie Rice had made this journey times without number, up the winding path that switchbacked the hillside, all the way from the river to the Town. She knew each landmark along the path: the broken rock whose face greeted her like a signpost af-ter the third turning, the stand of young oaks just beginning to hunch over the curve halfway up, the spot on the windward side where the path had eroded after years of taking the brunt of the winds that blew off the plains. At meeting last week, William Tear had talked about this spot; he said that they would have to shore it up, fortify it somehow. He had asked for volunteers, and a hundred hands had shot into the air.

Katie knew this path, but she still hated it. She hated the long walk, nothing to do but think. But the sheep farm was at the bottom of the hill, and Katie loved wool as much as she hated walking. She had been three years old when Mum first put a pair of knitting needles into her hands, and now, at fourteen, in addition to being the finest knitter in the Town, she was also one of the best spinners and dyers. To make and dye her own wool, this walk was the price.

She emerged from the treeline and there was the Town: hundreds of small wooden houses covering the gently rounded hilltop. The spread of houses dipped into the depression between hills as well, coming right up to the edge of the river where it curved in toward town before wending away again, south and then west. Mum said they had originally found this place by following the river up from the ocean. Katie tried to picture how it must have looked to Tear's settlers: just a group of hills covered in trees. Sixteen years had elapsed since the Crossing, which seemed like a long time to Katie, but she understood that it was really very short.

She turned around to walk backward, for this was her favorite view: the rows of trees carpeting the hillside, then the bright blue river fronting the green and gold of the farming plain. From here, Katie could see the growers, some fifty of them, working the wide rectangle of planted rows on the far side of the river. The growers would work right until sunset, and if the work wasn't done, they would continue by lamplight. Before Katie was born, there had been a terrible couple of years: the starving time, Mum called it, when the settlers couldn't figure out how to make crops grow. More than four hundred people—nearly a quarter of the population—had died. Now farming was the most serious business in the Town.

Next year, Katie would finally be of age to become an apprentice after school, and she could work at the farm if she chose, but she didn't think she would. She didn't like manual labor, lifting and carrying. But in September and October everyone worked at the farm, except the babies and the old people with arthritis. They didn't have enough career farmers yet, and the harvest had to be brought in before the frost. If anyone complained—and someone always did—the adults would inevitably bring up the starving time, and out would come all of the old stories: how they had to slaughter and eat all of the dogs except the puppies; how several groups fled in the night, seeking food elsewhere, and presumably perished in the snow; how William Tear had given away his portions to others until he became so painfully thin and malnourished that he caught pneumonia and nearly died. Now they had plenty of crops, potatoes and carrots and strawberries and cabbage and squash, as well as a healthy population of chickens, cows, and sheep, and no one starved. But every fall Katie was forced to relive the starving time, all the same, and now even the thought of the harvest made her sick to her stomach.

At meeting last year, William Tear had said something Katie would never forget: that someday all of the plains would be covered with farmland, as far as the eye could see. Katie couldn't imagine all of that wide grassland tamed into rows. She hoped the day wouldn't come in her lifetime. She wanted the view to remain just as it was.

"Katie!"

She turned and saw Row, about a hundred yards up the path. Katie hurried to meet him, feeling something thrill inside her. Row would make the walk interesting; he always did.

"Where are you coming from?" she asked.

"The south slope. I was looking for metal."

Katie nodded, understanding this instantly. Row was a metal-worker, one of the best in town. He apprenticed in Jenna Carver's metal shop, and people were always bringing him jewelry to fix, as well as more practical items like teakettles and knives. But repair was just Row's job. What he really loved was making his own pieces: ornaments and bracelets, ornate fire tools, utility knives with elaborate handles, tiny statues designed to sit on tables. For Katie's last birthday, Row had made her a little silver statue of a woman sitting beneath an oak tree. The carving on the leaves alone must have taken him days, and the statue was Katie's most treasured possession; it sat on her bedside table, right next to her stack of books. Row was a gifted artist, but the metal he loved to craft was hard to come by in the Town. Often Row would leave, sometimes for days at a time, and go prospecting outside town, in the woods and plains. One time he had hiked north for a week and found a great forest, the edges of which had yielded an impressive amount of copper. Row longed to return to the forest, and had even asked William Tear for permission to lead an expedition northward. So far, Tear had given him no answer.

They passed the graveyard, a one-acre patch of flatland beneath a stand of pines. Its perimeter was bounded by wooden fencing, a recent development. Something had been getting into the graveyard, wolves or perhaps just raccoons; in the past few weeks, Melody Banks, who was in charge of the yard, had found several graves torn open, their contents scattered across the yard. Melody would not say whose graves, and the corpses had already been reinterred. Katie was not particularly scared of graveyards, or of corpses, but even she didn't like the idea of animals digging into people's graves. She had been relieved when the Town had voted at meeting to fence the place off.

"Someday," Row said, "when I'm in charge, I'm going to dig this place up, cremate the whole lot."

"What makes you think you'll be in charge?" Katie asked. "Maybe I'll be in charge."

"Maybe both of us," Row replied, grinning, but Katie sensed a vein of seriousness beneath that grin. She had no interest in being in charge of the Town, in handling the eight hundred duties that William Tear juggled on a daily basis. But Row's ambitions were real. Even at fifteen, he was offended by the inefficiency of the Town, certain that he could run it better. He longed for responsibility, and Katie thought that he would be good at it; Row was a born problem solver. But so far, none of the adults in the Town seemed to have recognized this quality, and lack of recognition was a sore spot for Row.

The root of Katie's dissatisfaction was slightly different. She loved the Town, loved the beautifully simple idea that they all took care of each other. But in the past few years, she had sometimes felt hemmed in by her community, by its very niceness, the fact that everyone was supposed to watch out for everyone else. Katie didn't like many of her neighbors; she found them boring, or stupid, or, worst of all, hypocritical, feigning kindness because that was what was expected of them, because Tear was watching. Katie preferred honesty, even at the expense of civility. She longed to have everything out in the open.

The nicer half of herself she ascribed to Mum, who was one of William Tear's closest advisers and a true believer and a half. Katie didn't know who her father was; Mum liked women, not men, and Katie was almost sure that Mum had recruited some willing man to be the father, then forgotten him. Katie wasn't fussed over her father's identity, but she often wondered if this unseen, unknown man wasn't the source of her dissatisfaction, of the rising tide of impatience she sensed inside, an impatience that sometimes bordered on spite.

"Wobbling again?" Row asked, and Katie chuckled.

"Not wobbling, just thinking. It doesn't hurt."

Row shrugged. Her need to look at both sides of an issue, to be fair in her thoughts—*wobbling*, as Row called it—was an impulse that he simply didn't share. Whatever Row thought was certainly right, and he had never needed to look any deeper than that. It maddened Katie sometimes, but there was also a relief there. Row never needed to gaze backward, wondering whether he had screwed up, whether he had been unfair. The tiny mistakes he made didn't haunt him at night.

They turned the corner onto the High Road, passing the library, where the librarian, Ms. Ziv, was just shooing the last people out of the door. The library was a huge building, the only two-story structure the Town could boast. Unlike most of the Town's buildings, which were made of oakwood, this one had been built of brick. The library was Katie's favorite place, always dark and quiet, with books everywhere. Row liked it as well, though his taste differed from Katie's; he had already gone through the small section of books on the occult, but that didn't keep him from checking them out a second time, and a third. There were strict rules for touching and handling the books, and Ms. Ziv would descend like a hawk if she caught anyone bending the pages or, heaven forbid, taking a book out of its plastic dust jacket. Katie had once asked Ms. Ziv how many books there were, and Ms. Ziv had told her in a hushed voice that there were nearly twenty thousand. She had clearly meant for Katie to be impressed, but Katie wasn't. She went through two or three books a week. If that held true for her lifetime, she would have enough to read, but what if she didn't like most of them? What if the ones she hadn't read yet were checked out by other people? There were no more books, but there would surely be more people, plenty of them. Only Katie seemed to understand that twenty thousand was not many, that it was barely any at all.

Ms. Ziv finally got rid of the last stragglers. Katie waved to her, and the harried-looking librarian raised a hand in turn, then disappeared inside, shutting the library door behind her.

"Row!"

Katie turned and found Anita Berry heading toward them, nearly barreling down her porch steps. Katie didn't have much use for Anita, but she smiled all the same, for Row's effect on other girls never failed to entertain her. Row was extremely good-looking, even Katie knew that; it would occur to her sometimes, on those rare occasions when she looked at Row outside the lens of their friendship. Nature had gifted him with the face of an angel: high cheekbones with soft hollows beneath them, and a wide, somehow beautiful mouth. His thick hair, so brown it was almost black, fell over his forehead, nearly obscuring his black eyes. He had a magnetism that attracted a string of admirers, not all of them teenagers. More than once, Katie had seen older women flirting with him, and sometimes older men.

"Hi, Anita," Row replied. "We're in a rush; talk to you in school."

Katie smothered a grin as they walked off, leaving Anita looking crestfallen. Row elbowed her in the ribs, and she grinned at him. Row knew what he did to women; it was a game to him. Katie took a strange pride in all of this attention, a pride she didn't wholly understand. She and Row had bypassed attraction completely, moving on to something finer and stronger than sex: friendship, tight and loyal and bound, nothing like the friendships Katie saw among other girls her age, who seemed only interested in gossiping and backstabbing. Katie had never had sex—some quick, clumsy groping with Brian Lord was the nearest she had come—but her friendship with Row was such that she felt certain sex could only divide them.

When they reached Row's house, he paused, staring with distaste at the front door, where his mother waited. Despite Row's popularity, no one liked Mrs. Finn. She was a nervous, weepy sort of woman, constantly saying the wrong thing. Row could do no wrong in his mother's eyes, but he did not love her for her loyalty; the most he appeared to feel for her was contemptuous indifference.

"Don't want to go in yet?" Katie asked.

Row grinned ruefully, lowering his voice. "Sometimes I want to just move out, you know? Just build my own house, across town . . . except I think she would follow me there, knock on my door all day and night."

Katie didn't reply, but privately she thought that Row was right. Row's father had been one of William Tear's good friends, but Mr. Finn had died just after the Landing, and Mrs. Finn clung to Row with a desperation that was downright embarrassing. Mrs. Finn put things in perspective for Katie; Katie's own mother brooked no nonsense, but she was tough and fair, one of the most respected women in town. Mum gave Katie very little leeway, but she also didn't smother or humiliate her in front of other people.

"We could run away," Katie proffered. "Just run out into the plains and make camp. She would never find us there."

"Ah, Rapunzel." Row placed a hand on her cheek, and Katie smiled involuntarily. The first time they met, she had been crying behind the schoolhouse, because Brian Lord had pulled her hair, pulled it *hard*, and she didn't want to go back after recess because Brian would be there—he sat right behind her, and he pulled her hair all the time. Mrs. Warren had talked to him about it, but he would only wait until she wasn't looking before doing it again. The unfairness of this situation, the cruelty of it, had made six-year-old Katie weep, and she was just considering chopping off all of her hair, making it as short as Aunt Maddy's, when Row sat down beside her against the schoolhouse wall. Katie had been afraid of him—he was a third-grader—but he listened carefully to her complaint, inspected her head, and then told her the story of Rapunzel, whose long hair had allowed her to escape from prison.

If only we could, Katie thought now, an echo of her earlier impatience with the Town. *If only*.

"Row!" Mrs. Finn had come all the way out on the porch now.

She was a gaunt woman, with wide, needy eyes, the corners of her mouth pinched downward in disapproval. Katie, who had been thinking of inviting herself to dinner, suddenly decided to go home. "Row, come in now!"

"My mother might not find us," Row continued. "But yours would."

"You're right. Mum's a bloodhound."

"Row!" his mother called again. "Where have you been?"

Row smiled, trapped, and trudged away up the path to his porch. Katie turned and continued up the lane. Row lived on one of the higher slopes of the hill, but Katie's house was at the very top, right next to William Tear's. He was well protected, Tear was, with Mum's house on one side and Maddy Freeman's on the other. No one in town wanted to tangle with either of them.

"Katie!"

Mrs. Gannett, calling from her porch. Katie wanted to keep walking—Mrs. Gannett was nothing but a gossip—but that sort of thing always got back to Mum. She halted and waved.

"He's over at your house," Mrs. Gannett told Katie.

"Who?"

"You know." Mrs. Gannett lowered her voice almost to a whisper. "Him. *Tear.*"

With an effort, Katie kept from rolling her eyes. She knew she was supposed to worship Tear, as everyone did, but whenever she heard someone speak Tear's name with reverence, a rogue part of her longed to call Tear names and prove that he wasn't much. But she didn't dare. There was something about Tear, perhaps only the way he had of looking at her, grey eyes piercing. Those eyes scared Katie. They seemed to see right to the core of her, things she didn't want anyone else to know. She tried never to speak directly to him.

She liked Lily, Tear's wife—*not wife*, her mind reminded her; William Tear and Lily had never been married—but then, everyone liked Lily. She was one of the few genuine women in Katie's acquaintance, but Katie sensed that Lily's honesty had been hard-won, for there was something sorrowful about her as well, a melancholy that Katie glimpsed from time to time when Lily didn't think anyone was watching. Did William Tear see it too? He must, for he seemed to see everything.

The sun was just beginning to set as she crested the hill, but all of the lamps were already lit, flickering gently as the candles inside were buffeted by the light evening wind. That was another apprenticeship Katie could choose: learning to make candles. She had no interest in going anywhere near the Town beehives, but Mum had told her that beekeeping was separate, that candle makers only had to deal with the wax. Katie didn't know why the apprenticeship was so much on her mind today; it was still months away. Maybe because it would be a sure sign that she was growing older. She was so tired of being young.

"Katie!"

She looked up and found Mum waiting for her on the porch, her hands on her hips. Her hair was tied up into a messy bun and her shirt was splattered with bits of what looked like stew. Some days she drove Katie crazy, but on other days, like today, Katie was swept with a sudden wave of love for her mother, who was so stubborn that she even refused to wear an apron while she cooked.

"Come on, rags," Mum told her, giving her a hug and ushering her inside. "We've got company."

All of the lamps in the house had already been lit, and as Katie's eyes adjusted to the low light in the living room, she saw William Tear and Aunt Maddy by the fireplace, talking in low voices.

"Katie girl," Aunt Maddy said, turning around. "How are you?"

Katie hugged her happily; even though Maddy Freeman wasn't her real aunt, Katie loved her almost as much as she loved Mum. Aunt Maddy knew how to have fun; for as long as Katie could remember, she had always been the one who could think of a good game, or a way to pass a rainy afternoon indoors. But she was also a good listener. It was Aunt Maddy who had told Katie about sex when she was nine, two years before Mrs. Warren broached the subject at school and long before Katie could bring herself to raise the topic with Mum.

Aunt Maddy's hug nearly crushed her. She was strong enough to work on the farm, or in the stockyards for that matter, but if Aunt Maddy had any job, it was advising William Tear. Mum, Aunt Maddy, Evan Alcott . . . Tear never went anywhere without at least two of them along, and despite Katie's ambivalence about the man himself, she couldn't help being proud when she saw Mum or Aunt Maddy at his side.

"Come on out to the backyard with me, Katie," Aunt Maddy told her, and Katie followed, wondering whether she was in trouble. Aunt Maddy didn't have kids of her own to worry about, so she had far too much time to spend keeping an eye on Katie.

Their backyard was wide open, separated from the other houses only by a roundpole fence that Mum had built in order to keep out the Caddells' dog. The sun hung low over the houses, a blinding ball of orange just touching the horizon. Katie could still hear the shouts of other children, several houses over, but they would soon quiet down. The Town was always quiet at night.

Aunt Maddy sat down on the broad wooden bench under the apple tree and patted the space next to her.

"Sit down, Katie."

Katie sat, her anxiety increasing. She hardly ever misbehaved, but when she did, it was usually Aunt Maddy who caught her.

"You start as an apprentice next year," Aunt Maddy remarked.

So this was to be a discussion about her future, not her past. Katie relaxed and nodded.

"Do you have any idea what you'd like to do?"

"I want to work at the library, but Mum says everyone wants to work there and it's a fight to get in."

"That's true. Ms. Ziv has more helpers than she knows what to do with. What's your second choice?"

"Anything, I guess."

"You don't care?"

Katie looked up and found, to her relief, that she was not speaking to Aunt Maddy the disciplinarian. There were two Aunt Maddies, and this was the sympathetic one, the one who had helped Katie hide a dress she'd ruined in a mudfight when she was seven years old.

"I'm just not interested," Katie admitted. "I know there are some apprenticeships I'd hate for sure, like beekeeping. But even the ones I wouldn't hate, I just don't care about."

Unexpectedly, Aunt Maddy smiled. "I have an apprenticeship for you, Katie girl, one I think you'll like. Your mother has approved it, but it needs to be a secret."

"What kind of apprenticeship?"

"You can't tell anyone."

"Not even Row?"

"Especially not Row," Aunt Maddy replied. Her face was deadly serious, and the protest Katie had been formulating died on her lips.

"I can keep a secret," she replied.

"Good." Aunt Maddy paused for a moment, clearly choosing her words. "When we crossed the ocean, we left behind weapons, and therefore much of our ability to defend ourselves from violence. We didn't believe we would need such things here. You've read about weapons, haven't you?"

Katie nodded slowly, thinking of the book beside her bed, in which men shot other men with guns. There were no guns in the Town, only knives and arrows, and those were used for hunting and trades. No one was even allowed to carry a knife in the streets.

"Before the Crossing, your mother and I were both trained as weapons," Aunt Maddy murmured, her gaze fixed on some far-distant place. "We had guns, but we didn't need them. We learned to kill with our bare hands."

"Kill *people*?" Katie blinked, trying to wrap her mind around this idea. Such things happened all the time in books, but they were only stories. She tried to picture Aunt Maddy or Mum killing someone, and found that she had no idea what that would even look like. To her knowledge, only one man in town had ever died by violence, and he had been killed by a marauding wolf out on the plains, years ago. There had been an argument about it at meeting, though Katie had been too young to understand at the time. Several people had demanded that guards be posted around the edges of the Town, guards with bows. Such decisions were always made by democratic vote, but William Tear had spoken against the motion, and when William Tear said no, there was only one way for a vote to go. Katie looked down at Aunt Maddy's hands, then at her arms, muscular and dotted with scars.

"Is that why you always follow William Tear around?" she asked. "In case you have to kill someone?"

This time, it was Aunt Maddy who blinked. "Of course not. We just want to be there in case he needs anything."

Aunt Maddy had just lied to her, Katie thought. She did not take offense; adults lied all the time, their reasons often as silly as those of children. But it was odd that, in a conversation that had contained so many other surprising bits of honesty, Aunt Maddy would feel the need to lie about this.

"We want to start your apprenticeship early, Katie. Next month. We want to train you, just as your mother and I were trained, to meet violence when it comes."

"Why? What violence?"

Aunt Maddy's face seemed to shutter. Even her eyes became blank with concealment.

"Probably no violence at all, Katie. This is just a precaution."

Another lie, and Katie felt anger stir inside her now, a crouched animal, waiting.

"Does it have something to do with the graveyard?" she asked, thinking of those torn-open graves, their contents strewn pitifully across the grass. They said it was an animal, but privately, Katie had wondered. Wouldn't animals have torn up the entire place? Whatever had dug into the ground had apparently targeted three or four specific graves.

"No," Aunt Maddy replied. "But there may be other dangers. Consider yourself a preventative measure."

"Just me?" Katie asked, thinking of her size. She wasn't tiny, but she wasn't tall either, and she was slight. If she had to fight a man with her bare hands, she would probably lose, training or no.

"No. We've chosen several young people. Your friend Virginia. Gavin Murphy. Jonathan Tear. Lear Williams. Jess Alcott. A few others."

"But not Row?"

"No. Rowland Finn won't be a part of this, and he's to know nothing about it."

For a moment, Katie felt her anger begin to uncoil. Row had so many gifts; why couldn't the adults recognize them, at least once? The lack of acknowledgment hurt Row, though he did his best to hide it, and Katie felt that hurt as though it were part of herself.

"Do you want to do it?" Aunt Maddy asked.

Katie swallowed, trying to tame the animal inside her. She *did* want to do this, but it would mean keeping a secret from Row. Could she even do that? They had no secrets. Row knew everything about her.

"Can I think about it?"

"No." Aunt Maddy's voice was kind, but implacable. "You need to decide now."

Katie stared at the ground, her thoughts racing. She did want to do this. She had never hidden anything from Row, but she thought she could, just this once. She wanted to be in on the secret.

"I'll do it."

Aunt Maddy smiled, then crooked her finger toward the house. Katie turned and saw William Tear striding toward them. Without thinking, she hopped off the bench to stand up straight. Aunt Maddy gave her shoulder one final squeeze before she left, but Katie barely noticed her go. The only other time she could remember being alone with William Tear was last year at dinner, when they had both gone to the kitchen for seconds at the same time. Katie had waited, frozen, not knowing what to say to him, relieved when he took his plate back to the table. Now was no better.

"No need to be frightened, Katie." Tear settled himself into Aunt Maddy's spot on the bench. "You're not in trouble. I just want to talk to you."

Katie nodded and sat back down, though a muscle in her leg was shaking and she had to fight to keep it still.

"Do you want this apprenticeship?"

"Yes." Perversely, Katie felt her mouth wanting to open and let words tumble out: how she could keep a secret, how she would be a good fighter, never do anything to hurt the Town.

"I know," Tear said, making Katie jump. "That's a large part of the reason we've chosen you for this. It's not all fighting and knives, Katie. All the training in the world is worth nothing without trust. I've watched you for years. You have a gift, one we've all observed, a gift for seeing through artifice. The Town will need that, and I won't always be here."

Katie stared at him, bewildered. She had never given much thought to Tear's age, as she might do, idly, about the other adults in the Town. Tear had to be at least fifty, but that was just a number; Tear had no age, he simply was. But there was no mistaking the tone of his words.

"Are you sick, sir?"

"No." Tear smiled. "I have years left in me, Katie. Just being cautious. Which brings us to this."

Reaching beneath his wool sweater, Tear pulled out a tiny drawstring pouch that had been tied with a strip of deer thong. Katie had never noticed this pouch before, and she watched, interested, as Tear thumbed it open and dumped the contents into his palm: a sparkling, deep blue jewel—sapphire, Katie thought—its many facets reflecting the waning sun. Plenty of people in town had jewelry, brought with them in the Crossing, but Katie had never seen a gem of this size. Tear held it out to her, but for a moment she could only stare at it.

"Go on, take it."

She took the jewel and found that it was warm. Probably from Tear's chest, but Katie couldn't escape the odd idea that the stone was alive somehow, almost breathing.

"I want you to make me a promise, Katie. And be warned, it's quite a serious promise, not to be made lightly. The jewel you're holding has a way of making people regret their lies."

Katie clenched the sapphire in her fist and felt her hand heat around it, everything in her veins moving faster now. She looked up and saw something terrible: a drop of water trickling down Tear's cheek, incongruous with the world that Katie had always known.

"Promise me, Katie. Promise to do what's best for this town, always."

Katie's shoulders sagged in relief, because that wasn't such a hard promise to make. But Tear was so clearly upset that she forced herself to speak slowly and solemnly, as though thinking through every word.

"I promise to do what's best for the Town." She paused and, because those words didn't seem like enough, continued, "If anyone ever tried to hurt the Town, I'd stop them. I would . . . I'd kill them."

Tear's eyebrows rose. "A fierce animal. Your mother said so. But no more talk of killing, all right?" He held out his hand, and Katie dropped the sapphire back into it. "I'm hoping it will never come to violence. This wasn't supposed to be a killing place."

"Sir, can I ask you a question?"

"Of course."

Katie screwed up her courage. "You have visions sometimes. Everyone says so."

"Yes."

"If the Town is in danger, then from who? Don't you know?"

Tear shook his head. "My visions are often little better than shadows, Katie. It may even be nothing at all."

"But you don't think so."

"No. Even when I only see shadows, they're usually true shadows." He held up the sapphire, letting the last of the dying sun gleam through it. "This jewel is a powerful thing, but it has its limitations. It doesn't function on command. I can use it, but can't control it."

"Where did you get it? From the old world?"

"Yes and no."

She stared at him, confused.

"Someday, perhaps, I will tell you the story, Katie. But for now, just know that you've made a promise. A serious promise. We'll start next week, but until then, I'll ask you not to discuss this with anyone, not even your friends. We haven't spoken to everyone yet."

"Can I talk about it with Mum?"

"Of course. But no one else."

She hesitated, wanting to ask about Row, why he wasn't included. Row was surely the smartest teenager in town, except perhaps for Jonathan Tear . . . but Aunt Maddy had mentioned Jonathan too, Katie recalled now. He was only a year older than Katie, but three years ahead of her in school, and far more distant than his age would suggest. Jonathan never accompanied his parents when they came over for dinner, and though he lived next door, Katie hardly ever saw him. He was fearsomely intelligent; Katie had heard that even after advancing him several grades, they'd been forced to create a special math class for Jonathan, some kind of calculus that no one else was ready to learn. But he didn't have any friends, and the word around school pegged him as some sort of misfit. No one bullied him, because he was William Tear's son, but the fact remained that he was different, apart. Surely Row would be no more strange a choice.

"Katie?"

She turned and found Tear smiling at her, a bit sympathetically, as though he had read her confusion. The jewel and its little pouch had already disappeared back under his sweater, but Katie barely marked these things. Rather, she was struck by Tear's eyes, which were not grey or even light grey, but bright and translucent, almost silver in the fading sun.

"You don't have to be afraid of me anymore," Tear told her. "All right?"

Katie nodded, unable to stop herself from smiling back at him. She thought of all of her own sniping thoughts about Tear and Tear's sycophants, and felt suddenly ashamed. He was a good man, innately good; for a moment, Katie felt that goodness so powerfully that it almost seemed there was a rope binding them to each other, and she suddenly understood why Mum had followed this man across the ocean.

He only wants the best for everyone, she thought. *Beneath all of the whispering and idol-worship, that's the truth. I wish I could tell Row.*

"Thank you," Tear said, and for the rest of her life, Katie would never forget that moment: the tall man smiling at her, the hillside and river stretched out behind, and the bloodred sliver of sun hanging over them. She did not smile back this time, understanding somehow that it would undermine the gravity of the moment, in her own memories if not in fact.

"We'll go in now."

She walked beside him, listening to their feet scruff through the thin, scratchy grass, but her mind was elsewhere. Tear was right; this business needed to remain secret. Fighting and weapons . . . these things were so far outside the rules of the Town that Katie couldn't even imagine what would happen if people found out. Virginia Warren, Lear Williams, Gavin Murphy, Jess Alcott, Jonathan Tear, herself, a few others. But not Row.

Why not? she wondered, glancing sideways at Tear's long legs, his thick wool shoes. *What does he know that I don't?*

Mum was waiting for them, leaning against a wall just outside the kitchen door, her hands tucked behind her back.

"Done," Tear told Mum, settling a hand on her shoulder. "Fierce animal indeed, Dori. Just like her mother."

He went on inside, and Katie looked up at Mum, not sure what came next. Mum was unpredictable; she could be surprisingly rational about Katie's mistakes, but then the oddest things would set her off sometimes. Mum was smiling, but her eyes were watchful.

"You've never kept a secret in your life, Caitlyn Rice, that was as important as this one."

"I know." Katie debated for a moment, then blurted out, "Mum, Row's so smart! Why didn't they pick him too?"

"Ah." Mum leaned back against the wall, and Katie saw her searching for words. "Row is . . . an unpredictable boy."

"What does that mean?"

"Nothing. Come in and set the table."

Katie followed silently, still trying to puzzle this out. Row had a mischievous side, she knew that; he took delight in confounding others. But there was nothing malicious in it, nothing that the two of them couldn't look back and laugh at later. She wanted to be angry on Row's behalf, but all she could seem to feel was sadness. Only she got to see Row's real value, and part of her liked that; it was like a secret between them. But in this moment, she would have traded all of that carefully guarded intimacy to have the rest of the Town know him, see him clearly. And speaking of Row, how was she going to hide all of this from him? An apprenticeship took up a lot of time. How was she supposed to keep Row from finding out?

Tear will take care of it.

The voice came from somewhere deep inside her, a place that felt disturbingly adult, but Katie recognized the truth of the thought. Tear *would* take care of it. There was more than one secret being kept here; Katie sensed rings of concealment far outside herself, widening ripples in the deceptively smooth surface of the Town. She thought of the enormous sapphire, and shivered. She had promised to protect the Town, and she had meant it, but deep down, that other side clamored, the part that was tired of worrying about others, the part that longed only to look after herself.

I can do both, she insisted, but it was a shrill sort of insistence, desperate, as though something inside her knew even then that such equivocation was false, that one day she would have to choose.

Kelsea jerked to consciousness and found herself in darkness. The shadow of her jailor loomed nearby, making her tense up, but after a moment she saw that his head and chest swayed in time with the motion of the wagon. He was asleep. The sky over their heads was a deep, velvet black; Kelsea sensed that it was early morning, but there were no signs of dawn.

I saw.

Light flared above the wagon. Kelsea looked up and saw an ornate streetlamp passing over her head. At the same time she realized that the ragged, bumpy motion to which she had become accustomed had transformed into an easy glide. They were back on smooth ground. The night air was nearly freezing, and Kelsea tucked the ends of her cloak back over her shoulders. Another streetlamp danced by, a myriad of conflicting firelit shadows drifting across the floor of the wagon as it went. She should sit up, try to figure out where she was, but instead she merely lay there, frozen.

"I saw," she breathed, as though words would make the thing real. "I saw."

On impulse, she placed a hand on her chest, exploring, but of course there were no sapphires there. They were long gone, and yet when Kelsea closed her eyes, there it was, laid out before her: the Town, the forest, the Caddell, the Almont in the far distance. How was that possible? Even Lily's world had never been so clear.

She's not Lily.

No. This was a different girl, a child growing up in the Tearling, long before the kingdom had ever held that name. Her mother was Dorian Rice, who had once tumbled into Lily Mayhew's backyard with a bullet in her gut. The girl was Katie Rice. Years after the Crossing, this scene, Jonathan Tear only fourteen years old. The idea made Kelsea's heart ache, for she knew that, only five or six years later, Jonathan Tear would be murdered and William Tear's utopia would be plunged into chaos.

So little time. How could everything have come apart?

A puzzle, that, one with no solution, unless Kelsea went back and found the answers for herself. But she had learned through bitter experience that these little jaunts into the past could carry a terrible price.

It's not like you're doing anything else right now.

Kelsea smiled tiredly at the thought, a bit of pragmatism that reminded her of Mace. There was certainly very little she could do from this wagon. The cavalry had crossed the border and descended from the Argive Pass yesterday, leaving the bulk of the Mort army far behind. She didn't know whether the Red Queen had remained with her army or passed ahead in the night. She stared up at the sky, just beginning to lighten from black to deep blue, and for a moment she missed her country so badly that she thought she would weep again. She had left the Tearling in Mace's hands, yes, and that was a comfort. But she couldn't escape the feeling that her kingdom was in terrible trouble.

Above her head, another streetlamp passed, swinging slightly in the early morning wind. Even this bit of Mort organization galled Kelsea. Streetlamps had to be lit at night and doused in the morning, or they were a waste of oil. Who came out here, in the middle of nowhere, to tend to all of these lamps? Again Kelsea mourned her lost sapphires, for the streetlamps seemed to tell their own valuable lesson: fear bred efficiency.

Not lost.

The words made Kelsea jerk in surprise, for the voice deep in her mind was unmistakably Lily's. True, the sapphires weren't completely lost, but they were in the keeping of the Red Queen; they might as well be on the moon. The Red Queen couldn't use them, but neither could Kelsea.

Why can't she use them? Lily's voice was miles distant, buried in her mind, but still Kelsea registered the urgency there. *Think hard, Kelsea. Why can't she use them?*

Kelsea thought hard, but came up with nothing. Row Finn had said something about Tear blood; she struggled with the memory, which made her head ache. The Red Queen had Tear blood, Finn had said, but Kelsea's was stronger. She had given the sapphires away, so how could she still be seeing the past? She suddenly remembered the dream she'd had a week ago: the Crossing, the ships and the dark sky with a bright hole in the horizon. William Tear had opened a doorway through time, and in her own limited way, Kelsea had done the same thing, prying open an aperture and peering into the past. Was it possible that the aperture had stayed open, even now when the sapphires were lost? If the Crossing she had seen was real, it aligned neatly with what she had just seen here: Maddy Freeman, Lily's sister, years older but alive and well.

The sooner Kelsea got out of this wagon, the better. She was not in control during her fugues; both Mace and Pen had told her so. She twisted to lie on her back, feeling slivers of wood dig into her cloak. If only she could reach out to them, to William and Jonathan Tear, tell them of the storm-filled future, change history instead of just watching it play out—

A skull appeared over her head.

Kelsea bolted upright, clapping a hand to her mouth to stifle a gasp, and saw that the skull had actually been hung high in the air, mounted on a pike in between streetlamps. A few traces of flesh still dangled from its jawbone. The eye sockets were crusted with blood, long since aged black. She lost sight of the skull as the light from the streetlamp faded away behind them, but then another streetlamp appeared, and shortly afterward, another skull. This one was very old; wind and time had eaten away at the jawbone and the smooth curvature around the nose.

Well, there was at least one question answered. She was on the Pike Road.

As quietly as she could, Kelsea stood up in the wagon, holding her chains so that they would not rattle and wake her jailor. Dawn was coming quickly now, the eastern horizon lined with pink, but the land below was a vast darkness, broken only by their current road, which was lined with pikes and streetlamps. They were heading on a slight downhill slope, but in the distance, Kelsea could see that the road inclined sharply toward an enormous barrier: a wall, tall and well fortified, a black bulwark against the lightening sky. Above the wall, Kelsea saw the silhouettes of many buildings and, towering over all, a vast structure, tipped with spikes and oblongs that Kelsea identified as turrets.

Demesne, she thought, feeling something knot together in her stomach. Once it had been Evanston, the capital of New Europe, the city on a plateau, built brick by brick by settlers. But now it seemed like something out of a nightmare.

Kelsea sat back down in the bed of the wagon, keeping an eye on her jailor, who was beginning to stir, and wrapped herself up in her cloak. She tried to summon courage, but that well seemed to have dried up. She was in the middle of her own Crossing now, but this voyage was nothing like William Tear's.

This was a journey into a dark land.

When Ducarte walked through the door, the Queen knew it was bad. She had waited days for this report, trying to be patient—though it ran directly counter to her nature—understanding that it would take Ducarte some time to assess the situation. She had only sent him home from the border two weeks before. After the scene with the girl, Ducarte was no more use as a commander, for it seemed he could barely keep himself together. He jumped at loud noises, and sometimes the Queen had to speak his name two or three times to get his attention. She had hoped that a return to his old duties, the position that he had created and made his own, might bring him back to himself. But as soon as Ducarte entered her throne room, she saw that nothing had changed. If anything, he seemed worse than ever. Whatever the girl had done to him, she had done it well ... perhaps even permanently. And without Ducarte, the Queen's position became even weaker than before.

She was facing a revolt. Despite her best efforts, word had leaked out that she was gone, and the rebel leader, Levieux, had laid siege to Cite Marche. None of the overgrown prats to whom she had delegated responsibility had made even the slightest headway in stopping this Levieux, or even in discovering his identity. Her army had finally returned from the Tearling, but slowly, even more slowly than on the outgoing journey, and in this lack of speed, the Queen sensed treachery. Before she departed, she had given explicit orders to Ducarte's replacement, General Vine, that any man caught looting in the Tear be hung from the nearest tree. But General Vine was not a man to make an army tremble. Only fear of the Queen herself was keeping her soldiers in line now, and she sensed that fear steadily eroding. Her colonels and generals were loyal, for they knew they would be compensated for their share of plunder upon their return. But the rest of the army . . . damn it, she needed Ducarte now! How could he go and fall apart when she could least afford to lose him?

But the Queen allowed none of this rancor to show on her face. Even half of Ducarte's old competence, she reminded herself, was better than most men could boast. Behind him came two lieutenants, both of whom knew enough to take station behind Ducarte and stay quiet, their eyes cast respectfully to the floor.

"What news, Benin?"

Ducarte tossed his cloak away and collapsed into a nearby chair. Another disturbing sign. Ducarte had never liked to sit before; now he seemed to be constantly looking for the nearest support.

"Cite Marche is in chaos, Majesty. Last week, a mob broke into the Crown warehouses and removed everything, food and glass and steel and arms. The soldiers who were supposed to be on duty have disappeared. Mayor Givene has disappeared, and without him, no one has the authority to mobilize the city militia."

"I have the authority."

"Of course, Majesty. I didn't mean—"

"Get the militia out there and find my property."

"That might be a problem, Majesty. We've caught a few people with glass or steel, but only a piece or two at a time. That rebel bastard, Levieux, has already distributed all of the goods, and he seems to have done it citywide. The food is probably gone already, and we'd have to arrest half the populace to take back the rest."

"He stole only to give it away?"

"Apparently, Majesty."

The Queen remained still, but inside her muscles were jumping, galvanized by fury. It was not enough that she had expended a vast fortune to mount an invasion that had netted her nothing. Now she had to come home to this!

"When you find Givene, I want him hung from the walls of Cite Marche."

"Yes, Majesty." Ducarte hesitated for a moment, then asked, "His head?"

"His whole body!" she shouted. "His whole body, Benin! Alive! Once the crows have their way, we'll see how good a rebel he is!"

"Yes, Majesty," Ducarte repeated dully, and the Queen had to restrain the urge to leap from her throne and slap him. There had been a day once, almost twenty years ago now, when Ducarte had taken a traitor from Callae and skinned the man alive, working slowly and methodically, impervious to the man's screams, shaving flesh with his knife as a sculptor would shave clay. The old Ducarte would not have needed clarification. The old Ducarte would simply have understood. The Queen took a deep breath, feeling everything tip precariously inside her.

"What of Demesne?"

"At this moment, Demesne seems relatively calm, Majesty. But I'll wager not for long."

"Why not?"

"I sent several of my agents out into the countryside, Majesty, to assess the likelihood of a slave revolt. They found little to worry about from that quarter."

The Queen nodded. The penalties for runaway slaves had always been sufficiently severe to create an effective deterrent. "But?"

"There is a curious migration under way, Majesty. The villages of the Glace-Vert have been abandoned. People are taking their livestock and whatever valuables they can carry and moving southward. Many of them are already crammed into Cite Marche."

"Why?"

"My people were too spread out to conduct proper interrogations, Majesty. This is only the word they were able to pick up from voluntary statements. There is an old superstition in the Fairwitch—" Ducarte paused and coughed lightly. "A creature that supposedly stalks the mountains and foothills, seeking young prey—"

"The Orphan," the Queen murmured.

"Majesty?"

"Nothing. I know this superstition, Benin; it is older than I am. What has changed?"

"There are new reports, Majesty, of villages assaulted by not one, but an army of such things. My agent in Devin's Copse found blood and bones on the floors of the empty houses. My people have found eight villages so abandoned. Two of my agents have gone missing themselves, more than a week overdue."

"What is the alternate explanation?" the Queen asked. But her tone was hollow, for it was an empty question. The dark thing was on the hunt. She could tell Ducarte so, but then he would ask for an explanation, and what story would she tell?

Once, long ago, a frightened young girl fled from a village in the Glace-Vert. She was already in exile, and she had gone north to hide. But she found no comfort in the villages of the Glace-Vert, only abuse, so much so that she chose to starve in the mountains instead. She was prepared to die, but one night she saw a flicker of flame—

"Again, I had no resources to interrogate these people, but I tell you, Majesty, they believed what they were saying. Something is at bloody work in the north, and if it continues to move south, the entire country will be knocking at our door for asylum."

The Queen leaned back against her throne, a pulse drumming unpleasantly in her temples. Two weeks before, she had woken from a nightmare, the most terrible nightmare of her life, in which the dark thing, not phantom but solid, no longer bound by fire, chased her up and down the corridors of her castle, the length of the new world . . .

Free, she realized. Call it the dark thing, call it the Orphan—and those poor hunted villagers out in the Fairwitch certainly needed to call it something, to name the reason their children sometimes disappeared without a trace—but it was out now, free to roam . . . and would it be coming in this direction? Was there even any doubt?

Evie!

The voice rang inside her head, but the Queen pushed it away, staring sadly at her oldest and most faithful ally. Ducarte leaned forward now, resting his crossed arms on his knees and staring at the ground. He was not sixty yet, but he looked like an old man, worn and exhausted. The old General Ducarte, the Chief of Internal Security whose name had made her entire kingdom tremble, that man was dead, and the Queen mourned him. Ducarte had put down the Callaen rebellion, had helped to transmute the Queen's grasp on Mortmesne from wood to iron. But he was broken, and the Queen was only now awakening to the fact that sending Ducarte to the Tearling might have been the gravest mistake she had ever made. Without him, there was no one to shield her, not even from the army itself.

Have there been others? she wondered, feeling the question scurry in her mind, back and forth, like a panicked rodent. *Other failures? How many mistakes have I made?*

"What do you want to do, Majesty?"

The Queen tapped her fingers on the arm of her throne for a moment, then asked, almost idly, "Where's the girl?"

Ducarte's expression did not change, but his face paled a fraction, and in that moment, he seemed to grow older. The Queen didn't like to think of the girl either; the memory of that scene in the tent was terrible, so terrible that she had pushed it to the bottom of her mind. The girl knew so much now—

Evie!

—so many things that the Queen had meant to carry to her grave.

"They brought her in yesterday, Majesty. She's in the dungeons, safe and sound."

But Ducarte winced as he spoke.

"I want her well guarded."

"You worry about jailbreak, Majesty?"

"Of course not. I worry about her dying in custody. Your people don't have the best record in this department, Benin. I need the girl alive."

"Her name is a rallying cry for the rebels. Wouldn't it be better to simply execute her?"

The Queen slammed her fist down on the throne, and had the pleasure of seeing him jump.

"Did you hear me, Benin?"

"Yes, Majesty. Alive, I understand."

But the Queen no longer trusted him. Would Ducarte ever turn against her? No loyalty seemed certain anymore. She thought wistfully of Beryll, her old chamberlain, who would have walked into fire on her command. But Beryll was dead, and in his place the Queen now had Juliette, who seemed always to be whispering. Even now, Julie was forgetting herself, lounging against the wall and making eyes at one of the palace guards. The Queen's other pages were scattered around the room, barely even paying attention.

"What else?"

"The army, Majesty," Ducarte ventured, shooting an uneasy glance at the two men behind him. "It's a problem. Many of the soldiers refused to return home after they were discharged. Large groups of soldiers hold meetings which they believe to be secret. We have reports of widespread public drunkenness and brawling all over Demesne, and in the aftermath of broken furniture and abused women, the people blame you."

The Queen smiled, allowing some of her own spite to enter her voice. "Well, why don't you do something about it, Benin?"

"I no longer hold sway with my men, Majesty," Ducarte admitted stiffly. "They do not want platitudes or patriotism. They want their plunder, all the way down to the infantry. Failing that, they want to be paid in coin."

The Queen nodded, but what Ducarte asked was impossible. She had always acted as her own treasurer, and she knew down to the mark how much money was in her vaults. She had reserves, but the flow of money had slowed considerably since the Tear shipment had stopped. There certainly wasn't enough to pay the thousands of disaffected soldiers anything close to what they had expected to reap from the Tear invasion. Briefly, the Queen considered paying them all a small fraction anyway; such a gesture would empty the Treasury, but sometimes gestures were necessary. The Queen had gambled thus several times before, and the gamble had always paid off.

But something about the idea stuck in her craw. After all, she had not been paid either. The two Tear sapphires lay beneath her clothes, but they were only pretty baubles. All of the power, the invincibility, she had hoped to gain from the Tear invasion had been reduced to the empty trophies that now hung between her breasts. Upon her return to the Palais, she had tried everything, every enchantment she knew, but the jewels would not speak to her. It was maddening. She had Tear blood—at least the dark thing had told her so—and she should have been able to wield them. Where had their power gone?

Ducarte was still waiting for a solution, but the Queen had none to give. Her soldiers were children. She had compensated her high command, generously so. What they chose to do with that money was their own problem.

"This is my army," she finally replied. "They work for me. If they forget, I can remind them."

"Fear will only hold them for so long, Majesty."

"Just watch, Benin."

Ducarte wanted to argue further, she could tell, but after a moment he merely resumed his former defeated posture, hanging his head over his knees. For perhaps the hundredth time, the Queen wondered what in holy hell the girl had done to him. She hadn't even known that this man was capable of fear, and now he seemed to be nothing but a quivering mass of it.

"Anything else?"

"One disturbing report. When your soldiers meet in secret, my people are always watching. Two days ago, a group of ten lieutenants met down in an abandoned house in the southern district."

"And?"

"They met with two priests."

"*Tear* priests?"

"Yes, Majesty. We did not recognize the second, but the man in charge was Father Ryan, he who took over as the pope's right hand when Brother Matthew was executed."

The Queen's lips pulled back in a snarl. The Tear pope's principles were so flimsy as to be nearly transparent, and the bargain he had struck with the Queen now sat in limbo. The pope had failed to kill the girl, and the Queen had withdrawn her army. She would not touch the Tearling further; even though the jewels appeared lifeless, she had sworn an oath upon them, one she did not dare test. But she should have known that the two-faced bastard in the Arvath would now be seeking his own accommodation. She longed to have his neck in her hands.

"The substance of this meeting?" she demanded.

"I don't know yet, Majesty. I have two of the lieutenants in custody, but they have not broken."

"Break them *now*."

"Of course, Majesty." But Ducarte sounded discouraged, and the Queen heard his unspoken thought easily: it was so hard to keep people from plotting in the dark.

Evie!

"Christ God, shut *up!*" she whispered.

"Majesty?"

"Nothing." The Queen rubbed her temples, willing her mind to be silent. The girl had done quite a number on Ducarte, but he wasn't alone. The Queen, who believed she had killed off Evelyn Raleigh long ago, now found her mind peopled with Evelyn's unquiet ghosts. She needed peace, time to sit and think, to figure out what to do. Some tea and a hot bath. Answers would come, and if they didn't, she could at least take a nap, remove some of the muddle that seemed to cover her mind at all times these days. She had been so sure that the Tear sapphires would cure her insomnia, but of course they had not done this either, and now every day seemed to be about recovering the sleep she had lost the night before—

A light clang of steel echoed in the air. Out of old instinct, the Queen sprang from her throne and leapt off the side of the dais, landing in a crouch. Something thudded against the back of her throne, but she was already scurrying behind one of the enormous pillars that sat on either side of the dais. Her mind clocked glimpses of activity: Ducarte, grappling with one of his lieutenants; a knife lying at the foot of the stairs; the other lieutenant, stalking toward the pillar, sword in hand.

Assassination, the Queen thought, almost bemused at the idea. It was an old game, but it had been a long time since anyone had dared to play it here. She pressed her body against the smooth, rounded surface of the pillar, her mind working rapidly. The army was discontented, yes, but discontent alone would never drive them to such a drastic move. They thought her vulnerable, somehow. Did they think she had left the Tear intact out of weakness? Intolerable. Could Ducarte be in on it? She thought not; more likely, Ducarte was a secondary target. No one loved him, not even his own troops.

She sensed the second soldier coming for her now, could feel his heartbeat, light and rapid as a rabbit's, on the far side of the pillar. She could kill him easily, but two lieutenants had never hatched this plot on their own; she needed at least one of them alive. From the center of the room came the thick, gagging sound of a man being throttled. She hoped it wasn't Ducarte, but was forced to concede that it might be. The assassin was edging around the curve of the pillar now, approaching on her left, and the Queen tensed, preparing to go for his sword hand. But then something slammed into the pillar, an impact that the Queen felt even through ten feet of solid stone. The man's sword clattered to the ground in front of her.

"Majesty? You are well?"

The words were spoken with a heavy Tear accent. The Queen peeked around the pillar and found one of her pages, the new girl that Juliette had selected when Mina died. The Queen could not remember her name. Continuing around the curve, she found that the girl held the lieutenant up against the pillar, his face smashed into the stone and a knife to his throat. The Queen couldn't help being impressed. Though tall and muscular for a woman—all of the Queen's pages were built so—the girl was still smaller than the soldier. But she held the lieutenant immobilized.

The state of the throne room said a great deal. Juliette had not moved, nor had the rest of the pages. The Queen's guard captain, Ghislaine, was just pulling Ducarte from beneath his attacker, and even from here the Queen could see the ugly bruises forming on Ducarte's throat. The other lieutenant was dead, knifed in the back. Most of the Queen's private guard still lined the walls, sharp eyes watching her every movement. They had barely even stirred.

Good God! the Queen thought. *My own Guard!*

She turned back to the new page. "What is your name?"

"Emily, Majesty."

"Benin! Are you well enough to take a prisoner?"

"I'm fine!" Ducarte spat, nearly snarling. "He blindsided me."

The Queen's lips tightened. No one ever took Ducarte by surprise. She turned back to the girl, Emily, sizing her up: good Tear stock, tall and blonde, tightly corded muscles in her arms. Pretty, but not bright; her face had that dull look which the Queen had always associated with the Tear underclass.

"You came in the shipment," the Queen remarked.

"Yes, Majesty," the girl replied in a mixture of Tear and broken Mort. "A page I'm chosen, last month only."

A page who couldn't even speak the language properly! Juliette must have been desperate. And yet, given the events of the past few minutes, the Queen couldn't really fault the choice. She could have dealt with the assassins herself, but that didn't matter. Of all the people in the room, only two had acted: Ghislaine and the slave. Competent Mort speakers were abundant, but loyalty was in very short supply these days. What a pity the girl was a Tear!

"Give him to General Ducarte," she told Emily. "Benin! I want names!"

"Yes, Majesty," Ducarte replied, dragging himself to his feet. The new page handed the prisoner over while the Queen kept a careful eye on Juliette, who was working hard to conceal her anxiety. Whether that indicated guilt, the Queen couldn't say. Treachery seemed to surround her now. It was like the old Tear tale: the lonely dictator, safe in his castle, so well guarded that he could not leave. Ducarte had warned her that withdrawing the army would cause a real problem, and now she realized that he had understood his men better than she had. She should have listened. As Ducarte began marching his prisoner toward the door, the Queen found herself forced to face an unpleasant truth: this miserable man was the closest thing she had to a friend. Alone, neither of them would last very long.

"Benin!"

He turned back. "Majesty?"

The Queen took a deep breath, feeling as though she had to coax each word from her throat. Asking for help . . . it was the most difficult thing, the most terrible thing. But she had run out of options.

"It is only you and I now, Benin. You see?"

Ducarte nodded, his face twitching, and the Queen made a startling discovery: he found her just as unpleasant as she found him. That would be something to think on, but later, when this crisis was over, when she'd finally had one good night's sleep.

"Go."

Ducarte left, pushing the army lieutenant in front of him. There was probably nothing to be extracted from the man anyway; a dissatisfied army made for fruitful recruiting, but the clever conspirator never told the assassin anything, and her unseen adversary, this Levieux, was nothing if not clever. The Queen seated herself on her throne again, staring at the menagerie of potential traitors before her: guards, pages, soldiers, courtiers, at least thirty people, all of them scheming to bring her down. Juliette had begun to arrange for removal of the corpse on the floor, but her eyes darted constantly to the Queen, fearful.

The Queen sought out the Tear girl, who had retreated to stand against the wall with the other pages. She should dig into the girl's background, find out where a Tear woman had learned to handle a knife like that. But that was for later; there were too many things to worry about now. Entire villages had disappeared, fleeing from the Glace-Vert. The Queen no longer commanded an army, only a bunch of cutthroats. The Orphan, the dark thing, whatever name he traveled under, he was coming, and she had nothing with which to stop him. The girl might be of use, but she was a dangerous uncertainty, and the Queen hated uncertainty above all things. She felt a sudden urge to scream, to throw something, anything to stop all of these people from staring at her, waiting for her to make another mistake.

"Emily, is it?" she asked the slave.

"Yes, Majesty."

The Queen stared at her for a moment longer, sizing her up. She could not trust anyone, she realized now, but perhaps a Tear slave was a better choice than most. By and large, the Tear who came in the shipment retained no loyalty to their kingdom; they were more likely to feel active hate. It was a risk, and a large one, to give a Tear slave access to the Tear Queen, but the girl had at least *acted*, damn it . . . and that was more than the Queen could say for most of the room, even her own guards. Again she thought with longing of Beryll, of a time when loyalty had not been a choice between evils.

"You are no longer a page," the Queen told her. "Yours is a special assignment. Go down to my dungeons. I want a full report on the status of the Tear Queen. Where is she, what are her conditions. Find out if she has made any requests of her jailors."

The girl nodded, shooting a triumphant glance at Juliette, whose face darkened further. No love lost there; a good sign.

"And get yourself a Mort tutor. Learn fast. I want to hear no Tear words out of your mouth."

Another good sign: Emily neither talked back nor asked questions, only nodded and left.

The Queen returned to her throne, but once there, it seemed she could do nothing but stare at the fresh bloodstain on the floor. Rebellion and revolt. No ruler had ever held such things down for long, not by force. Levieux and the dark thing . . . for a moment she wondered if they might be working together. But no, the dark thing would never condescend to work with anyone. Even the Queen, who had thought they were partners, had only been a pawn to him. The dark thing would wait until she was weak, until the rebellion raging across Mortmesne had taken its worst toll, and then it would come for her.

I could flee, the Queen thought, but it was an empty idea at best. She was equally hated in both Cadare and Callae. That left the north, where the dark thing waited, and west, the worst option of all. If the Tear got hold of her, they would stretch her to ribbons just to watch her scream. And even if she could flee, into dark holes and shadowy corners, what kind of life would that be, when she was used to watching kingdoms dance at her command?

Evie! Come here!

"No," she whispered. Long before the Tear had sent its first shipment, she had already been a slave, and now she could never go back. She would rather be dead. She thought of her recurring nightmare, which had plagued her for months now: the last flight, the girl, the fire looming, and the man in grey behind them. *You will flee*, the dark thing had told her, and perhaps she would, but only at the very end, when she had nothing left. She lifted her chin, staring at the room of traitors before her.

"Next."

Chapter 3

Demesne

These people are so damned proud of their hatred! Hatred is easy,
and lazy to boot. It's love that demands effort, love that exacts a
price from each of us. Love costs; this is its value.
        —*The Glynn Queen's Words*, AS COMPILED BY FATHER TYLER

In all his years of sneaking in and out of every venue imaginable,
the Fetch had found that the most valuable skill was the correct
stride. Too fast was suspicious. Too slow was lost. But the right
pace, the confident gait of one who belonged there, these things
had an almost magical power to set guards and sentries at ease.

He padded stolidly up the stairs, the walk of a much heavier
man who did not relish his destination. He wore the cloak of one
of the Arvath guards, but beneath the hood his eyes darted everywhere, looking for movement. It was half past three in the
morning, and most of the Arvath was asleep. But not all; the Fetch
could hear the activity far above him, the sound of many voices
drifting down the center of the staircase from the upper floors. A
new mob. When the Holy Father had been anointed, the devout of
the city had hailed the event in a three-day waking fast before the
Arvath. These same people thought the Holy Father would restore

the glory of the Church, a glory that had steadily eroded since the Glynn Queen took the throne. It was from this demographic that the Holy Father assembled his mobs.

I could tell you, the Fetch thought, the thought tinged with black inside his head, and now, instead of the Holy Father, he saw Row, swathed in white. *I could tell you about God's Church.*

The mobs were bad; they had already slaughtered several "sinners" in various corners of the city. But there was worse to come. The new Holy Father had hired more than twenty-five bookkeepers for the Arvath, but even a casual observer could see that these men were not accountants but enforcers. Howell had followed several of them around the city, into the Gut and the warehouse district, even down into the Creche, where they dealt in whatever obscenity would give a good rate of return. Intuition told the Fetch that a vast criminal empire was being assembled here, under the streets, in the dark.

Of course, there were many gangsters in the Tearling; the Queen's treasurer was one of them. But this was the Church, and the Fetch, who had once been a member of God's Church in its infancy, felt the difference deep inside himself. Criminals and panderers . . . he didn't know why this fact should continue to surprise him. But the shame he felt now was the same shame he had felt then.

Before he died, Thomas Raleigh had told the Fetch that the crown was in the keeping of the Holy Father. Thomas had offered an infinite number of minor bribes to get it back, but he had at least had the presence of mind to withhold what the old Holy Father had really wanted: a permanent income tax exemption for the Church. It was, after all, only a crown, though the Fetch, who had always been able to read Thomas easily, saw a different truth in the condemned man's eyes: he had wanted the crown terribly. He had no idea of what it could do—for that matter, neither did the Fetch—but the silver circlet symbolized something that Thomas had needed to prove. In that final moment before execution, the Fetch had pitied him, but not enough to withhold the axe.

Several weeks ago, just before the Queen's capture, Howell had picked up word that something had been stolen from the Arvath. The Holy Father's enforcers didn't know that something from Adam, but they knew that it was kept in a polished cherrywood box; it was this information that had made Howell prick up his ears. The Fetch's men had never seen that box, but the Fetch had, long ago, in the hands of the man he had thought was his friend. Keeping it out of Row's hands was paramount, but there were other hands almost as bad. The entire Church was on the lookout for the Keep priest, Father Tyler, and the bounty on his head seemed to go up every day. If the Keep priest had taken the crown, then the Fetch would not find it by skulking around the Arvath. But yesterday he had spotted something interesting, and if life had taught him nothing else, it had taught him that more information was never a bad thing. The small facts one learned by accident often became useful later.

Before him was a dark-haired woman sitting on a bench in the hallway that ran the length of the brothers' quarters. Her face had been sliced to ribbons by what looked like a straight razor. The cuts had not been stitched, leaving the woman's face a seamed patchwork of dried blood and infected flesh. She stared at the ground as the Fetch approached.

Howell had not said anything about this woman, but the Fetch had picked up enough gossip in the kitchens to know that her name was Maya, and she had been one of the Holy Father's concubines. The Fetch, who knew a comer when he saw one, had kept a weather eye on Cardinal Anders for years; the man always had women, two of them, no more and no less. Though well hidden from the populace, these women were no secret in the Arvath. They came from prostitution and usually went back there when Anders was finished with them. But this one, Maya, would never be able to work again. Like all of the Holy Father's women, she was addicted to morphia, and the Fetch guessed that her addiction was the only thing that kept her sitting obediently on the bench. She might be looking no further than her next fix, but the Fetch knew that her death could not be far behind.

Still, she was a puzzle. Anders had never been one to cut his women. He was a violent man, for certain, but he had always reserved that violence for his antisodomy demonstrations. There was no attempt to hide Maya; she was out on full display. She was being punished, made an example of. He was determined to find out why.

The Fetch tapped her on the shoulder, and she looked up. The slashes on her face were cruelly visible, even in the dim torchlight; one of them traveled up and over the bridge of her nose, very near to the corner of her eye. It looked as though her eye had wept blood, and this made the Fetch think again of Row. In the excitement of discovering this woman, he had forgotten about the hell that was currently raining down on the northern end of both kingdoms, Tear and Mortmesne. That was one of Row's many dangers; he was so damnably easy to ignore until it was too late.

"You are the Fetch," Maya murmured.

For a moment he was stunned, and then he remembered that he was wearing his mask. He often forgot about it; he was so used to its leathery feel that it often seemed like part of his face. Far away, deep in the bowels of the Arvath, he heard a clock strike two.

"What do you want with me?" she asked.

The Fetch touched a light hand to her hair, brushing it away from her forehead. He had often used artifice to get what he wanted, particularly from women, but there was no art here. The Tearling was full of battery, but the Fetch had rarely seen any woman so poorly used as this one. For a moment, the Fetch seemed to hear William Tear's voice, deep in his mind.

God does not keep his hands to himself. Believe, or not; your neighbor's belief will wound you just as surely as your own.

The Fetch nearly groaned. They had heard, all of them; they had heard William Tear speak these words—or some variation thereof—many times, but they had never listened. To all of them, born after the Crossing, with no frame of reference, Tear's words were merely so much breath. The Fetch had belonged to God's Church long enough to know that the carnage before him was nothing to do with God, or good. Brutality found such great camouflage under the cross.

We didn't listen.

No, you didn't listen. Katie listened.

That was true. She had. And she had paid for it, forced into exile, her belly great with Jonathan's child. More than anything, the Fetch suddenly wished that he might have five minutes with Katie, just to apologize, to tell her that she had been right. The younger Gavin had been too proud even to think of apologizing, but the Fetch had found that age brought that need, to even scores and make things right. But it was many long years too late to beg forgiveness of Katie. There was only the woman in front of him, her face a path of razors.

"Why has he done this to you?" the Fetch asked.

"Because I let the Keep priest get away."

"Why?"

Maya stared at him blearily. "The old man was kind. He listened. He said the Queen was good—"

She paused, looking around her, and the Fetch realized that he'd been wrong; she was immobilized not by morphia, but by withdrawal. The skin of her neck and shoulders was damp with sweat.

"Good," Maya continued, her voice growing hoarse now; her muscles were spasming, constricting her vocal cords. "He said she was good. And I thought, well, if she is good, then Anders shouldn't be allowed to keep it from her. He shouldn't be allowed to do that."

"Keep what?"

"The crown. He liked to try it on when no one was looking, and even when I was deep under the spoon, I would think: it's not his; it belongs to the Queen. He shouldn't get to wear it." She blinked slowly; the Fetch thought that she must be very close to sinking into unconsciousness. "When the old man came, I saw my moment, and I jumped."

The Fetch needed to ask her more, but his time was running out. "This crown. What did it look like?"

"Silver. A circle. Blue sapphires. In a pretty box."

"And the Keep priest took it away?"

She nodded.

"Where is he?"

"I don't know. They said he got away, took Father Seth with him. When Anders found out, he cut my face."

The Fetch frowned, his stomach twisting. Few in the Tear knew that the silver circlet the Raleighs had worn for centuries was only an imitation. The real crown had disappeared completely, along with its cherrywood box. The Fetch suspected that Katie had taken it with her, but he had never been sure. Regardless of where the crown was now, for at least a brief moment it had been here in the Arvath, and he had lost it. Two cloistered Arvath priests, on their own, in New London? The thought made him shudder.

"Do they feed you?" he asked Maya.

"Yes. Every day a tiny dose, not nearly enough . . ."

The Fetch grimaced.

"You will not stay, keep me company?" Maya asked. "I'm not afraid of your mask."

"Then you would be the first," the Fetch murmured. Even he

himself had become afraid of the mask, for he no longer knew which was the real man beneath. The outlaw? The rueful traitor who had been forced into hiding, donning the mask only because he could no longer stand the idea that he might be recognized? Or was it a boy named Gavin, a boy who had wanted so badly to be right, to be clever, that he had been easy pickings for the cleverest manipulator of them all?

Which are you?

He didn't know. He had been walking the Tear for more than three hundred years, and sometimes he felt that he was not one man, only a collection of phases, several different men with their own lifetimes.

But which are you now? his mind hammered relentlessly. *Which man have you become?*

Ah, there was the question. The boy, Gavin, would have left the mutilated woman before him on the bench, her purpose served, information extracted. The man, the Fetch, might have rescued her, but only to increase the glory of his legend, as when he had once stolen an unhappy concubine from right under Thomas Raleigh's nose.

He dug deep into the inner pocket of his shirt and came up with a cloth-wrapped packet. Inside were several needles and a good quantity of high-grade morphia. He had not expected to need these things, but had brought them along just in case. Now he unwrapped the cloth and snapped his fingers before Maya's face.

"Listen." He pressed the vials into her hand. "These are for you. Hide them away, and hide them well."

Her gaze sharpened as she focused on the needles.

"For me?"

"Yes. Just in case." He patted her cheek to make her look at him. "This is the Grandmile grade. Powerful, far more powerful even than what you were getting from the Holy Father. If you took it all at once, you wouldn't live out the night."

She looked up at him steadily, clenching the packet in her fist.

The Fetch tiptoed backward, leaving her on the bench. Briefly, he considered going upstairs and ending the Holy Father once and for all, but then he realized that he could not; he might need the man in the end, and even if not, there were ranks of eager priests, perhaps worse, waiting behind him. No, better to simply fade away, vanish, as he had always done. And yet he couldn't help loathing himself.

"Dear God," he whispered, and even though he was currently walking through the oldest house of worship in the new world, he knew he was talking to no one at all. If God had ever been in the Tearling, he was long gone.

Javel could not stand still. He had spent most of the morning pacing in front of the window, which was spattered with tiny droplets. Cold rain had been falling in Demesne on and off for the past two weeks, and the unpaved streets of this neighborhood, the Breen, were nothing but a wet bog. Winter came to the Mort capital several weeks earlier than it did to New London; Javel was grateful that Galen had insisted they bring heavier clothing. Sometimes Galen's caution was annoying—like having a mother along—but more often than not, that caution was also justified. Javel had learned to trust the man's instincts, and several days ago, when Galen suggested that it was time to move along to new quarters, they had packed up and moved into the Breen.

Javel had not expected to like Demesne. Even before it had taken Allie from him, Mortmesne had been a dark realm, evil kingdom in the fairy tales Javel had heard growing up. But Demesne was, after all, only a city, buildings and alleys and streets, and Javel had been a city dweller all his life. Demesne was bigger than New London, and boasted impressive construction, most of its buildings made of brick instead of wood. The streets gleamed with windows, for glass was nearly as cheap as brick in Mortmesne, the result of a glut of supply from Cadare. The Red Queen was no fool; she'd made sure that glass was affordable even for Mortmesne's poor. The city was filled with such small gestures, the trappings of quality of life, plazas and public parks. It was the facade of an easy, open land, incongruous with the image of Mortmesne that Javel had always carried in his head.

But the plazas and parks were actually under close surveillance by the Queen's Internal Security, watching to see who gathered with whom. The windows meant that very little could be hidden.

"Calm yourself, Gate Guard," Galen murmured from the desk, where he was busy writing a message to the Mace. "You'll wear out the rug."

Javel halted in front of the window. Once still, he could feel steady pounding under his feet. Steel foundries, brick kilns, and many other types of industry operated beneath the streets, and the noise was horrendous, even indoors. The racket made ground-floor space extremely cheap, and they had been at Meiklejohn's Pub for two days now, paying daily rent to the extremely bad-tempered publican. Galen, ever cautious, had expressed some concern about asking Javel to stay in a pub, but Galen needn't have worried. Demesne's pubs were not like those of New London, dark holes where a man could get lost and drown. And Javel had never felt less like drinking in his life. Dyer had been gone all night, but soon he would return, and if he'd been successful, he would return with Allie's location.

They were a badly mismatched group. Queen's Guard or not, Galen was too old for such an enterprise. Dyer and Javel had reached an uneasy balance of civility and mistrust, but Javel knew that, all things being equal, Dyer would like nothing better than to run him through. Dyer often baited him, and it was an easy business, for Javel could not argue with Dyer's two recurring themes: Javel was a traitor and Javel was a drunk. Several times,

Galen had broken them up when the argument was just about to tip over into violence—though Javel knew he would come off badly in such a brawl—but any truce they made was no more than temporary. Dyer loathed him, and Javel often considered telling the truth and saving him some time: Dyer could not possibly hate Javel more than he hated himself.

But their odd partnership was often effective. Galen, who had grown up in a border village, spoke excellent Mort, good enough to blend in with the people of the city. They let him do most of the talking—Dyer spoke good Mort, but with a slight accent that might be picked up by a keen ear, and Javel, who did not speak Mort, was not allowed to talk at all. Javel had to admit that Galen was a savvy negotiator. He'd gotten them the rooms in Meiklejohn's for next to nothing, and even more importantly, he'd ensured that the landlord would leave them alone.

Then there was Dyer. Javel had assumed that Dyer had been sent along primarily as a sword, for he was well known to be one of the Queen's best. But he had other talents: it had taken him only two days to pick up a girl in the Auctioneer's Office. Since then, there had been several more meetings, from each of which Dyer returned with an increasingly unbearable air of having made sacrifice for Queen and country. The three of them were posing as merchants up from the south, and Dyer was also feigning a gruesome interest in the slave trade. Last night, the girl had been meant to show him the Auctioneer's Office itself, but when Javel woke this morning, Dyer still hadn't returned. Now Javel could do nothing but pace in front of the window. The Auctioneer's list held the name, location, and origin of every slave in Mortmesne, for Gain Broussard's office was nearly as efficient as Thorne's former Census Bureau. Word had reached Demesne almost a month ago: Arlen Thorne was dead. The Glynn Queen had ended him, and even the Mort consensus seemed to be good riddance. But for Javel, news of Thorne's death had not brought the satisfaction he might have expected, only a sense of futility. He would have bet his last pound that Thorne had died believing he had done nothing wrong, but even if the man had discovered some late form of repentance, the world remained full of Thornes.

"You're pacing again," Galen remarked. "If you can't keep it together, I'll have to tie you to a chair."

"Sorry," Javel muttered, forcing himself to be still. It was a terrible thing, having hope. Sometimes he longed for the old days. The last six years in New London had been miserable, yes, but at least there had been a cold certainty there.

Outside, the rain had changed from a steady drizzle into a downpour, and on both sides of the street, the vendors hawking their wares had begun to close up shop. Just beneath Javel, on the sidewalk outside, was a pile of curdled horse droppings that no one had bothered to clean up. Abundant windows or not, this wasn't a good neighborhood. Although Demesne didn't have an area comparable to the Gut, where nearly everyone was up to no good, in his exploration of the city Javel had found plenty of neighborhoods that the Red Queen's improvements had failed to reach, where decay had set in. He had plotted these places on a map in his head. This was his usefulness, the reason he didn't feel like completely dead weight on this enterprise. Dyer had spent most of his life in the Keep, and Galen was more or less a country boy turned Guard. Both of them were intimidated by Demesne's size, its navigational difficulty, and whenever they had a question about the city's geography, they turned to Javel.

In his twenty minutes next to the window, Javel had already seen three troops of Mort soldiers go by. Despite the lack of a Gut, in some ways the vast majority of the city was nothing else, everyone doing what they had to and looking the other way. The people of Demesne didn't seem to consider themselves under martial law, but the city's standing police force roved the streets ceaselessly. Javel had seen no real unrest, though Galen had pointed out that the Tearling, even under Thomas Raleigh, had always had a much higher tolerance for civil unrest than Mortmesne. Galen said the soldiers were an anticipatory measure, and he was right. Even three strangers could feel the difference in the city now, the rumblings of discontent in quiet quarters. Galen, who never forgot that he was a Queen's Guard, liked to sit in the pubs at night, making a mug of ale last for hours while acting as the Mace's ears, and lately he'd heard plenty. The Queen of the Tearling— widely acknowledged by Demesne to be a fearsome sorceress— had marched into the Mort camp and turned back the Mort army at the very gates of New London, just as her mother had done, though no one quite seemed to know how. Javel wondered briefly if the Queen had reinstituted the shipment, but then dismissed the idea. He was no sycophant, like Galen and Dyer, but he had never forgotten the woman he had seen on the Keep Lawn, the woman who had opened the cages. She would cut her own throat before reviving the slave traffic.

Both Dyer and Galen were anxious over the Queen—though each tried to hide it—but there was no more news to be had of her, not in any pub. The rest of the gossip was of Mortmesne's difficulties, and they were many. Some sort of plague was crossing the northland, emptying villages and scattering the inhabitants. A rebellion was raging in the northern cities, Cite Marche and Arc Nord. The rebels were moving their resistance down to Demesne, and Demesne was waiting for them. Without flesh to peddle, many in the city had lost their jobs, and many more in other industries had temporarily lost their regular subsidy of labor from the Crown. Even the girl in the Auctioneer's Office had confided to Dyer that she lived in fear of being sacked. Demesne's economy grew increasingly shaky, and all corners of the city placed the blame squarely on the Red Queen. The invasion of the Tearling, which should have injected some badly needed wealth into the city when the army returned, had yielded nothing.

Javel had assumed that the return of the soldiers would calm the city's unrest. But instead, the Red Queen had found her problems compounded. The two guards seemed to think that all of this chaos was good, that it would make their job easier. Javel hoped they were right.

"Sir!"

A fist pounded on the door. The voice was Dyer's, and Javel realized, disgruntled, that Dyer had snuck past him somehow. At a nod from Galen, he went to unlock the door and was nearly thrown backward as Dyer burst into the room, panting.

"Sir, come. Now."

Galen stood and grabbed his cloak. This was a thing Javel had learned to admire about the Queen's Guard: no arguing, not even petty bickering, all questions cleared to one side in the expedience of the moment. He wanted to ask about Allie, but Galen's professionalism had shamed him into silence. No one had invited him, but he followed them anyway, carefully locking the door of their rooms behind him. He was forced to hurry, for the two guards pounded past the glaring publican and did not slow until they reached the street. The rain had reduced to drizzle again, almost a mist. The air was rank with the acrid smell of steam from the steel foundries. Above the buildings to their right, Javel could just glimpse the topmost turrets of the Palais, the crimson flag that flew over all, lest the people of Demesne forget that the Red Queen's reign had begun in blood.

The two Queen's Guards maintained a steady jog, brisk enough to make Javel feel as though his lungs would collapse, but after a mile or so their progress slowed. They were nearing the Rue Grange, the enormous boulevard that bisected Demesne. Javel enjoyed exploring the city, but he tried to avoid the Rue Grange when possible, for it was the main entry through Demesne's western gate, the beginning of the Pike Road. Javel could not forget that Allie must have gone down this very boulevard in a cage, years ago. But Dyer led them in that direction, and Javel had no choice but to follow. The crowds intensified as they closed on the Rue; a throng of people seemed to be stuffed down every side street, but the two big Queen's Guards were able to push through easily, Javel trailing in their wake.

When they emerged onto the Rue itself, they were forced to halt; there was simply no more room. The middle of the boulevard had been cleared of people by the approach of hundreds of heavy horse, all marching in neatly ordered lines toward the Palais. The ground shook with the impact of their hooves, but Javel could hear nothing over the roar of the crowd.

"What is it?" he shouted in Dyer's ear. He half expected Dyer to turn and clout him in return—it had happened before—but Dyer paid him no heed. His eyes were fixed on the endless columns of horse, searching.

"There!" he cried.

Javel stood on his tiptoes, trying to see over the big men's shoulders. After a few seconds, he spotted something: an open wagon, buried deep in the center of the Mort column. Hopping slightly to peer over Galen's shoulder, he saw a figure seated inside the wagon, facing the rear, a hood drawn low over his face.

"What is it?" he shouted again, and this time Dyer deigned to notice him, though his lip curled in disgust as he spoke.

"It's the Queen, you fucking drunk."

Javel wanted to shout back that he wasn't a drunk; he had been sober for six months now. But then Dyer's words struck him.

"The Queen?"

"Yes, the Queen," Dyer snarled, "taken prisoner while we were stuck here playing at nonsense with you."

Javel stood on his tiptoes again, staring at the wagon, which was now nearly in front of them. The line of the shoulders did suggest a woman, and so did the thin wrists, chained to the wagon. As she approached, the roar of the crowd increased, and a piece of what looked like raw meat flew from the other side of the Rue, narrowly missing her head.

"What do we do?" Dyer shouted at Galen.

Javel felt the lightest of touches at his waist. He looked down and found a pickpocket, little more than a child, busily exploring beneath his cloak. He shoved the boy away.

"Ah, Jesus!" Galen cried.

Javel looked up again and found the wagon past them now, far enough that they could see under the prisoner's hood. Someone had worked her over; her lower lip was busted and the mother of all shiners adorned her right eye. But those green eyes could not be mistaken; they darted over the crowd, even as the people cursed her and clods of mud landed almost in her lap. For one interminable moment, Javel was certain that her gaze had swept across the three of them, her good eye fixing on his. Then the wagon dropped out of sight.

Dyer began to draw his sword, and Javel felt panic clutch his heart. Was Dyer really going to bring the Mort army down on them all? Now? What about Allie?

A hand snaked from behind them to clamp Dyer's wrist, and a voice hissed in Tear, "Do nothing!"

They whirled to find a group of dark-garbed men standing behind them. The leader was not big, but he was surrounded by larger men, one of them far too big for either Dyer or Galen to take. If this was a Mort patrol, they were all likely dead. Javel considered begging Dyer to tell him where Allie was, in case there was no other chance.

Galen had pulled a knife, but the stranger only marked it for a moment before returning his gaze to Dyer.

"She's beyond your reach at this time, Queen's Guard. Save your strength for another moment. She's bloodied, but not broken; look!"

The three of them turned to look, but the wagon had long since disappeared. The Mort cavalry marched onward, seemingly endless.

"Who are you?" Galen demanded, turning around again.

But the man and his companions had already faded into the crowd.

K elsea's dungeon was eight feet by eight feet. She had discovered this by walking the length of each wall, measuring paces. Three of the walls were stone, well built; Kelsea's fingers could detect no cracks or leaks. The fourth wall was made up of iron bars and a door, beyond them a hallway of indeterminate length. The sounds from this hallway were not good: some screaming, some moaning, and, down the corridor, one man who could not stop babbling, holding an interminable dialogue with someone named George. The fact that George was not there to hold up his end of the conversation was no impediment to this poor soul, who seemed determined to convince his invisible friend that he was not a thief.

There was no way to measure time. They had taken her watch in the camp, and Kelsea was already finding out that the worst of a bad situation was the uncertainty of hours passing. Meals provided some respite—though not much, as they were usually cold vegetables, occasionally combined with some sort of meat that Kelsea could not identify. She forced it down all the same. Meals did not seem to conform to any set schedule, and it could be a long while before the next arrived. Water also came erratically; Kelsea had learned to ration her drinking bucket.

She could see very little; the Mort did not allow prisoners so much as a candle. Some of these inmates were undoubtedly being kept alive against their will, for Kelsea had heard more than one voice down the hallway beg for death. She saw the logic behind the deprivation of light; the darkness was in itself a terrible thing. She had shown greater kindness to her own prisoners, even to Thorne.

But thinking of Thorne was a mistake. By her best guess, Kelsea had been down here for four days, and she had discovered that a dungeon was of little use for anything but reflection. Over those last weeks in the Keep, watching the Mort draw closer, there had been no time for self-assessment, but here there was nothing else, and she thought often of Arlen Thorne, kneeling on the platform, his face twisted in agony. He had been a traitor and a trafficker, a brutal man who did not blanch at torture. He had presented a clear danger to the Tearling. And yet—

"George, you must believe me!" the man down the hall shouted. "I did not take it!"

Kelsea wondered why there was no one to quiet him. She rarely saw anyone here, only jailors and the servants who brought the food. They provided a brief moment of light with their torches, enough for Kelsea to have mapped out her cell, with its empty floor and two buckets. She had not seen her own jailor since her arrival, and was just as happy to have it so. The darkness, the monotony, the unscheduled nature of meals . . . these things were at least gloomily predictable, but the jailor was a pure variable, and Kelsea preferred the grim certainty of her solitude.

It was cold down here, and dank—she had seen no moat around the Palais, but moisture was certainly leaking in from somewhere— but Kelsea was relatively fortunate. She had worn a warm dress for the early morning excursion across the bridge, and the heavy wool had taken minimal wear on the long road. She only felt the chill on rare occasions when wind moaned through the dungeons, a sure sign that there were either multiple entrances and exits or a failure in the structure somewhere. She spent much of her time near the bars, listening, trying to understand the spatial distances in this place. The Palais was not as tall as the Keep, but it covered an enormous acreage. She might be as far as half a mile from the outer walls.

At this moment, Kelsea sat against the wall beside the bars, trying to judge whether she was really hearing a certain sound: scratching and scraping on the far side of the wall. Based on the dim, torchlit glimpses she'd gotten on her way in here, there was another barred cell over there. The Mort didn't like to waste space, nor did they like to give prisoners the barest sliver of privacy. There was someone there, and that someone was scraping something against the wall, repeatedly and without pattern.

Kelsea cleared her throat. She hadn't had a drink in several hours, and her voice seemed to feel each syllable as its own special rasp.

"Hello?" she called in Mort.

The scraping stopped.

"Is someone over there?"

The scraping resumed, slower now. Kelsea felt that whoever was over there was doing it deliberately, to show her that he'd heard but simply wasn't answering.

"How long have you been in here?"

The scraping continued, and Kelsea sighed. Some of these people had undoubtedly been imprisoned for years, long past the time when they would have retained any interest in the world outside their cells. But she could not shake her own sense of urgency. The Tearling was safe, she told herself, safe for the three years she had purchased, so what did it matter if she rotted in here? Vague thoughts of William Tear flitted through her head, images of his utopia, his Town, already beginning to rot from the inside. But that would happen whether Kelsea was locked up or not. The past in her head could be seen, but it could not be changed.

Why not?

Kelsea jumped, but before she could continue the thought,

her ears caught a faraway sound: boot heels, more than one set, coming down the hallway on her right. As they came closer, the scratching sound against the wall ceased. The heels descended two small sets of steps—staircases, as yet unseen, at the far end of the corridor. Somehow, Kelsea knew they were coming for her, and she scrambled to her feet, so that when the torchlight came around the corner it found her standing proud and straight inside her cell.

There were two of them. One was Kelsea's jailor, his eyes as mindlessly jolly as before, holding a torch, and the other was a woman, well dressed in blue velvet. She was very tall of frame, with sharp eyes and the extra consideration of movement that told Kelsea she'd been trained somehow, perhaps in combat. Kelsea cast back and found a nugget of information told to her by Mace, long ago: the Red Queen's pages had to know how to handle themselves.

"She's filthy," the woman remarked in badly accented Mort. "Did you not wash her up?"

The jailor shook his head, and Kelsea was pleased to see him looking slightly embarrassed.

"When did she last eat?"

"Yesterday, I think."

"You're a joy to your profession, aren't you?"

The jailor gave her a befuddled look, and that was when Kelsea knew that it was all an act. There was something wrong with her jailor, deeply and fundamentally wrong, but he wasn't stupid.

"Give me that!" the woman snapped, grabbing the torch and holding it high, her narrowed eyes locked on Kelsea's face. "This woman has been beaten."

The jailor shrugged, staring at the ground. "She was disorderly."

"This is a high-value prisoner. An underjailor does not lay fingers on her except to save her life. Do you understand?"

The jailor nodded sullenly, a low gleam of anger in his eyes.

But the anger itself did not frighten Kelsea nearly as much as how quickly he hid it, there and then gone, tucked neatly from sight.

"Bind her hands and bring her up to the third floor," the woman ordered.

The jailor unlocked the cell, and Kelsea tensed as the woman disappeared around the corner.

"Pretty is special," the jailor muttered to himself. "But not special to them like she is to me. Pretty is mine."

Kelsea's lip curled in disgust. It seemed the safest time to correct this particular misconception, since he could hardly beat her again without incurring the wrath of the woman in blue. She spoke carefully in Mort, enunciating every word.

"I belong to no one but myself."

"No, no, they would not have locked pretty up if she wasn't meant for me, all my own."

Kelsea resisted an overpowering urge to kick him in the kneecap. She had seen Mace demonstrate the maneuver, one of the most painful wounds an unarmed man could inflict: right on the dome of the knee, shattering the bones into so many fragments. Kelsea had no magic these days, only her own force to work with, but she thought she could do it, and hearing this man howl in agony suddenly seemed the loveliest idea in the world. But there would be nowhere to go afterward.

"Hands," the man demanded, putting the torch in its holder. Kelsea held them out and allowed him to place manacles around her wrists.

"Pretty does not move quickly enough."

"Perhaps not," Kelsea replied. "But before pretty leaves this dungeon, she is going to deal with you. Know that for a certainty."

The man looked up, startled. "Nonsense. She is only a prisoner."

"No. She is a queen."

"Yes." The man finished locking her manacles and ran his palm over her hair. There were certainly worse places he could have chosen to touch, but the possessiveness in the gesture made Kelsea's skin crawl. "My very own queen."

She rolled her eyes, sickened. "Christ, let's go."

"Women shouldn't curse."

"Get fucked."

He blinked in surprise, but did not react, only took her arm and led her out of the dungeon. Kelsea would have given the world and all of its riches for her sapphires in that moment. Just the tiniest push with her mind, and the jailor would die screaming. She could make it last for days if she wanted to.

Brutality, her mind whispered, and Arlen Thorne's face flashed behind her eyes, there and then gone. *You meant to leave all that behind, remember?*

She did remember; that moment in the Red Queen's tent had put paid to all of Kelsea's easy ideas about the use of violence. But hatred was stronger than memory, infinitely stronger, and in her hatred Kelsea felt an echo of the woman she had become in those last few weeks in the Keep: the Queen of Spades. Kelsea had meant to lay that woman to rest, but she did not rest easily.

Beyond the corridor, they went up several flights of steps. It was a different route than Kelsea had taken coming into the dungeon, and at the top of the last flight she was disheartened to see a massive iron-barred door, two guards inside and two guards outside.

So much for my ideas of escape, she thought grimly. A man could batter his brains out against those iron bars and get nowhere. She kept her eyes down as the inner guards unlocked the door. The jailor's hand brushed her bottom, and she jumped. The longing for her sapphires felt like a physical thing, almost a fever.

They emerged into a long, high hallway draped in red silk, the bright sheen of the fabric glowing in the light of many torches. The effect was beautiful, and Kelsea felt, again, the incongruity with the Red Queen, the witch-queen she had heard of throughout her childhood, the woman with no mercy, no heart.

That's not so, her mind whispered. *She does have a heart, and it's a complicated one. You know that.*

Kelsea knew. As the jailor led her up another flight of stairs, she wondered if the Red Queen had finally decided to kill her. Kelsea had spared the Red Queen's life, but felt sure that this fact would not enter into consideration. The Red Queen would view Kelsea as a pure liability now, for she knew too many things that the woman had tried to bury. She knew the Red Queen's name.

I need to survive, Kelsea thought, *else how will I ever get home?* And beneath that, quieter but no less powerful: *How will I ever hear the end of the story?* The Red Queen wanted something, or she would never have carted Kelsea to this hellhole in the first place, and Kelsea felt her mind girding itself up, putting her bargaining face on. They had bargained once before, she and the Red Queen, and Kelsea had won, but only by luck. She did not underestimate the woman in red.

At the top of the third flight of stairs, the Red Queen's page waited. She waved the jailor away with a sweep of her hand.

"I will take her from here."

The jailor frowned, the pout of a child denied a treat. "I should stay with her."

"You should do as you're told."

His eyes burned, and Kelsea, who had briefly considered sticking her tongue out at him, thought better of it. She had no intention of putting up with the worst of the man's abuses and delusions, but there was also no percentage in antagonizing him further.

Just one moment, she thought, as the jailor—with poor grace—handed over the key to her manacles. *One moment with my jewels and I could turn you inside out.*

"Come along," the page told her. She had switched to Tear now, and her Tear was very good. "I have a bath for you, and some clean clothing."

Kelsea brightened at this prospect, increasing pace behind the woman until she was nearly jogging along. The jailor had at least left her boots to her, the good riding boots she had worn on that long-ago morning. They had stood her in good stead when she fled across the New London Bridge. Would Mace rebuild the bridge? There was very little money in the Treasury, and an enormous building project seemed like an extravagance.

Look at you! her mind jeered. *Trying to govern even from here!*

Taking a bath in front of the woman was difficult. Kelsea had long ago banished Andalie from her bath chamber, but at least Andalie was sometimes helpful, whereas this woman merely leaned against the wall, watching her without expression.

"What is your rank?" Kelsea finally asked.

"I am Her Majesty's page."

So Kelsea had been right. But still, a Tear page! Kelsea herself had no real pages; Andalie covered the job well enough. But the Red Queen had a well-known disdain for all things Tear. This woman must be something special.

"What is your name?"

"Emily."

"How do you come to be here? Were you in the lottery?"

"Wash your hair, please. We'll check for nits when you get out."

Kelsea stared at her for another moment before dunking her head. Her hair, long and straight now, Lily's hair, was a tangled mess lying halfway down her back. It took a long while to comb out, but to Kelsea's relief, she had no lice. They gave her a black dress to wear, whether by design or accident Kelsea didn't know, but she accepted the garment gratefully and found it made of comfortable, undoubtedly expensive wool.

"Come," the page told her. "The Queen waits."

Kelsea followed her down another long corridor, this one lined with dark fireplaces. There seemed to be guards everywhere, and while they wore the Queen's red, they did not have the feel of close guards. Unlike Kelsea, the Red Queen did not have to barricade herself in a single wing of her palace with a handpicked group. What would it feel like, Kelsea wondered, to be that secure on the throne?

They were headed for two black doors at the far end of the corridor, blocked by a man who clearly was a close guard. He seemed vaguely familiar, but there was something else: a sense of pride in his station, even though it merely consisted of standing there. For the men in the long hallway just past, guarding was merely a job, but not for this one. At a nod from the chamberlain, he knocked twice before opening the door.

Kelsea had expected a throne room of some sort, but only a few steps in she realized that this was a private chamber. Everything was hung with crimson silk: walls, ceilings, even the enormous bed that dominated the room. The room also held a vast oakwood desk and a sofa upholstered in red velvet. Nothing here was gold, and that forced Kelsea into a reassessment of the Red Queen. Velvet and silk were luxuries, certainly, but the space was not gaudy or tasteless. It was a room that conveyed a forceful personality.

"Kelsea Glynn."

The Red Queen stood in the far corner. Her dress matched the hangings so perfectly that Kelsea had missed her the first time around, but now she saw that the Red Queen was unwell. Her skin was pallid and waxy, as though with fever. Her eye sockets had the bruised look of someone who had not slept soundly in a long time.

That makes two of us, Kelsea thought ruefully.

"That will be all, Emily. Ghislaine, leave us."

Pen would have argued with Kelsea at this point—ah, but thinking of Pen was a mistake as well; the image of his stricken face on the New London Bridge would be with Kelsea all of her days—but the Red Queen's close guard merely bowed and left the room. He was the man who had manacled her in the tent, Kelsea remembered suddenly. She had thought he meant to cut her throat, but he had merely clamped her in irons and taken her away. How could that day seem so long ago?

"Sit," the Red Queen commanded in Mort, indicating the crimson sofa. She might be ill, but her dark eyes remained as unperturbed as ever, a calm port in a raging storm. Kelsea admired that outward serenity, wished she knew how it was done. She was trying to hold on to her bargaining face, but it was difficult. Her sapphires were here somewhere, and though Kelsea had willingly given them away, the Queen of Spades wanted them back.

She seated herself—a clumsy experience with bound wrists—and found that the sofa was the softest piece of furniture she had ever encountered. She seemed to sink into the plush velvet. The Red Queen sat down in a nearby chair, staring at her for a long moment, until Kelsea was acutely uncomfortable.

"You used to be a plain thing," the Red Queen remarked, "when I saw you in dreams. But you are not so plain any longer, are you?"

"You neither, Lady Crimson."

The Red Queen's jaw firmed, a sign of irritation.

"How are your accommodations?"

"None too comfortable, but I've been in worse places."

"Really?"

The Red Queen's gaze sharpened, interested, and Kelsea reminded herself to watch her step. In the tent, the Red Queen had recognized her out of Lily's portrait. She didn't know Lily, but her fascination with the portrait, and with its subject, might be an important bargaining chip. But what was the bargain? What could Kelsea possibly offer that would make this woman set her free?

"It was worse to be stuck in a doomed city with my hands tied."

"Your hands weren't tied."

I didn't know that, Kelsea almost answered, but then she thought of Mace, Mace who, when dealing with a known enemy, would have given nothing away. Thinking of him steadied her, allowed her to find her own authority. She would never see Mace again unless she got home.

The Red Queen reached into the pocket of her dress and came out with both sapphires, dangling them from her fingers. "I wish to know what you've done to these jewels. Why won't they work for me?"

Kelsea stared at the two jewels, trying to understand her own feelings. She had been longing for them for days, thinking of the hell she could rain down if she only had them in her hands again. But now that she saw them, she felt nothing, just as she had felt nothing when she had taken them off. What did that mean?

Seeing that she was not going to reply, the Red Queen shrugged. "No one understands them, the Tear jewels. Not even those who wear them. Elyssa never had the slightest idea. She merely thought them pretty pendants to wear around her neck, but she was attached to them as such. I could never get her to take them off, not even as the price of her kingdom."

"I've heard many opinions of Queen Elyssa now, but I'm curious: what is yours?"

"That she should never have been given a kingdom to rule."

"That much is obvious to everyone. But what was she like?"

"Shallow. Careless."

The very words Kelsea would have chosen. She shrank into the cushions.

"Let me give you some free advice, Glynn. You are too invested. The tie of blood is only as strong as you want it to be. Some parents are poison, and it's best to simply let them go."

"Did you find it that easy?"

"Yes." The Red Queen moved to sit at the far end of the sofa. "Heir and spare or no, my mother, like yours, should never have borne children. Realizing that, I left her behind and did not look back."

She's lying, Kelsea thought. She had seen into this woman's mind, if only briefly, and the Beautiful Queen was littered all over the landscape.

"Who is your father?" the Red Queen asked. "I confess, I am curious to know."

"So am I."

"You do not know either?" The Red Queen shook her head, smirking. "Ah, Elyssa."

"You won't attack me by attacking my mother."

"Who attacks her? I have a different man in my bed every night. We are not the Tear, to demand that women ignore all the pleasures of the world. But it was unlike Elyssa to keep secrets. And even more strange," the Red Queen mused, holding up the sapphires, "that these did not tell you."

Kelsea shrugged. "Perhaps not so odd. I've never had a burning need to know."

"You do not care who your father is?"

"Why should I? He did not raise me, did not shape me. I had others for that."

"But blood does tell, Glynn." The Red Queen smiled sadly, and Kelsea was alarmed to find herself almost sorry for the woman. She would not delve further into the Red Queen's memories, but she could not unstring the connections she had already made. The Beautiful Queen had traded away her daughter, as one would trade a steer at market, and that betrayal still loomed over the Red Queen's mind, darkening it, scorching the earth beneath. "Blood raises us and shapes us in ways we don't yet understand."

"Ah, yes. I've heard that you call yourself a geneticist."

"It is only a word. In truth, I know very little of genes themselves. We have not regained that technology, not yet. But traits, Glynn, traits . . . these I watch, and these I analyze. We are back at the level of Mendel, but still there is much to be learned and understood about behavior."

"Mendel dealt in physical traits."

"He was not ambitious enough. There are mental traits to be passed down as well."

"This from the woman who tells me blood means nothing."

The Red Queen smiled in acknowledgment, but the smile gave Kelsea no ease. What did the woman want from her?

"You said yourself that no one understands these jewels. What makes you think I do?"

"You must. They have been rendered lifeless. I've never heard of such a thing, but there it is. What have you done?"

"I don't know," Kelsea answered truthfully. "Why don't you ask Row Finn?"

"Who is Row Finn?"

Kelsea narrowed her eyes. If the woman meant to play with her, she would not converse at all. But then, searching back through the memories she had glimpsed in the Red Queen's mind, she realized that it was perfectly possible that the Red Queen had never known Row Finn's real name. The two of them had a mutual history, clearly, and Kelsea had glimpsed something about a dead child . . . but it was already gone. Her foray into the woman's mind had been too brief.

"Stop."

The Red Queen grabbed her wrist.

"I know what you're doing. It's unfair."

"Unfair? You're holding me in a cell."

"What you're examining is not yours. You stole it. I did not look through the contents of your mind."

"But you would if you could, Lady Crimson."

"What difference does that make?"

The question startled Kelsea. She felt very sure that it did make a difference . . . but did it really? Mace would have said yes, but Kelsea was no longer sure. Just because she could, just because others would have done the same, did that actually make it right?

"I get a weekly report on the state of your kingdom," the Red Queen continued, her voice laced with mockery. "Kelsea Glynn, a queen of great principle. Your government trumpets the value of privacy. Even your laughable new judiciary has decided cases on this basis. Privacy is privacy, Kelsea Glynn. Now, are you a queen of principle, or are you not?"

Kelsea grimaced, finding herself checked. There was hypocrisy in the Red Queen's argument, but that did not change its underlying logic. She could not believe in privacy for some and invade it in others. After another moment's pause, she dropped the fabric of the Red Queen's memories, and they seemed to puddle, a shapeless mass at the foot of her mind, as when she stepped out of a dress.

The Red Queen nodded, a hint of triumph in her voice. "Principle weakens you, Glynn. It will always be used against you at the most inconvenient time."

"Lack of principle is worse."

"There is a middle ground."

"That would be the Mort way, I suppose. All things inconvenient discarded."

"What have you done to these sapphires? I demand to know."

"What is the information worth to you?"

"Don't test me, Glynn. You live only on my sufferance."

She does want something, Kelsea realized, *not just information but something else.* The idea elated her, and she leaned back against the sofa, crossing her legs.

"You do not speak."

"Why should I? I haven't heard an offer."

The Red Queen's face twisted. She reminded Kelsea of a dog stuck in front of forbidden food.

"I could curl up and sleep in the hollows under your eyes, Lady Crimson. What ails you?"

"You are right," the Red Queen admitted slowly. "I do not sleep well. I am beset by visions."

"Of what?"

"The future, what else?"

The past, Kelsea nearly replied, but kept her mouth shut.

"A plague has descended on my land."

Kelsea blinked. "Disease?"

"Not in the way you mean. This plague comes out of the Fair-witch."

A cold hand seemed to steal inside Kelsea's chest.

"In your Tear, he is called the Orphan. An ancient monster, filled with spite." The Red Queen eyed her narrowly. "But I think you have seen him differently, Glynn. A young man, perhaps? A young man, handsome as the devil himself."

Kelsea kept very still, for she did not trust the woman in front of her even an inch, but without volition, her mind moved backward, far back into the past, where a boy named Row Finn already felt slighted by William Tear's town.

He's always been here, Kelsea thought. *Always here, waiting to wreck my kingdom, perhaps the whole new world. And I let him out.*

"A horror moves across the north, sweeping my people south. Entire villages have disappeared."

"What sort of horror?"

"Children," the Red Queen replied, her face twisted with distaste and something else; guilt? "They're moving from village to village, slaughtering the old, scavenging the young."

Kelsea closed her eyes. In the moment she had forgiven Finn, she had *felt* the badness of the bargain, had known that she was once again being tricked by exigency into making a terrible decision. Behind her closed lids, she glimpsed the cages in front of the Keep, the special cages made for small children. The memory brought not comfort but a sense of great futility. Had she done anything of value since taking the throne? Anything that would mean something in the long run?

Ozymandias, king of kings, her mind whispered, the words not snide but plaintive, the tone of a wind that scraped the landscape, sweeping all before it, leaving nothing behind. Carlin had made her memorize Shelley's poem, and now she saw why, for certain.

"Why children?" she asked.

"I don't know. Always, the man has wanted children. For years, I had to keep back a portion of the shipment for times when I needed his help."

"What sort of help?"

"He knows things. Simply knows them. If I had a rebellion brewing somewhere, he knew, and I could act before conspiracy found its legs. If I needed to find someone, a fugitive, a traitor, he would know where. Except for you, Glynn. He has protected you all your life. He was happy to give information on other matters— for a price, always a price—but he would never give me anything about you, your location. Why do you think that is?"

Kelsea turned away, feeling sick again.

The badness of the bargain!

"Fire allows him to travel where I could not, but he no longer needs the fire. He comes, and the children come with him, moving from village to village, using my people as meat."

The words seemed to stab a soft place behind Kelsea's ribs, but she merely shrugged and asked, "What do I care? He told me his hatred lay here."

"In Mortmesne?"

"With you, Lady Crimson. What do I care if he comes for you?"

"Don't be a fool, girl. The damage these children inflict is not random. One village at a time, they tear apart. Houses wrecked, fields churned to mud, graves disinterred . . . they search for something."

Disinterred graves . . . another echo of the Town. Kelsea was disquieted, if only because past and present were supposed to remain separate. Even Lily's time, powerful though the vision had been, had always been distinct. What business did Tear's people have in the current world?

She shook her head to clear it. "Search for what?"

"Who can say? But if they don't find it in my kingdom, they will come for yours."

"Finn can't be so powerful as all that."

"He can be, and you know it. This creature has survived for centuries on spite alone."

"Well, what am I to do about him?"

"You idealists are all the same," the Red Queen spat. "You assume that because you wish no harm, your decisions are always harmless. This thing was restrained, Glynn . . . bounded by magic so dark that even I could never discover its source. Now that spell is broken, the Orphan is free, and I know that you have done it. This plague is yours."

Kelsea sensed her own temper stirring, roiling beneath the surface calm she projected, and she welcomed it as though it were an old friend at her door.

"You have a nerve, Lady Crimson. You wish to discuss responsibility? Let's talk about yours. Thousands of people stolen from my kingdom, men and women and children, brought here to be worked and screwed until they dropped dead of abuse. And how many did you hand over to Finn yourself? You've been taking a disproportionate number of children since the shipment started, and I'll wager my crown that's where they've been going. If my hands are bloody, you're swimming in it."

"Will that allow you to sleep at night?"

Kelsea gritted her teeth. Arguing with this woman was maddening, for hypocrisy seemed to shame her not at all. "Perhaps not, but I don't need fear to rule my own kingdom. I have no secret police, no Ducarte."

"But you wish you did."

"You think I'm jealous?" Kelsea asked incredulously. "Of *you*?"

"I have kept my people safe and fed and housed for more than a century. You can only dream of such an accomplishment. Instead, you've wrecked us all, without a second thought."

"You don't know me. I agonize over every decision I make."

"No decision so damaging as this one. The dark thing—"

"His name is Row Finn. You really don't know very much about him, do you?"

"Neither do you."

"Oh, but I do," Kelsea replied, seeing a sudden glimmer of a path. "I know more about him than you could imagine. He grew up in William Tear's town. His mother was named Sarah. He was a gifted metalworker."

"You're lying."

"I am not."

"He would never tell you these things."

"He didn't."

The Red Queen stared at her for a long moment. "What is your source?"

"You're not the only one beset by visions." Kelsea hesitated—it was second nature, by now, to deny the truth of her fugues—then continued. "I see the Landing, the time when New London was no more than a village on a hill, ruled by William Tear."

"What use is a vision of the past?"

"That's a fine question, but I see it all the same: fifteen years after the Landing, Tear's town just beginning to rot from the inside." As she said the words, Kelsea realized that history had failed them; always, in Carlin's classroom, the fall of Tear's utopia had been ascribed to the death of Jonathan Tear. But it had begun much earlier than that, all of humanity's old vices creeping back in. Kelsea sensed them, even in Katie, who had been raised by one of Tear's oldest and most trusted lieutenants. Even Katie had doubts.

Maybe we aren't capable of being satisfied, Kelsea thought, and the idea seemed to open a chasm inside her. *Maybe utopia is beyond us.*

But no, she didn't believe that.

"And the Orphan—Finn, as you say—he was there?" the Red Queen asked.

"Yes, little more than a child."

"But vulnerable," the Red Queen murmured, her eyes beginning to gleam. "Everything is vulnerable in infancy."

"Perhaps. But I must live long enough to discover that vulnerability. My visions are not unified. They progress in time, sometimes by leaps and bounds. Like a story in chapters."

"How strange," the Red Queen mused, but then her gaze sharpened. "You still have these visions, even though I hold the Tear sapphires?"

"Yes."

"How can that be?"

"I don't know."

"This Row Finn. Can he be killed?"

"I think so," Kelsea answered truthfully, for she sensed that this was so. Young as she was, Katie's sight was very clear. The boy, Finn, was undeniably arrogant, but there was fear there too, carefully hidden, driving him. But fear from what source?

"But you don't know how to kill him."

"My visions come unbidden. I don't control them. You have to give me time."

"Time, with this creature breathing down my neck?" The Red Queen turned away, but not before Kelsea had seen something extraordinary: the Red Queen's knuckles locked together, so white that they seemed as though they might split and begin to bleed.

"What is it you're afraid of?" Kelsea asked softly. She didn't expect an answer, but the Red Queen surprised her, the words muffled as she spoke over her shoulder.

"You think I don't care about my people, but I do, just as you care about yours. I have built this kingdom from nothing, from a disordered mess into a machine. I won't have it torn down. I care about my people."

Not as much as you care about yourself, Kelsea thought, but she kept the words locked behind her lips.

"I need time," she repeated firmly. "Time to find out what *he's* afraid of. And I want a different jailor."

The Red Queen stared at her for a moment, her brow furrowed, then barked, "Emily!"

The page entered, bowing.

"Yes, Majesty?"

"Who is her jailor?"

"Strass, Majesty."

"Strass? Why do I—"

"Three years ago, Majesty, there was an incident," the page replied in her poor Mort. "I was not here, but heard it told of. A female prisoner."

"Ahhh." The Red Queen grimaced, gesturing toward Kelsea. "Did he do that to her face?"

"And elsewhere, Majesty."

The Red Queen shook her head and turned back to Kelsea. "That should not have happened. I will give you another jailor, a woman with no such tendencies."

"Why do you keep a jailor with such tendencies at all?"

The Red Queen waved Emily away, and waited until the doors closed to answer.

"Because he is good at his job. Prisoners do not escape."

Kelsea thought of Ewen in the Keep, who had never let a prisoner escape either, who would hurt no one by his choosing. "That's no excuse."

"Who are you to judge? A mad dog captains your Guard."

"Another word about Lazarus, and I help you with nothing, jailor or no."

The Red Queen's eyes lit with anger, and Kelsea realized how novel this must be for her, to seek aid. With her temperament, it must be nearly intolerable.

"If you want me to help you with Row Finn, then the exchange goes both ways. You must tell me what you know about him."

The Red Queen nodded, and Kelsea was astonished to see that her hands were trembling.

I'm not the only one who fears the past, she thought. *She has even more to regret than I do.*

"And I want my sapphires back."

"Not yet."

"Why not? They're of no use to you."

"But of great use to you, Glynn. We must have some basis for trust first."

Kelsea laughed. "There can be no trust, Lady Crimson, only mutual self-interest."

The Red Queen frowned, and Kelsea had the odd feeling that the woman wanted to trust her. Clearly, she had missed much on her brief venture through the Red Queen's mind. There were still many things here that she did not understand, but beneath the woman's superficial poise, Kelsea sensed a desperate unhappiness.

Could she be lonely? Kelsea wondered, and then: *Is that even possible?*

The Red Queen held out a hand. Kelsea stared at the offering for a moment, feeling uneasy. If the recent past had made anything clear, it was her inability to recognize a bad bargain.

"Well?"

Instinct is your best adviser. Barty's voice in her head, calm and undemanding, the very opposite of Carlin's. *Learn all the knowledge in the world, but your gut will always know best.*

"Look on my works, ye mighty, and despair," Kelsea murmured. She grasped the Red Queen's hand and shook.

Chapter 4

Brenna

No more tears now. I will think upon revenge.

—MARY STUART (PRE-CROSSING ANGL.)

There was blood on her hands.

She stared at her palms, trying to remember. The past few days were a blur, but then everything had been a blur since her master had died. From that moment on, she did not remember time as a concrete thing, only a river in which she occasionally bumped against the shore. She remembered killing the Queen's Guard, but not how she had escaped afterward. She did not know how she had gotten here.

To her left was a small stream. Brenna bent and rinsed her hands, scrubbing at her nails to get rid of the dried blood. She had killed a man in Burns Copse, she remembered now, killed him for food and coin. She had caught him before he had time to pull a weapon, and he had merely stared at her, hypnotized, until she slipped a knife between his ribs. He had a horse as well, but she could not ride, and there would be no way to sell the horse without attracting attention. The entire Tear thought her albino, and the master had said that was a good thing, a good secret to keep.

But she was no more albino than she was madwoman, and since the master had died, she had already begun to recover some of her color, her life. But not enough to sell a horse without anyone noticing, not yet. Not enough to blend into a crowd.

The master.

She had shed no tears for him, but that was only because tears were such a cowardly way to grieve. First one sought vengeance, and then, long years later, when all ledgers were balanced, one could wallow in sorrow. The master's voice still echoed in her head, screaming; she could not quiet the sound. She had felt him die, felt his agony and, worse, his absolute panic in that final moment when he had realized that there was no way out, that he had finally met a force with which he could not strike a deal. She had been taking on his pain her whole life, ever since they were children; the effort had turned her white.

She straightened from the stream and turned east again, seeking her quarry. She did not use her sense of smell, not precisely; rather, it felt as though she were cutting through distance, wading through thousands of people, all their myriad feelings like muddy water, until she found exactly what she sought. This particular gift had been quite useful to the master, for whenever someone tried to flee the shipment, there was no way to hide from the tracker inside Brenna's head. It was a powerful skill, and when she was young, the Caden had tried more than once to acquire her, to cleave her from the master. She had killed three of them before they finally gave up. Last year, they had tried again; several of them had come to the master, requesting a temporary loan of her services to find the Raleigh heir. But they would not pay what the master demanded.

If they had only paid! Brenna thought fiercely. This particular path was one that her thoughts had trodden many times before, but it grew no less bitter, no less urgent. *If they had only paid, perhaps the master would still be alive!*

She turned her face into the wind, sensing its movement on her tongue. The bitch was out there still, but no longer moving. Now she was in a cold, dark room. Brenna tested the walls, tasted them on her tongue, and found them to be thick stone.

"Imprisoned, are you?" she whispered. She could not be sure, but she fancied the bitch could hear her. There was power in her, great power; Brenna could sense it even now, distant and faint, just as she'd always been able to sense the force up in the Fairwitch. She had briefly considered turning her steps northward on this journey, traveling up to the mountains and seeking assistance. Whatever was up there was powerful, for certain; Brenna felt its pull beneath her feet. But there was some sort of upheaval going on in the Fairwitch now, and she could sense the lines of force that had always underlain the Tearling beginning to shift. Too uncertain, and she wanted no distractions. She had food enough to get her to the Mort border, and really, she needed very little to sustain her. Rage was more nourishing than food.

But if the bitch was in the Demesne dungeons, she might be beyond even Brenna's reach. It would serve the master nothing if Brenna died trying to get into the Palais. There must be another way.

After another moment's thought, Brenna began to look around the woods. Most of the animals had fled at her approach, but they were beginning to creep out again, now that she was still. A few minutes' searching found her a grey squirrel, peeping out from behind a tree. She was on it before it could blink. The squirrel bit and tore at her, but Brenna ignored the sting—pain was only a trick of the mind, after all—and wrung its neck. Pulling out the dead man's knife, she slit the squirrel from throat to belly, allowing the blood to drip and puddle on the ground. She had to be quick. Blood would bring other predators, and they might attract a hunter. She could deal with such a person, but had no wish to leave a trail behind. She was free now, yes, but the master had often told her never to underestimate the Mace.

Tossing the squirrel aside, she bent to the small puddle of blood, taking a deep copper breath. Knowing where someone was, that was easy. Finding out where they were *going to be* was more difficult, but it could be done, and probably far more easily than getting into the Mort dungeons on her own.

What if she dies there?

Brenna refused to consider that idea. The bitch's death in Mort custody would not be pretty, but it would be a holiday compared to what Brenna had in mind. Brenna had suffered, the master had suffered, and she did not believe the future would rob them of revenge.

She remained very still, staring into the scarlet puddle for a long time, her eyes wide, each breath a hiss of pain. A quarter of a mile away, on the Mort Road, traffic continued, an exodus of wagons and riders heading east, refugees from New London returning to their homes on the border. None saw Brenna, but all of them shuddered as they passed, as though they had hit a pocket of freezing cold.

Brenna finally straightened, smiling. A further hint of color had come back into her cheeks. She grabbed the bloody knife and the bag of food, then turned her steps southeast.

Javel wrapped his cloak more tightly around himself, wishing he could somehow draw into the shadows of the overhanging building. Another Mort street patrol had passed him only a few minutes ago. Sooner or later, someone was going to notice that he was simply standing there, not moving, and assume that he was up to no good.

The address Dyer had discovered sat opposite: a stately brick house, three stories, surrounded by a high stone wall with iron gates. Javel could not even peek in the windows, for two guards stood just inside the gates, opening them only for certain people.

According to Dyer, Allie's buyer had been a Madame Arneau, but that was the only information Javel was going to get. Ever since they had seen the Queen on the Rue Grange, Allie might as well have dropped off the face of the earth. Dyer and Galen had moved their base to an abandoned factory in the steel district, and their evenings seemed to be taken up entirely with unexplained errands and secret nighttime meetings with men Javel did not recognize. These men were Mort and carried steel, but they were not soldiers. There was a rescue attempt under way, and Javel felt like more of a nuisance than ever.

Across the street, an open wagon circled around the house from the back. They must have stables back there, for when men arrived, one of the guards on the door was quick to take their horses around the side. Javel had already seen several men come and go. Two of them had been drunk. An awful realization was growing upon him, turning his stomach and weakening his knees.

It could be any sort of house, he told himself. But that was nonsense. This neighborhood might be cleaner than the Gut, but some things were the same everywhere. He knew what he was looking at. He rubbed a hand across his brow and found that he was perspiring, even in the late autumn chill. He had known that these were the odds, he reminded himself. No one bought a pretty woman like Allie to make her into a servant, and he had done his best to accept the fact that she might be a whore. But now he had begun to wonder if his best would be good enough. When he imagined his wife under another man, he wanted to kick and punch, to break things.

High, merry laughter made him look up. A group of five women had emerged from the front of the house, chattering among themselves. They carried bags on their shoulders. All of them were tarted up, dressed in glittering fabrics, their eyes painted, their hair piled atop their heads.

Allie stood in the middle.

For a long moment, Javel couldn't move. It was his Allie, all right; he could see her distinctive blonde curls, now gathered in a bunch on top of her head. But her face was so different. Older, yes, lines at the corners of her eyes, but that wasn't the real change. His Allie had been sweet. This woman looked ... sharp. There was a tightness about her mouth. She laughed as merrily as the rest, but not the laughter Javel had known: broad and secretive, cold as the skim of ice on a dark lake. Javel watched, astounded, as she climbed into the wagon of her own free will and seated herself beside the other women, still laughing.

A man, tall and burly, had followed them out the door. As he climbed into the wagon, Javel saw the flash of a knife beneath his coat. Another guard, then, although Javel had already noticed in his explorations of Demesne that most prostitutes were treated far better here than in New London. Even the street girls were not molested. He did not know why five high-end whores should need a guard in Demesne, but with both the guard and the driver to take into consideration, Javel could not take the chance of approaching the wagon.

The driver clicked to the horses and left the enclosure of the walls. As though in a dream, Javel followed, forcing himself to stay more than a hundred feet behind. A dark hole had opened inside him. Over the past six years, he had imagined Allie's life often, many images pouring through his head, driving him into the pub just as surely as a man would drive goats to market. But he had never pictured her laughing.

When the wagon halted for traffic at the next intersection, Javel crept closer, ducking into an adjacent alley, and made a second unpleasant discovery: all five women, including Allie, were speaking Mort. The wagon turned into the Rue Grange and Javel followed, though he was forced to duck and dodge. This was the marketing segment of the Rue, and the street was always busy, crowded with vendors' stalls and customers for the shops. He was beginning to lose the wagon when, miraculously, the driver slowed, pulling to one side so that the women could alight and spread along the sidewalk. Two of them crossed the street, and Javel realized, astounded, that this was a shopping excursion. Allie went straight into an apothecary.

The driver remained with the wagon, and the guard stayed with him, but his eyes roved the street continuously. Javel got the sense that he would be ready to move at the first sign of trouble. Javel slipped closer, not even sure what his plan was. Part of him wanted to flee back to the safety of the warehouse, to the time when he knew nothing of Allie's fate at all.

Keeping a weather eye on the guard and driver, he strolled casually toward the apothecary. People jostled him, but he ducked and dodged around them, watching the door. The driver was telling some story now, the guard smirking, and Javel slipped past them and inside the shop.

He found Allie in a darkened corner, waiting in front of the counter. The apothecary was nowhere in sight, but Javel could hear the sound of bottles being moved behind a small green curtain. He wished that he could do this in other circumstances, without an audience that might reappear at any moment, but he also realized that he might never get such a chance again. It was now or never.

"Allie."

She looked up, startled, and Javel felt the world shift on its axis as he saw her eyes, cold and distrustful beneath their violet-painted lids. She looked at him for a long moment.

"What do you want?"

"I've come—" Javel felt his throat lock, cutting off the words. He summoned his memories: those nights sitting half asleep in pubs, Allie's face floating behind his eyes, the hatred for himself that had washed over him in endless waves. Six long years he had left her here, so that she could become the woman before him. If he left her here again, how would he live with himself afterward?

"I've come to take you home," he finished awkwardly.

Allie emitted a brief, throaty sound that he finally realized was a chuckle.

"Why?"

"Because you're my wife."

She began to laugh, the sound like a slap to Javel's face.

"We can get you out of here," he told her. "I have friends. I can keep you safe."

"Safe," she murmured. "How sweet."

Javel flushed. "Allie—"

"My name is Alice."

"I've come here to rescue you!"

"A knight in shining armor!" she exclaimed brightly, but her eyes did not change, and Javel heard a great deal of anger just beneath her bright words. "And where were you six years ago, Sir Knight, when your bravery could have done me some good?"

"I followed you!" Javel insisted. "I followed you all the way down the Mort road!"

She stared at him for a long, cold moment. "And?"

"Thorne's people were too powerful. I couldn't do anything. I didn't think we could get away."

"And in all the years since?"

"I was—" But there was nowhere to go from there. What could he tell her? That he'd been at the pub?

"I tried," he finished brokenly.

"All right, you tried," Allie replied. "But since you were a coward then, you don't get to claim bravery now. You're six years too late. I have built a life here. I am content."

"Content? You're a whore!"

Allie gave him another long, measuring look. That look had always been able to make Javel feel about two feet tall, but he had only seen it a few times during their marriage, usually when he had promised to do something and forgotten. He felt as though a spell had been cast upon her; if he could only get her away from here, he could surely break it and change her back.

"Is anything wrong, Alice?" a voice asked. Javel turned and saw the burly guard who had been on the wagon, standing just inside the doorway. His gaze was fixed on Javel, and the look in his eyes made Javel shudder. The man would like nothing better than to beat him to a pulp.

"Nothing at all," Allie replied brightly. "Just trawling."

At this, Javel's mouth dropped open, and he suddenly understood the dual purpose of the shopping trip, the reason for the women's fine dresses and heavy paint.

"Well, let me know if you need anything, ma'am." Clearly disappointed, the guard backed out of the shop.

Javel suddenly realized that he had understood the man perfectly, that he had been speaking in Tear. Violence in every muscle, that guard, but his manner toward Allie was utterly deferential. Javel turned back to Allie, wishing he could take his last words back, but he sensed that it wouldn't matter.

"I am a whore indeed," Allie replied after a long moment. "But I am *working*, Javel. I earn my own money and answer to no one."

"What about your pimp?" he shot back, hating the venom in his own voice but unable to control it.

"I pay rent to Madame Arneau. Reasonable rent, far more reasonable than the rent on a similar space in New London."

Javel could not reply. He only wished that he might have this Madame Arneau's neck in his hands, even once.

"In return, I get a suite of beautiful rooms and three cooked meals a day. I am well guarded from predators, I work my own hours, and I choose my own clientele."

"What sort of whorehouse gives a whore that much freedom?" he demanded. "It's bad business, if nothing else."

Allie's eyes narrowed, and if possible, the coldness in her voice became even deeper, sharper. "The sort that realizes a happy, healthy prostitute is a more profitable one. I earn three times your salary as a Gate Guard."

"But we're still married! You're my wife."

"No. You gave me away when you watched me climb into the cage six years ago. I want nothing from you, and you have no right to demand anything from me."

Javel opened his mouth to protest—surely marriage could not be dissolved so easily, even in Mortmesne—but at that moment the apothecary reappeared from behind the green curtain. He was a tiny, balding man with spectacles, holding a small box in his hands.

"Here you are, Lady," he said, offering the box to Allie. He, too, spoke Tear, and this puzzled Javel, who had heard no Tear on the streets of Demesne and had been forced to pick up his tiny smattering of Mort word by word. "Two months' worth, this is, and you want to make sure to take each one with a substantial meal. They may increase your sickness otherwise."

Allie nodded, producing a purse full of coin. "Thank you."

"Come back in two months' time and I will mix you another batch, but you want to discontinue use after the sixth month, else they may harm the baby."

At the final word, Javel felt a wave of unreality wash over him. He barely marked Allie handing over several coins and tucking the box into her bag. The apothecary looked between the two of them and then, clearly sensing the tense atmosphere, disappeared behind his curtain again.

"You're pregnant," said Javel, not so much to question Allie as to convince himself.

"Yes." She stared at him, as though daring him to continue.

"What will you do?"

"Do? I will have my baby and raise a fine child."

"In a brothel!"

Allie's gaze pinned him like sunlight. "My child will be cared for and then schooled by three women Madame Arneau keeps for no other reason. And when my child gets older, there will be no shame in knowing that Mother was a whore. What do you think of that?"

"I think it's criminal."

"You would, Javel. I might once have thought so too. But this city is better to women than New London has ever aspired to be. Perhaps it was brave of you to come here, I don't know. But yours is a low-risk bravery. It always was, and I deserve better than that. If you value your skin, don't ever approach me again."

She swept outside, banging the door shut behind her, leaving Javel still pressed against the wall. Claustrophobia gripped him; the shop seemed suddenly tiny, but he didn't dare go outside, not until he knew she was gone. He prayed the apothecary would not emerge from behind his curtain, and by some miracle, the man did not. Finally, when it felt as though hours had passed, Javel peeked through the glass-paned door of the shop and saw that the wagon was gone. He took a deep breath and went outside.

The Rue went on just as ever, which seemed strange to Javel; how could the city continue to function normally, when everything had changed? A sweet smell was in the air, pastries from the bakery nearby, but to Javel the smell was cloying, sweetness over filth, just like this entire city. He had spent six years worrying about Allie, suffering for Allie, and now he had no idea what to do. Going back the way he had come seemed intolerable. Going forward seemed worse. And night was coming down.

He stood on the footpath, cradling his head in his hands like a man deep in thought, but his mind was empty. He took his hands from his eyes, looked up, and found everything clear before him.

He was standing in front of a pub.

E ven the Mace could not find the two priests.

The Queen's Guard was supposed to stay with the Mace at all times. They had been charged to do so by the Queen herself, and Aisa could not imagine that any of the others took that charge less seriously than she did herself. But the Mace was the Mace, and if he wanted to disappear, they could not stop him. Yesterday he had gone, and now he reappeared, just as suddenly, through the secret door in the kitchen, causing Milla to scream in fright as she tended a pot of stew.

The Mace's disappearances were maddening, but even Aisa understood that the Mace tolerated them all by only the barest margin, that he was made to guard, not be guarded. Sometimes he just had to leave, to be somewhere else without any of them around. Aisa had assumed that the Mace went out drinking, or spying, but an overheard conversation between Elston and Coryn told her different: he was out looking for the Keep priest, Father Tyler, and a second priest, Father Seth, both of them bountied by the Arvath.

"The Caden are looking for them too," Coryn remarked. "They want bounty, ours or the Arvath's, makes no difference. Who knew that two old men could stay so well hidden?"

"They won't hide forever," Elston rumbled. "And every time the Captain leaves the Keep, it becomes more likely that the Holy Father will get wind of it."

Aisa would have liked to hear more, but in that moment Coryn noticed her in the doorway and shooed her out.

Each time the Mace returned from one of these expeditions without the two priests, he seemed more discouraged. Aisa thought it likely that Father Tyler was dead, for it seemed unlikely that the timid priest could hide for long. She wasn't the only one

who held this view, but no one quite dared say so to the Mace.
They had learned to leave him alone at such times, but today, as
soon as the Mace collapsed in one of the chairs around the table,
he began bellowing.

"Arliss! Get out here!"

The words reverberated through the floor of the audience
chamber.

"Arliss!"

"Be patient, you thick bastard!" Arliss shouted down the corridor. "I can't run!"

The Mace settled into a hunch, an ugly look on his face. His
inability to find the two priests was only part of the problem,
Aisa thought. The real problem was the empty silver throne. The
Queen's absence weighed on all of them, but heaviest on the Mace.
Aisa thought that, beneath his impassive exterior, the Captain
might be suffering even more than Pen.

Arliss dragged himself from the mouth of the corridor. "Yes,
Mr. Mace?"

"What's the latest from the Holy Father?"

"Another message this morning. Unless we produce Father Tyler and renew the Arvath's property tax exemption, he threatens
to expel us all from the Church."

"Who is 'us'?"

"The entire Keep, from the Queen on down."

The Mace chuckled, rubbing his red eyes with one hand.

"It's no laughing matter, man. I've got no use for God, but this
place is full of devout people. There are practicing Christians in
the Guard. They will care, even if you don't."

"If they're fool enough to take the word of God from that piece
of shit in the Arvath, they deserve the flames."

Arliss shrugged, though Aisa could see he would have liked to
say more.

"They demanded only Father Tyler? Not Father Seth?"

"Only Father Tyler. And the bounty has doubled again."

"Strange. Still no word on what happened when he fled the Arvath?"

"A scuffle. Some sort of alarm in the Holy Father's chambers. That's all I could dig up."

"Strange," the Mace repeated.

"By the way, he's no longer Father Tyler, or even the Keep priest, in these little missives. The Holy Father's given him a new name."

"What's that?"

"The Apostate."

The Mace shook his head. "Anything else while I was gone?"

"Another village was attacked in the foothills."

"What kind of attack?"

Arliss shook his head. "We only have two survivors, sir, and their reports don't make much sense, monsters and ghosties. Give me a few more days."

"Fine. What else?"

Arliss turned to Elston, who suddenly looked acutely uncomfortable.

"We have to talk about Pen, sir," he muttered.

"What about Pen?"

Elston looked down, searching for words, and Arliss took over.

"The boy's been drinking too much—"

"I know."

"I'm not finished. Last night he got into a brawl. A public brawl."

Aisa's eyes widened, but she said nothing, lest they remember she was there and shoo her out, as Coryn had the other day.

Pen, she thought, and shook her head, almost sadly.

"Lucky he was in one of my gaming pubs, or he might have been killed. He took on five men without a sword. As it is, he's taken a good beating. I tried to keep it quiet, but news will probably leak out. It always does."

"Where is he?"

"In the quarters, sleeping it off."

The Mace stood, his face grim.

"I'm sorry, sir," Elston said miserably. "I've tried to wrangle him, but—"

"Never mind, El. This mess I made myself."

The Mace headed down the hallway toward the guard quarters, moving in vast, purposeful strides. After a moment, Elston followed, then Coryn and Kibb, and Aisa trailed warily behind them. They reached the far end of the hallway, and were brought up short by the sharp *crack!* of a palm smacking flesh.

"Get your ass up!"

Pen mumbled something.

"We've coddled you long enough, you lovesick brat. Get out of that bed, or I will kick you out, and I won't be careful what I break on the way. You're embarrassing yourself and this guard. You're embarrassing me."

"Why?"

"I picked you, you little shit!" the Mace roared. "Do you think you're the only boy I saw on the streets who was good with a blade? I picked you! And now you fold, right when I need you the most!"

Pen mumbled something else. He was still drunk, Aisa realized, or at least deeply hungover. She had heard a similar mush of words from Da many times. Now, louder: "I'm a close guard, and you don't need a close guard." Pen's voice rose. "We sit here, doing nothing, while she's over there! There's no one for me to guard!"

Wood splintered, and there was a thump, followed by Pen's bellow of pain.

"Should we go in?" Aisa whispered, but Elston shook his head and raised a finger against his jagged teeth. A hissing, sliding sound came through the doorway; the Mace was dragging Pen across the floor, his breath roughened with exertion.

"You were the smart one, boy. You were supposed to captain

this Guard after the rest of us get too old and slow. And here you are, wallowing in misery like a pig in shit."

Aisa felt a tug on her shirttail and looked down to find her sister Glee peering up at her.

"Glee!" she whispered. "You know you're not supposed to be down here."

Glee continued to stare at her, unseeing, and Aisa realized that she was in one of her trances.

"Glee? Can you hear me?"

"Your chance," Glee whispered. Her eyes were so empty that they seemed hollow. "You'll see it clear. They turn the corner and you grasp your chance."

Aisa's lips parted. She could not pay attention to Glee now, for the business between the Mace and Pen continued violent; she heard more breaking furniture, followed by the thud of a punch.

"Go find Maman, Glee." She turned Glee around and gave her a gentle push, sending her down the corridor. Aisa watched her for a few seconds, troubled, before turning back to the guard quarters. Elston and Kibb were leaning around the doorframe, and Aisa, screwing up her courage, got down on all fours and stuck her head past Elston's legs to peek into the room.

Pen was bent over, his head inside one of the basins that lined the far wall. The Mace stood over him, holding the back of his neck, and Aisa had the impression that if Pen tried to come up too soon, the Mace would shove him under. Elston signaled, asking if they should leave, but the Mace merely shrugged.

Pen came up and took a great gasp of air, his brown curls plastered slickly to his head. Aisa winced as she saw his face: a bright sunrise of bruises, both eyes black, and a wide slice of dried blood on his cheek. The Mace did not seem concerned.

"Are you sober now, boy?"

"Why do we not act?" Pen howled. "We stay here, waiting and waiting, while she's over there being—"

The Mace slapped him.

"You have a nerve, Pen. If you had ever looked past your own misery, you would see it plain. We have a city of people who need to get home. A Church that wants to crack this throne down the middle. And a festering boil under the Gut. You know the Queen, Pen. If we left this mess here, untended, just to get her back, she would kill us both."

"Without her here, it all grows worse—the Church grows worse—"

The Mace's eyes flickered. "True. And you could be of great help, but instead you drown your sorrow in drink and brawling. You think the Queen would enjoy seeing you like this? Would she be proud of you?"

Pen stared at the ground.

"She would find you pathetic, Pen, just as I do." The Mace took a deep breath, folding his arms. "Have a wash and put on some clean clothes. Then get out of here. Do what you need to do, think about whether you want to remain a part of this Guard. You have two days. Come back at your best, or don't come back at all. Understood?"

Pen drew breath in a sharp hiss, his bloodshot eyes wounded. Aisa hoped the Mace would slap him again, but the Mace merely headed for the doorway, shooing them all out.

"I'm sorry, sir," Elston repeated.

"Not your fault, El," the Mace replied, shutting the door of the quarters behind him. "I bent an old rule, and I shouldn't have."

"Do you think he'll come back?"

"Yes," the Mace replied shortly.

Arliss was waiting for them outside his office, holding his usual sheaf of papers, but now Ewen had joined them, peeping around Arliss's shoulder like a bashful child.

"We have estimates on the harvest—" Arliss began, but the Mace cut him off.

"Ewen, what ails you?"

Ewen emerged from behind the Treasurer, his cheeks flushed a dull red. "I would like to talk to you, sir."

"Go ahead."

Ewen took a deep breath, as though commencing a speech. "I'm not a Queen's Guard. You have been very kind to me, sir, you and the Queen, to let me wear the cloak and act the part. But I'm not a real Queen's Guard, and I never will be."

The Mace looked sharply at Elston. "Has someone been speaking to you about this, Ewen?"

"No, sir. Everyone has been as kind as yourself," Ewen replied, blushing harder. "It took me some time to work it out in my head, but I have now. I'm not a *real* Queen's Guard, and I should like to be useful again."

"And how would you do that?"

"The same way I always have, sir: as a jailor. You have a prisoner loose."

"A prisoner—" The Mace stared at him for a long moment. "Jesus, Ewen. No."

"I should like to be useful again," Ewen replied stubbornly.

"Ewen, do you know how we captured Brenna the first time? Coryn came upon her by accident, dreaming deep in one of Thorne's morphia dens. You've heard what happened to Will downstairs. Knowing what we do now, I think Coryn was very lucky that Brenna didn't see him coming. I wouldn't send the best sword in the Tear to lay hold of that witch. I certainly can't send you."

Ewen firmed his shoulders until he stood very straight. "I know what she is, sir. I knew it the day I first saw her. And I heard about what she wrote on the wall. She means to harm the Queen."

The Mace frowned. "Have you spoken to your father about this?"

"My father is dead now, sir. But even dying, he told me to do whatever I might to protect the Queen."

The Mace did not reply for a long moment, but Aisa could see that he was troubled.

"Ewen, she's not an ordinary prisoner. You can't kill her, for the Queen gave her word to keep her alive. But if you try to take such a witch alive, I think you will die in the attempt. I appreciate your courage, but I can't let you do this. The Queen would say the same. I'm sorry."

Ewen stared silently at the ground.

"We will find something else for you to do. Something to help the Queen. I promise."

"Yes, sir."

"Dismissed."

Ewen went down the hall toward the audience chamber, his shoulders slumped.

"Perhaps you should have let him go," Arliss remarked quietly.

"That would be a fine legacy for me as Regent, wouldn't it? Sending a child on a suicide mission."

"He wants to do something honorable, sir," Elston broke in unexpectedly. "It might be good to allow it."

"No. I'm done with being a killer of children."

Aisa froze, but no one else seemed surprised by his words.

"Those days are long gone for you," Arliss murmured, but the Mace chuckled bitterly, shaking his head.

"You mean to be kind, old man, but no matter how we try to outdistance the past, it's always very close. I'm done with those days, but that doesn't mean they're done with me."

"You're a good man now."

"Aye, I am," the Mace replied, nodding, but his eyes were hollow, almost damned. "But it does not wipe out what came before."

They continued down the hallway, discussing the harvest, but Aisa remained where she was, almost rooted to the floor, her mind running over the words again and again, trying to make sense of them. She could not. She thought the Mace was the best man in the Queen's Wing, except perhaps for Venner, and she was unable to reconcile the Captain of Guard she knew with the picture his words had planted: a man who strode through ranks of small forms, wielding a scythe.

A killer of children.

Two hours later, they assembled in the throne room for the Regent's audience. Elston, Aisa, Coryn, Devin, and Kibb were grouped around the dais, the rest of the Guard scattered around the room. The Mace sat in one armchair atop the dais, and Arliss beside him in another, as they began to let the petitioners in. The empty throne gleamed in the torchlight.

"God help me," the Mace muttered. "I used to wonder why the Queen couldn't keep her temper at these things. Now I wonder how she managed at all."

Arliss chuckled. "Queenie's rage was a powerful thing. Entertaining, too. I miss that girl."

"We all miss her," the Mace replied gruffly. "Now let's be about her business."

Aisa turned toward the doors, fixing her face into the mask of impassive stoicism that Elston recommended. The nobles came first, an old custom that, more than once, Aisa had heard the Mace and Arliss discuss discarding. But in truth, it made business move faster. Fewer nobles attended the Mace's audiences now, and today there were only two, both petitioning for tax relief. No one was working the fields, and even Aisa saw that this must be remedied, and soon; not only would there be no food, but the empty fields and farms gave every noble in the kingdom an excuse to dodge tax. Lady Bennett and Lord Taylor listened, their faces glum, while the Mace explained, with extraordinary patience, that changing events made it impossible for him to decide the issue yet. Aisa knew that Arliss was working on the problem of the harvest, of getting people home, but it was a slow business to provision families for such a journey on foot. Both petitioners left empty-handed and disgruntled, just as so many had before.

After the nobles came the poor. Aisa liked them better, for their problems were real. Unredressed crimes, missing livestock, disputes over property . . . the Mace often came up with solutions that Aisa would never have thought of. The Guard tended to relax a bit during this portion of the audience, even Aisa, who was almost enjoying herself, right up until the moment the crowds parted and she found herself facing her father.

Aisa's hand went automatically to her knife, and she was beset by such a conflicting mixture of feelings that at first she could not separate them. There was relief, relief because she had grown several inches since the spring, and Da no longer seemed quite so tall. There was hatred, a long-burning fire that had only sharpened with distance and time, searing through her head and gut. And last and most urgent, she felt a need to find her younger sisters, Glee and Morryn, to find them and protect them from everything in the world, starting with Da.

The Mace had clearly recognized Da as well, for a muscle had begun to twitch in his jaw. He leaned down and asked in a low voice, "Do you wish to leave, hellcat?"

"No, sir," Aisa replied, wishing her resolve was as firm as her voice. Da no longer loomed over her, perhaps, but he looked the same as ever. He laid stones for a living, and his top half seemed twice the size of his bottom. As he approached the throne, Aisa drew her knife, clenching it in a fist that was suddenly wet with perspiration.

The Mace beckoned Kibb and murmured, "Make sure Andalie doesn't come in here."

Da was not alone, Aisa saw now; he had emerged from the crowd with a priest beside him. The priest wore the white robes of the Arvath, but the hood was pulled low over his brow and Aisa could not see his face. After a glance in her direction—a single, sharp look that Aisa could not read—Da ignored her, focusing all of his attention on the Mace.

"You again, Borwen?" the Mace asked in a tired voice. "What's on the menu today?"

Da looked as though he meant to speak, but then the priest moved forward and pushed his hood back. Aisa heard the low hiss of the Mace's breath, and she drew her knife automatically as Elston jumped forward. The rest of the Guard quickly moved to surround the foot of the dais, and Aisa went with them, jumping up two risers to tuck herself behind Cae and Kibb.

"Your Holiness," the Mace said slowly. "What an honor to have you here. The last time was thrilling."

The Holy Father himself! Aisa tried not to stare, but she couldn't help it. She had thought that the Holy Father would be old, but he was much younger even than Father Tyler, his hair still nearly black, his face traced with only the lightest of lines. The Mace said that the Holy Father never went anywhere unguarded, but Aisa didn't see any guards in the crowd around him. Still, she took her cue from the men around her, who had ranged themselves in a defensive posture around the Mace.

"I come to demand justice from the Queen's government," the Holy Father announced in a deep, carrying voice, and now Aisa noticed his eyes: blank, almost reptilian, betraying no emotion. "Our brother parishioner, Borwen, came to us with a grievance some weeks ago. The Queen has denied him his parental rights."

"Has she now?" The Mace leaned back in his armchair. "And why would she do that?"

"For gain. She wished to keep Borwen's wife as her servant."

The Mace pinned Borwen with a long stare. "This is your tale of the week? It's a foolish one. Andalie is no one's servant."

"I am confident in the truth of Borwen's tale," the Holy Father replied. "Borwen has been a good member of Father Dean's parish for some years, and—"

"You didn't come here to plead a case for this nonce. What do you want?"

The Holy Father hesitated, but only for a moment. "I also come to personally demand the return of the Apostate."

"As I have told you perhaps ten times now, we don't have him."

"I believe otherwise."

"Well, this wouldn't be the first time you believed something without evidence, would it?" The Mace's tone was mocking, but a large vein had begun to pulse in his forehead. "We don't have Father Tyler, and I will not discuss the subject further."

The Holy Father smiled blandly. "Then what of Borwen's case?"

"Borwen is a pedophile. Do you really wish to tie the Arvath to his cause?"

"That is slanderous," the Holy Father replied calmly, though Aisa noted that his smile had momentarily slipped. Perhaps they had believed that the Mace would not raise the subject in a public audience. Aisa didn't know whether to be relieved or disappointed that he had.

"Borwen lives the life of a good Christian. Each morning he attends dawn services. At night he donates his time to—"

"Borwen has no choice but to be a good Christian," the Mace growled. "Because he knows that for the past six months, I have had a New London constable on him like glue. I understand his neighbors are greatly relieved."

This took Aisa by surprise. She wouldn't have thought the Mace would take an interest in anything that didn't directly affect the Queen. She wondered if Maman knew. Da was certainly no good parishioner; their family had attended church only a few times a year.

"Borwen has repented sincerely for all of his past acts," the

Holy Father replied. "He has reformed, and now he wants only to be with his wife and children."

"Reformed," the Mace sneered. "Tell whatever story you like, Borwen. Sooner or later, we both know that the sickness inside you will have its way, and when we catch you in the act, I will put you away for good."

"My children belong to me!" Da bellowed. "You have no right to keep them from me!"

"You gave up your children the moment you laid a hand on them. On their mother."

Distant movement caught Aisa's eye: Maman, standing at the mouth of the hallway, her arms folded. Kibb had not noticed her—or was pretending not to—and Aisa said nothing either. How could the Mace know about Maman? Had she told him about those days? It seemed unlikely. They didn't get on at all.

"My daughter stands there!" Da snapped. "Ask her! Ask her how badly she was treated!"

Aisa froze, for all eyes in the room were suddenly upon her.

"Your daughter works for me," the Mace replied quickly, and Aisa could tell that he had not been prepared for this turn of the conversation. "She speaks on my command, not yours."

Aisa met Da's gaze and found triumph there. Da still knew her well. This was a well-calculated gamble he took, that she would not want to reveal her own misery, their terrible past. To tell her shame to strangers, so many of them staring at her now . . . how could she do that and then go on? Even if they believed her, how could she go through the rest of her life, knowing that this was the first thing everyone would know about her: that she had endured these things? Who could do that?

The Queen, her mind answered suddenly. *The Queen would speak and face whatever came afterward.*

But Aisa couldn't.

"Aisa has been through enough," the Mace said. "And no true Christian would force her to recount the tale here."

"Indeed, God loves children," the Holy Father replied, nodding. "Except the liars."

"Watch yourself, Father." The Mace's voice had dropped a note, a danger signal to those who knew him, but the Holy Father didn't seem to care. Aisa wondered whether the priest meant to get himself beaten here, or arrested; that would surely be a useful event for the Arvath. The Mace was too smart to oblige him . . . or so Aisa hoped. This low, quiet anger was much worse than when he yelled. She felt Da's eyes on her again, and resisted the urge to meet his gaze.

"Surely if the child had an accusation to make, she would make it," the Holy Father remarked, his voice dismissive. "These baseless charges against Borwen are meant to obscure the fact that the Queen's laws are arbitrary, designed to serve her own needs. All men of God should defend him."

"Her own needs. When the Mort came, the Queen opened the Keep to over ten thousand refugees. How many refugees did the Arvath take in?"

"The Arvath is sacred," the Holy Father replied, but Aisa saw, relieved, that the Mace had broken his rhythm again. "No layman may enter God's house without the Holy Father's permission."

"How convenient for both God and Your Holiness. And what does Christ say about taking in the homeless?"

"I would like to return to the Apostate, Lord Regent," the Holy Father said quickly. Aisa stole a glance at the crowd, but she could not say whether they had noticed the man's quick retreat. Most of them merely stared at the dais with open mouths.

"What about Father Tyler?"

"If he is not handed over by noon on Friday, the Church will excommunicate all employees of the Crown."

"I see. When all else fails, blackmail."

"Not at all. But God is disappointed in the Crown's failure to address sin in the Tearling. With the Queen gone, we had hoped that you would take this opportunity to criminalize unnatural acts."

Elston twitched beside her; Aisa sensed rather than saw it. But when she looked up at him, he looked the same as ever, his face blank and eyes pinned on the crowd.

"How's the money for that property tax payment coming?" the Mace asked suddenly. "Going to be ready for the new year?"

"I don't know what you mean," the Holy Father replied, but his tone was uneasy.

The Mace burst out laughing, and at the sound, Aisa relaxed a bit, the tension easing from her shoulders. She stole another glance across the room and found Maman's eyes pinned on the Mace, a tiny smile curving Maman's lips.

"You know, Anders," the Mace said, "for a few minutes, I wasn't sure what you were doing here. But now I see perfectly. Let me take this opportunity to tell you plain: come hell and vengeance, that tax payment *will* be due on February first."

"This is not about money, Lord Regent."

"Everything is about money, always. You impose a tithe on the Tear and then seek to keep it all, pouring money into luxury, feeding off the credulous and the starving. You *profit*."

"People give freely for a holy cause."

"Do they now?" The Mace's face broke into an ugly grin. "But I know exactly where the money goes. We picked up two of your enforcers last week. You've been doing business in the Creche."

At this, a ripple went through the crowd, and the Holy Father's smile slipped a notch before he recovered.

"Baseless accusations!" he cried. "I am God's messenger—"

"Then your God is a trafficker in child flesh."

The audience gasped.

"And you!" The Mace turned to Borwen. "I wasn't sure what you were doing here either, but now I see you plain. You thought that you would have a better shot at your ridiculous argument with a man on the throne. If you ever try to come near your wife and children again, I will—"

"What? Kill me?" Borwen shouted. "What threat is that? I am already dead, my children lost to me, and hounded wherever I go! Why not just kill me now?"

"I will not kill you," the Mace said quietly, his dark eyes cold. "I will take you into custody and allow your wife to decide your fate."

Da turned white.

The Mace descended the steps, focusing his attention on the Holy Father. "You will not blackmail me with threats, nor will you distract me from the Queen's agenda. Don't send any more of this nonsense to my door. The next priest to set foot in here may not fare so well. And you, Borwen . . . you never want to be in my sight again."

Aisa felt as though her heart would burst. Maman and Wen had always defended her from Da when they could, but it was different to have someone outside their family do so. If it had been permissible to hug the Mace, she would have done, for she loved him suddenly, with the sort of fierce love she had never felt for anyone but her mother.

"Come, Brother Borwen," the Holy Father commanded. "It's just as I have always said: the Glynn crown drowns in its own pride. God knows of this injustice, but we will take your case to the public courts also, and expose this place for what it is."

"You may try," the Mace replied evenly. "But beware, Your Holiness. Borwen's children are hardly his only accusers."

"No one has accused him of anything, Lord Regent."

"I accuse him."

The words were out of Aisa's mouth before she could stop them. The eyes of the crowd were on her, and she wished, more than anything, that she could take it back.

"Did you say something, child?" the Holy Father asked. His voice was honey-sweet, but his eyes glared. Strangely, this forced Aisa to speak again. She thought that each word would be worse than the last, but once started she found, relieved, that the opposite was true: the first words had been the hardest to say, and everything afterward came easier, as though a dam had broken inside her throat.

"I was three or four years when you started." She fought hard to meet Da's eyes, but could only focus on his chin. "You went after Morryn at the same age. We finally had to hide under the floor to get away from you." Aisa heard her own voice rising in distress, but now it was like running down a hill, arms spinning like pinwheels. She couldn't stop. "Always pushing, Da, that's you, and you wouldn't leave us *alone*, that's what I remember best—"

"Lies!" the Holy Father snapped.

"*It's not!*" she screamed. "It's true, and you just don't want to hear it!"

"Hellcat," the Mace said gently, and she stopped, drawing a thick, angry breath.

"You're not in trouble, child. But I want you to go, now. Coryn, take her to her mother."

Coryn tugged gently at her arm, and after a moment, Aisa went with him. She snuck a last look back and found an ocean of eyes still upon her. Da remained beside the Holy Father, his face red with anger.

"Are you all right?" Coryn asked her in a low voice.

Aisa didn't know how to answer. She felt sick. Behind her, she heard the Mace tell the two men to get out.

"Aisa?" Coryn asked.

"I embarrassed the Captain."

"No, you didn't," he replied, and she was grateful to hear his businesslike tone. "You did a useful thing. The Arvath won't dare put your father in front of a public judge now. Too many people were here."

Everyone will know. The thought seemed to scald Aisa.

"The Caden won't care," Coryn remarked casually, and Aisa halted.

"Why do you say that?"

"I saw your face, girl. I know we're going to lose you one day. But grey cloak or red, do yourself a favor: don't let your past govern your future."

"Is it that easy?"

"No. Even the Captain struggles with it, every day."

A killer of children, Aisa remembered. Maman was there suddenly, her arms open, and everything inside Aisa seemed to mercifully collapse. She had been ready to kill Da, ready for years, but now she was amazed to find that she had done something even more difficult: she had spoken aloud.

Tyler did not believe in hell. He had decided, long ago, that if God wanted to punish them, there was infinite opportunity right here; hell would be superfluous.

But if there *was* a hell on earth, Tyler had certainly found it.

He and Seth were tucked into an alcove, a hidden recess deep within a tunnel, buried in the bowels of the earth. They had squeezed in here through a tiny crevice in the stonework. The floor and walls, lit only by the tiny, flickering match in Tyler's fingers, were covered with mold. In the last moment before the match died, Tyler saw that Seth was looking worse than ever today, his cheeks hectic with fever and corneas yellowed with infection. Tyler had not looked at Seth's wound in several days, but if he did, he knew that he would see the red streaks climbing up Seth's belly toward his chest. When they had first escaped the Arvath, Tyler had taken Seth to a doctor, using most of the money he had saved. But the man was not a real doctor, and though he had given Seth something to ease his pain for a few days, he had not been able to stop the progress of the infection.

The match guttered, and not a moment too soon, for now Tyler heard the sound of running footsteps, several pairs, in the tunnel outside.

"The east branch!" a man panted. "To the east branch, and we can meet up in the road."

"They're Caden, I know it," another man said, his voice weak with fear. "They're coming."

"What would Caden want down here? There's no money for them."

"All of you, the east branch, quickly!"

The footsteps took off running again. Tyler leaned back against the wall of the recess, his heart pounding. He and Seth were already in a great deal of trouble, but if there really were Caden down here, their problems would multiply. In the early days of their flight, Tyler had gone up to the surface several times, to trade coin for food and clean water, and it had not taken long to hear the news: the Arvath had placed bounties on them both. Tyler and Seth had long since discarded their Arvath robes, but even in layman's clothes, they no longer felt safe above ground. Tyler had not been out of the tunnels for more than two weeks, and their food supply was nearly gone.

"Ty?" Seth asked in a whisper. "Do you think they've come for us?"

"I don't know," Tyler replied. He had thought they were safe down here, but that safety brought its own price. In his trips through the tunnels, Tyler had seen many things, and as he came to understand what this labyrinth really was, he had begun to lapse back into the spiritual darkness that had gripped him during his final few weeks in the Arvath.

God, why do you allow this? This world is yours. Why do you suffer these people to remain?

Not surprisingly, he received no answer.

He knew he must get Seth out of here, and soon. He had been

looking for a subterranean route to the Keep; surely the Mace must have used such a route to slip in and out of the Arvath unnoticed for his reading lessons. But Tyler was afraid to venture too far from the safety of their crevice. The price on Seth was only a thousand, but on Tyler's last trip topside, the bounty on his own head had stood at five thousand pounds. No Caden would allow such an opportunity to slip through his fingers. From the gossip Tyler had picked up in a shadowy pub, he knew that his bounty also included his possessions, and this told Tyler that while the Holy Father surely wanted them both dead—and would pay good money to be able to send Tyler to judgment himself—his primary interest was not Tyler or Seth, but the polished cherrywood box that Tyler kept in his satchel. Tyler longed to take it out and open it again, but they could not afford to waste any more matches; they were down to their last packet. All the same, he could not help holding the satchel close, feeling the comforting edges of the box inside.

After several weeks in the tunnels, Tyler had pieced together some of this business. The Tear crown had not been seen since Queen Elyssa died. She must have gifted it to the Church—an odd move for a monarch who did not attend services more than once a year, but Elyssa would not be the first to have found Jesus at her deathbed. Tyler had never met the Glynn Queen's mother, but she was accounted the sort of woman who might attempt to buy her way into heaven. The crown was undoubtedly valuable, made of solid silver and sapphire, but its value to Tyler went far beyond money. This crown had sat on the heads of every ruler since Jonathan Tear, and had anchored many bloody battles of succession. It was rumored to have magical properties as well, though Tyler thought that was little more than fancy. To him, the crown was an artifact, a witness to the wild, brawling, extraordinary history of the Tear, and Tyler could no more be careless with such an artifact than he could leave Seth behind. Besides, he had a promise to keep. The thought of the woman, Maya, nearly wrenched him in half. She had given him the crown, and he had left her there, sitting in front of the table of drugs. He could not have taken her with him, or the game would have been up; he knew this, but the knowledge brought him no peace. Anders was not one to spare the rod, and Tyler could not imagine what fate had befallen Maya after his escape. If nothing else, he meant to keep his promise and deliver the crown to the Queen. But he could hardly do that down here.

Footsteps pounded on the stone above Tyler's head, causing him to shudder. It might be the Caden, or another group of the lost and damned souls Tyler had seen down here. But the footsteps continued, many of them, and Tyler could not help thinking of another piece of information he had heard in the pub: mobs now roamed the streets of New London, carrying swords and carpentered crucifixes, praising God and threatening violence to all who would not do the same. There was nothing explicit tying these mobs to God's Church, and yet Tyler smelled the Holy Father's stink all over them. He would have bet his Bible that these people took their orders from the Arvath.

It was a good Church once, Tyler thought, and that was true. After the Tear assassination, God's Church had helped to keep order. The Church had worked with the first Raleighs, kept William Tear's colony from scattering to the four winds. In the second century after the Crossing, an enterprising preacher named Denis had seized on Catholicism, recognizing the great value of theatricality and ritual in capturing imaginations. Denis had overseen the design and construction of the Arvath, a life's work that had drained the Church coffers and made the man old before his time. Denis had died only three days after the final stone was laid, and the Church now recognized him as the first true Holy Father, but there had been plenty of men before him, guiding God's Church along the same path. Tyler, who had gathered as much oral history as he could, knew that his church was far from perfect. But not even the darkest chapter in its history approached the state of the Arvath now.

Of course, the Holy Father would not have dared to do any of this with the Queen in residence. Anders feared Queen Kelsea, feared her so greatly that, not so long ago, he had handed Tyler a vial of poison and ordered him to a terrible purpose. The Queen had surrendered herself to Mortmesne—that news had been impossible to miss, even in Tyler's briefest trips to the surface—and the Mace was in charge of the kingdom. But the people of the Tearling did not love the Mace, only feared him, and fear was not nearly so dangerous. In the Queen's absence, the Holy Father was emboldened.

She must come back, Tyler thought, almost in the form of a prayer. *She must.*

New footsteps echoed in the tunnel outside, and Tyler pressed back against the wall. Several men ran by the tiny opening, but they made no sound beyond their steps, and even through the wall Tyler could sense the military efficiency that underlay their movements, all of them unified in purpose.

Caden, his mind whispered. But in search of what? Were they here for Tyler and Seth, or someone else? It hardly mattered. All it would take was one sharp pair of eyes to spot the narrow opening in the tunnel wall, and they would be discovered.

The footsteps passed without slowing, and Tyler relaxed. Seth huddled against him, shivering, and Tyler wrapped his arms around his friend. Seth was dying, slowly and painfully, and Tyler could do nothing for him. He had helped Seth to escape the Arvath, but what good was escape to them now? All hands were turned against them.

Dear God, Tyler prayed, though he felt certain that the words were going nowhere but around and around the dark chasm of his mind. *Dear God, please show us your light.*

But there was nothing, only darkness, an endless drip of water, and, somewhere nearby, the fading footsteps of assassins.

Chapter 5

Tear's Land

The mistake of utopia is to assume that all will be perfect. Perfection may be the definition, but we are human, and even into utopia we bring our own pain, error, jealousy, grief. We cannot relinquish our faults, even in the hope of paradise, so to plan a new society without taking human nature into account is to doom that society to failure.

—*The Glynn Queen's Words*, AS COMPILED BY FATHER TYLER

William Tear was deeply worried about something. Katie was sure of it.

Even after almost a year of working with him, she didn't know Tear well. He wasn't a man one came to know, for he guarded himself too closely. Katie didn't think even Mum completely understood him. Some days Katie felt as though she could almost see the thing, weighing on Tear, bowing his shoulders and making him age, and because he was worried, Katie was worried as well.

She was seated on the ground in the middle of the Belt, the narrow strip of dense woodland that bordered the northern side of town. The tree cover was thick here, allowing only rare patches of sunlight to dapple the dry grass.

"Push!" Tear barked. "His footing is weak, you see? This is the moment when you use the weight of your body to close on him and put him down. Get a man solidly beneath you with a knife in your hand and you've already won."

Katie wrapped her arms around her knees, trying to concentrate on the sparring area in front of her, where Gavin and Virginia were locked, straining. Each had a knife in hand, but right now weapons were secondary; this lesson was about leverage. Katie wasn't fantastic with a knife, and she didn't have the size to overpower anyone, but she was one of the quickest among them, and she had an easier time trusting her own body, her reflexes and balance. Virginia was taller and better muscled, but she couldn't find the place to push, and a few seconds later Tear called a halt and began to point out what she had missed. Virginia looked disgruntled, but Katie didn't think it would be counted against her. There were nine of them in training here: Katie, Virginia Warren, Gavin Murphy, Jess Alcott, Jonathan Tear, Lear Williams, Ben Howell, Alain Garvey, and Morgan Spruce. They all had different strengths, but Virginia's was the most valuable: she feared absolutely nothing. Katie had learned much in the past year, but fearlessness couldn't be taught, and she coveted the quality.

"Virginia, sit and watch. See if you can spot it this time." Tear snapped his fingers. "Alain, have a go at Gavin."

Alain got up from his spot across the circle and approached Gavin warily. The two were good friends, but Alain was the weakest fighter among the group, and Gavin knew it; a gleam of overconfidence had entered his eyes. Katie shook her head. Gavin was a good fighter, but he tended toward arrogance, and it had gotten him in trouble more than once.

"Shrink your size, Garvey!" Aunt Maddy called from beside Tear. "Or he'll knock you flying!"

Alain tucked his shoulders toward his chest and pulled a knife from the sheath at his waist. Their knives were crude, little more than pointed spears with handles, the same tools that workers used to slaughter cattle. But Katie had overheard Mum talking to Aunt Maddy, who said that Tear had made them all real knives, fighting knives. Such weapons had to be made in secret, and carried in secret—sometimes it seemed to Katie that, in the long year since she had sat on the bench with William Tear, her life had filled up with secrets, like a pot beneath a leak—but they would receive the knives when they were ready. Katie could barely wait.

Alain was taller than Gavin, but Gavin was the best knife handler among them, and he could move like a tree lizard to boot. Within only a few seconds, he had maneuvered behind Alain and grabbed his knife hand, rapping Alain's wrist over his knee, purposefully and methodically, trying to make Alain drop his knife.

"Hold!" Tear called, stalking into the ring. Mum came with him, her eyes snapping with disapproval.

"What would happen in a real fight, Gavin?" Mum demanded.

"I would have kept hold of him," Gavin replied, his voice toneless. "I would have broken his wrist and then busted his knee."

"Failure means little in this ring," Tear told Alain. "But in the real world, the real fight, failure is swift death. This is a thing to understand and remember."

From the corner of her eye, Katie saw Virginia nodding grimly. They were friends of a sort, though Virginia was a bit too fierce to ever be a real friend. Last week, at the big argument over the distribution of the harvest, Virginia had actually grabbed Mr. Ellis by the throat, and if several adults hadn't pulled her off, Katie was quite sure that Virginia would have strangled him with her bare hands. In the Town of Katie's childhood, there had been no fighting; if people had problems, they argued them out. Now, it felt as though there was an incident every week, and Katie often wondered whether they were training for peacekeeping, whether this was the trouble that William Tear had foreseen.

Next to Virginia, Jonathan Tear was staring at the two figures in the center of the ring, his eyes clocking and learning. Every-thing about Jonathan was William Tear in duplicate, except for his eyes, large and dark. Lily's eyes; Katie had often noted the re-semblance. Jonathan was neither a good nor a bad fighter; Katie had beaten him before, though he was a year older than she was. But that hardly mattered. Every moment of his life, Jonathan was *learning*. Katie could see it, see those dark eyes recording infor-mation and sending it to be processed back in the enormous room that was Jonathan's brain. Room? Hell, it was an entire house.

"Gavin, swap out. Lear, you have a go at Alain."

Lear scrambled up from his place, and Katie almost saw Alain groan. Lear was not the best fighter among them, but he got the most respect, because he was smart. His father, who had died in the Crossing, had been one of William Tear's most trusted peo-ple, and Mum often said that Lear had gotten his father's brains. He was apprenticing with old Mr. Welland, the Town historian, and Lear was working on his own history of the Town. Not the Crossing; none of them knew enough about that period, and the answers they got from adults were maddeningly vague. But ac-cording to Gavin, Lear meant to chronicle the history of the Town for his entire lifetime, before publishing the document at his death. No one wanted to fight a boy who was capable of thinking so long-term.

"Close the circle a bit," Mum ordered. "Less room for error."

They all scooted inward.

"Go."

Lear circled Alain, who stood nearly frozen. He was a weak-ness among them, and Katie resented that weakness; there was no room for it here.

That's Row talking.

She scowled, wishing she could force her mind to be quiet. There was an almost schizophrenic quality to her thoughts these days; it seemed as though each discrete idea could be categorized as belonging to either Row or Tear. Alain was not a great fighter, no, but, like so many Crossing children, he had other skills, particularly a phenomenal gift for sleight of hand. You never played Alain at cards, not for anything more than bragging rights; he had won several skeins of Katie's best marled yarn before Katie learned to stop betting. Each fall, at the harvest festival, Alain would put on a magic show that impressed the adults and absolutely thrilled the smaller children. He might not be much of a fighter, but Katie recognized the great value of having so many different people in one community, each of them singular, each with gifts and faults and interests and oddities. They created a tapestry, all of them, just as the characters in a book might. It was the lesson of the Town, taught to children before they could even walk: *You are special, everyone is special. But you are not better. All are valuable.*

But Row couldn't quantify the value of that tapestry. Katie often tried to explain it to him, but she wasn't sure she was getting through. Row had no patience for inefficiency, and sometimes his thoughts would entwine with Katie's, strangling Tear's voice, killing it off.

Lear stopped circling and moved in, quick and silent. In moments, he had slipped behind Alain and wrapped his arms around his friend's neck, headlocking him.

"Hold."

William Tear stood with crossed arms, his eyes pinned on Alain. Those eyes were not without pity, but they were cold, and Katie suddenly knew that Alain was on thin ice.

"That's enough for today. All of you go to your regular apprenticeships."

Lear released Alain, who stumbled away, rubbing his throat. Lear placed a hand on his back and Alain smiled good-naturedly, but there was grimness there as well; Katie felt certain that he, too, knew he was on some sort of probation. Gavin began to give him a hard time, but that was Gavin, so convinced of his own gifts that he sometimes tipped into cruelty by accident. Gavin had asked her to the summer picnic last year, and even though he was good-looking, Katie had said no. There was something relentless in Gavin, ready to crush everything on the path to his objective. Katie didn't trust him to put anything before himself.

Come on now! her mind mocked. *Is Row any better?*

No, but Row knew he was worse, harbored no illusions about himself. That made a huge difference. Row might be unkind, but Gavin was a fool. He didn't even like to read.

Tear, Aunt Maddy, and Mum left the clearing, heading west, back up toward town. Mum nodded to Katie as they went, a subtle signal that Katie had done well today. Gavin, Howell, Alain, and Morgan disappeared into the trees, heading eastward, around the hill and south, down to the cattle farm. Jess went downhill, toward the lumber site, and Virginia followed; she was part of a large group that was just beginning to explore and map the vast land outside the Town—Tear's Land, they were calling it now, though Katie knew from Mum that William Tear didn't like that at all. They all had apprenticeships to camouflage these sessions; even Jonathan Tear had a day job, working at the dairy. But no apprenticeship could match Tear's lessons. He was teaching them to fight, but that was only half of it. In some indefinable way, Katie felt that Tear was also teaching them, not by word but by example, to be better. Better people, better members of the community. During their sessions, Row's voice was still present in Katie's head, but muted. In Row's world, Alain would have been booted a long time ago, but Row's ideas of exceptionalism, his dog-eat-dog vision of the world, these things seemed to have no place in this clearing.

Katie waited a minute before she got up, brushing the prickly grass from the bottom of her pants. She could afford to be a bit late to the sheep farm; she worked hard, and Mr. Lynn, who was in charge of the spinners and dyers, thought she practically walked on water. She could probably ditch for a week before he would say something.

Across the clearing, Jonathan Tear was still sitting on the ground, staring straight ahead. His face was clouded and dull, almost sleepy, and Katie walked away, leaving him alone; Jonathan was so damned *weird*! Even in a community that valued individuals, Katie wasn't sure what place Jonathan held. He was his father's son, and that could have given him a great status, but Jonathan would accept none of the adulation the Town longed to shower upon him; he didn't seem to know how to handle it. He spent all of his free time in the library, curled up with a pile of books in a dark recess on the second floor. Even in their practice sessions, Jonathan was isolated, shut out of the jocular familiarity that the rest of them enjoyed, that happy sense of group-elite that defined them. He was odd, simply odd, and Katie's first impulse was to simply leave him alone.

But as she reached the edge of the clearing, her steps slowed until she came to a halt. Mum's voice was in her head, the voice of Katie's childhood, the voice that said when you saw your neighbor in trouble, no matter how much you disliked him or disagreed with him, you stopped. You *helped*.

Jonathan Tear didn't look at all well.

With an exasperated sigh, Katie turned and marched back to him.

"Are you all right?"

Jonathan didn't answer, merely kept staring straight ahead. Katie squatted down on her haunches and stared at his face, realizing that the look she had mistaken for dullness was really fixation, as though Jonathan saw something in the distance. Katie looked behind her, but there was only the wall of trees on the far end of the clearing.

"Jonathan?"

She snapped her fingers in front of his eyes, but he didn't blink. His pupils were dilated, and Katie wondered if he was having an attack of some kind, if she should call someone. But the rest of the group had disappeared. Even the sounds of their passage had gone, and there was only the melody of the woods, birdsong and the low rustle of the tree branches as early afternoon wind sighed through their leaves.

Slowly, hesitantly, Katie reached out and placed her hand on Jonathan's shoulder. He jumped, but his pupils did not contract, and when he turned to look at her, his gaze was just as blank and distant as before, staring straight through her, making Katie shudder.

"It's gone bad," he whispered. "Bad town, bad land. You and me, Katie. You, me, and a knife."

At the last word, Katie jumped, her hand reaching automatically for the knife at her waist. Jonathan reached out and grasped her wrist with ice-cold fingers, the edges of his mouth lifting in a ghastly grin.

"We tried, Katie," he whispered. "We did our best."

With a low cry, she tore her wrist free. Jonathan blinked, his pupils contracting in the sun-dappled light. He stared at her, brow furrowed.

"Katie?"

She scooted backward. Her heart was still racing, and she didn't want to be so close to him. She felt danger coming from him, radiating off him, almost like heat.

"You were dreaming," she ventured.

Dreaming, her mind replied mockingly. *He was in a trance, some kind of trance, like Annie Fowler gets sometimes when they ask her to tell tomorrow's weather.*

But Annie would merely close her eyes for a moment before predicting the weather, usually correctly. What happened to Jonathan had been something else entirely. It was almost like—

"Is practice over?" Jonathan asked.

"Yes." She straightened, then offered him a hand. She would pull him to his feet, and that would be the end of it. She had fulfilled her neighborly requirement for today. She would get out of here, go down to the sheep farm, dye some yarn, and forget about this entire creepy scene.

Instead, she felt her mouth open and say, "What did you see?"

His expression drew inward. "What do you mean?"

She pulled him up. "Your father goes into trances. Mum's told me about them. You were in one too. What did you see?"

"You can't tell anyone about this."

"Why not? It's not my fault you decided to do it right in the middle of practice."

He grabbed her shoulders and Katie tensed, suddenly realizing that he was nearly a foot taller than she was. She reached for her knife, but before she could pull it free, Jonathan released her and backed away.

"I'm sorry," he said stiffly. "But I don't want anyone to know."

"Why not?" Katie asked, bewildered. "I would love to have the sight. I didn't get any gifts from the Crossing."

Jonathan gave her a measuring look. "All my life, people have been watching me, waiting for me to become my father in miniature. And that's fine; I understand why they do it. But dynasties are dangerous. Whoever they elect to lead this town next, it shouldn't be simply because he's someone's son. They'll make a better decision if they think I'm like everyone else."

"Isn't it a little hard to hide?"

"Not really. I spend most of my time alone."

Katie looked down, embarrassed. She had always assumed that Jonathan's isolation was merely a function of social awkwardness; it had never occurred to her that it might be self-imposed. Thinking of the snide comments that she and Row had traded back and forth about him, she felt ashamed.

"Don't," Jonathan said, making Katie jump. "It's the impression you were meant to get."

Katie retreated, frightened again. Had he heard what she was thinking? Several teenagers in town had a little bit of that talent; Katie had overheard Mum and Aunt Maddy talking about it once. Mum said that William Tear had ordered them not to talk about these things, not to make the Crossing children feel singled out. Row could do extraordinary things with fire; it was his gift, just as Ellie Bennett could find water and Matt van Wye could make things vanish. Row did not showcase his ability either; only Katie—and perhaps Row's mother—knew that this skill was what made Row such a fine metalworker. Katie, who had been born nearly two years after the Landing, had no such gifts, and had often envied them. But she sensed that the Crossing children, with their little magics salted around the Town like hidden eggs at the spring festival, were very different from Jonathan. Power seemed to surround him. Katie looked down and found that the hair on her arms was standing on end. She kept her hand on her knife.

"I'm no danger to you," Jonathan told her.

Maybe not, but there was danger in him, all the same, and Katie struggled to analyze it. Hadn't she just been thinking that the Town was a place where everyone was equally valuable, where all of their gifts came together to make a tapestry?

Equally valuable? What about William Tear?

Katie blinked. She wondered what Row would say if he knew what she had discovered here, and the answer came back instantly.

We don't need another William Tear.

Yes, that was Row's voice, but Row hadn't been there that night, hadn't sat on the bench and felt Tear's greatness, the majesty of him. Tear had arranged with all of their mentors to shield this time, to pretend that they were all working at their apprenticeships when they were not, and so far the story seemed to be holding. But secrecy from Row was a different story entirely; he knew that Katie wasn't being entirely truthful, and it had created a tiny divide between them. Katie hated this divide, but could do nothing about it. Although she still chafed occasionally at the strictures of the Town, its innate hypocrisy, she knew that she could never go against William Tear. Tear didn't want to be worshipped as a god, or even a king; there was danger there, something innately hostile to the democracy he prized. But Katie worshipped him, all the same. And now here was Tear's son, the odd duck of Katie's school, a boy she had always dismissed as utterly unimportant, standing here with William Tear's power flowing off him in waves. A new thought occurred to Katie, one she had never considered: what would happen to the Town when William Tear was gone?

"Will you take your hand off your knife?" Jonathan asked.

She did. Jonathan relaxed, sinking to his haunches, and Katie suddenly remembered that he was only a year older than she was. For a few moments there, the gap had felt like decades.

"I won't tell anyone," she said.

He looked up and smiled. Katie had to look away, for the smile was brilliant, almost blinding in its goodwill. For a moment she wanted to beg his forgiveness. Again she thought of that night in her backyard, sitting beside Tear on the bench and realizing that she would do whatever he might ask. The Tears were dangerous people, but theirs was not a danger of knives.

"Thank you," said Jonathan.

Katie looked at her watch. She should have been at the sheep farm long ago, but something in her still hesitated, and when she identified that hesitation, it stunned her: she was waiting to be dismissed.

"Go," Jonathan told her, and Katie stumbled toward the edge

of the clearing. Her mind would not quite focus, and her skin was puckered with gooseflesh. It was the way she imagined trees felt after being struck by a bolt of lightning.

She looked back, but Jonathan had already vanished. Katie turned and continued on her way, cutting steadily eastward, looking for the path that wrapped around the slope, the path that would take her back to the Hill Road. She eventually found it, but that lightning-struck feeling persisted.

What happened? she demanded, though she knew she would get no answers. *What happened to me back there?*

She didn't know, but one fact, at least, had solidified in her mind: she now had another secret to keep. Not from the Town—that was easy—but from Row. Another secret to divide them, and Katie felt the wedge drive a bit deeper into her mind: Tear and Row, so distant now that they might as well have been on opposite sides of a ravine, and where did Katie plant her flag?

I can be both! she insisted, but even in her mind her voice was shrill, the high, anxious tone of someone covering a lie.

Tapping.

Katie woke abruptly from a dream of flight, and found herself in darkness. The tapping continued, and for a moment she felt her dream morph, smoothly and seamlessly, as dreams often did, into something new, a poem Mum had read to her when she was young. There was a raven outside, tapping away, and Katie could not open her window. Only madness waited there.

Another soft set of taps. She realized that she was awake, that the sound was real fingers on her window, a large board that Mum had built to swing outward on hinges. Unlike the glass windows in her books, this window was only opaque wood, and Katie could not see what was out there.

Nothing, her mind whispered. *Nothing good. Ignore it and go back to sleep.*

But the tapping could not be ignored. In fact, it was beginning to increase, both in speed and volume, and soon it would wake Mum. Katie took a deep breath, reminded herself that she was a fierce animal, drew the bolt, and cracked the window.

Row was crouched beneath the windowsill, his dark eyes peeping up at her in the moonlight.

"Bundle up and come on."

"Where?" she asked.

"Out."

"What time is it?" She fumbled on her bedside table for her watch.

"Two thirty." Row held up a black, shapeless mass. "I brought us cloaks. I figure in these, we should be able to pass as grown-ups."

Katie didn't move. Every instinct in her body told her not to go, yet there was a terrible fascination in the darkness behind Row. He could break the rules and not get in trouble. But Katie wasn't as brave.

Row smiled. "Why not? You know me, Katie; I never get caught."

She drew back, suddenly chilled, remembering the moment that afternoon with Jonathan Tear. Could *anyone* read her mind now? She looked at Row suspiciously, wondering if he had been holding back on her all these years.

"Did you—"

"I know you, Rapunzel. When have we ever needed magic to read each other's minds?"

That was true. Sometimes the two of them achieved such perfect simpatico that they didn't need to talk at all.

"What are you afraid of, anyway?" Row demanded, crossing both arms on her windowsill. "Me?"

No, not Row precisely, but Katie couldn't explain. As always, what Row offered was dark and wild and off-limits: the night outside her window. If she got caught out after curfew, her punishment wouldn't end with Mum. It would go all the way to William Tear. He might even take her off the guard.

"Why are you even here?" she demanded. "What about Mia?"

Row shrugged, an entire conversation that Katie read easily. He might be sleeping with Mia Gillon this week, but Mia would wait, just as all the women in town seemed to wait on Row. He had his choice of beds, and he made good use of them, but none of the women mattered. Katie found the idea comforting. The magic circle that had surrounded the two of them since childhood was solid, far too solid to be broken by anyone as ridiculous as Mia Gillon.

Row leaned in even farther, dangling the cloak in front of her. "Last chance, Rapunzel."

With fingers that were not quite steady, she took the cloak. "I have to get dressed."

"I'll be out front. Hurry up."

Trembling, Katie closed the window. Her stomach had twisted into knots, as it always did when she knew she could get into trouble. She felt as though she might throw up.

"What are you doing?" she whispered to herself, drawing on her thick wool pants and warmest shirt. "Why are you doing this?"

There was no answer. Katie thought again of Jonathan Tear, his father, Mum, books . . . but these were things of the daytime, and now it was night.

"So stupid," she whispered, swinging a leg over the windowsill. "Stupid, stupid, stupid."

She dropped to the ground and swung the window closed behind her. The hinges screeched a bit, making her wince. Without the bolt shot the wood would not lay flush, leaving a gap of perhaps half an inch, but there was no help for that. The grass under her window was wet with night dew, and she could already

feel it beginning to soak through her thick wool shoes. But her
feet seemed to carry her forward of their own accord, out into
the lane in front of the house, where Row waited silently, cloaked
and hooded. He took her hand, and Katie felt an odd thrill course
through her veins.

"Come on."

They hurried up the lane and then down, toward the southern end of town. Mist had covered the hillside, obscuring all but
the occasional brightly lit lamppost. Everything was quiet, and
the silence brought home to Katie, as nothing else had today, the
strange hybrid status of her age, right on the cusp of growing up.
All of the children were in bed, but here were she and Row, neither
children nor adults, darting through the streets without permission, interlopers in a deep blue world.

After a few minutes the lane began to slope downward for
good. Katie had lost her bearings in the mist, but Row seemed to
know where they were going, for he tugged at her hand, leading
her off the road and into the space between a cluster of houses. Katie didn't know how he could be so sure of their path; she couldn't
see more than five feet ahead. Her shoes were soaked through,
the tips of her toes going numb. The houses ended and they were
into the woods now, trees and shrubs that Row darted around,
pulling Katie with him. The mist began to clear as they continued
downward, and soon Katie was able to find her own footing. They
were in the Lower Bend, the last section of town before the eastern
slope went back into forest. Row did his internship down here, at
Jenna Carver's metal shop, and Katie soon realized that was their
destination.

"Row, what—"

"Shhh."

Jenna's shop was a rickety wood building, unprotected from
the relentless wind that battered the eastern slope. Katie assumed
that the door would be locked, since Jenna had many people's

valuables in there, but as they climbed the worn steps, Row produced a key.

"Where did you get that?"

"I duped it."

Katie shook her head at the foolishness of her own question. Among many other metal items, Row and Jenna also made locks and keys. Not many people locked their doors in town, but all of them *had* locks. Katie suspected that this oddity, like so many others, had something to do with the pre-Crossing, but she could not be certain. All of the adults were the same: happy enough to talk about the Crossing itself—though they were maddeningly vague about geography—or about world history, but the period immediately before the Crossing, some thirty or forty years, was a dark hole in the Town's consciousness. Whatever had driven them all here, they had decided to bury it.

She followed Row inside the shop, then waited, shivering, as he lit a lamp.

"This had better be good, Row. I'm freezing."

"It is," Row replied, rummaging through a drawer in Jenna's desk. "Look here!"

He held up a dark gemstone, its many facets gleaming. Even in the dim light, Katie had no trouble recognizing this stone as William Tear's, the same one she had held in her fist more than a year before, but she stared at it as though it was new to her.

"What is it?" she asked. Part of her felt sorrow, the same sorrow she experienced when she lied to Row about where she had been in the afternoons. There were so many secrets now!

"It's William Tear's," Row replied. "He gave it to Jenna, wants her to set it in a necklace with a silver setting. I'm not supposed to know."

"Then how do you know?"

"I eavesdropped," Row replied, grinning. Katie knew that grin well, but in this moment it struck her as almost grotesque. She didn't like seeing William Tear's sapphire in Row's hand.

"*That's* what you dragged me out here to show me?"

"It's not just any stone!" Row protested. "Here, take it."

Katie took it. She felt none of the sensations she remembered from that night on the bench, only the cold heft of the thing, its many points biting into her palm. Row stared at her eagerly, but after a moment his brow quirked.

"Don't you feel it?"

"Feel what?"

"Magic," Row replied.

"Magic," Katie replied, her voice laced with sarcasm.

"It's real magic, Katie! I can feel it when I hold it!"

Katie threw him a disgusted look, but beneath the sadness at her own deception, she felt a sudden, deeper pain. Row's enthusiasm wasn't false; Katie hadn't seen him this excited about anything in a long time. When he held the jewel, *something* happened to him . . . magic, as he put it. Why wasn't anything happening for Katie? She squeezed the jewel tightly in her fist, but there was nothing, not even that warming tingle she remembered from the night on the bench with Tear. The jewel was an inert rock in her hand.

"What kind of magic?"

"It shows me things!" Row's eyes were bright with excitement. "The past. The Crossing. I know what happened, Katie! I know why they kept it a secret!"

He paused, waiting for her to ask what, but Katie did not. Anger bubbled inside her, anger that began with a sickly, acid trickle she recognized as jealousy.

"Get real, Row," she replied, turning away.

Row grabbed her arm. "I'm not lying! I saw it!"

"Sure you did." Part of Katie felt sick at this exchange, at lying, once again, to her oldest and best friend. But she couldn't help it; the trickle of jealousy inside her had quickly widened into a raging river. Katie was the one who had promised, the one who followed William Tear, who killed herself to learn his lessons, and now she was even keeping Jonathan Tear's secrets as well. Row hated William Tear. So why did he get to see?

Row stared at her, his face both angry and hurt. "You think I'm lying?"

"I think you're having some sort of delusion."

Row's eyes narrowed. He held out his hand, silently, and Katie returned the sapphire, relieved when he tucked it back into the drawer. As the drawer was closing, Katie caught sight of something else there—a dull gleam of unpolished silver, almost circular—and then it was gone.

"I'm sorry I wasted your time," Row said stiffly. "I'll take you back home now."

Katie nodded, just as stiffly. She wished she could just walk out, but the idea of going back up through town alone, in the dark, gave her the jitters. She waited silently as Row doused the lamp, then followed him out the door.

The wind had picked up again, hissing through the pines. Katie's night vision was gone now, and she saw only a black world beyond the timbers of the porch.

The Town is darker now, she thought, but didn't know what the thought meant.

Row locked the door of Jenna's shop, and in each movement Katie sensed the sudden deep gulf between them, a gulf that had never existed before. They argued sometimes, certainly, but nothing like this. She felt an absurd impulse to take it back, tell him she believed him, but pride wouldn't let her utter the words. What the hell was Row doing playing with William Tear's sapphire anyway? He wasn't supposed to know about it, he had said so himself.

Crap. At least admit that you're just jealous.

Katie grimaced. She could admit it, but not to Row. She walked faster, overtaking Row and then passing him, following her breath in the frosted air. She wished she could just not speak to him until morning, when she would surely have calmed down. Why was she so jealous, anyway? She was content to be Katie Rice. She didn't need to have magic, to be one of the Crossing children with their strange assortment of gifts. It was Row who couldn't bear to settle for the hand life had dealt him, Row who wouldn't rest until he brought down William Tear's entire town—

Katie halted. That last thought hadn't been her own, but someone else's, as though there were a stranger inside her head. Not Row, not Tear, but a third party, a voice she had never heard before.

Hearing voices. You're about two steps from crazy.

But Katie didn't believe that. She turned to look at Row, to see whether that voice had been correct, whether she could find destruction in his face.

The road behind her was empty.

Katie turned in a slow circle. She was at the very edge of the Lower Bend, just where the road inclined sharply to begin switch-backing the hill toward the center of town. The area was lit with sporadic lamplight, but this only served to highlight the many pools of shadow behind her. On either side, long-weathered buildings creaked and groaned under the assault of the wind. This end of the Lower Bend was the closest thing to an industrial row that the Town could boast: Mr. Eddings's forge; Ellen Wycroft's flour mill; the ceramics shop, which held ten potter's wheels and two kilns and was open to all via a sign-up sheet; and Mr. Levy's all-purpose art store, full of leads and canvas, homemade paints, and plain, well-made oak picture frames. These were good buildings, friendly buildings, but now they leaned and groaned in the darkness, and Katie felt a trickle of unease at how different they were, how easily certainty became uprooted in the dark. Where was Row? If he was playing a trick on her, she would make him regret it.

"Row?" she called. The wind picked up her voice and carried it; it seemed to slip down the street, around corners and into shadows, places she didn't want it to go. She thought of the graveyard, bones strewn every which way by an animal that thought nothing of tearing into graves and carrying off corpses. Her imagination, so vivid that Mrs. Warren often read her creative writing assignments to the class, was coming to life, sparking and popping. She sensed movement all around her, behind her, in each pool of shadow.

"Row!" she cried out, her voice cracking mid-syllable. She didn't care if they both got caught now; in fact, she would welcome it, welcome some disapproving adult to escort her back up to the Town for a talk with Mum about being out after curfew. Ahead of Katie were deep woods, broken only by the almost imperceptible glimmer of the path. She would rather face getting caught than enter those woods alone.

"Row!" she screamed, but the wind grabbed her voice and seemed to shred it to tatters. No one lived down at this end of town. All of the buildings were closed up and empty at night, but that very emptiness seemed suddenly terrible to Katie, a void waiting to be filled. She would never forgive Row for this, ever. He had snuck past her, taken one of his secret ways through the woods, and now he was probably halfway home, laughing all the way. They both liked to read horror stories, but the stories didn't frighten Row the way they did Katie. He probably thought nothing of leaving her stranded here in the dark, thought it was a wonderful joke.

Don't you think he knows you better than that?

Yes, he did. Row knew Katie's imagination, knew that she wouldn't like to be alone in the windy dark. He had done this on purpose. Katie had behaved badly at Jenna's shop; she knew it. She had meant to apologize. But what Row had done here was deliberate, spiteful.

Katie heard something.

Beneath the high, cold cry of the wind, her ears picked up the stealthy sound of something moving. Not behind her, but in front, somewhere beyond the mill and the ceramics shop. There was plenty of movement out there; the wind on this slope was so strong that the trees were always talking and rustling in their own secret language, but these were not tree noises. Slow and clumsy, but purposeful, the sounds getting closer. Katie heard the sharp crack of a disturbed branch snapping back into place.

"Row?" she asked faintly. The sound barely left her lips, and she was glad. She might not have any gifts; she couldn't see in the dark, like Gavin, or move with the quick, animal silence of Lear, but her intuition worked as well as anyone's, and what she heard out there was bad. Not Row's kind of bad, charming and seductive, but something terrible. Katie thought longingly of her knife, still sitting on her dresser next to a pile of clothing. They weren't supposed to wear their knives anywhere but practice, but Katie would have given anything to have a blade with her now.

There was no hope for it. She turned and began walking up the path into the woods, tucking her head, trying to step quietly, determined not to look backward. The woods would be bad, but she could manage; she was fifteen years old. The path was longer than Row's shortcut, but at least it was a way that Katie knew; she wouldn't get lost. She would walk back up to town and crawl into her own bed, and the next time Row came knocking, she would keep her window shut.

Even in the dark, she made decent progress; the tree cover was thick, but enough moonlight shone down through gaps in the branches that Katie could pick her way along. Despite her best intentions, she kept glancing behind her, but she saw nothing. Whatever it had been—and she had no intention of dwelling on that question, not until she was safe in her bed and the sun had risen and flooded the Town with light—it hadn't followed her up here.

The path curved. Ahead of her, Katie saw a wide break in the trees, giving on to a broad, leveled field. Moonlight limned the field clearly, revealing the dark, rounded shapes of tombstones. The graveyard. The Town, worried about contaminating the water supply, had always buried its dead near the bottom of the hill. William Tear encouraged cremation—he and Row agreed on that, at least—but there were too many people whose religious faith demanded that they go into the ground. The last time the subject had come up at meeting, Paul Annescott had rallied a large contingent of Christians; they had won the vote to keep the graveyard, and won it fairly, but for a moment, Katie hated them all. That wide expanse of field glowed ghostly in the moonlight, but it was the markers that bothered Katie most. Bad enough to put people in the ground to rot; did they have to commemorate it as well?

A branch snapped behind her.

Katie whirled around. Through a tiny hole in the foliage, almost impossibly distant, she could see the dim lights of the Lower Bend, but the portion of path she had just traversed was a long carpet of shadow. Her heart thundered in her ears, but even over its wild pounding, she could hear that sound again, the stealthy push of branches being moved out of the way. Something coming toward her. But on the right, or the left?

"Row!" she screamed into the woods, her throat raw with fright. "If this is you, I'll fucking kill you!"

There was no answer, only that same sound of approaching progress, measured and deliberate. Katie dropped to the ground and began scrabbling, digging through the dirt until she found what she sought: a good-size rock, smooth and rounded but heavy, a rock she could wield. One side was jagged; a geode, perhaps, its crystals broken through the rock's cracked surface. Katie straightened, clutching the rock in her hand, then froze as something moved on the path, perhaps thirty feet away, covering a patch of moonlight and blocking it out.

It was big, whatever it was, the height of a tall man. Katie could just make out a hint of silhouette, rounded shoulders and the protrusion of a head, but the shape, the posture, were wrong, slumped over, almost as though it was crouching. In desperation, her mind tried to convince her one last time that it was Row, having her on, but Katie knew better. Her *gut* knew better. She could smell the thing, dank and rotten, like vegetables gone bad in the cooler.

It stood still, regarding her silently, and in that silence Katie felt menace, not the charged, barely contained menace of a wolf or other wild animal, but something much worse: a *thinking* menace. Katie was suddenly certain that it knew who she was, that it had come looking specifically for her.

It knows my name, Katie thought, and her nerve broke. She turned and fled.

Whatever it was, it was quick. Branches whipped and cracked behind Katie with the speed of its passage. Katie heard her own gasping breath, tearing in and out of her throat, but beneath that, she heard the thing behind her, not breathing but snarling, a low buzzing noise like the wind made when it crossed the pinwheels in front of the school. Katie wasn't used to running uphill. She sensed that it was gaining.

She ran through the lumber site, sprinting now, laying herself out, hearing a clatter of metal and wood as the thing behind her knocked aside one of the logging stations. She chanced a look back, hoping that it had gone down, but the thing was still behind her, even closer than before, a black shadow that loped along, bent low to the ground. The tree cover thinned and Katie bit back a scream as she glimpsed white flesh and staring eyes, hands that felt along the ground like those of an animal. It was a man, but not a man, not with its spine bent that way and that inhuman buzzing in its throat.

Bad, Katie thought. *I know what bad looks like and there it is and will it eat me? Is that where this ends?*

Then the trees closed again and Katie was back into the deep woods. Her breath rasped inside her throat like sandpaper. She leapt over the trunk of a fallen tree, its branches reaching up to scrape at her legs, but she barely felt it. She kept her eyes on the path, dimly visible ahead of her, knowing that if she blundered into the woods she was lost. The line of the path was becoming clearer in front of her, a long, light groove in the night, limned in blue. Yes, now she could see everything! If she hadn't been so scared, she might have laughed, because Gavin wasn't the only one who'd received night vision in the Crossing. But a moment later she realized that it wasn't night vision. The light was coming from her right hand, which was still clenched around the rock she had picked up. Tiny blue lines of light gleamed between her fingers, bright enough to illuminate the path.

The thing behind her snarled and Katie screamed because it was right on her, its voice had been *right there*, behind her left ear. Something grabbed her hip and squeezed and she shrieked, a sound like the town firebell, and now she broke free through the treeline and there glimmering in the distance was the Town in all of its dull communal glory, but now Katie was dying to embrace that dullness; if she could have found the Town's stolid, thudding heart she would have kissed it right now—

She chanced another glance behind her and came to a halt, such an abrupt halt that she fell sprawling in the dirt, scraping the skin from her left elbow.

Nothing was behind her.

The treeline was perhaps one hundred feet back from where she had fallen, right at the bottom of the High Road, where the houses began and streetlamps glimmered merrily in the dark. The trees at the edge of the woods were rustling, but it was only the natural sound that Katie had heard all of her life, leaves and branches rubbing together in the wind that came off the plains. There was no sign of anything moving.

"Katie?"

She rolled, gasping, drawing the rock back, prepared to throw it even though she was on her belly. The blue light had faded now—had it even been there at all?—but the lamps were still flickering, and she didn't need extra light to recognize Row, standing several feet up the High Road, not a hair out of place.

"Katie, what happened to you?"

"Row!" She pulled herself to her feet, sobbing, and flung herself at him. "Where were you?"

"I went back up on my shortcut, and all of a sudden I looked around and you weren't there. What happened?"

Crying, Katie told him. Row kept his arms around her, but there was something distant about the embrace, and a few minutes into her story, Katie realized that he wasn't giving comfort. He was simply listening, his face turned away.

"—and then I got out of the trees and turned around and there was nothing, it was *gone*, Row, but it was there and—"

"I wouldn't worry about it," Row replied mildly.

"What?"

Row turned toward her, and Katie saw that his mouth was crimped upward in a smile, triumphant and cruel. She had seen that smile on Row's face, many times, but never directed at her, and it hurt so much that she pulled free of his arms and backed away, looking up at him with wide, wounded eyes.

"I wouldn't worry about it," Row continued. "In fact, Katie, I'd say you were probably just having a delusion."

She gaped at him, but Row had already turned and trudged away, up the hill.

Kelsea broke from the past and found herself trapped in the dark. For a moment she could not escape her vision, and she rolled, gasping, until she recognized the hard stone floor beneath her. She was still in her cell, and for a long minute all she could feel was blessed relief that she was not back there, with Katie, out in the woods.

There was no one outside the bars, which was a relief as well; the Red Queen knew about her fugues, but still Kelsea didn't like the idea of being observed. Through the wall at her back, she heard her neighbor working, shuffling paper and what sounded oddly like the scratching of a pen. She still hadn't gotten him, or her, to say a word, but there were occasional silences over there that suggested he might be listening when she spoke. Now, though, there was nothing but that scratching. The rest of the dungeon was silent. Kelsea thought it might be the middle of the night.

There was something in her hand, hard and rounded. She blinked for a moment, trying to think what it might be, but she was stumped. She was receiving special treatment now; the page, Emily, had given her a candle and a few matches. Kelsea hesitated to waste one of them, but curiosity was too strong. She felt around on the floor until her fingers encountered the candle, and after a bit of fumbling, finally lit it. The flame was weak, at hazard from the many drafts that crisscrossed the dungeons, but it was enough for Kelsea to see, and she stared at the object in her hand for a very long time, her mind working, trying to grasp what it meant.

She was holding a smooth, oval stone, shot through with blue quartz.

Book II

Chapter 6

Aisa

The future cannot be divorced from the past. Trust me, for I would know.

—*The Glynn Queen's Words*, AS COMPILED BY FATHER TYLER

Hellcat. Time to go."

Aisa looked up from her saddlebags. Venner was in her doorway, his long, dour face shadowed with concern.

"You have everything?"

"Yes, sir."

"Well, say good-bye to your mother."

She scrambled up.

Maman was in the Queen's chamber, changing the bed linen. She did this every two days, though no one slept there. For a moment, Aisa hung in the doorway, watching Maman work. She would miss Maman, yes, but she longed to be out in the world. The Mace had already told her that she was not going all the way to Demesne; she would stay in the Almont, with General Hall, and be relatively safe. But she had still been surprised that Maman had given her permission to go. A small, nagging voice inside her even wondered if Maman wanted her gone.

"Maman. I'm leaving."

Maman dropped the pillowcase she was fighting with and came around the corner of the four-poster bed, her arms open. Maman's face was as composed as ever, but Aisa was shocked to see that her eyes were sorrowful. Maman had not looked that way since before they had escaped Da's house.

"Have you seen something, Maman?" she asked. "Have you seen whether we'll bring the Queen back?"

"No, love. I don't know."

"Have you seen something about me?"

Maman hesitated, then said, "I see many things about you, Aisa. You have grown up too quickly already, but I would be a poor parent if I kept you from a course you're clearly meant to follow."

"I'm meant to rescue the Queen?"

Maman smiled, but Aisa sensed bitterness behind it. "You're meant to fight, my girl. Just be careful. You go to a dangerous place."

Aisa sensed Maman hedging, but could make no sense of these dodgy answers. For a rogue moment she wished that Maman could go with them. But no, that would be disastrous. A woman with Maman's sight would command a heavy price in Mortmesne; the Mace had said so more than once.

"Andalie!"

Elston's voice roared outside, making them both jump. Aisa grabbed her knife and they hurried out into the hallway, where Elston beckoned.

"It's your little one. She's having a fit."

Maman broke into a run. Following into the audience chamber, Aisa found Maman bent over Glee, who was in one of her trances. Aisa had seen this phenomenon so many times that she found it routine, and was almost amused by the reactions of the men around her, who had drawn back from Glee, their faces mirroring a nearly identical superstitious dread.

"Poppet?" Maman asked. "Will you come back to us?"

But Glee shook her head vigorously. Her wide eyes roved the room for a moment before fixing on the Mace, staring at him so long and raptly that even he looked unnerved.

"You seek a prize," Glee murmured, her tone musing, as though she were working out a problem in her head. "But you will not find it in Demesne."

One of the new guards, whose name Aisa did not know, crossed himself.

"Look to Gin Reach," Glee told the Mace.

"Poppet!" Maman put her hands on Glee's shoulders. "Poppet, can you hear me?"

"Gin Reach," Glee repeated. "But we cannot know—"

"Glee, wake up!"

"Get her out of here, Lie," the Mace growled. "Before she spooks us all."

Maman gathered Glee up in her arms and carried her down the hall. Aisa thought of following them, but did not. She had already said good-bye to Maman.

I'm ready to leave, she thought, marveling. *Really ready now.*

The Mace turned to Arliss. "Are you sure our intelligence is sound?"

"It's sound!" Arliss replied, exasperated. "You handpicked the girl!"

"What if they've moved the Queen in secret?"

"They haven't. Not unless it happened in the last two days."

"Find out."

Arliss got up and headed for his office.

"Go through Levieux rather than Galen!" the Mace called after him. "We'll get quicker answers!"

Arliss waved him off. Aisa wondered what the Mace would do. Glee's visions sometimes ended up empty, meaning nothing, but Aisa had never known one of her predictions to actually be wrong. She had never heard of Gin Reach.

"El? What do you think?"

Elston shrugged. "The little one sees, for certain, but I'll take concrete information over vague any day. I say we head on to Demesne, like we planned."

The Mace nodded. "I agree. We can't miss our window."

He turned to the rest of the room, and Aisa found that disturbing phrase—*a killer of children*—echoing inside her head. She had asked Maman about it, and Maman had said she didn't know, but Aisa had seen a different truth in her eyes. Aisa had asked Coryn where the Mace came from, and Coryn had said he didn't know. There was a secret here, and Aisa was determined to ferret it out.

"All of you who remain here," the Mace announced, "Devin is in charge of Guard business! All other matters belong to Arliss or Andalie!"

At this, Aisa's mouth dropped open. The Mace, leaving Maman in charge? Several of the guards clearly didn't like it either, but their mutters died under the Mace's gaze. Looking around the room, Aisa suddenly noticed Pen, standing several feet behind the Mace. His eyes were circled dark, but he looked sober. He was armed and dressed for travel, his sword at his hip.

"Have this place ready for our return," the Mace told the guards. "We're bringing the Queen home. Don't let her find you napping."

But despite the confidence of his tone, the Mace still looked troubled. Ten minutes later, when Aisa went to fetch her saddlebags, he was still bent over the dining table, staring at a map.

It was thrilling to be out in the city after dark. The Mace had chosen the quietest hour of the night, after the drunks went to bed but before the early laborers were out, and the streets were nearly empty.

But all was not quiet. As they approached the outskirts of the Gut, Aisa became aware of a growing din, men shouting to each other and the occasional clash of swords.

"What is that?" Ewen asked. He was riding beside Aisa, near the back of the troop.

"I don't know."

"It's the Creche," said Bradshaw, who was riding on Ewen's other side. He was a last-minute addition to the Guard, but in the end, even the Mace had been forced to admit that a magician might make himself useful in a jailbreak. Aisa still did not know why the Mace had decided to bring Ewen. The three of them, Aisa, Ewen, and Bradshaw, existed in a strange twilight, armed but not real guards, and Aisa wondered if they would serve the same function on this journey: essentially ballast. But that was the life of a Queen's Guard. The Queen's safety came first, even if all three of them were nothing more than human shields.

"What's the Creche?" Ewen asked.

"The tunnels beneath the Gut. The Caden have gone to work in earnest, clearing the place out."

Ewen still looked confused, but of course he would; how would he even know what the Creche was? Now they were close enough that the battle noise echoing from the Gut was horrendous. Aisa wondered how the people who lived there could stand it, how they got any sleep.

"Why are they working at night?" Ewen asked.

Bradshaw's mouth curled in disgust. "Because at this hour, there's a better chance of catching the clientele."

Aisa grimaced as well. She found herself able to picture the Creche with extraordinary clarity: the tunnels, the fleeing men, the torches. Red cloaks. All of it was somehow tied up in her head with Da, because of all the children down there, all of them in danger.

"Aisa?"

She blinked and found that she had brought her horse to a stop. Ewen and Bradshaw were some ten feet ahead, beckoning her to catch up.

"Aisa?" Ewen asked again.

She opened her mouth, meaning to explain this thing to him. After all, Ewen was not a real Queen's Guard either. He knew what it was like to be only halfway part of this world. But no, she could not burden Ewen; his imagination would not extend so far, would not be able to encompass the human ugliness that played out only a few streets away. But Aisa's could, and did. To her left, a man screamed, and there was a sound of running footsteps. Aisa's temperature was rising, and she suddenly remembered something Glee had said, days ago: *They turn the corner and you grasp your chance.*

"Aisa? Are you all right?"

She smiled. The Guard had turned the corner. Her chance was before her, clear and bright and shining, and she only regretted that she could not apologize to the Mace personally, explain to him that this was something she simply had to do. Her hand wandered to the knife at her waist, and she gripped the hilt, feeling something titanic rise inside her. She was not a Queen's Guard, not really, for she suddenly saw that there were more important things in the world than one woman's life. She had wanted to stride the world, stabbing out evil, had been dreaming of it for months. But she knew that the root of these dreams went back further, all the way back to her childhood, back to Da. She had been waiting for this chance her entire life.

"Tell the Captain I'm sorry. Tell him I had no choice."

Ewen's face pinched in confusion, but Bradshaw asked, "What are you going to do?"

"What the Queen would have done." Aisa turned away and found the memory right behind her eyes: the cages; the soldiers;

Glee's face, bewildered and frightened behind the bars; Maman screaming. It had felt like the end of the world, and then the Queen had come. She had released Glee from the cage, but there were cages everywhere.

"Child, you can't go in there!" Bradshaw protested.

"I'm not a child," Aisa replied, and knew as she said the words that they were true, that she had finally crossed over that mysterious border in her mind.

"Tell the Captain that I'm about the Queen's business."

Ewen's mouth widened in dismay, but before he could say anything more, Aisa had grasped her chance and disappeared, deep into the shadows of the Gut.

Y ou! Girl!"
  Kelsea looked up, startled. The voice was a man's, speaking good Tear, but she couldn't see the source. She sat cross-legged on the floor, perfectly still, but her brain had been working steadily for the past hour or more, trying to assemble information into a unified theory. She was just starting to get somewhere—something about the sapphires and William Tear—but at the sound of the man's voice, her thoughts fell into disarray.

"You next door!"

It was her invisible cellmate. She went to the bars.

"What?"

"You're the marked queen?"

Kelsea raised her eyebrows. "I suppose so."

"My jailor said your army was destroyed. A massacre. Is it so?"

"Yes," she replied, lowering her voice to a whisper. She could hear footsteps now, descending the shallow stairs at the end of the corridor. "We were heavily outnumbered."

"Did none survive?"

Kelsea did not reply as the footsteps approached and torchlight came around the corner. She had assumed that it was Lona, her new jailor, come for her, but the steps paused at the next cell, and a man's voice said in Mort, "Up, you. You're wanted."

Kelsea leaned through the bars, trying to peek down the corridor as the guard unlocked her neighbor's cell. She could not see much, only the far wall and, after a moment, the back of a man's bald head. He went down the corridor, followed by the shadowy form of his jailor, and the light disappeared behind him.

Kelsea retreated to the back wall of her cell and slid down to the floor. She considered lighting her candle again, then discarded the idea. Thinking was always easier in the dark.

Eight months ago, she had had no magic at all. She had been a young girl with a decent brain, a good education, and a strong conviction that some things were definitely right and others definitely wrong. One sapphire had lain around her neck since her infancy, but it had only been a jewel. She had been royal, perhaps, but not remarkable. Life had been ordinary. She had never felt like a queen.

On the journey to New London was when she had felt the first difference. It was early one morning, she remembered, perhaps the day of the hawk, perhaps some other. But everything had begun to change from that moment onward. Because she was nineteen, the age of ascension? It seemed as good an explanation as any, but still it rang false. Nineteen-year-olds were fools, and William Tear would have known that.

They were together, Kelsea recalled suddenly. *Both sapphires. I held them together, in my hands.*

Could that be it? She didn't know. Where had the second sapphire come from? In Katie's town, two exploration parties had already gotten as far as the foothills of the Fairwitch; surely one of those parties would eventually come across sapphire in the mountains, where it was nearer to the surface. Easy to make a necklace, once you had the raw jewels. Row Finn was the best metalworker in the Town, but by no means the only one.

How does this help you? her mind demanded. *All of this history, how has it ever helped?*

But that voice carried no weight with the adopted daughter of Carlin Glynn. History always mattered. There was a pattern here, and sooner or later, it would begin to repeat itself. Both Kelsea and Jonathan Tear had inherited kingdoms that were falling apart. They were falling apart for different reasons, true, but—

You're wandering. You've had one of the jewels around your neck since you can remember. So why did it lie there for so many years, doing nothing?

Perhaps there was nothing to do.

This felt right. All of those years, she had been hidden in the Reddick, safe in anonymity. Many people had been hunting her, but none of them had found the cottage. If they had, would Kelsea's jewel have lain, meek and quiescent, around her neck? The same jewel that had killed the assassin who dragged her from her bathtub?

He was trying to take my necklace off, she remembered, but this fact only seemed to confuse the matter further. Where did such power come from? How could a sapphire act as its own enforcer? Kelsea had given the jewels to the Red Queen of her own free will, but the Red Queen had not been able to use them, though she certainly knew more of magic than Kelsea did herself. Did the jewels have a mind of their own? If so, why choose Kelsea? The Raleighs had worn the jewels for years, but as far as Kelsea knew, there had been no hint of magic about them.

She looked up, broken from the run of her thoughts. She had heard something, down the hallway on her left. She had the measure of this dungeon now, and this sound did not belong: a sliding rasp, as though something had scraped the wall of the corridor.

There was no other sound, not even from the accused thief up the corridor, and Kelsea realized then that she had not heard from him in days. People probably died in these cells all the time. The Red Queen's page, Emily, came down to check on Kelsea at least twice a day . . . but these sounds were not hers.

Another rasp, this one soft, almost furtive, definitely closer. Something inside Kelsea went cold, and without thinking, she reached over to the small pile of provisions by her bedding, feeling around for the rock, Katie's rock. Katie had thought it was blue quartz, but Kelsea had examined it for a long time in the candlelight before deciding that it was sapphire, like those in her necklaces, the same sapphire that seemed to run through the bedrock of the Tearling. It might be easiest to get at in the Fairwitch, but it was everywhere, anchoring her kingdom, shaping the ground beneath the Town, and Kelsea had recognized the blue glow lighting Katie's path with no problem at all.

But though Kelsea scrabbled on the floor, she could not find the rock, only her matches and the remnants of her last meal. She forced herself to be still. Down the hallway, she heard one footstep, and then another. Soft, as though someone were barefoot—or walking on tiptoe. If they had been carrying a torch, Kelsea would have seen the light by now; whoever it was traveled in the dark. A cold hand seemed to rest on the back of her neck, making her think of Brenna, Thorne's creature, who could lower the room temperature by her very presence. But Brenna was locked safely away in the Keep. The footsteps moved directly in front of her cell and Kelsea held still, not even breathing, caught in the momentary hope that if she didn't move, no one could find her. The bars thrummed gently as fingers ran lightly across the front of her cell. Her nerve broke.

"Who's there?" she asked, then wished she hadn't. There was something terrible about asking questions of the faceless dark. She thought of Katie, calling into the night, and closed her eyes.

"They thought they could keep pretty from me."

Kelsea froze.

"They thought I wouldn't have my own key."

Kelsea backed up against the wall. She had forgotten about the jailor, and that was a bad misstep. She heard the jingle of a ring of keys, felt the thrum of her pulse racing.

"Stay away from me."

"As though pretty could belong to anyone except me."

At the words, Kelsea's fear suddenly morphed into anger, beautiful and welcome anger. Vague memories tugged at her, echoes of the day she had ripped Arlen Thorne to pieces. She had promised never to do that again, but now she was ready to jump.

The jailor slid his key into the lock, and with the sound of the tumblers falling, Kelsea felt the last of her fear disappear. Fury swelled inside her, bright and shining, until her chest felt twice its actual size. Oh, how she had missed her rage in these past weeks, missed it in a way she would not have imagined possible, and now she felt as though she were reuniting with herself, becoming whole.

"Where is she?" the jailor mused. This was a game to him, one he had played before. How many prisoners had been forced to endure this? As he moved into the cell, Kelsea suddenly realized that she could *see* him, a vague figure cast in dim blue light. It was the rock, Katie's rock, Katie's sapphire, lying in the corner of the cell, glowing a thin blue. But Kelsea had no time to reflect upon it, for the jailor was moving closer.

"There she is," he murmured. His gaze flicked to the corner, marked the glowing piece of sapphire, then seemed to dismiss it.

"You do not want to come near me," Kelsea said, speaking slowly. She had meant the words as a bluff, but she also felt a certain truth in them. Something enormous was gathering force inside her, a boulder careening down a hill, picking up speed and power. The jailor pulled a dagger from his waist, and somehow this angered Kelsea most of all. He had at least fifty pounds on her, but still, he didn't want even the semblance of a fair fight. She considered various parts of his body and settled on the eyes, visible in the thin blue light. What a pleasure it would be, to claw them from his head.

No sooner had she thought this than the jailor stumbled, clapping his hand to his eyes. The dagger clattered to the floor and Kelsea snatched it up. The jailor sank to his knees, howling, and Kelsea darted forward and knocked him over, using her full weight to drive him off his knees and onto the floor. His head clanged against the bars, but Kelsea barely noticed. Whatever had incapacitated him could end at any time, and the urgency of that thought allowed her to straddle him—though she hated to touch him at all—take a good grip on the knife, and bury it in his throat. The jailor groaned and gagged, while Kelsea held tight to the dagger's hilt, driving it downward.

"No one owns me," she whispered.

It went on for a long time, somewhere between five minutes and forever, but finally, the jailor's struggles ceased. Feeling the muscle beneath her go slack, Kelsea relaxed.

The glow from the rock, if it had even been there at all, had vanished, and Kelsea felt as though her anger had drained away with it. Groping around under the edge of her mattress, she found her matches. The candle took longer, for the struggle had knocked it all the way into the far corner of her cell. When Kelsea finally got it lit, she stood over the man on the floor, staring down at him. She felt very little, only a mild disappointment that she remembered from killing Thorne, and now she heard Andalie's voice, echoing from a dark corner of her memory.

This, I think, is the crux of evil in this world, Majesty: those who feel entitled to anything they want, anything they can grab.

There was the disappointment. Kelsea longed to eradicate true evil, but she could not. All she could do was kill men like the jailor, like Thorne, men who represented evil's weak and worthless implements. True change danced beyond her grasp.

"How do I fix it?" she whispered to the corpse. "How do we get to the better world?"

She remained silent, hoping against hope that someone would hear her and answer. William Tear himself, perhaps, possessed of so much power that his voice might echo across the great twin voids of time and death. But after a moment's thought, she realized that Tear had already answered her, long ago. There was no quick and easy eradication of evil. There was only the passage of time, of generations, of people raising children who would hold all other lives just as valuable as their own. Tear had known that was the answer, but even his best efforts had failed.

Because they forgot, her mind answered. *It took them less than a generation to forget everything they should have learned.*

But that wasn't strictly true. The parents, the generation that had made the Crossing, they had deliberately hidden the past from their children. Katie had learned something of world history in her schoolwork, but the brutal period just before the Crossing—the guns, the surveillance, the poverty—Katie had no sense of these things, and neither did her peers. The generation that was beginning to rebel against Tear's socialism had no familiarity with the flip side of the coin. Tear had had access to the ultimate cautionary tale, but he had wasted it, allowed the warning to vanish.

But you remember, Kelsea, Carlin whispered. *By the end, you might even know it all.*

What can I possibly do with that knowledge?

There was no answer, only the jailor's face, staring up at her. His corneas were a deep, dark red; he had tried to claw his own eyes out. Kelsea cast around for the piece of uncut sapphire and found it still lying in the back corner of her cell.

"What are you?" she asked. She began to pick it up and then

froze, feeling her breath halt. The door of her cell was wide open, the jailor's key ring still dangling from the lock.

Her first impulse was simply to bolt from the cell, but Kelsea forced herself to hold still, to assess the situation. She had some sense of the layout of the dungeons, but none of the castle beyond. How far would she really get?

Don't be a coward. You have an open door!

At the thought of the Tearling, longing seemed to wrench her heart. She generally avoided thinking of her kingdom in concrete terms; in this dark cell, it seemed like a good way to go mad. But now she closed her eyes and saw the Almont stretching before her, miles of farms and river, and then New London, her city on a hill. Very different from Tear's, this city, and sinking just as surely, but there was still good there. When the Mort had reached the city and they had brought the last refugees inside, the Keep had been filled to capacity and there were still two thousand people without shelter. They could not sleep in the streets, for the temperature was dropping to freezing at night. Arliss had been at his wits' end, but at the last moment, Kelsea remembered now, the merchants had come forward, the guild of New London shopkeepers, and offered to house them all in their homes and shops. Her kingdom might be flawed, but it was still worth fighting for, and more than anything, Kelsea simply wanted to go home.

But acting on desire had gotten her into trouble before. Thorne's face flashed before her again; sometimes Kelsea felt that she would never escape him, and perhaps that was fitting, for when she had killed him, she had been thinking not of the kingdom, but of herself. She could not afford to make such a mistake here. She could not help her kingdom when she was dead, and she was currently alive on the Red Queen's grace. An escape attempt would crush their fragile détente. As much as she wanted to, Kelsea could not simply flee and hope for the best. For her kingdom, she had to stay.

She could at least get her jailor's body out of her cell. But another look at him convinced Kelsea of the futility of that. The floor around his corpse was covered with blood. No, they would find him, and they would find him in her cell. There was no way to prevent it.

You have an open door! her mind hectored.

"Maybe just a look around," Kelsea whispered, and realized in horror that she was speaking to the jailor as she skirted his corpse to reach the door. "Just a quick look around, see what's what."

She tiptoed out of her cell. The corridor to her right was dark, but to her left, far down the hallway, there was a hint of flickering torchlight near the stairs. Otherwise, the long line of cells was still, and she heard no sounds of movement. The jailor had made plenty of noise as he died, but screams were hardly uncommon in these dungeons. It didn't sound like anyone was coming to investigate. Cupping her hand around her candle flame, Kelsea moved toward the light.

Even a brief survey of her neighbor's empty cell showed that seniority did have its privileges. The bald man had clearly been here for a long time; he had not only a pallet and several buckets, but a desk and chair. The desk held a stack of paper and a jar of pens, as well as about ten candles. The walls were not bare, as in Kelsea's cell, but hung with drawings. Kelsea lifted the candle higher, then stilled.

Not drawings, but schematics. Every inch of each sheet seemed to be covered with measurements and directions. Most of the work was too far from the light to be clearly seen, but even near the bars, Kelsea could make out several designs. A siege tower, measuring well over sixty feet. A double-layered device with some sort of locking mechanism in the middle. Two different types of bows. The desk itself, which sat near the bars, was covered with a half-finished plan that Kelsea could not make out. She held the candle as high as she could, hissing as a bit of hot wax dripped on her hand, and was rewarded with a clear view of the schematic pinned over the desk: a diagram of a cannon, identical to those she had seen in the Mort war train. Kelsea's breath halted as the implication of all of these drawings sank in: she had found the Red Queen's weapons designer.

But what in God's name was he doing down here? The bald man spoke perfect Tear. It was a good bet that he was a slave, and if so, he must be one of the most valuable slaves that the Red Queen could claim. So why on earth would she keep him in the Palais dungeons? Why open him up to brutality, to rats, to the pneumonia that must surely beset this damp, drafty place in winter? An engineer this gifted should be living the most pampered life a Mort slave could imagine.

The empty cell provided Kelsea with no answers. She stood before the bars for a moment longer, making sure there was nothing she'd missed, and then crept down the hallway.

The next cell boasted not even a pallet. A young woman, Kelsea's age, was curled up on the bare floor, fast asleep. She was naked, and even in the thin candlelight, Kelsea could see her shivering. Her arms were covered with red welts that looked like puncture wounds. Kelsea's anger, which seemed to have died with the jailor, bloomed again, deep in her stomach.

How can you do this? she asked the Red Queen inside her head. *You're not stupid, you know right from wrong. How can you live with yourself?*

But it was Carlin who replied.

Don't waste your time, Kelsea. Some people are simply broken.

Surprisingly, Kelsea found that she did not want to think this of the Red Queen. She did not like the woman, but she had come to respect her. The child Evelyn had not had an easy life.

If you make apologies for the Red Queen, you should have made them for Thorne . . . perhaps even for your jailor, as well. None of them could have had happy childhoods.

Kelsea shrugged this off. The death of the jailor would not weigh on her. The world was better off without him. As for Thorne—

A door banged open at the top of the staircase. For a moment, Kelsea stood paralyzed. Escape was now impossible, if it had ever been an option at all, but she mustn't let them know how close she had come. She might face some sort of punishment for killing the jailor, but there was nothing to be done about that now. Her legs unlocked and she scampered down the corridor to her cell. The candle guttered as she ran, and she took the last few steps by feel, grabbing hold of the open door and slipping inside. The jailor's key was still hanging in the lock, and for a moment she debated taking it out, then decided against it. The fact that the jailor had let himself in would only bolster her story, and Kelsea had a suspicion that the jailor's death would not trouble the Red Queen overmuch anyway.

As torchlight spilled down the hallway, she moved to the back of her cell and stood very still, waiting. As she looked down at the jailor's body, relief filled her, the emotion so much an echo of Lily's memories that Kelsea almost felt that the world had doubled back on itself. No matter what happened, at least she wouldn't face the jailor, ever again.

The torch appeared, and beneath it was the tall form of Emily, the Red Queen's page. She took in the scene in one quick scan, then set the torch in its bracket and hurried into the cell.

"Poor timing," she murmured in Tear. "Simply poor timing."

She looked up at Kelsea, a hint of impatience in her gaze. "You are unharmed?"

"I'm fine."

"Well, help me then. We must get him out of here."

"What?"

"If the Red Queen finds that you've killed your jailor, she will increase your security. We cannot have that now. Not so close to the date."

"The date of what?"

"Help me!" Emily hissed. "Take off your dress."

"There's too much blood."

"We can clean up afterward. But we mustn't leave a trail. Let me have your dress."

After another moment's indecision, Kelsea pulled her dress over her head and tossed it to the other woman, who began to swaddle the jailor's neck. Reflexively, Kelsea covered herself, before she realized how little modesty mattered in this moment. She dropped her hands and simply stood there, shivering, in her boots and underclothes. Emily pulled the jailor's key ring from the lock, removed the key to Kelsea's cell, and then tucked the ring into her pocket.

"Grab his legs."

Kelsea took the jailor's legs and helped Emily haul him off the ground. The page was much stronger than Kelsea, carrying more than her share of weight. Kelsea stared at her, honestly confounded. Was it possible that she remained loyal to the Tearling?

"Not a sound," Emily murmured. "The cell to your right is empty, but the rest are occupied. The prisoners may not be asleep."

"What about light?" Kelsea whispered.

"I have mapped this dungeon well. Just follow my lead, and don't make a sound."

More questions sprang into Kelsea's mind, but she swallowed them and followed Emily out of the dungeon. They turned right, and Kelsea saw that Emily had been correct: the cell on her other side was empty. The light waned as they turned a corner, and finally they were traveling in total blackness. Beneath Kelsea's fingers, the jailor's legs were still warm, and with each step Kelsea became more and more tormented by an irrational certainty: he was not dead, only asleep, and at some point she would feel his hands slide over hers, hear his voice only inches away.

Pretty.

"Who's there?" a man screamed to Kelsea's right, so close that she veered left, stifling a cry, and nearly dropped the jailor's legs. Sweat had broken out on her brow. She could hear other people in their cells, coughing and crying, and her mind called up the Security compounds she had seen in Lily's time, vast black labyrinths of suffering.

We've learned nothing, she thought again. *We all forgot.*

Ahead, Emily cleared her throat, bringing Kelsea to a halt. She felt the other end of the jailor's body begin to drop, and lowered his legs to the ground. Metal clinked beneath her: Emily, depositing the jailor's key ring on his body. She was very cool under pressure, this woman; she reminded Kelsea of Andalie. A moment later Emily grabbed her arm, guiding her back the way they had come. Kelsea wondered what Mace would say if he could see her now, wandering the Palais dungeons in her underwear. She was truly cold, her teeth chattering behind her clenched lips. She thought of the naked woman down at the far end of her hallway, shivering on the bare floor. Kelsea would need some clothes, and quickly.

They turned a final corner, and Kelsea saw that they were back on her hallway. Looking down, she found her hands and arms covered with tacky patches of drying blood. But the corridor was clean.

"Get back in there," Emily murmured, shooing her into her cell. She held the stained remains of Kelsea's dress in her hand. "I'll bring back cleaning supplies and a new dress for you."

"Then what?"

"It will be as though he never entered your cell." Emily held up the silver key to Kelsea's cell. "He was not supposed to have this key. I will dispose of it."

Kelsea hesitated, reminded again of Andalie's terrifying efficiency. Emily began to swing the cell door closed, and Kelsea grabbed the bars, holding it open.

"Who are you? Do you serve the Tear?"

"No. I serve the Mace."

Emily jerked the door from Kelsea's hands, locked it behind her, and disappeared down the corridor.

W ake up, you pathetic sot."
Javel bleared his way back into reality. It was a slow process. There were so many sensations to ignore: headache, backache, the heavy, empty feeling in his stomach. The Mort brews were much stronger than those of the Tear. He almost remembered trying something the bartender had laid on him, a very brief period of the mindlessness that drink always gave him, and then nothing more. He became aware of wetness on his cheek: a line of drool.

"Wake up, damn you!" Something slapped the back of his head, and Javel's headache intensified, becoming almost blinding. He groaned and batted the hand away, but then his hair was seized and he was yanked bodily upward, the pain in his head making him screech. He found himself staring at Dyer.

"You. Stupid. Fuck." Dyer shook him with each word, his voice a low hiss. "We're here to do a job, a discreet job. And here I find you passed out."

Javel's mind was a muddle. What was he doing in a pub? He'd been sober for months. Did he really have to start over now, at the bottom of the ladder?

Allie.

Memory came tumbling back, painfully clear. Allie had brought him here. Allie, in a whore's dress and makeup, no longer herself but someone else. She wanted no part of him. They had been in Demesne for months, chasing a ghost. Javel wished Dyer would go away so he could order another drink and start the carousel all over again. At least another drink would ease the headache that threatened to crush his skull.

"What ails you, traitor?"

"Allie," Javel mumbled. "My wife. She . . ."

"Oh, for God's sake." Dyer grabbed him by the collar and pulled him to the floor, and Javel realized that he had spent the night on a barstool, his head on the counter. It would not be the first time, but oh, he thought he had put those days behind him.

"My wife—" But he hesitated at that. Could he even call Allie his wife anymore? "She was dressed like a—"

"A whore?" Dyer asked. He looked at Javel frankly, no sympathy in his gaze.

"Yes," Javel whispered, thankful that he did not have to say the word out loud. But a moment later his eyes flew open as wetness dashed across his face. Dyer had doused him with water. Dimly, Javel noticed the publican behind the bar, watching them with the disinterested gaze of a man who has seen everything.

"Let me get this straight, Gate Guard. You found your wife in a Mort knockhouse."

"Yes."

"Then what?"

"She said to leave her there. She said she was happy. She said—" Javel swallowed, for this last was the worst to admit. "She said she wanted no part of me."

"My God." Dyer hauled him toward the door, tossing a few marks on the counter as he went. The publican didn't even blink, merely nodded and cleared the money from the surface in one smooth motion.

Outside, the sunlight seemed to cleave Javel's skull. He moaned, clutching his head.

"Shut up, you waste of space." Dyer yanked him along. They passed the apothecary, and Javel restrained the urge to spit in the doorway.

"She was laughing," he told Dyer. He didn't know why he was talking to this man of all people, a Queen's Guard who would have liked to watch him swing for treason. There was no one else to listen. "She was happy."

"And that makes you angry?"

"Of course it does!" Javel shouted. "Why shouldn't I be angry?"

Dyer grabbed him by the neck and slammed him into a wall. In the moment before pain flooded in, Javel wished he were dead.

"Since you're a fucking idiot, Gate Guard, I will explain it to you. Your wife was taken more than two hundred miles in a cage. When she got to this city, she was stripped naked, searched, and placed on a platform in front of the Auctioneer's Office. She may have stood there for hours, while strangers debated her worth and children catcalled her for being a Tear. If she was purchased by the knockhouse outright, as the Auctioneer's documents seem to suggest, she was expected to perform on command, and if she didn't, she was likely beaten, or raped or starved. Six years." Dyer's voice deepened and roughened. "Six years, and where were you all that time? Working your day job and drinking your pay away at night."

"She's still my wife."

Dyer shook him, hard, rapping his head against the brick.

"Your wife is doing what she has to. Did it never occur to you that pretending to be cheerful about it makes her life easier here?"

"Cheerful!" Javel snarled. "She's pregnant! She's going to have another man's child!"

"I really don't know where you get the gall, Gate Guard." Dyer released him, his voice disgusted. "Your wife was shipped to Mortmesne while you stayed behind, a free man, and you think you have the right, any right at all, to question how she survived?"

"I love her," Javel repeated brokenly. "She's my wife."

"She seems to have moved on."

"But what about me?"

"You should do the same. Let her go." Dyer's gaze was still pitiless, but when he spoke, his voice had softened a bit. "The Queen saw something in you, though for the life of me, it escapes my vision. Your purpose here is gone, but you might still be useful to us. To *her*."

"To Allie?"

"To the Queen, jackass." Dyer shook his head. "The Captain is coming, and when he arrives we will break the Queen out of the Palais or die trying. We need more men."

"What does that have to do with me?"

Dyer held up a sealed letter. "These are the Captain's latest orders. He wants to send a messenger back to New London to bring more guards, but none of his people can be spared. Galen and I cannot go either."

Spared, Javel thought bitterly.

"The Captain will arrive in four days. We will need reinforcements no more than two days after that. Therefore, we need a messenger who can ride like the wind." Dyer stared at him, measuring. "I watched you on the way here. You're a fine rider, when you're off the slop. If you leave early tomorrow, you could make it."

Javel frowned, calculating time, though it hurt his head. He would have to reach New London in no more than three days. Not long, but it might be long enough.

"You'll need to stay out of the pubs along the way, of course."

"What about Allie?"

"Well, that's the choice before you, Gate Guard. Serve the Queen, or serve your own nonsense. The Captain has put your fate in my hands, and I can leave you here to drown, if that suits you better. It certainly suits me." Dyer looked over Javel's shoulder, his eyes narrowing. "Either way, we've spent enough time loitering on this street."

Javel followed his gaze and found that some sort of commotion was building down at the next intersection. Another riot. The streets of Demesne were full of them. The rebels rioted, Demesne's security forces broke them up, and then another riot began the next day. Galen said that the city was heading for open revolt.

Dyer walked up the street, away from the trouble, and Javel followed. His mind was a tumult: two parts hangover, two parts Allie, and a tiny, uncertain corner that had begun to turn Dyer's words over, to examine them like a raw jewel unearthed from a mine.

You might still be useful.

He had been useful once. Before the drink had gotten hold of him, and long before Arlen Thorne had shown up with his poisonous bag of bribes, there had been a Gate Guard named Javel, ordinary but competent, content to simply do his job well and go home to his wife at the end of the day.

Serve the Queen, or serve your own nonsense.

He had not thought of the Queen in weeks, not since they had seen her go by in the wagon. But he realized now—and felt a fool for not realizing it before—that the two Gate Guards had thought of nothing else. The Queen could have stretched Javel's neck for treason, just as she had done to Bannaker and the Arvath priest, or even mutilated him, as she had done to Thorne. But she had not. Death would have been a kindness to Javel, but there was no way for the Queen to know that, and now here he was, miserable perhaps, but alive and free, while the Queen rotted in a Mort dungeon. Javel considered this a moment longer, dodging a cart that had come trundling down the footpath, then hurried to catch up to Dyer.

"I'll leave tomorrow."

Dyer halted, and Javel, who had prepared himself for a sarcastic remark, looked up and found the Queen's Guard honestly considering him, perhaps for the first time. After a long moment, Dyer pulled the sealed letter from his pocket again and offered it to Javel.

"Keep it close and show it to no one until you reach New London. It should get you past the Gate Guard and into the Queen's Wing. Present it to Devin, him that was left in charge of the wing."

Javel took the letter, sliding it into the inner pocket of his shirt. They began walking again, narrowly missing a splash of mud from a passing wagon. Dyer's gaze was distant, almost sorrowful, and Javel knew that he was thinking of the Queen. Javel would be thinking of Allie, this night and many nights after, and the thoughts would undoubtedly be painful, but she was no prisoner.

"Will you be able to get her out?" Javel asked quietly.

Dyer slammed a fist into his palm. "I don't know, Gate Guard. But dear God, if we fail . . ."

Javel peeked at Dyer's face, wary of the rage he sensed in the man, fuel just waiting for a match. But what he saw there was more alarming still.

Dyer was crying.

Chapter 7

The Fall

It is difficult to fight the cult of sycophancy that has sprung up around the Glynn Queen. Too many historians fail to question her decisions. This historian, however, finds that the Glynn Queen made several disastrous mistakes. The Tearling is invested in the myth of the infallible ruler, but the fact remains that the Glynn Queen abandoned her kingdom at a crucial point, leaving it in the charge of the Mace, who then abandoned it as well. These decisions had catastrophic results, and true historians should admit that fact.

—*An Alternate History of the Tearling,* ETHAN GALLAGHER

I am under assault," the Red Queen remarked. "Each day, it grows closer."

They were standing on a balcony, the highest in the Palais, so far above the rest of the turrets that Kelsea could turn in a wide circle and see everything, unobstructed, in all directions. Demesne stretched out like a carpet beneath them, a vast tapestry of red brick and grey stone, and beyond it lay the Champs Demesne, a massive open field encircling the city. Mortmesne was a far greener country than the Tearling; much of the land was covered with pine forest, but even the farming fields had abundant greenery, rather than the dirt base that Kelsea was used to seeing in the Almont. It was an extraordinary land, this, and Kelsea could only regret the bitter history that divided Mort and Tear, made them enemies. The waste was terrible.

To the west, Kelsea could just glimpse the twin peaks of Mount Ellyre and Mount Willingham, their summits nearly hidden under the haze of the late autumn day. Both mountains were already covered with snow, but Kelsea's eyes were locked on the divide between them: the Argive Pass. The longing to be back in her own land, standing on Tear soil, was so sharp that it wrenched something inside her.

"My army can't stop this rebellion," the Red Queen continued, bringing Kelsea back to herself. "Look down there."

Following her gaze, Kelsea saw an enormous plume of smoke in the north section of the city below.

"What is that?"

"My armories," the Red Queen replied tonelessly. "Always, these rebels are able to get past my soldiers. The precious few that are left, anyway. More of my army desert to join this Tear lunatic every day."

"Levieux?"

"You know the name?"

"I have heard it," Kelsea replied carefully.

"Why would a Tear want to do this to me?"

Kelsea turned to face her and realized, astonished, that the Red Queen was serious. "You invaded our country."

"I withdrew."

"This time, yes. The last time, your pet general left a trail of rape and slaughter. And even if any Tear could forget that, they would not forget seventeen years of the shipment."

The Red Queen shook her head. "Populations are pawns, Glynn. It is but the movement of pieces."

"Surely you know that people don't think of themselves that way?" But a moment later, Kelsea wondered if the Red Queen did know it. She had spent more than a century disconnected from her own populace. The beginnings of sympathy that had been stirring in Kelsea's mind faded and disappeared.

"People don't think of themselves as pawns. The suffering wreaked by the shipment—relatives divided, spouses taken from each other, children torn from parents—do you think anyone can forget?"

"They will."

"No," Kelsea replied firmly. "They won't."

"People have been trafficked since the dawn of time."

"That doesn't make it better. It makes it worse. We should have learned something by now."

The Red Queen stared at her for a long moment, her gaze almost wistful. "Who raised you, Glynn?"

"A good man and woman." Kelsea felt her throat tighten, as always when she thought of Barty and Carlin. She hesitated to say their names, then realized that there was no point in keeping secrets. No one could harm them any longer. "Bartholemew and Carlin Glynn."

"Elyssa's tutor. I should have known."

"Why?"

"The rigid morality. Far too rigid for Elyssa; Lady Glynn fell out of favor before you were born." The Red Queen shook her head. "Anyway, I envy you."

"You do?"

"Of course I do. You were raised to believe in something. Many things."

"And you believe in nothing?"

"I believe in myself."

Kelsea turned back to the edge. Far below, a dark tide emerged from the gates of the Palais: soldiers, heading for the inferno on the north side of Demesne. Was the fire truly the Fetch's work? What could he possibly want with this place?

No one had connected Kelsea with the death of the jailor. There had been an uproar when he was found, a huge increase in traffic through Kelsea's corridor, but she had not been questioned. Strass had clearly not been well liked; the furor over his death soon died down. Life in the dungeon went on as always, with Kelsea turning the strange rock over and over in her hand, trying to sort out what had happened. Her invisible fellow prisoner, the weapons designer, had lapsed back into silence.

"Why did you bring me out here?" she asked the Red Queen.

"Because we have lost contact with Cite Marche. The last three envoys I sent up the Cold Road have not returned." The Red Queen stared at Kelsea, almost hungrily. "So what news, Glynn? What do you know of him now?"

"Not as much as you'd like."

"Why not?"

"I can't speed up the past. I've only seen the boy."

"And what is he like?"

"Cruel," Kelsea replied, and for a moment she was right back there with Katie, standing frozen in the industrial row of Tear's town in the dead of night. "Spiteful."

"What else?"

"I'm not sure." Kelsea closed her eyes, thinking of the Town graveyard, the torn-open graves. Katie had not yet put two and two together, but then, Katie didn't know her best friend as well as Kelsea did. "He dabbles."

"In what?"

"The occult. I think he means to raise the dead."

"Well, he's figured it out now," the Red Queen replied bitterly, gesturing toward the northeast. "Every new group of refugees arrives with some terrible tale. These children cannot be killed by swords. Only magic will reach them."

"What do you know of him?"

"He's a drinker of blood," the Red Queen replied flatly.

Kelsea blinked in surprise, but said nothing.

"I used to offer him children, from the shipment, in return for his help. None of them ever came back."

"How did you meet him?"

"I was on the run."

"From your mother?" This much, at least, Kelsea had drawn from the woman's mind. There was a great betrayal there, though the exact circumstances had not come clear.

"Yes. From the Cadarese as well." The Red Queen shook her head, as a dog would shake off water. "At any rate, the dark thing gave me shelter, saved me from starvation in the Fairwitch."

"Why would he do that?"

"He thought I could set him free." The Red Queen grinned bleakly. "But it wasn't me, Glynn. It was you."

"I did what I had to do to save my kingdom."

"Temporary salvation at best, Glynn."

"Why did you really bring me out here? To gloat?"

"No," the Red Queen replied, suddenly subdued. "I wanted to talk to someone."

"You have an entire kingdom at your disposal."

"I can't trust them."

"You can't trust me, either."

"But you are not double-faced, Glynn. This entire castle, these people, all of them look for ways to tear me down."

"People have always plotted against you. That's the nature of being a dictator."

"I do not care about that. It's the artifice I can't stand. You may despise me, Glynn, but your hate is open and clear. These people, they smile, but underneath . . ." The Red Queen's voice hoarsened, her hand tightening on the balcony railing, her knuckles white. Tear legend said that the Red Queen had been born without a heart, but nothing could be further from the truth. What Kelsea was now seeing were the first cracks in decades of iron self-control. She considered putting a hand on the Red Queen's shoulder, then wondered what she was doing. There was no friendship with this woman.

Why do I give her so much leeway?

Because you were inside her head.

Kelsea nodded, recognizing the truth of this. The sapphires provided the ultimate experience in empathy. It was impossible to hate someone after having watched the long tale of her life: the mother, beautiful and terrible, who had rejected Evelyn Raleigh for years . . . until the time came when the mother needed something to sell. Then the girl had been thrown into the whirlwind. The Red Queen had made her own terrible decisions, but the deck had been stacked against her from birth.

You've made your own terrible decisions, Carlin whispered darkly. *Who are you to judge?*

Kelsea closed her eyes, beset by images: the screaming mob in the New London circus, their faces so twisted by hate that they appeared not human but monstrous; Row Finn's smile as he stood in front of the fireplace; Arlen Thorne's face, bleeding from multiple seams as he died in agony; and, last of all, Kelsea's own hand holding a knife, her fingertips running red with blood.

"Who raised you?" she asked suddenly, opening her eyes, willing the images to be gone.

"Don't you know?" the Red Queen asked.

"I didn't see it all," Kelsea admitted.

"I had a nursemaid, Wright. She was a very smart woman, but she scared me too. She seemed to take it as her job to teach me that life was going to be hard."

Like Carlin, Kelsea thought, marveling. She had caught flashes of this woman in the Red Queen's mind; her hair was long and dark, not white like Carlin's, but there was a similarity. Both women had sharp, hawklike eyes.

"My mother was happy to leave me to Wright. Elaine took all of her time."

"Who was your father?"

"I don't know." The Red Queen looked sharply at Kelsea. "I didn't want to know. Do you want to know yours?"

Yes, Kelsea began to say, then *No.* She did want to know, but that was only her academic curiosity speaking. She wouldn't like the answer, or Mace would have told her.

"Never mind, Glynn. I had not meant to say so much to you, but it has been a long time since I had anyone to talk to. Not since Liriane."

"Your seer. Was she as gifted as they say?"

"More. We were friends, or I thought we were." The Red Queen's brow furrowed in sudden confusion. "Such women are difficult to know, which brings me to the matter. I have received a most interesting offer from your pope."

"His Holiness? Deal with that man and you'd better have a knife in one hand."

The Red Queen smiled, but the smile did not touch her eyes. "I think your kingdom is in a great deal of trouble, Glynn. The pope is asking for mercenaries, an entire legion of my army."

Something inside Kelsea seemed to turn over. She needed to warn them all, warn Mace . . . but of course, she could warn no one.

"For what purpose?"

"Who knows? But his hatred for you is plain."

"Will you give him soldiers?" Kelsea asked through numb lips.

"Perhaps. It depends greatly on the value of the trade."

"What trade?"

"The pope tells me that you, Queen Kelsea, have a seer of your own."

Kelsea's mouth dropped open. Who had talked? She whirled away, to look over the far parapet, but it was already too late.

"It's true!" The Red Queen's voice revealed genuine astonishment. "And the child, too?"

Something broke in Kelsea then. Before she knew it, she had crossed the balcony, grabbed the shoulders of the Red Queen's velvet dress, and lifted her bodily off the ground, wondering if she actually had the strength to heave the woman over the side.

The Queen of Spades! her mind cried, but the sound was faraway, despairing.

"Don't even think about it," she snarled. "Don't even think about touching them."

"Be careful, Glynn. Think about what you're doing."

Kelsea paused. The air around her had grown taut, almost electric, her skin tightening uncomfortably. It was suddenly difficult to breathe. Her throat had closed.

"Put me down, Glynn." The Red Queen patted Kelsea's cheek, as one would do with a child. "Put me down, or I will choke you to death."

After another moment, Kelsea relaxed her hold on the red velvet and lowered the woman to the ground. Her throat remained closed for perhaps ten more seconds—the slight, victorious twist of the Red Queen's mouth told her that this was deliberate—and then loosened. Kelsea gasped, whooping as her lungs took in a great breath of air.

"You have balls, I give you that." The Red Queen looked down at her dress, which now sported ripped seams beneath both arms. "I once whipped a page for ruining a dress of mine."

"I'm not one of your servants." Kelsea leaned on the parapet, gasping. The pillar of smoke that bloomed from the burning armory was blurry now; her vision had doubled. She felt the start of a headache at her temples.

"You tipped your hand far too easily," the Red Queen remarked, joining her at the edge. "I can hardly send soldiers to the Tearling now, to the pope or otherwise. I merely wanted to know whether the information was correct. Your dame of chamber and her youngest daughter! I've always thought the sight was hereditary, but I've had no chance to study it before."

"Good luck with that. This particular seer would kill her child before seeing her in your hands."

"You have bigger problems, Glynn. Benin tells me that the Holy Father has been double-dealing. He's also made direct overtures to my army, behind my back."

"Your soldiers want a seer?"

"No, my soldiers want their plunder. But a seer, a proven seer, would fetch a high price on the open market, high enough to compensate an entire legion. I no longer—" The Red Queen broke off, and Kelsea sensed that her words were costing her. "I no longer control my army, not completely."

"How terrible for you."

"Laugh if you like, Glynn, but this problem belongs to you as well, if my soldiers go rogue."

Kelsea winced, thinking of the Keep, unguarded now, most of her army dead in the Almont. General Hall couldn't have more than a hundred men at his disposal, no match for a legion of Mort. She thought she had bargained for three years of safety for her kingdom, but had she really accomplished anything at all? If only she could contact them! Something seemed to glimmer in the back of her memory, but then it was gone.

"You have nothing useful to give me on this thing, the Orphan?"

Kelsea shook her head. "Not yet."

"Emily!" the Red Queen called, and the page appeared from the staircase in the center of the balcony. Her eyes darted briefly to Kelsea, then away, and Kelsea did not acknowledge her either. Ever since they had cleaned up the jailor, Emily had refused to answer any more questions.

"I'm done with her for now. Take her back downstairs."

The words were said offhandedly, but the tone was wrong. Looking back at the Red Queen as she descended the stairs, Kelsea again received an impression of deep unhappiness, of a woman on the edge of something. She had heard that tone often enough in her own voice during those last few doomed weeks in the Keep.

She didn't try to talk to Emily during the journey downstairs. There were too many people in the hallways, too much chance of being overheard. *So close to the date*, Emily had said, and only now did Kelsea allow herself to consider that there might be a prison break under way. She hoped for it, and hoped against it; if the Holy Father was preparing to move against the Keep, Mace had bigger problems. Kelsea longed to give Emily a message, to warn Mace, to warn Andalie, who needed to know that she and Glee were no longer safe. And how had the Holy Father found out about Andalie, anyway? Was there another traitor in the Queen's Wing?

I must get out of here, Kelsea thought. *No matter what it costs. My kingdom is wide open.*

When they passed her neighbor's cell, Kelsea snuck a glance inside and found him at his desk, hard at work by candlelight, his face less than an inch from the canvas. She could see only a fraction of his profile, but enough to tell her that he was much younger than she had taken him for. Bald, yes, but a closer look at his head suggested that his hair had been shaved. Kelsea longed for a decent look at him, but the man did not acknowledge either her or Emily as they went past.

As Emily shut the door of her cell, Kelsea grasped her arm and gestured her closer, meaning to tell her about Andalie, ask her to get a message to Mace. But Emily drew back, placing a finger to her lips, and departed. Kelsea wanted to scream in frustration. As the light from Emily's torch disappeared, Kelsea lit one of her own candles, placing it carefully on the floor beside the bars. It was a waste of wax, but the thought of Mace, Pen, Andalie, all of them, going blithely about life in the Keep while a deathweight hung over their heads . . . these visions had undone her, and she could not bear to sit in the dark.

A drinker of blood.

If the Red Queen was telling the truth—and though Kelsea did not trust the woman, she believed the desperation in the Red Queen's voice—then Kelsea had loosed a nightmare upon the world. She seemed to feel the slickness of blood on her hands.

"I have done murder before," she murmured, and strangely, it was not Thorne or the jailor she thought of now, but Mhurn. Killing him had been a mercy . . . or so she had thought at the time. The silence of her cell bore in upon her, and after a moment she got to her knees, clutching the bars.

"You there! The man with the drawings!"

Silence from the next cell.

"How long have you been here?"

More silence. How to make him speak? Kelsea thought for a moment, then ventured, "I have seen your cannons on the battle-field. Extraordinary pieces of equipment."

"You've seen them fired?" he asked.

Kelsea frowned, thought about lying, then replied, "No. They never used them on us."

The man began to laugh, bitter and hollow. "That's because they couldn't. They were never able to make them fire. My design was sound, but the Red Queen's chemist was supposed to come up with an answer to gunpowder, and it didn't work."

Kelsea sat back from the bars. All of the time and energy they had expended on the cannons, on finding a way to disable them; she could have kicked herself.

"You got played," the man said, then, after a long pause: "Was the Tear army really wiped out?"

"Yes."

"The general?"

"Bermond was killed," Kelsea replied. Intellectually, she knew that she should grieve a lifelong soldier, but she could not; Bermond had been reactionary, a thorn in her side. "His second commands what's left of my army. Not really enough even to make a decent city police force."

"That's a misfortune. It takes generations to build a good army from scratch."

"We have three years." *Perhaps less*, her mind remarked. At the thought of the Holy Father commanding an armed legion, she felt something burn inside her. Even if the Holy Father failed, there was Row Finn, Finn and his creatures, coming along right behind.

"Three years, eh?" Her neighbor chuckled. "Good luck."

"Why are you in here?" Kelsea asked, more to keep the conversation going than anything else. She didn't want to sit alone in the dark. "You're a slave, yes?"

"Yes."

"I was told that the Red Queen treats exceptional slaves like free men. You're a gifted engineer. Why are you in a dungeon?"

He remained silent for a long moment. Kelsea's heart sank, and she grasped the bars again, feeling the stone dig into her knees. "Please talk to me. I'll go mad in the quiet."

"The plea of a queen is no small thing, I suppose. Even a queen in a dungeon." A chair scraped on stone as the man got up from his desk, and Kelsea heard the rustling of paper. "It doesn't matter anyway. They search my cell once a week, just to make sure I'm not building anything too creative. But when they moved me in here, they simply grabbed all of my stacks of drawings and plans. So far this has escaped them, but it's the real reason I'm here. Have a look."

A moment later, a crumpled sheet of paper landed in front

of Kelsea's cell. She stretched out to grab it, then opened and smoothed the paper on the stone floor. It had the look of an advertisement, but when Kelsea brought her candle closer, she saw that it was a political flyer, beautifully lettered in both Mort and Tear.

> **People of Mortmesne!**
> **Do you tire of being slaves? Do you tire of working endless days to satisfy the whim of a corrupt few? Do you tire of watching your sons go to war and come home empty-handed, if they come home at all? Do you wish for something better?**
> **Join our fight.**

"You belonged to the rebellion," Kelsea murmured. It was a clever piece of business, this flyer. Blunt and simple language, but she guessed that its appeal would be very broad.

"I didn't belong to the rebellion," her neighbor replied. "I only did this work for them from time to time, making advertisements so that I could earn a few marks for myself." His voice was laced with self-mockery. "It was a wonderful way to rebel without putting myself in any real danger."

"Yet here you are," Kelsea remarked absently, still examining the flyer. The paper was ordinary enough, normal highstock, the same thickness as Arliss had used for her Bill of Regency. But something about the text struck her as odd. Kelsea held the candle as close to the paper as she dared, squinting as she examined individual letters. The two *e*'s in *Mortmesne* appeared identical, exactly the same size, with no variation whatsoever. Even the color consistency of the black ink was the same. Kelsea's eyes jumped from one word to another, vowel to vowel, consonant to consonant, looking for flaws, looking for faults . . .

"Great God," she breathed.

The flyer had not been lettered by hand, but printed.

⟶❄ ❄⟵

Ewen had never imagined that the Tearling could be so vast. He had grown up in New London and had never been outside the city. Always, he had thought of the kingdom as the distance between the Caddell River and the horizon. But when the Queen's Guard reached the end of the Caddell, the land kept going. Eventually the Crithe River, too, stopped being a river and turned into just grass. There were mountains in the distance, mountains that Ewen had never seen, drawing nearer. This was a serious business, going to rescue the Queen, and Ewen understood that. But all the same, he felt as though he were on a grand adventure.

They had built camp in the cup between two high hills. The Mace had placed Ewen on guard duty, looking out toward the west, in case anyone should approach. They had seen several large parties of people, and from Coryn, Ewen knew that they were refugees from the city, returning home. If he saw anyone approach, he was to keep them away from the camp, for no one was supposed to know that the Mace had left New London. Ewen took his guard duty very seriously, but all the same, he wished there was time to sketch. He'd brought his paper and leads in his saddlebags. He'd never known how much of the world one could see out here, from hill to hill.

The Mace was in the center of camp now, holding a meeting with General Hall and the man from Mortmesne. Ewen hadn't been chosen to attend the meeting, but he wasn't offended. He didn't know why the Mace had brought him along on this journey in the first place, but he was happy to be here; it saved him from thinking of Da. Two months ago, Da had died, and the next morning Ewen, with his three brothers, had put Da into the ground. Ewen tried not to think of that day, but it often came back to him. He had cried, but that was all right; Peter had cried too. Ewen did not like to think of Da lying there in the light brown box, only a layer of oakwood to protect him from the dark underground.

"Ewen!"

He turned and found the magician, Bradshaw, coming up the hill behind them.

"They want us to come back down."

Ewen nodded, gathering up his cloak and canteen. Bradshaw waited, and they walked down to the camp together. Ewen liked Bradshaw; he could make things disappear and come back, and he was always able to guess what Ewen had in his pockets. But Bradshaw was patient as well, willing to explain the things that Ewen didn't understand.

"Were you at the meeting?" Ewen asked.

"No. I was sent to find a deer for dinner. I think they believe I talk to animals as well."

"Do you?" Ewen asked, thinking how wonderful that would be.

"No."

Feeling chastised, Ewen didn't say anything else.

The camp was a bustle of activity. There were twelve Queen's Guards, eight soldiers who had come in with General Hall, and then several more men who had come with the man from Mortmesne. Elston and Kibb were cooking the deer, and the air was heavy with the smell of roasting meat. The rest of the men milled around the fire like hungry vultures. Ewen heard snatches of conversation as he and Bradshaw walked the perimeter: the Queen, the Mort rebellion, something about an orphan. Ewen knew of no orphans among the Guard, though now that Da was dead, he supposed he was an orphan himself. On another day, he might have asked Bradshaw, but now he thought it best to stay quiet.

"You two!" the Mace barked. "Over here!"

Ewen and Bradshaw followed him to the tent at the center of the camp. Inside, the small folding table was covered with maps and surrounded by chairs from the just-finished meeting. As the Mace sat down, Ewen saw that he had dark circles around his eyes. Normally, Ewen would not even dare guess what the Mace was thinking, but now he thought he knew. The first night out of New London, they had ridden hard, and so it was not until dawn that the Mace had noticed Aisa missing. The entire Guard had taken the news badly, though none so badly as Venner, who pitched what Da would have called a fit, cursing and throwing things from his saddlebags. The Mace did not say a word, but his silence frightened Ewen. He had worried that the Mace might blame him, or blame Bradshaw; after all, they had been the last to see her. But no one said anything, and gradually Ewen realized that he was not in trouble.

"We need to do this quickly," the Mace said. "Sit down."

They sat.

"Levieux confirms that the Queen is still in the Palais dungeons. But we cannot enter Mortmesne via the Argive. General Hall tells me that a legion of Mort remained behind, to hold the eastern end of the pass. They mean to regulate traffic from now on. So we will be moving straight east, crossing over the border hills."

Not all of this made sense to Ewen, but he nodded anyway, following Bradshaw's lead.

"You two will not be going with us."

Bradshaw drew an angry breath, but Ewen merely waited. He hoped he was not to be sent home, for he loved it out here. In the Keep, he could not help thinking of Da, who had worked in the dungeons for his entire life.

The Mace frowned. "Andalie's little one is only three years old, and I am not a man to base strategy around a child's dreams. But the fact remains that Glee is often correct."

"She does have a gift," Bradshaw ventured.

"This is my dilemma. Levieux says that the Queen is in the Palais dungeons; he saw her there himself, and I trust his word. Glee says the Queen is in Gin Reach, and Andalie tells me that Glee is correct. So what am I to do?"

"Where is Gin Reach, sir?" Bradshaw asked.

"It's a tiny village in the southern Almont, just north of the Dry Lands, a way station for fools who mean to cross the open desert and try to get into Cadare without paying the King's tolls. There can't be more than two hundred souls in the town, and I don't know what the Queen would ever be doing there, but all the same . . ." The Mace's voice trailed off.

"You must cover your bases," Bradshaw supplied.

"Yes. As strange as it sounds, I want the two of you to go down to Gin Reach and simply keep your eyes open. Look for anything out of the ordinary." The Mace rustled through his saddlebags and tossed Bradshaw a bag of coin. "That should keep you in a good room for three weeks. If nothing happens and you see nothing, then come home."

"What if we see something?"

"Then use your judgment. Our priority is the Queen. If we recover her, we mean to head for the Keep as soon as possible, and we won't have time to come looking for you down in the Dry Lands. If anything should happen, send word back to this camp. Several of the Guard and most of Hall's people will stay here."

Ewen didn't like the sound of this errand. It seemed as though they would be all alone in a tiny village in the desert. Bradshaw might have magic, but neither of them knew how to wield a sword.

"You will leave tonight, quietly, after dinner. Follow the irrigation system off the Crithe. A good night's ride and a bit, due south, should see you down to Gin Reach."

"How will we know it?" Ewen asked.

"By asking, I suppose. Bradshaw is in charge."

Bradshaw looked surprised by this, and Ewen was too. Aisa had told Ewen that the Mace didn't like magic, though Ewen didn't understand why. Surely the world was better when unusual things could happen.

"I am going to trust you, magician, though I trust none of your ilk."

Bradshaw shrugged. "The Queen did me a good turn, Captain. I will do her one if I can."

"Dismissed."

The two men wandered out of the tent. Ewen had the feeling that Bradshaw was just as surprised as he was. Bradshaw could do many amazing things; perhaps that was why the Mace had chosen him. But after thinking about it for a moment, Ewen was fairly sure that the Mace didn't expect anything to happen to them at all.

"Pack yourself up," Bradshaw told him. "I'll see about food and water."

Ewen nodded and went to find his horse. From the noise around the campfire, he could tell that the deer was finally ready, but he had lost his appetite. He had been terrified of the very notion of Mortmesne, the wicked kingdom that Da spoke of in all of his fairy tales, but at the same time, he had been proud to be chosen to venture there. He knew he was not smart enough to be a Queen's Guard, and he had been ready to bow out and go on the hunt for the witch, Brenna. There was honor in that. But this mission did not feel real.

As he neared the horses, he saw a solitary figure: Pen, sitting alone, facing east, on one of the rocks that bordered the corral. More than once, Ewen had heard others in the Guard say that Pen was the Queen's favorite, and he had noticed that Pen did not seem himself since the Queen had left. Ewen thought it best not to talk to Pen, so he merely dug through the pile until he found his saddles and saddlebags, then took them over to his horse. Ewen was not a good rider; he had learned with his brothers when he was young, but he had never taken to it the way Peter and Arthur had. Bradshaw was not much of a rider either, and the two of them had often lagged behind on this journey, hurrying to catch up while the others rested. Now they were being sent away, off to some place Ewen had never heard of. His horse, Van, stared at him, almost as though he understood, and Ewen stroked Van's neck for a long moment. It was one thing to go to Mortmesne himself, another to drag an animal there; at least Van would be out of danger as well.

When he slung his saddlebags over the horse's back, his grey Guard cloak fell to the ground. They hadn't been allowed to wear their cloaks on this journey, but Ewen had brought his anyway. It was the dearest item he owned, though he understood that it had never really belonged to him. He went to the Mace's horse, folded the cloak, and draped it over the Mace's saddle.

"Ewen."

Pen was beckoning him over. Ewen touched the cloak one last time and then went to Pen. As he neared, he saw that Pen's eyes were red, as though he'd been crying.

"You're going to Gin Reach."

Ewen nodded.

"I don't think you'll find anything there, and neither does the Captain. But if you do . . ." Pen was silent for a long moment. "If you do, you're a Queen's Guard now. A real Queen's Guard, you understand? You protect the Queen, no matter the cost to yourself."

Ewen was too bewildered to do anything but nod, and Pen clapped him on the shoulder.

"Draw me some pictures while you're down there. When we all get back to the Keep, we'll sit and have another look through your portfolio."

Ewen smiled. Pen had been the first one to tell him that his pile of pictures had a name.

"Luck to you, Ewen."

"And you," Ewen replied. As Pen walked away, he tried to puzzle out what Pen had said. Queen's Guards were supposed to lay down their lives to protect the Queen, and Ewen understood that. But Pen seemed to be talking about something different.

Bradshaw was approaching the corral now, a heavy pack over one shoulder. Ewen waited for him, still considering Pen's words. There was a word for these things . . . it danced right on the edge of Ewen's mind for a moment before he retrieved it. Sacrifice. That was what it was. For Pen, being a Queen's Guard was a matter of sacrifice, and from the look of him, it was hurting him badly. Ewen hesitated for a moment longer and then, not quite knowing why, he grabbed his grey cloak from the Mace's saddle and stuffed it back into his own saddlebag.

J avel woke to shouting.

The voice was a woman's, and for a moment he was confused, until he remembered where he was: in the Keep. He had ridden hard for three days, with only brief breaks to water his horse, and at the moment he put the Mace's letter into Devin's hand, he had not cared whether the man believed him or not, had only felt great thanksgiving that the ride was done.

Now a man was shouting. Javel sat up in bed, scrubbed a palm across his face, and found at least four days' growth of beard. He had been asleep for some time. The argument continued to rage outside, unintelligible but rancorous, and Javel sighed and grabbed his boots.

When he emerged into the hallway, he found it lined with Queen's Guards. The guard in charge, Devin, was squared off with a tall, dark-haired woman just outside Javel's door. Javel did not recognize the woman, but he marked how hard the rest of the Queen's Guard were working not to look at her, their gazes fixed on the floor or the ceiling or anything else.

"I tell you, they are coming!" the woman shouted at Devin.

"Calm down, Andalie! You'll wake the wing!"

"Good! We must get out of here, now!"

Devin glanced at the men around him, his face reddening. "Are you giving me an order?"

"Yes, you great ass! Get these people out of bed!"

"Shut up!"

The voice echoed down the hallway. On Javel's right, a new figure emerged from one of the rooms farther down the corridor, and this was someone Javel did recognize: Arliss, one of the biggest bookmakers and dealers in New London. If a man spent any amount of time drinking in the Gut—and Javel, of course, had spent plenty—he could not fail to encounter Arliss's ubiquitous, gnomelike figure, in and out of various pubs, wheeling and dealing, making money hand over fist.

"This had better be good," Arliss growled. "I'm trying to resettle nearly a hundred thousand people who still don't want to leave. The provisioning alone would make you cry."

The woman, Andalie, said, "We must leave. Now. Immediately."

"To go where?"

"Anywhere," she replied flatly.

"The woman had a nightmare," Devin told him. "I will clear this up, sir. Never mind."

But Devin's voice had weakened, and he would not look directly at Andalie either. Even Javel could feel the aura of strangeness around her, her eyes so distant that they seemed to see beyond this world. The group of Queen's Guards shuffled uncomfortably, looking from Devin to Arliss.

"Andalie?" Arliss asked.

"The Holy Father's people are coming here, now. We must get out of here."

"I warned you, Andalie." Devin lowered his voice, for now doors were beginning to open up and down the hallway. "Get yourself back to your children."

"I will not," Andalie replied coldly. "The Mace put you in charge of the Guard, not of me."

"How do you propose the Holy Father means to enter the Keep? He has no soldiers!"

"Yes, he does. The Mort."

"The Mort are gone!"

"No."

"She's right!" said a younger guard. Javel vaguely remembered him from that long, dreamlike trip back from the Argive. He could not be more than twenty. There was a bow slung across his back. "Andalie always knows! We must get out of here!"

"Shut up, Wellmer!" Devin snapped. At the same moment, a thundering blow shook the floor beneath their feet. Javel cried out, and he was not alone.

"A ram," Arliss muttered. "Too late."

Devin grabbed one of the guards. "Find out what's happening down there."

The guard disappeared. Javel watched him go, picturing the scene at the gate below; the Gate Guard would be scrambling to bolster the doors, to pull the drawbridge. They knew how to repel invaders; it was part of the standard training for a Gate Guard. But if there were too many people on the bridge, it would not rise, and the gates, while strong iron, would not hold forever against a steel ram. Even the moat was not deep enough to act as an impediment. If Vil was still in charge of the Gate Guard, he would be down there, calm and competent as ever, directing men as they bricked the gate and strained to raise the bridge. But if the attacking force was large enough, every guard on the gate would know that these were holding actions only.

Arliss turned to Devin. "What about the Mace's back way out? The tunnels?"

"I don't know them," Devin replied, looking shamefaced. "He never told me."

"Andalie?"

She shook her head. Another blow shook the walls around them, and Javel blinked as grit silted down from the ceiling into his eyes.

"Have the Mort invaded again?" Devin demanded. "How could we not know?"

"It's no invasion," Andalie replied. "This is the Arvath."

Javel felt a tug on his trouser leg, and looked down to find a small girl staring up at him. She was tiny, little more than a toddler, but her eyes were strangely adult. Javel tried to ignore her, but she kept on tugging, her small face determined, and finally he bent down and asked, "What is it, child?"

"Gate Guard," the girl whispered, and her voice did not match her age either; the tone was mocking, somehow familiar.

"Yes?"

"You might still be useful."

Javel recoiled, but the child had already released his leg. She toddled over to the woman, Andalie, and climbed up into her arms. They stared at each other for a long moment, as though speaking, and a shudder worked its way up Javel's spine. For the past few days, he had been riding too hard to even think of drink, but in that moment he would have given anything for a shot of whiskey. Perhaps ten.

A rhythmic thrumming echoed beneath their feet, and Arliss shook his head. "The gate won't hold forever. We have to barricade the wing."

Andalie nodded. "We need furniture. The heavy pieces."

Thinking of the heavy armoire in his room, Javel headed back there. But he paused in the doorway, struck by the pitiful pile of belongings at the foot of the bed. He had brought only a few things with him to Mortmesne, preferring to leave their house just as it was, so that when Allie came home, she would see that nothing had changed. The idea made him smile now, but it was a smile full of winter. His old life was gone, wiped away, and the sad, half-full state of his baggage seemed to prove it.

Gate Guard, the girl's voice, Dyer's voice, echoed inside his head.

"I was," Javel replied, almost absently. He had been a Gate Guard for more than ten years, and a decent one. Going to a job every day, a job that needed doing, and performing it competently . . . there had been honor in that. But a man eaten up by his past mistakes could not see it. Javel bent to his baggage, picked up his sword, and stared at it for a long moment, feeling as though he stood on the edge of a precipice.

Useful.

He turned and strode down the hallway, into the great open room that housed the Queen's empty throne. When he turned the corner, he saw the Guard preparing to barricade the great double doors with heavy furniture, several pieces already grouped on the far wall.

"Hold!" Javel shouted. "Let me pass!"

"You don't want to go out there," Devin told him. "There's a mob, at least two hundred, plus the Mort."

"I'm a Gate Guard," Javel replied. "Let me pass."

"Your funeral." Devin knocked four times on the door, then raised the bar and opened it wide enough for Javel to slip through.

"We can't let you back in!" Devin called after him.

"Right," Javel muttered, increasing his pace. The sound of the ram was much louder out here, a steady thudding that shook the walls. More dust drifted down from the ceiling, a light snowfall in the torchlight. As Javel descended the stairs, the thudding increased until it was strong enough to make his teeth clatter, each blow punctuated by the metallic clang of wood on iron. Part of Javel, the weak part that always retreated into the shadows of the pub, wanted to turn around, to run right back upstairs.

"No," he whispered, trying to convince himself. "I can still be useful."

When he reached the first floor, he ran down the main hallway, passing several wide-eyed Keep servants along the way.

"Sir, what's happening?" an old woman demanded.

"Siege," he replied. "Make for the upper floors and hide."

She fled.

Javel came around the final corner and found the Gate Guard preparing to brick the gate. This was a contingency for which they all prepared, and a small storeroom was kept just off the gatehouse for this purpose. Guards moved back and forth from the storeroom, carrying piles of bricks, and several more were already laying a triple layer of bricks and mortar behind the barricade. Javel was relieved to recognize two of them: Martin and Vil. As he approached, Vil straightened, holding a trowel.

"Javel! What—"

"What's happening?" Javel shouted. The blows of the ram were so loud out here that they seemed to make his spine shudder.

"They came out of nowhere!" Vil replied, shouting as well. "We dropped the gate, but we didn't have time to get the bridge up! The gate won't hold unless we brick!"

Javel nodded. "Give me work, Vil!"

"I thought you were with the Queen's Guard!"

"I'm a Gate Guard!" Javel shouted back. "Give me work!"

Vil stared at him, measuring, for a long moment, then said, "I could use another man to mix mortar! Gill's already in the storeroom. Go!"

Javel nodded, smiling, for in this simple order he felt somehow blessed. He belted his sword to his waist, stepped lightly over Martin's back, and went to work.

Aisa crouched in the shadows of a recess, her hand on her knife. She was filthy, covered in the grime of the tunnels, and she could smell herself, a mixture of long-congealed sweat and the rotten dampness that seemed to reign down here. Her arm throbbed dully from a long scratch she had taken yesterday. But the song of the fight was upon her; her blood coursed with it.

Merritt stood behind her, and across the tunnel, in another recess, were the Miller brothers, barely visible in the thin torchlight.

Daniel's neck was wrapped and bandaged; he had taken a terrible burn when he surprised a woman who was cooking chicken in a pot of boiling oil. She had thrown the pot at him and then tried to flee with her charges, two boys and three girls, all under the age of ten. They had managed to save the children, removing them to the large holding area up in the Gut. But the woman had fled into the dark. Another of the handlers, a man, had tried to club Christopher with a shovel, and ended up with the shovel buried in his ribs. Aisa didn't know whether the Miller brothers were typical Caden or not, and she no longer cared. She meant to join them or die trying.

But that dream was still years away. The first step, the one she could accomplish now, was to have them treat her as though she were anyone else, a tool to be wielded.

Christopher leaned into the light, pointing to Aisa. Merritt poked her in the back.

"That's you, girl. Give us another good show."

Aisa tucked her knife into the back of her trousers, covering it with her shirttail. She took a deep breath and darted out into the main tunnel. It was a wide bore, perhaps twenty feet from side to side, and another twenty to the arch of the ceiling over her head. Water seeped through the cracks and dripped down to form wide puddles on the floor. Aisa thought they must be somewhere near the Keep moat, perhaps even underneath it.

Ahead, the tunnel branched into three passages, each leading into darkness. Down one of these three passages were several men, a pimp and his clients, holding at least ten children. Aisa and the four Caden had been tracking them for more than a day in this underground labyrinth. The upper levels were lit by scattered but consistent torchlight; down here, there was none but what they brought themselves. Aisa held her torch higher, but she could see nothing of the three passages beyond their entrances, vast black mouths opening into more dark.

"Hello?" she called. "Is anybody there?"

Silence. But Aisa could feel eyes upon her. She tottered forward, wrapping one arm around herself in the manner of a cold child. In the five days she had been down there, she had seen many children, both living and dead. James had explained to her, in a quiet, matter-of-fact voice, that some pimps chose to slaughter their stables, so that the children could neither implicate them nor slow them down in flight.

"Hello?" she called again. "Mrs. Evans?"

They had put Mrs. Evans under arrest three days ago, and she was now being held at the New London Jail. She had not gone easily; it was she who'd given Aisa the knife wound on her arm. But her name was very useful, for she seemed to be well known in the Creche, and no one knew that she'd been arrested. Aisa had already pulled this trick successfully twice.

"Mrs. Evans? I'm hungry."

She sensed movement ahead, but could not tell which tunnel it came from. Fear welled within her, but adrenaline was stronger. It was the song of the fight, yes, but there was something else at work here. Aisa was doing something important. She didn't know whether the Caden would have accepted her if they hadn't had use for a child, dangling bait to draw out the difficult prey. But it no longer mattered. She was *helping*, helping to save the weak and punish those who needed punishment. The song of the fight was a great thing in itself, but the song of the righteous fight was exponentially more powerful, allowing Aisa to ignore her fear and limp forward a few more feet.

"Hello?"

The shadowy form of a man emerged from the left-hand tunnel. Aisa blinked up at him. Instinct told her to give the alarm, but she held silent. When they spooked the prey, the prey would panic, and that made them more likely to kill the children.

"Mrs. Evans left me," she told the man, pitching her voice high for the Caden behind her.

He smiled; she could see the white of his teeth in the dim light. But the rest of him was a large shadow, holding out a hand.

This was the most difficult part for Aisa. She would have liked nothing better than to lop his hand off at the wrist, but there were more than ten children down that tunnel. The man could not be given the chance to scream.

She took his hand, grimacing inwardly at the sweaty feel of his skin. The man took the torch from her and held it high, pulling her with him into the tunnel. With her free hand, she reached behind her and grasped the hilt of her knife. The man was much taller, and it would take a movement both sharp and seamless to get the knife to his throat. The people in the Creche, both adults and children, were like animals, skittish and overly sensitive to danger. Merritt said it was the result of a life lived in the shadows, but Aisa wondered. She was skittish herself.

They rounded a corner and Aisa found herself in a small, enclosed chamber with a low ceiling, barely tall enough for the man beside her to stand up straight. The chamber itself was lit by two torches, but on the far wall was another door that led into blackness. The floor was covered with children sitting cross-legged; a quick scan of the room gave Aisa fourteen of them. The oldest could not be more than eleven. Five more men were scattered along the walls, and Aisa marked that three of them carried swords before she halted, dumbfounded, her eyes locked on the fourth: Da, staring right back at her.

His eyes widened, and he opened his mouth to shout. Aisa tried to jerk her hand free, but the tall man had already whirled her around and thrown her against the wall. Aisa went down, half dazed, and felt a bloom of pain in her chest as the man kicked her in the ribs.

"A trap!" Da shouted. "Run!"

The children began to scream, and the echo of all of those voices against the tunnel walls made Aisa clap her hands to her ears. The children scrambled to their feet and rushed through the far doorway. The blows to her rib cage stopped, and Aisa looked up to see the last of the men disappearing behind them.

Da, she thought fuzzily. And she wondered why she had not expected him. Pimp or client, neither would surprise her.

The four Caden burst into the room, swords drawn, and she pointed to the far doorway as she tried to sit up.

"You're all right, girl?" Daniel asked her.

"Fine," she wheezed. "Go, go."

They tore through the doorway, and Aisa began the slow process of dragging herself to her feet. Her ribs ached, and her head was cut open where she had hit the wall. She heard the ring of swords in the tunnel beyond and pushed herself up. The Caden could take care of themselves, but later on they might remember that she had not been there with them.

Da here, her mind repeated, and the thought had a sharp edge to it now. She pulled one of the torches from its bracket and cast around until she found her knife, lying across the room. The screams of the children were muted now, growing distant. With her knife in one hand and a torch in the other, Aisa took a deep breath, feeling something pull at her ribs, and charged after them.

The tunnel was narrower on this side, and soon it began to wind, snakelike, ever upward. Ahead, she heard a man shouting, and then there was only the scuffling of her own feet. The closeness increased until Aisa would have given anything for a breath of fresh air. She thought she was gaining on them, but could not be sure. Her head ached. Every few seconds, she had to wipe blood from her eyes.

She skidded around a turn and came to a halt. At her feet lay a man's body. She crept closer, then used her foot to roll him over: Da, still breathing. He, too, had taken a blow to the head; she could see the beginnings of an ugly bruise on his temple.

Aisa squatted and placed the torch on the floor, her knife held at the ready in case it was a trick. But Da lay still, hoarse breath hissing in and out through his thick black beard.

"I could kill you now," Aisa whispered, brandishing her knife before Da's closed eyes. "I could cut your throat, and no one would care. I could say I was defending myself."

And it would be true, she realized. She couldn't even imagine how it would feel, to walk the earth knowing that Da was no longer doing the same. To know that she no longer had a lurking enemy out there, a danger to them all . . . that would be freedom indeed. Aisa had never killed anyone before, but if she was going to start, she could hardly make a better choice than this.

Still, she hesitated, clutching her knife, as her knees began to ache and her palms became sticky with sweat.

"Why?" she whispered, watching Da's eyelids twitch. "Why did you have to be this way?" Even more than she wanted to kill Da, she wanted answers, wanted to call him to account. Killing him seemed far too easy, particularly when he was unconscious. It was no punishment.

Several childish shrieks echoed up the hallway, making Aisa jump. For a moment, she had forgotten why she was here: the children. One day, less than a year ago, she had walked into the kitchen and found Da with his hand up Glee's dress, and Glee not three years old.

"Too easy," she muttered. "Just too easy."

The Caden had the manacles, but she didn't know when they would be back. Using her knife, Aisa cut the sleeves from Da's shirt, being careful not to touch him. She wrapped his wrists and ankles, tying the knots as securely as she could. Da stirred and groaned as she tightened the bonds, but his eyes remained closed, and Aisa stared down at him for a long moment, wishing she were older, old enough to get past it all.

Someone was coming back up the tunnel now, and Aisa straightened, raising her knife. But as the noise resolved itself into many footsteps, walking at a steady pace, she relaxed and slipped the knife out of sight. The other part of her job was about to begin, and she was determined to do it well.

The group of children came around the corner, followed by all four Caden, holding torches. Christopher and James were each hauling a prisoner as well, men whose faces had been badly beaten. The children were frightened; many of them were crying, and they looked fearfully up at the four red-cloaked men. Aisa held up her hands.

"Listen to me," she said. "These men are good men. They're here to help you, I swear it. We're going to take you out of the tunnels."

She said this last as gently as possible, for they had already discovered that this news alarmed the children more than anything else. Many of them had lived their entire lives down here, and had no concept of the world above.

"We have plenty of food," Aisa continued, and saw their eyes brighten with interest.

"We'll get sick if we go up the stairs," one of the older girls announced. "My pa said so."

"Your pa lied," Aisa told her, glancing down at Da, whose chest still rose and fell in the easy rhythm of unconsciousness. "I have lived up there my entire life."

The girl still looked faintly mutinous, but said nothing else.

"You should follow us, and stay together. If you stray, you may get lost down here in the dark." For the first few days, this possibility had haunted Aisa as well, but Daniel always marked the walls well, with special chalk that did not dissolve under the drip of water. As long as they didn't run out of light, they were fine.

Christopher had bent to Da now, examining his bonds. "I'll have to teach you to tie a knot, girl. If he'd woken, he would have been out of this in seconds."

If he'd woken, I would have killed him.

But Aisa didn't say it. She didn't want to alarm the children, but even more, she didn't want the Caden to know Da was her father. Coryn had told her that the Caden, like the Guard, allowed new recruits to wipe their pasts clean. But she didn't know what status she really held with them, and besides, did that leeway include a past as ugly as this?

Christopher snapped a pair of manacles on Da's wrists before hoisting him to his feet. Da's eyes opened, bleary and red, and they wandered the room for a moment before finding Aisa and locking on her.

"Want to do the honors?" Daniel asked.

Meeting his eyes, Aisa froze, because she saw that he already knew. They all knew. It was the audience, the damnable audience, where she had revealed her shame to the entire world. Merritt was looking at her with poorly concealed pity, and James had put his hand on her shoulder.

"Go ahead," he murmured. "It will do you good."

Aisa took a deep breath. The children's faces calmed her, reminded her of how much was at stake here, and her own shame receded. She did not even need to dig for the words; she had heard them so many times in the past week that they were right there, within easy reach.

"In the name of Her Majesty, Queen Kelsea Glynn, you men are under arrest for pandering, trafficking, and facilitation of assault. You will be held in the New London Jail until such time as you account for yourselves before a judge. You will not be harmed further unless you attempt to escape."

"Come on," Daniel said brusquely. "Let's get them topside. You keep an eye on the children, girl. Make sure they don't stray."

They started back the way they had come, James and Christopher in the front and Aisa, Merritt, and Daniel bringing up the rear. Aisa's arm throbbed, and she saw that the long scratch, which had sealed itself yesterday, was beginning to swell beneath its reddening seam. As adrenaline wore off, the pain from this scratch became difficult to ignore, but Aisa swallowed it as best she could, holding a child's hand in each of hers.

After more than an hour of walking uphill, they came to a broad intersection of six tunnels. Aisa recognized this place; they were only some thirty minutes from regaining the surface. Blue light filtered down, diffused through several layers of gratings, and Aisa realized that up there, topside, it must be dawn already. The idea of sunlight seemed almost fanciful; down here long enough, one forgot that there was anything more than the amber glow of torches.

The children were tired; one little boy, who could not be more than five, had begun to lag every few steps, and Aisa had to lightly jerk his hand to bring him along. The entire group walked without speaking, no sound but their staggered footfalls echoing against stone, and it was this void that allowed Aisa to hear a man's voice, low and urgent, somewhere behind her on the right.

"Please God."

Aisa halted. The acoustics in these tunnels were strange; sometimes she could hear distant voices clearly enough to understand the words, while at other times she could not hear Daniel's murmured commands from ten feet away. The voice she had just heard had been clear, with no peculiar quality of distance or dead air. The speaker must be very close.

"What is it, girl?" Merritt asked, turning back to wait for her.

"Give me your torch."

"Hold!" he shouted to the Miller brothers, then handed his torch to Aisa. Holding it high, she wandered a few feet down the tunnel, examining the walls. The intersection was now at least a hundred feet behind them, and she didn't think the voice could have been so far off as that. A hidden nest, perhaps? They had found one of those already, cleverly concealed under a drainage grate. The Caden had been forced to kill the six men and women who ran that particular pod, but Aisa counted them no loss; one woman, realizing she was cornered, had put a dagger to the throat of a young girl, little more than a toddler. But Daniel could throw a knife just as well as he could wield one, and the woman went down with the blade planted squarely in her jugular, the child not even scratched. Aisa ran her fingers over the uneven surface of the tunnel, working her way backward, and her breath halted as she felt a gap in the stonework, not more than ten inches wide.

"Light!" she shouted up the tunnel. "More light!"

The Caden ushered the children and prisoners backward, crowding close to examine the gap. It would barely admit a thin man, but would certainly admit children. Aisa fancied she could hear—not with her ears, perhaps, but with her mind—a rapid heartbeat on the far side of the wall.

"There's someone in there," she told Merritt.

"Can you squeeze through?"

She gave him the torch. Her own heartbeat had increased, for there was certainly danger here, but she was pleased that none of them protested sending her in, on her own, where they could not follow.

Holding her knife in front of her, she bent down and eased through the crack. It was a squeeze, but not too tight. At any moment she expected to meet resistance: adult hands, grabbing her. But nothing came, and then she was on the far side of the wall, reaching back through so that Merritt could hand her the torch.

"Be on your guard, child!" Daniel called outside.

Aisa held the torch high, looking around. She was in a narrow room, almost a tunnel itself. The smell was much, much worse in here, enough to make her eyes water. The walls dripped with mold. Trash littered the floor, and in the near corner Aisa saw what appeared to be a pile of human waste. She jumped, gasping, as a rat's thick body scuttled over her foot, and for a moment she wanted to simply flee, flee this room and these tunnels and run the long road back up to the Keep. Her arm ached, her mind ached, and she was only twelve years old.

Pain. The voice was little more than an echo, deep in her mind, but still it made Aisa stand up straight, for it belonged to the Mace. *Pain only disables the weak.*

A killer of children, her mind returned, but that thought had no power here. What happened in the Creche was worse than murder. Far worse.

"Only the weak," Aisa whispered to herself. "Only the weak."

She held the torch higher and stepped forward, seeking the far end of the long, narrow room, and as the light hit the far wall, she halted, instinctively raising her knife.

Two men sat there, leaning against the wall, their clothing so streaked with mud and filth that it told Aisa nothing. One man's eyes were closed; he appeared to be asleep, but Aisa knew instinctively that he was dead. The other simply stared with wide, distant eyes. His face was smudged with mud and he was bone-thin, gaunt hollows beneath his cheekbones. His wrists looked like sticks where they emerged from his sleeves. He stared up into the light, his pupils dilating, and Aisa gasped as she recognized the Keep priest, Father Tyler.

"All right in there, girl?" one of the Caden called from the tunnel outside.

"Yes."

"Well, hurry it up! These children need food, and we need sleep."

The priest opened his mouth to speak, and Aisa put a finger to her lips. Her mind was moving, not sluggishly as before, but lightning-quick. Father Tyler, who had helped her to find books to read in the Queen's library. The Mace wanted Father Tyler returned to the Keep, but had not been able to find him. The Arvath had laid a bounty on Father Tyler's head, ten thousand pounds, the last Aisa had heard. Of course, the Mace had laid a bounty too, but the two amounts were constantly in flux. The Mace would surely match the Arvath's offer, Aisa knew that, but the Caden might not. If Aisa told the Caden that ten thousand pounds lay behind this wall, would they help her return Father Tyler to the Keep, just on her say-so? Not a chance.

As quietly as possible, Aisa dug into the pockets of her grey cloak. She had half a loaf of bread, only two days old, and some dried fruit, and these she placed at Father Tyler's feet. He grabbed the bread and began to wolf it down. She produced her canteen and handed it over as well, and then, placing her finger to her lips again, she backtracked toward the gap in the wall.

"My mistake!" she called. "Rats, a good-size nest."

"Well, get out here!" James shouted, irritated. "We're tired."

Aisa flattened her palm at Father Tyler, indicating that he should stay where he was, and then worked her way back into the main tunnel.

"I'm sorry," she muttered. "I thought I heard a voice."

Daniel shrugged. "Good to check every corner. Let's get going."

For a moment in there, Aisa had forgotten about Da, but now, as she emerged, his voice echoed across the tunnel.

"Aisa girl."

She looked up, and a part of her hated herself for it, for the fact that Da's voice was still the voice of God inside her head, impossible to ignore.

"What, Da?"

"Surely you won't let them do this to me?"

"Shut up!" Christopher snapped, shaking Da like a rag doll.

"I'm speaking to my daughter."

Aisa stared at him, sickened. His hair was mussed, his beard soaked with blood, but beneath these things he looked just as he always had. Manacles or not, Aisa was suddenly frightened, for she remembered this exactly: Da's voice, wheedling, full of slippery oil.

"Aisa? You don't want to see me in jail?"

She clouted him across the face. "I'd like to see you in a hole, Da. But prison will do for me. You'll never see any of our family again. I hope you die in the dark."

She turned back to Christopher. "Do me a favor and gag him."

"Do us all a favor," Merritt echoed, his voice disgusted. The group of children around them stared wide-eyed at this exchange, and the little boy wormed his hand back into Aisa's, staring up at her, as Christopher anchored a length of cloth in Da's mouth. The gag brought Aisa no relief; she could only stand there miserably, wishing that she were the child of someone else, fighting not to look backward at the hole in the wall. She would have to come back down here, slip the Caden somehow and return with more food . . . alone, down here in the dark. The idea terrified her, but she saw no way around it; the priest must be returned to the Keep. She felt much loyalty to these Caden, who had taken her in and put her to work. But her loyalty to the Mace, to the Queen, these were greater, and both the Queen and the Mace wanted Father Tyler back.

Which am I? she wondered. *Caden, or a Queen's Guard?*

She didn't know, but whichever she chose, it would be dangerous work. Her arm throbbed insistently, and when they got topside, Aisa saw that the seam of her wound had begun to weep clear fluid. The surrounding flesh burned an angry shade of red.

Infected, Aisa's mind whispered, and her stomach tightened. At their little house in the Lower Bend, they'd had a neighbor named Mrs. Lime who had cut herself with a dirty blade. No one in the Lower Bend could afford antibiotics, and Mrs. Lime had finally simply disappeared from the landscape, her house standing empty until some squatters took it over. Aisa had always remembered the word, which rang like a death knell in her mind.

Infection.

Chapter 8

The Tear Lands

My tables—meet it is I set it down—
That one may smile and smile, and be a villain.
    —*Hamlet,* WILLIAM SHAKESPEARE (PRE-CROSSING ANGL.)

In her more selfish moments, Katie wished only for the harvest to be over. She hated the farm, the smell of manure, the back-breaking work of picking vegetables only to reap the reward of food that would simply be eaten. She hated manual labor. Sometimes she wished that the fields would catch on fire.

She was not alone. She seemed to hear complaints all around her, more than she had ever heard before, and most of it was directed toward the people at the top of the hill: those too old or sick to work, or parents with children too small to be left. These people were always excused from the harvest, but this year such exemptions were causing more ill feeling than usual.

Maybe Row's right, she thought, late one afternoon, when her back was screaming and her hands blistered from lugging her basket of corn down the row. *Maybe none of us are selfless enough to live here.*

Row and Katie had not been assigned as harvest partners this year; Row had been stuck with Gavin on the squash patch, more than an acre away. Katie wondered if Mum had interfered to bring about this result; lately, Katie had begun to feel as though Mum were actively working to disengage her from Row, to keep them apart.

"Good luck, Mum," Katie snarled quietly, digging into the corn plants. Her friendship with Row was very different than it had once been; Row had never admitted what he had done that night, and between them they maintained the polite fiction that Row had simply lost her in the dark. But they both knew that wasn't so, and the knowledge had changed their friendship irrevocably. No longer did the two of them seem bound in a magic circle, inviolate by the outside world. They were still friends, but now Katie was one of many, perhaps no more special to Row than Gavin or Lear or anyone else. Sometimes that hurt, but not much. The memory of that night in the woods was too strong.

"Did you say something?" Jonathan asked, leaning around the cornstalk.

"Nothing."

He ducked out of sight again. Katie didn't know why they had been assigned as partners, but she could have done worse. Jonathan was a hard worker, and he didn't disappear—as Row so often did—when it was time to lug the full baskets back toward the warehouse. For the first few days of the harvest, Katie had waited to see if Jonathan would fall into another trance, but when nothing happened, she gave up. Two years had passed since that day in the clearing, and she had kept her word, telling no one, not even Row. But she wasn't even sure whether Jonathan remembered. He was unfailingly serious, keeping all of his attention on the task at hand. He reminded Katie of his father.

Several rows over, someone was talking to himself. Katie listened for a moment, and the words resolved themselves into a prayer. Here was another new development. Katie had never heard anyone pray in public during her childhood; there was no penalty for doing so, but William Tear discouraged it, and Tear's disapproval had always been enough to shut down any behavior. Now Katie seemed to hear prayer constantly, and it irritated her no end. Mum was death on religion, and her views on the topic had shaped Katie's as well. She wanted no invisible sky fathers hanging over the Town, mandating irrational behavior. She didn't want to hear prayer around every corner.

Jonathan was listening too; he had paused in picking, cocking his head.

"—and God protect us from all demons and spirits, thieves of children, God bless us and keep us safe—"

"*Shut up!*" Katie shouted, louder than she had meant to. Her voice echoed over the rows, bringing silence in its wake. Jonathan peered at her around the corn plant, his eyebrows lifted.

"Sorry," Katie muttered. "I can't stand that."

"They're frightened," Jonathan replied, snapping off another ear of corn.

"Everyone's frightened. But not all of us are dumb enough to go looking for Jesus."

Jonathan shook his head, and Katie felt color come to her cheeks. Even five minutes' conversation with Jonathan was enough to reaffirm that he was a much better person than she was, kind and understanding and tolerant. Katie was seventeen now, Jonathan eighteen, but she still felt as though he were years— perhaps centuries—older.

"Don't you think it's dangerous?" she asked. "All of this religious nonsense springing up everywhere?"

"I don't know," Jonathan replied. "But I would like to know *where* it's coming from. Even my father can't find the source."

"What about Paul Annescott? His Bible meetings get bigger all the time."

"Annescott's a fool. But my father says he's not the real problem."

"Can't your father make it stop?"

"Not yet. Not while children are disappearing. Fear is fertile ground for superstition."

Katie's heart sank, but deep down she knew he was right. They had studied the same history in school. Religion always rode on the back of turmoil, like a jockey. The Town might not be panicking yet, but panic could not be far away. Two weeks ago, Yusuf Mansour, seven years old, had disappeared from the park during a game of hide-and-seek. The Town had combed the woods, all the way down to the river, but they had found no trace of him.

Katie's first thought had been of the creature she had seen in the woods, the one that had chased her up toward town. She had never talked about that night with anyone but Row; she tried not to think of it herself. For a few weeks, there had been nightmares, but in time they had faded away. The depredations in the graveyard had stopped long ago and had never been repeated. Katie made sure to never be alone outside town after dark. Most days she could even pretend that she had imagined it. But when Yusuf disappeared from the park, Katie had realized that it might be time to tell someone about that night, even if they thought she was crazy. She had no right to withhold the information from the community, simply to make things comfortable for herself. She might not be a perfect member of the Town, but she knew that much.

But who to tell? Mum? Katie shrank from that option, for many reasons. Mum would be furious that she had been out with Row after curfew, but even more, Mum was one of the toughest people Katie knew. Mum would not have turned tail and fled; she would have fought the thing, and if it would not submit, Mum would have dragged it back to town, kicking and screaming, to present it to William Tear . . . or she would have died trying. Katie didn't want Mum to know that she had run away from danger.

Next, she had debated telling William Tear himself. It would be a bit of a challenge to speak to him alone, but it could probably be done. But again, Katie shrank from the idea. Tear had chosen her for the town guard, chosen her over many better and smarter—and taller!—people. Did she really want to tell him that this was how she'd repaid him, by remaining silent for the past two years? Anyway, Yusuf had been gone for more than two weeks. It seemed impossible that he could be alive.

What could Tear have done? her mind demanded. *What could anyone do, against that thing you saw?*

But Katie ignored the question. William Tear was William Tear. There was no problem he couldn't solve.

"What's wrong?"

She looked up and found Jonathan staring at her with that gaze of his, the one that could almost strip flesh. Again, she was reminded forcibly of his father. Behind them, the unseen penitent had started up again, a steady stream of pleas to God, and Katie felt as though she could cheerfully brain him with her shovel.

"What did you see?" Jonathan asked, and Katie found herself telling him, just like that, telling him in a low voice because she didn't want the Christer across the way to hear. She told Jonathan everything, even about Row at the end, that cruel and vindictive side of Row that had never been turned on her before. It hurt in the telling—even now, the memory of that night was enough to freeze Katie's heart—but when it was all out, Katie knew that she had picked the right person. She didn't know Jonathan well at all, but she felt better, almost comforted, as though she had handed him a burden and he had shouldered it without being asked.

"Row Finn had my father's sapphire," Jonathan said, almost a question, when she was done.

"Yes," Katie replied, bewildered; of all the things she had just told him, the sapphire was what he cared about? She had betrayed Row, she realized now, but the whole thing was years old, and William Tear's sapphire had been set to a necklace and returned long ago; she had seen it around his neck, many times. No harm, no foul.

"Well, you're not crazy," Jonathan finally replied. "There was something in the woods. Your mother, my father, Aunt Maddy, they were out hunting it for months."

"What? When?"

"Almost two years ago. They used to go out on expeditions, late at night. I wanted to go, but Dad said I had to stay with Mum."

"Did they find anything?"

"No. Whatever it was, it always prowled around the graveyard, and once the grave robbing stopped, it stopped too."

"Grave robbing?"

Jonathan looked at her, his face kind but also a trifle impatient. "Of course grave robbing. You didn't really believe that bit about wolves, did you?"

"No, I didn't!" Katie snapped. "But I didn't think . . . who would rob a grave? For what reason?"

"For silver." Jonathan smiled grimly. "None of the corpses we found had any jewelry left."

"No one in town would rob a grave."

"Are you sure?" Jonathan smiled again, but this smile was different, almost sad.

"Well, no, but–"

He took her hand. Katie jumped and tried to jerk free, but Jonathan held on. For a moment they might have been back in that clearing two years ago, but now it was Katie, not Jonathan, who was in a trance. She stared at her small hand, covered in Jonathan's large one, but she wasn't seeing these things; her vision stretched far beyond, to a dark and windswept patch of ground, dotted with tombstones. Lightning shattered the sky overhead, briefly illuminating the graveyard, and in that flash Katie saw a man digging at one of the graves. But his head was down; she couldn't see his face.

With a tremendous yank, she pulled her hand free of Jonathan's. The connection between them broke with a sizzling flash that made Katie cry out. Her hand tingled as though it had been asleep.

"Why did you do that?" she demanded.

"This town is in danger."

"I know that." But she suddenly wondered if they were talking about the same thing. She had been thinking of Yusuf's disappearance, but now her mind brought up all of the complaining she had heard this week, all of the vitriol directed toward those who had been exempted from the harvest, the same ideas she had heard from Row for so many years: there was no point in treating everyone as equal when they simply weren't. Some people were more valuable than others. This sort of thinking was anathema to the Town, of course, and Row was careful never to say such things where William Tear might overhear. But Row's ideas were steadily gaining ground. Sometimes Katie felt as though there were two towns: the community she had known all of her life, where all were equally valuable, and a second community springing up beside it, inside it, a dark cousin growing in the Town's shadow. The outbreak of religious fervor, a phenomenon that Katie had never seen before, seemed to have lodged itself inside this second town like a parasitic growth.

"I don't agree with everything my father says," Jonathan remarked, breaking off another ear of corn. "But I believe in his vision. I believe we could reach an equilibrium where everyone has an equal chance at a decent life."

"I believe that too," Katie replied, then paused, surprised at herself. All the times she and Row had discussed a different sort of town . . . those years were not so far off, but they seemed very distant, as though Katie had shed a younger skin and left it behind.

"But we'll never get there unless we commit to it," Jonathan told her. "Doctrines of exceptionalism will have to go."

Katie blushed, thinking he had read her mind, but a moment later she realized that Row's wasn't the only such doctrine knocking around the Town. The underground religious movement was full of people who claimed that they were better because they believed. Even Gavin had started mouthing some of this nonsense, though he, too, was careful to keep it out of William Tear's earshot. Those who had been saved—and there was a word, *saved,* that Katie had never trusted—had apparently earned the right to forget that they had once been sinners, too, as though baptism could erase the past. Why had William Tear never put a stop to it? He disapproved, yes, but he did not forbid. Every time Katie thought she was coming to understand Tear, even a little, she realized that she didn't understand him at all.

In the distance, the bell gonged, signaling the end of work for the day.

"Come on," Jonathan said, and they each picked up a basket of corn. Katie's lower back protested, but she did not complain. The first day of the harvest, when she had tweaked a muscle, Jonathan had offered to carry her basket for her, and that could never happen again.

They hauled their baskets down the row toward the warehouse, where Bryan Bell stood waiting to take the count. Bryan's was only one of about twenty lines that had formed as pickers streamed in from the other fields; two lines over, Katie spotted Gavin and Row, each looking just as filthy and disgruntled as herself, each hauling a basket of dirty squash.

Katie had never been inside the enormous warehouse, which stood more than two stories high. But she knew from Mum that there was a long trough in there, and every morning it was filled with fresh water. Later, Bryan and the other checkers would count all of the produce, wash it free of dirt and insects, and then divvy it up. Some would go to everyone in town, a fair portion for each citizen, but most of the drying vegetables, like corn, would be taken for storage or seed. The bulk of the warehouse consisted of storage bins, constructed in Dawn Morrow's wood shop, their lids so flush that they were effectively airtight.

"Do you want to come over for dinner?"

Katie blinked. For a moment, she thought that Jonathan must have been speaking to someone else.

"Wake up, Katie Rice. Do you want to come over?"

"Why?"

"For dinner."

"Why?"

Jonathan grinned at her, though the grin turned to a grimace as he hefted his basket another few feet forward. "The soul of manners."

Katie was not diverted; she narrowed her eyes as she hauled her own basket forward. "Why would you ask me over for dinner?"

"To eat."

"Am I in trouble with your father?"

"I don't know. Should you be?"

"Oh, piss off," she panted, setting her basket down. "It's not like you're so well behaved. I know you've been skipping classes. It's all over school."

"Sure, you know that. But you don't know why."

"Well . . . why?"

"Come to dinner and find out."

She frowned, still sensing something off about the invitation. She had never heard of Jonathan inviting anyone over to his house, not even to play when they were younger. Again she remembered that day in the clearing, Jonathan's eyes staring miles away, seeing all the way to nowhere.

We tried, Katie. We did our best.

"Haul 'em forward!" Bryan Bell shouted, making her jump. She grabbed her basket and scurried to catch up with the line.

"Well?" Jonathan asked.

"What time?"

"Seven."

"All right." Katie wiped her forehead, feeling as though she were covered in dirt. If she was going to dinner at William Tear's, she would need to take a bath first.

"I'll see you then," said Jonathan. He dumped his basket on the counter, waited for Bell to check it off, then walked away. Katie was left staring after him, thinking of that day in the clearing, wondering: *What did we try?*

And then: *How did we fail?*

D espite the proximity of the Tears' house to her own, Katie had been there fewer than a dozen times in her life. Except for Mum and Aunt Maddy, and sometimes Evan Alcott, people were rarely invited to Tear's; when there was something to discuss, Tear usually went to them. Katie had an idea that he was trying to act like a normal man, to avoid the appearance of a king demanding audience from his subjects. If so, he had failed. People dressed more formally for a visit to the Tears' than they did for a festival.

Katie had taken a bath and combed out her long amber hair. The latter was no small feat; she hadn't combed her hair since her last bath, and it was utterly tangled and ratnested from two days of sweating in the fields. After some thought, Katie pinned it up, not wanting Tear—or, somehow worse, Jonathan—to think that she was trying to look pretty.

She had been dreading a barrage of questions when she told Mum that she was going next door for dinner, but Mum merely shrugged and went back to kneading her bread dough. Katie wondered why she had been so worried; after all, she was seventeen now, no longer accountable for all of her movements, even to Mum. At eighteen, she would begin building her own house somewhere in town, and at nineteen she would move out. Row, whose twentieth birthday was only a week away, had decided to hang in with his mother well after the usual time—Katie couldn't quite picture what Mrs. Finn would have done if Row had moved out early—but he had already designed his house and bartered for most of the lumber. He couldn't wait to get away, but Katie was more ambivalent. A part of her didn't want to leave Mum, but a second part of her loved the idea of being out on her own, responsible only for herself, answering to no one.

The Tears' house was almost the duplicate of Katie's: one floor, fronted by a high, raised porch to accommodate their basement. Katie tromped up the steps, and the front door opened to reveal Lily. She, too, had been in the fields today, but now she looked ill, and Katie wondered if she had caught a touch of the fever running around the town.

"Katie," Lily said. She sounded genuinely pleased, as though Katie were bringing her a present.

"Mrs. Freeman," Katie replied politely. She always thought of Lily as Mrs. Tear in her mind, but any misstep here, and Mum would surely hear about it.

"Come on in."

Katie followed her into the Tears' living room, a small area filled with comfortable wooden chairs that had supposedly been built and finished by William Tear himself. The eastern wall of the room was dominated by a broad brick fireplace, though no fire burned there now, in early Ocobter. Two portraits hung above the mantel, and, as she always did on her rare visits to the Tear house, Katie paused to have a look at these.

One was of William Tear. It had been painted by John Vinson, who was understood to be the best artist in town, but it was not a particularly good picture. Tear was standing next to a small bookshelf, staring at the artist with shoulders drawn back. The posture and setting were right, but Tear himself looked annoyed at having to stand for a portrait.

The other picture was of Lily. William Tear had painted it himself, and while he didn't quite have the technical skill of Mr. Vinson, Katie thought that he had captured Lily much better. She was standing in a sunny field, dressed for hunting, so pregnant that she seemed likely to burst. She was looking backward over her shoulder, her face only an inch from laughter.

Mum said that Tear hadn't painted this portrait from life, but from memory. Nevertheless, it was very lifelike, and it had always conveyed a sense of freedom to Katie. The Lily in the portrait seemed happy, extraordinarily so, but Tear hadn't missed the subtle lines around her eyes and mouth, lines that spoke of long-buried pain, the hard life before the Crossing. Katie had no idea what that life had entailed, but it had taken its toll on Lily, sure enough.

"Eighteen years ago," Lily remarked, moving up beside Katie to stare at the portrait. "I was pregnant with Jonathan, and we had just gotten over the starving time. It seemed like everything was ahead of us."

"What happened?"

Lily looked sharply at her, and Katie wished she could take it back. Was she the only one who sensed something wrong in the Town?

No. Jonathan knows too.

After a moment, Lily relaxed and turned back to the portrait. "We forgot. We forgot everything w should have learned."

Katie looked down and saw that the older woman was rubbing at the scar on her palm.

"What—"

"Come on in to dinner," Lily said abruptly, and beckoned her forward.

The meal surprised Katie. She would have thought the Tears would eat better than any other family in town—though why she thought that, she couldn't say; perhaps something Row had told her once—but their dinner was as simple as those she ate at home: roast chicken, broccoli, a loaf of five-grain bread. They drank water, rather than ale or juice. Tear and Lily sat at opposite ends of the table, Jonathan between them, and Katie sat on the other side. When she pulled the fourth chair out, she saw that the seat was covered with dust.

Katie had always assumed that the Tears must talk about deep, weighty matters at dinner, but here, too, they surprised her. Lily was full of gossip, good-natured, but gossip all the same. Melody Donovan was pregnant. Andrew Ellis had finished his house, but he wasn't much of a carpenter; the walls in the kitchen were so drafty that they would need to be torn out and reworked before the winter set in. Dennis Lynskey and Rosie Norris had decided to go ahead and get married after the harvest.

At each of these pronouncements, William Tear nodded, rarely commenting, though he shook his head at the news about Andrew Ellis's house, and Katie remembered something she had heard last year: that Ellis had refused all help from the Town's better build-ers. He was determined to do all of it himself, and Katie had re-spected that. But now she wondered if Mr. Ellis was merely foolish. Even more, she wondered what she was doing at this table. Why had Jonathan invited her here?

Jonathan asked his father if they had found any trace of Yu-suf Mansour yet, and Tear shook his head wearily. The shadow that Katie had seen over his shoulder, years ago, seemed more pronounced than ever now, as though he was somehow start-ing to fade. She wondered, again, whether Tear might be ill, but shelved the thought just as quickly. The Town without William Tear . . . that was nothing to think of. Fever usually traveled through entire households; if Lily was ill, chances were that Tear had been too.

"Wherever Yusuf is, he's hidden well," Tear told them.

"Do you think he's dead?" Lily asked.

"No," Tear replied. He looked about to say something else, but he firmed his jaw and remained silent. Fading sunlight slanted through the open kitchen window, glinting off the silver chain that hung around his neck, and Katie remembered something else from that long-ago night: Tear had said that his visions were often no more than shadows. Were Jonathan's visions the same? She looked between the two of them, seeing a few differences—eye color, the red cheeks that Jonathan had gotten from Lily, in contrast to his father's pale complexion—but far more similarities. Both tall, both lanky, but even more, Jonathan had his father's air of observation, of sitting quietly and watching until it was time to make a decision, a decision that would undoubtedly be correct.

It was a pity that no one else saw this side of Jonathan. He barely came to school anymore, but he was still an object of distance. If people would only talk to him, he would get more respect. Not as much as his father, perhaps, but at least as much as he deserved. This sense of hidden value was familiar, and a moment later Katie identified it: it was the same way she'd always felt about Row.

The talk turned to the mountain expedition, which would be leaving next week. So far, there had been two expeditions to chart the vast land outside the Town, and on the second, they had come upon mountains, but not small mountains like those to the west. According to Jen Devlin, who had led the previous expeditions, the northern mountain range was vast, with peaks so massive that they appeared impossible to cross. But Jen was champing at the bit. She meant to climb.

"Sounds dangerous," Lily remarked.

"It is," Tear replied, and a shadow seemed to cross his face. "But you know Jen. She never met a challenge she could ignore. It's not the worst thing in the world, I suppose. The Town needs people like that, people who aren't daunted by the unknown."

Katie frowned, trying to decide whether she was such a person.

Disgruntled, she was forced to admit that she wasn't. She liked things to be certain, decisive.

"I've made my decision," said Jonathan, and Katie looked up, surprised. He had an annoying habit of guessing her thoughts, but he wasn't looking at her. He was speaking to his father.

"Have you?" Tear asked.

Jonathan pointed to Katie, who jumped as though she'd been pinched. All three of them were looking at her now, and that was too many.

"What decision?" she asked her plate.

"Katie, didn't you ever wonder what I was training you for?" Tear asked.

Katie nodded mutely. She never had reached a satisfactory answer about that, but over the years the question itself had begun to seem unimportant. They were learning to fight, because someone had to know how, and that knowledge had gradually become its own reward. But Tear was waiting for an answer, so she said, "I thought we were meant to be some kind of police force."

"If only that would solve our problems," Tear replied.

"Why won't it?"

"Police forces are designed to protect the many, not the one."

Katie digested this for a moment, but reached no understanding. She didn't think the Tears meant to speak in riddles; it was merely their way. She considered pretending to understand, then shrugged and asked, "Who's the one?"

"Jonathan."

Katie looked up, her eyes widening. She glanced to her right and found Jonathan watching her, his gaze coolly amused.

"Protect him from what?" she asked.

"That's the bitch of it. No one knows." Jonathan threw a wry glance at his father, who smiled back. "Magic is wonderful, but it never works when you need it."

Katie frowned, feeling slightly disillusioned. What good was magic that didn't work on command?

"There's a knife out there, hanging over Jonathan's head," Tear replied, "but I can't see it, and neither can he. Jonathan needs protection. He needs guards."

Katie sat back in her chair. She wondered if Tear was having her on, but there was no joke in his eyes, and beneath Jonathan's smile, she sensed a dark pocket of worry. Jonathan was a great one for gallows humor, but even in their brief conversations, Katie had observed that he used such humor defensively.

"All of us?" she asked.

"As many as you choose."

"Me?"

"A guard needs a leader, Katie."

"I thought you were our leader."

Tear paused, looking to Lily, who shrugged and poured herself another glass of water. Tear turned back to Katie, and she saw something grim and hopeless in his eyes, the look of a doomed man with his fingers full of straw.

"I'm leaving."

"Leaving where?"

"Leaving the Town."

Katie gaped at him, once again sure that he must be joking. But Lily and Jonathan were both staring at the table, and in their downcast gazes, Katie sensed the ghost of many arguments, already lost.

"This community is a good one," Tear continued. "I believe in it. But the White Ship was a terrible loss. We have medics and midwives, and they're doing hero's work, but we need doctors. We need medicine."

"Why?"

"We're running out of diaphragms, for a start."

Katie blushed, dropping her gaze so that she wouldn't have to look at Jonathan. Mum had taken her to Mrs. Johnson, the midwife, when she was fourteen, just like every other girl in town, and Katie had come out with a diaphragm and instructions on how to use it. It had never occurred to her that there wasn't an inexhaustible supply of such things.

"I had hoped that the doctors would be able to find a substitute for birth control here, something in the local plant life, before we ran out. But now we have no doctors, no chemists. We have no one who knows how to perform an abortion. Think on that for a moment."

"Where can you find doctors?"

"Across the ocean."

Katie was already shaking her head, because this was a mistake. Tear shouldn't leave the Town now, not when there was so much whispering and muttering, so much discontent.

"Can't someone else go across the ocean? Why does it have to be you?"

Tear and Lily looked at each other, almost furtively, and then Tear replied, "No. It has to be me."

"Why?"

Tear took a deep breath, then turned to Jonathan and Lily. "Leave us alone for a moment."

The two of them got up from the table and disappeared into the living room, Lily closing the door behind them.

"You know the Crossing as a simple matter of sailing across the ocean," Tear murmured. "But it was more complex than that. I have to be on the ship."

Katie didn't understand this, but she thought it explained at least one thing: why, in the large, illustrated atlas in the library, she had never been able to find the new world, the Town. From all she understood, the new world should have been right in the middle of the Atlantic Ocean, but there was nothing there, only tiny archipelagos. None of the adults would talk about it, and Katie knew now that she'd been right: the Crossing was a secret, deliberately kept.

"A long time ago," Tear continued, "I made a great mistake, an error of judgment. I didn't even know how large it was at the time."

"What error?"

"We put all the medical staff on the same ship," Tear replied. The pallor that Katie had noticed earlier had deepened now, and his face looked ghastly, almost skeletal, in the candlelight. "I assumed that all of the danger would come before the Crossing, not after. When the storm hit us, I knew. I *knew*. But it was too late. We all watched the White Ship go down. I couldn't save them."

Katie nodded. Everyone knew about the White Ship.

"Now the Town suffers for my mistake."

"We're not suffering!" Katie protested. All her life, Mrs. Johnson had taken care of her, through illness and injury, and she had done fine. People died of illness sometimes, but they were usually old. The Town's population had doubled since the Landing.

"We suffer," Tear repeated, and Katie wondered if he had even heard her. His hand gripped the tablecloth, twisting it. "I failed, and my mistake has come back to haunt me."

"What do you mean?" Katie demanded. Normally, she would not have dared to demand answers of William Tear, but in this moment he seemed almost like a child in a daydream. If he had been anyone else, she would have slapped him to snap him out of it.

"Lily's pregnant."

Katie stared at him, startled. She had always thought of Jonathan's mum as young, but she had to be at least forty, maybe more. That was old to have a baby, but not impossible. Many women in town had done it.

"Nyssa says she's three months along," Tear continued. "She's healthy right now, but it's going to be a difficult birth, and dangerous." He swallowed. "She may not survive it, either way. But she'll have a better chance if we have an obstetrician."

Katie narrowed her eyes. The Town didn't need a doctor; *Lily* needed a doctor, and now William Tear—the same William Tear who had always told them to think of community before themselves—was going to charge off in search of one, leaving the Town behind.

Selfish, she thought, watching him narrowly. *And do you know it? Are you lying to me, or to yourself?*

Tear didn't answer, but Katie thought that some of what she'd been thinking must have gone through, because he dropped his gaze.

"I see what you're thinking," he told her. "You think this is about me."

Katie wanted to say yes, but she couldn't bring herself to go so far.

"You don't understand, Katie. The White Ship has been with me for almost twenty years. You're young, but smart enough, I think, to understand the need to right a wrong."

Katie didn't, but strangely, in that moment, her anger faded. It was no small thing, to see an idol teetering, but Tear's lessons were still true, and no one had the right to judge the pain of another. Katie had learned that long before she ever stepped foot in Tear's classroom.

He doesn't need to be perfect, she decided suddenly. *The* idea *is perfect, and the idea is bigger than the man.*

"Don't go," she begged for the last time. "Not now, not when the Town is so weak."

"I have to go."

"The religious people . . . they're getting worse—"

"I know that."

"Why don't you stop them, then?" she blurted. "Why don't you make them stop?"

"Then I would be a dictator, Katie. I can discourage, but no more."

Katie paused, furious. Her first thought was that the Town *needed* a dictator, needed someone to step in and stop the bad behavior . . . but that was Row's voice again. She swallowed the words, looking down at her lap.

"When will you leave?"

"Next month," Tear replied. "As soon as the harvest is finished."

"Alone?"

"No. Madeleine will come with me. I'm leaving your mother in charge."

"Then let me come too."

"No. You need to stay here. Stay here and protect Jonathan."

Katie frowned. She didn't like to think of Jonathan in danger, but the idea of many people protecting only one, or even two, seemed to go against the very grain of the Town.

"You pick your own people," Tear told her. "Anyone in our classes. I would say five or six at most; any more will be unwieldy."

"When do we start?"

"When I leave."

"What about the people who don't make the cut? How do we keep it a secret?"

Tear began to reply, but Jonathan cut him off; he had returned to stand in the doorway. "It's too late for that. Everyone will know, sooner or later. An armed guard is hard to hide."

"Why me?" she asked, looking between the two of them. "I'm the smallest of us. Lear is smarter. Virginia's tougher. Gavin's better with a knife. Why me?"

"Because I trust you, Katie," Jonathan said simply. "I've been watching all of you for years, and you're the one who doesn't change course with the wind."

This was news to Katie, who thought she changed her mind all the time, and sometimes for the most ridiculous reasons. She wanted to disabuse Jonathan, but Tear was nodding agreement, and the idea that they saw her so differently from the way she saw herself stunned her into silence. Later, she would think that it was as if she'd known that this was coming all along, that there had always been something much larger here than nine children in a clearing, playing with knives. The past three years had only been preparation for the next phase.

Jonathan moved forward, extending a hand across the table, but for a moment, Katie could only stare at him, this odd unknown, her eccentric classmate, strange sometimes friend who didn't get along with anyone and didn't want to. At times she sensed William Tear's grandeur in him, masked, carefully hidden because being a Tear was dangerous, because in the days to come all of the Tears would have a target on their backs—

How do you know that?

Jonathan's hand closed over hers, and Katie blinked, her mind suddenly filled with a vision: she and Jonathan, alone in a lightless place. He released her hand and, mercifully, the vision faded. But the feel of his hand did not; Katie felt as though she'd been branded.

What happened to me?

Her mind returned an answer immediately, unbidden, as though from a deep well that stood outside Katie's control. She was bonded to Jonathan now, and she suddenly understood that she had taken on much more than an internship, or even a career. A tiny, cowardly voice spoke up inside, protesting that this was too much, that she was only seventeen, but Katie fought the voice, furious. She had always known this was a serious business, even at fourteen, sitting with Tear on the bench in her backyard. She had promised to protect the Town, but William Tear and the Town had always been inextricably intertwined. Now Tear was leaving, and all the Town would have left was Jonathan, an unknown.

I'm a guard, Katie thought. Jonathan might reject the title—and he wouldn't be the only one—but she was a guard protecting a prince. She thought of the incessant whispering she heard everywhere now: discontent, avarice, judgment. Superstition creeping into the Town like tendrils of mist. The air of trust and goodwill that had been an omnipresent part of Katie's childhood seemed to have drained away from the Town, little by little, and now it was almost gone.

"You've made a good choice," Tear told Jonathan. "If she guards your back half as well as her mother guarded mine, you should be safe as houses."

He smiled at Katie, but Katie couldn't smile back, for a terrible premonition was suddenly upon her, a certainty she could not shake, and it seemed to seize her heart.

"Katie? Are you all right?"

She nodded, forcing a smile, but she wasn't all right. She knew, and Jonathan knew too; his dark eyes were grim as he met her gaze across the table.

William Tear wasn't coming back.

K atie."

She looked up from her book. She had come out into the middle of the woods to read, in a quiet area that she and Row had discovered as children: a small, relatively flat clearing, ringed by oaks, on the western slope. But she hadn't seen Row here in ages.

"What are you reading?" he asked.

Katie lifted her book to show him the cover. She had just been getting to the good part, but she was just as happy to put the book down for a while. King's work could always scare her, even on a bright sunny day. Row dropped down beside her, and as he sat, Katie caught sight of a flash at his throat.

"What's that?"

Row held the pendant up, and she saw that it was a crucifix, bright silver on a fine chain. Katie felt a tremor of disquiet; it had been so long since she and Row had actually talked. Even though

Row had finished school, they ran into each other often. But the days when the two of them would spend an entire weekend together, out of sight of the rest of the Town, were long gone.

"What's that for?"

Row shrugged. "I've been saved."

"You're kidding me."

"Nope. I'm a bona fide believer."

Katie looked up sharply, but relaxed as she saw the twinkle in his eye.

"It must have taken quite a while to save *you*, Row."

"Oh, it did. I had to confess my sins."

"To who?"

"Brother Paul."

"*Brother* Paul?"

"I'm part of his congregation."

She stared at him, waiting for a sign that he was joking, but none came, and her relief melted away. Brother Paul was undoubtedly Paul Annescott, who fancied himself a Bible scholar. He had reading groups in his home every week, but they were supposed to be academic, not religious. Katie wondered what William Tear would think if he knew there was an active Christian congregation in town . . . but no, Tear had said he would not intercede.

"You're no more Christian than I am, Row. What is this?"

"I've been saved," he repeated.

"Does that mean you'll stop sleeping with half the town?"

"I've left my impure ways behind," he replied, with a grin that Katie couldn't decipher. She felt as though he were inviting her in on a joke that she couldn't identify. When *was* the last time they'd been together, just the two of them? It had to be at least six months gone.

"What do you want, Row?"

"I'm leaving next week."

Katie's jaw dropped. Her first thought was that Row was going with Tear, but no, Tear would never take him along. After a moment she realized what he meant.

"You're going on the mountain expedition?"

"Yes."

Katie nodded, but that touch of disquiet inside her intensified. Jen Devlin's expedition had been meant to leave this week, but they had pushed the date back now that Tear was leaving too. He had announced his plans to cross the ocean at meeting last week, and predictably, the Town had erupted in protest. Everyone seemed to sense disaster, but even the pleas of the entire Town could not sway Tear to stay.

"You're no explorer, Row. What do you want with Jen's expedition?"

"I want to get away."

This made sense. The closer Row drew to moving out, the more officious his mother became. When Row was at work at the shop, Mrs. Finn would show up with something she claimed he'd forgotten, his lunch or his jacket. When Row went out with friends, his mother could sometimes be seen following him, tagging along perhaps a hundred feet behind, her eyes squeezed down into small, jealous triangles. Mum said Mrs. Finn was becoming unhinged, and it made perfect sense that Row would want to get clear of her hawklike vigilance; even the mountain expedition seemed like a good choice, since Mrs. Finn wasn't hardy enough to attempt such a journey. Everything was utterly plausible, but Katie, who knew Row well, sensed a great falsity in his answer, some other reason glimmering just beneath. She wanted to dig for it, grab his shirt and demand the truth, but even then, he might not tell her. And Katie suddenly realized just how far their friendship had eroded in the past few years. She had no idea what Row was thinking, what he meant to do. The effortless simpatico they had enjoyed when they were younger was gone, and now Katie could only imagine what lay beneath that angel's face. For a terrible moment, she wondered whether she had ever known Row, or whether she had simply invented the boy she thought she knew from whole cloth. Nothing seemed certain any longer.

"I'm going to miss you, Katie."

She looked up and found Row watching her, a small smile playing on his lips.

"I'll miss you too, Row," she replied, not sure whether she meant it. After Tear left, she would begin guarding Jonathan in earnest, and though she had never guarded a person before, she understood the security problems posed by uncertainty. Her mind tipped sideways, and for a moment she was standing in the woods, staring at a monster in the moonlight. Uncertainty was dangerous, and Row was nothing if not a wild card.

What is a childhood friendship really worth? she wondered, staring at the ground. *How much loyalty do I owe?*

"When will you be back?"

"Jen estimates two months, three if we get caught in bad weather. They saw snow on top of those mountains, and that was in spring."

"Well," Katie said awkwardly, and in that awkwardness she felt as though a door was closing somewhere, walling off everything that had come before, all of the times they had snuck away from their parents and decided to run away, the forts they had built in each other's backyards, the times Row had helped her with her maths homework, all the way back to that day against the wall of the schoolhouse when Row had smoothed a hand over her aching scalp and made her forget that someone had been cruel. The door closed, deep in her mind, with a hollow boom that Katie heard rather than felt, and when she blinked, she found that her eyes were full of tears. Row opened his arms and she stumbled into them, trying not to weep. Row wasn't crying; she wouldn't either.

"Be safe, Row," she told him.

"You too, Rapunzel," he replied, smiling. Reaching for one of her long curls, he gave it a tug, then turned and walked back into the woods, heading east, toward town.

He never apologized, Katie realized suddenly. *All these years and he never apologized for stranding me there and leaving me for that thing—*

The thought tried to crystallize, to become anger, but before it could, Katie shoved it away. She still loved Row; she always would. She would miss him while he was in the mountains.

But why is he going to the mountains? her mind demanded, hammering her with the question, refusing to relent. *Why is he going to the mountains, Katie? Why is he going to the—*

"Shut up," Katie whispered, and picked up her book.

Three weeks passed, then four, and still William Tear did not return.

Katie knew that Tear was dead. She had no gift of vision; the answer was much simpler. She knew because Jonathan knew. He still kept himself very close, but by now, Katie had learned to read him better than anyone, to parse his words, to extrapolate from the little he revealed. In the fifth week, when the knock came on Jonathan's door in the middle of the night, it was Katie who answered, because she knew.

The woman outside the door was almost unrecognizable as Aunt Maddy. She was in the final stages of starvation, each bone visible in her pallid face, even by candlelight. When Katie grabbed her arm, Aunt Maddy's skin burned beneath her fingers. Katie's mind registered these things, but even then her first priority was to get Aunt Maddy inside, to get the door closed. She knew that Aunt Maddy was dying, because no one could survive the condition Katie saw before her. But even in that early moment, some part of Katie had already focused on the greater priority: keeping a secret.

Aunt Maddy told them her story in a hoarse, rasping voice, her skeletal hands clasped in front of her. All of the muscle that had roped her body was gone now, and her forearms were little more than twigs.

"He couldn't do it," she murmured, and though she didn't look at any of them, Katie knew that she was talking to Lily. "You remember last time, it almost took everything out of him. Whether he was too old, or whether it was harder in the other direction, I don't know. But I saw that he wasn't going to make it, that he would kill himself trying. I tried to help him, grabbed his hand, thought he could draw on me for some of it. And he did. But it still didn't work. The door wouldn't open."

Katie didn't understand much of this, but a quick look around showed that she was the only one in the dark. Jonathan and Lily wore identical expressions of resignation, their eyes downcast.

"In the end, I saw that it was killing him. He knew it too, because he shoved me away. But before he died, he gave me this."

She reached into her pocket and came up with Tear's sapphire, dangling on its fine silver chain. The chain had become tangled, the silver dulled by tarnish, but the jewel gleamed as brightly as ever.

"He told me to give it to you," Aunt Maddy croaked, offering it to Jonathan. "And now I have."

Jonathan took the jewel on his palm and stared at it for a long time. Katie could usually tell what he was thinking, but in this moment, she had no idea. At some point, Lily had gotten up and left the room, and now she came back with a plate, piled high with bread and cheese. But Maddy only stared at the food for a moment, then looked up at them, her eyes dark and flat. "I'm dying. I know I am. I made it back here because I had his share of the food, but whatever he pulled out of me, it's gone forever. Every day I weaken."

"What about his body?" Lily asked.

"Gone," Aunt Maddy replied. "I had to dump it overboard."

At this, Lily turned away and didn't speak. Jonathan was still staring at the jewel in his hand. Katie longed to grieve for William Tear, but she could not, for Tear himself had already directed her thoughts toward the more important issue: how would this affect Jonathan? What would the Town do when it found out that Tear was dead? The others might not have traveled so far in their thinking, but a deep part of Katie's mind had already grasped the implications and begun to think of concealment.

"We can't tell anyone," Aunt Maddy announced, and Katie looked up gratefully.

"What are you talking about?" Lily asked. "We can't keep this a secret."

"Of course we can," Aunt Maddy replied, her rasping voice closing off all argument. "This is the last thing the Town needs right now."

Katie nodded. William Tear had always been the stopgap for the worst impulses of the Town. Without him, there would be nothing to stand in the way of Paul Annescott or any one of the countless other forces grappling for influence. Sooner or later, people would conclude that Tear was dead, but even uncertainty was preferable to the facts.

"How can we keep something like that a secret?" Lily demanded. "What will people say when they see you've come back without him?"

"They won't see anything. I don't have long." Aunt Maddy pushed herself up from the sofa. Even in the soft candlelight, Katie fancied that she could see the bones of Aunt Maddy's arms through her skin. "I'm leaving. Now, before the sun comes up."

"You can't!" Aunt Lily cried, her voice cracking.

"Lil." Aunt Maddy grabbed her shoulder, squeezing it until Lily winced. "Stop."

"But where will you go?"

"It doesn't matter," Aunt Maddy replied. "This is more important than either of us. It always was, and you knew it as well as I did. He told me you were always one of us, even way back then, in Boston."

She turned and limped down the hallway.

"She's right, Mum," Jonathan said quietly, turning the sapphire over in his hands. "Dad dead, and this town falls apart."

"We have to stop her!" Lily insisted. But neither Katie nor Jonathan moved, and when Lily made to get up, Katie grabbed her arm and pulled her back down. A few seconds later, the front door clicked shut, and Lily began to sob. Katie wanted to cry as well, for William Tear, for Aunt Maddy, and even more, for what they had all lost, the entire Town. But in the face of Jonathan's stoicism, she had no choice but to swallow her own tears, turning her thoughts to the immediate future.

No one was ready to hear that William Tear was dead. Tear had left Mum in charge, but that was an interim solution; Mum was not the woman to hold the Town together for the long term. It would have to be Jonathan, but the Town wasn't ready to accept that either. Aunt Maddy was right. Tear's death would have to be concealed at all costs. Katie was a guard now, and secrets were her business, but a rogue part of her mind could not help wishing that this charge had fallen to someone else. She loved the Town, and she was no good at telling lies.

You'll learn, Tear whispered inside her head, and Katie shivered, realizing the truth of that voice: she was working for a dead man now.

Chapter 9

Flight

Even at this late date, we have been unable to discover any con-
clusive proof of the origins of the Red Queen. This historian be-
lieves that she was born in one of the small villages of northern
Mortmesne, but this is guesswork only, for how can we research
a woman about whom so little is known, not even her true name?
  —*The Tearling as a Military Nation*, CALLOW THE MARTYR

When the Queen woke, she lay still for a moment. She was sure she'd heard something, a rustling on the far wall. Once, during a particularly cold winter, the Palais had become infested with rats. They'd taken care of it with poison bait, but perhaps the rodents had come back.

They have indeed.

The Queen's mouth stretched in a cold smile. More of her people deserted every day. Her throne room had not been cleaned for a week, since most of the Palais cleaning staff had run off. Half of her own personal Guard could not be found. Ghislaine, her Guard captain, was the only reason the Queen dared to sleep; at this moment, Ghislaine stood watch outside her chamber door. Beyond her windows, she could hear the distant sounds of battle in the city. Demesne was in anarchy.

That odd, rustling sound came again.

The Queen uttered a low curse and reached for her candle. She slept very little at night anyway; it was so much easier to fall asleep in the daytime, in the light. The room beyond her covers was ice-cold, full of drafts from the many broken windows in the Palais. Three weeks ago, the King of Cadare had missed his first shipment in more than twenty years. Even the thought of it made the Queen's blood boil. The old bastard had sensed her weakness, and the Queen, who had not had to worry about Cadare for years, suddenly had a problem on her southern border. Glass, once cheaper than food on the streets of Demesne, was about to become a priceless commodity, and the Queen, who had once had the best-insulated bedroom in the kingdom, now shivered beneath her blankets. The treasury couldn't spare the money to repair windows. The Palais was wide open to the early winter air, as well as whatever vermin might crawl inside.

The Queen found her matches, sat up, and lit the candle. Her chamber looked as always, crimson walls and furniture. They'd had to replace almost all of the furnishings after the dark thing's fire this past summer, but her furnishers had done an admirable job, making the new room almost identical to the old. Where were those furnishers now? Fled, most likely, to join Levieux and his band of traitors. A civil war raged in Demesne, and on some days the Queen could convince herself that she was winning. But most days she knew she was not.

This is what the fall feels like, the Queen thought, wrapping herself in her robe. As a child, she had read her history; her nurse, Wright, had forced her to read many pages on the fall of dictators throughout the world. But no one ever mentioned how soporific the experience was, almost narcotic, like being lulled to sleep. She was fighting an invisible enemy, one who did not announce his victories but stole away into the night. Gradually, more and more of her city was being annexed by Levieux and his rebels, and she only found out about specific incursions after the deed was done. Paralysis was setting in, for it was easy, so damned easy, to simply sit here, barricaded in, clutching her crown, her throne, until someone came and took them away.

On her bedside table, twinkling darkly in the candlelight, lay the two Tear sapphires, and the Queen stared at them for a long moment, hearing the girl's voice inside her head: *You lost.*

Yes, she had lost. Whatever the girl had done, she had done it well. The sapphires were a broken tool, just like Ducarte. When the Red Queen went to bed, Ducarte had been down the hall, closeted with several of the Queen's generals. To the outward eye, it looked like a strategy meeting, but the Queen knew what it really was: hiding. All of her generals were now hunted, for it was common knowledge that she had compensated them out of the treasury. If the regular army got hold of any of the high command, their fates would be no prettier than her own.

More rustling from the far wall.

With a sigh, the Queen tucked the sapphires into her pocket, then tiptoed toward the far corner of the room. If a rat was here, she would kill it. There was nowhere for it to hide, except beneath the bed or the sofa. As a child, she used to kill rats to pass the time when she was left alone.

Evie!

She placed her fingers against her temples, willing the voice away. But these days, it seemed that all the power in the world would not give her command of her own mind. Her mother's voice was always there, hectoring, criticizing, finding fault. The girl had woken the Beautiful Queen, and she would not go back to sleep. The floor was freezing against the Queen's feet, and she cast around for her slippers, finding them beneath her desk. She was halfway across the room when the rustling came again, directly over her head.

Evie!

The Queen looked up and felt her blood turn to ice.

There was a little girl on the ceiling. Her thin limbs were white and bloodless. Her grimy fingers appeared to be latched to the wood, allowing her to cling there like an insect. Her back faced the Queen, dark hair hanging beneath her. She was dressed in rags.

The Queen forced herself to take a deep breath, deep enough to make her muscles unlock. She backed toward the wall and the little girl followed, scuttling across the ceiling like a spider. The rustling sound was the child's knees, scraping against the wood. It reached the join of wall and ceiling and began to crawl down the wall. Again the Queen thought of a spider, not the webbed spiders of southern Mortmesne but the hunting spiders of the Fairwitch foothills, which would stalk their prey for long minutes across grass and rocks. They were slow in the early going, but could move like lightning as they closed in.

Keeping her eyes on the girl, the Queen backed toward her desk. She had a knife in the top drawer, though she was unsure whether a knife would be of any value here. This creature belonged to the dark thing; she could sense the similarity in the strange, shifting texture of the girl's form. Not wholly solid, this child, almost as though she were not real, and the Queen, who had the ability to turn a man inside out in a hundred different ways, could not find anywhere on the child's body to begin. If she could not reach it with her mind, then she was unlikely to reach it with a weapon, but a knife was better than nothing, and she fumbled in the drawer, pushing aside paper and pens and stamps, searching for the sharp edge of the blade. She tried to call up what she remembered from conversations with the dark thing, so long ago when they had been allies . . . or at least, when it had still considered her useful. There wasn't much. The dark thing had taught her a great deal, but about its own history, the strange transformation that had made it what it was, it remained silent.

The girl reached the bottom of the wall and clambered to her feet. The Queen shuddered, for she recognized the rags the girl wore: remnants of one of the cheap blue uniforms that had once been used to clothe auctioned slaves. But Mortmesne hadn't used such uniforms for more than forty years, long before Broussard's tenure as Auctioneer. This child would have been in one of the earliest loads sent north to the Fairwitch, back when a much younger Queen of Mortmesne still thought she could placate the dark thing, buy him off with homeless children culled from the city streets. The girl's eyes were dark and empty, and when she spoke, her voice was hoarse, as though she hadn't used it in a long time.

"I don't want to go," she rasped. "Don't make me get on the wagon."

The Queen scooted away, around the back end of the sofa. She tested the girl again, gently, pushing with her mind, and found that she had been right: the girl's flesh was like the dark thing's, low and humming like a hive, not entirely there. The Queen looked down at her candle, wondering if the girl would burn . . . but no. Nothing that belonged to the dark thing would ever be vulnerable to flame.

"I want my Maman," said the girl, her voice plaintive. "Where are we going?"

"You're no ghost," the Queen countered. "You're a pawn. He told you to say this to me."

The girl vaulted over the edge of the sofa, reminding the Queen again of a hunting spider. The child's size was deceptive; it had tricked the Queen into expecting a child's speed and reflexes. The Queen backed across the room, nearly stumbling on the hem of her nightgown, and the girl darted forward, her blank face becoming eager and hungry. The Queen suddenly remembered a long night out in the Fairwitch, the snow steeping into drifts and the wind howling across the frozen wastes of the mountainside. The dark thing had wrapped her with fire, keeping her warm, and the Queen had been astonished to find that even though she was inside the blaze, she felt no pain. She had reached up to touch the flames, and the dark thing had grabbed her hand.

Don't be fooled by the reprieve, he told her. *In the end, we all burn.*

"Burn," the Queen whispered, almost wondering. Her entire acquaintance with the Orphan had been a history of fire held in abeyance, but now the flames were upon her.

She turned and fled for the door, heard the slap of the girl's running feet right behind her. She got the door open and slipped through, but then her trailing hand was seized as though in a vise, and she screamed as she felt the girl's teeth sink into the flesh of her wrist. She caught a wild glimpse of the sofa beside her doorway, and there was Ghislaine, dead, his skin bleach-white. The cushions beneath him were soaked with blood.

We all burn.

"Not yet," the Queen snarled. She jerked her arm forward, ramming the girl's head against the far side of the door, and felt the teeth dislodge from her wrist. Then she was fleeing down the corridor toward her audience chamber, the rabbit-patter of the girl's feet right behind her. The hallway in front of her was empty and endless.

What can I do? the Queen wondered. She recognized the voice of incipient panic, but could not seem to control it.

Where is everyone?

Through an open doorway on her left, she saw several of her generals piled against the far wall, their limbs haphazard, as though they had been thrown there. Blood had puddled and trailed on the chamber floor.

I heard nothing, the Queen thought, almost marveling, before the girl caught the trailing end of her robe and the Queen was suddenly jerked backward, landing painfully and thumping her head on the floor. The girl jumped on top of her, giggling, the laugh of a child playing a particularly good game. The Queen grabbed the child's throat, holding her off, but the girl was stronger than a man, and she wriggled free of the Queen's grasp. The Queen summoned what strength she had and shoved the girl away, across the corridor to slam into the wall, but a moment later the girl was back up again, her grimy face full of white teeth. She didn't even appear dazed.

Can't win, the Queen realized. Already, she felt herself weakening. Her wrist was pouring blood; she pressed it against the waist of her robe, trying to staunch the flow, and felt something hard and unyielding in her pocket: the Tear sapphires.

"You are fun to hunt," the girl lisped, her eyes no longer dull and lifeless but bright, sparkling with a glee so dark it was almost madness. "More fun than the others."

The Queen turned and fled down the corridor. Behind her came the girl, giggling. The Queen reached a connecting door and slammed it behind her, then turned and ran, the breath tearing from her throat. Behind her, she heard a cracking sound as wood shattered, but she was nearly to the door of her throne room now, and that door was made of good Mort steel with an answering steel deadlock. It would not hold forever, but it would give her some breathing room, time to figure out what to do. She stumbled through the door, limping, gasping, and slammed it shut behind her, shooting the bolt.

Behind her came the sound of stifled gasping. The Queen turned and found a naked man and woman on her throne, intertwined, oblivious to her entrance.

"On my throne," the Queen murmured, her voice a series of ghastly echoes that faded into the far corners of the room. The woman looked up and the Queen saw that it was Juliette, her brow shining with sweat.

"M-Majesty," she stammered.

"On my throne!" the Queen howled, her wounds and weakness forgotten; even the child forgotten. She shoved out with her mind, flinging Juliette across the room and into the far wall. Juliette's spine shattered and she fell to the floor, her corpse still twitching.

The Queen turned to the man, curled up now on the throne, clutching his legs, trying to shield his rapidly wilting erection. The spectacle was so sad that the Queen began to laugh. She thought he was one of the Palais guards, but could not be sure, and either way he seemed so insignificant that the Queen could not even recover her anger. Normally, the throne room would have a full complement of guards, even in the middle of the night. But not now. The Queen ignored the man as he crept off the throne and crouched behind it, his terrified eyes peeping over the arm. She turned to Juliette's broken body and felt a brief moment of regret; even Julie would have been better help than no one at all.

A thundering blow slammed against the steel door of the throne room. The Queen looked around wildly, seeking any weapon, only to realize the futility of that; no sword would take the girl down. Even her own magic was not enough. She reached into her pocket and pulled out the Tear sapphires; perhaps now, in her peril, they would respond . . . but nothing. Their power was as far beyond her reach as ever. Only one person knew how to use them.

Another blow at the door. This time, the impact sent a long blister down the steel surface. The Queen turned and fled, through the great double doors, into the wide hallway that led to the Main Gate. She could not go out the Gate; a massive mob had been gathered around the Palais for days, a mob that would probably tear her to pieces if given an opportunity. But there were other routes out of the castle; the Queen, who believed in prudence, had prepared well for this day, though she had believed it would never come.

Running, her mind whispered as she ran, her bare feet slapping against the flat stones of the hallway. *Running away*. The idea made the Queen snarl, but she could not deny it. She *was* running, fleeing the seat of her power, the Palais she had built brick by brick. The construction had taken more than fifteen years, and she had given the architect, a man named Klunder, a lifetime pension for his work. The Palais was the seat of her government, but it was much more than that: it was the place that had allowed her to forget her youth, to wash away her childhood in the Tearling, to build her own history from scratch. She could not believe how quickly the fall had come.

Ahead of her, around the next corner, a man screamed, and she heard the sounds of a struggle, muffled by the thick stone walls. Her feet slowed automatically, and she turned to look behind her. There was only a long, empty hallway, dappled with patches of darkness where the torches had been allowed to burn out. But now, distant and yet not too distant, she heard a high, happy giggle.

Damned either way.

The Queen took off running again, breath tearing from her throat. But as she careened around the corner, her feet came together in a flat halt.

Some twenty feet in front of her was Ducarte, veering madly from side to side, bashing himself against the walls. Two children, a boy and a girl, were attached to his body; they twined around him like serpents, hands and arms seemingly everywhere, and Ducarte screamed as the girl bit into the back of his neck. The Queen remained frozen for a long moment, trying to sort out what she was seeing—did they drink blood, these children, or were they trying to feed?—but then the giggle came again, and the Queen whirled around. There was nothing behind her, but the sound had been very close.

Ducarte stumbled to his knees, and the boy made a low, growling noise, the satisfied grunt of an animal that had brought down prey. The Queen could not outrun these children forever; they were too strong, and while the scattered reports from northern Mortmesne had become increasingly bizarre over the past month, they were very clear on one thing: there were a lot of these things, too many to repel. The Queen needed help, but her only ally was dying before her eyes.

You lost.

The Queen's eyes opened wide. She had thought she was out of options, but no. One remained. She felt suddenly galvanized, new life in her legs. Leaving Ducarte to his fate, she turned right and darted down a nearby staircase, heading for the dungeons.

The man in the next cell knew more science than anyone Kelsea had ever met, including Carlin. His name was Simon, and he had been a slave since his sixteenth year. Upon his arrival in Mortmesne, he had been sold from master to master for heavy labor, until his fifth master finally realized that Simon had a great aptitude for building and fixing. The next sale had been to a scientist, a man who designed weapons for the Mort army. The scientist—whom Simon spoke of with real affection—had also loaned Simon out to several like-minded men, all of whom had taught him something. Elementary physics, a bit of chemistry, even the properties of plants, a subject on which Simon seemed to know as much as Barty. He had quickly surpassed his new master and begun to design more complex offensive weapons. It had not taken long for him to come to the Red Queen's attention.

"The footbridges?" Kelsea asked. "The platforms the Mort used to cross the river. Were those your handiwork?"

"A group effort," Simon replied. "The design was mine, but I needed the help of a physicist to understand weight ratios and leverage. My gifts are mechanical, not theoretical."

"Yet you made a printing press," Kelsea mused, still marveling at the idea.

"It's a simple press, hand-operated. But it will output twenty pages a minute if run properly. The hourly rate goes down, as you need to include loading time for the plates. And each page needs at least several minutes to dry properly; someday a better man than I will invent ink that doesn't smear."

"Twenty pages a minute," Kelsea repeated faintly. The man on the far side of the wall seemed suddenly more valuable than all the gems in Cadare.

It was the middle of the night, but Kelsea had been awake for more than two hours. Emily, the page, sat outside her cell, apparently standing guard. It was almost like having Mace himself there, except that Emily had fallen asleep, her knife clutched in her hand.

Kelsea's mind continued to run busily on the same track it had run so many times before: what were the sapphires, really? Why could she use them, when the Red Queen could not? The small chunk of sapphire from Katie's world was in Kelsea's lap, but it merely lay there, inert. She felt that she was very close to an answer of some kind, but every time she reached out to grasp it, it danced just beyond her reach. The dungeon was wearing on her, on her ability to think critically. A few more months in here, and even rudimentary thinking might feel like slogging through mud. She lashed a vicious kick at the bars, hating them, hating the Red Queen, the Palais around her, this cursed country, all of them conspiring to keep her from her home.

"You'll break your foot doing that," Simon remarked mildly, and Kelsea drew her feet beneath her with a low oath. She sensed a storm brewing, but whether that storm gathered in the present, the future, or the past, she could not say. William Tear's town was beginning to crumble. Kelsea looked down at the rock in her lap, considering it. So much sapphire underlying the Tearling; was it all the same? And did it even matter? Tear had understood his sapphire, controlled its power, so much better than Kelsea did, but he still hadn't been able to save his town, or his son. A few more years, and the dark-eyed boy who only wanted what was best for everyone would be dead.

How did Jonathan Tear die?

Kelsea didn't know why, but sometimes she felt that everything hinged on this question. Row Finn was the obvious suspect; even if Katie couldn't put two and two together, Kelsea could. Corpses stolen, silver stolen, Row's bright fascination with Tear's jewel . . . Kelsea would have bet her kingdom that the second Tear necklace had come from Row's talented metalworking hands, but that wasn't all. In the dark of the Town, Row was up to no good. Katie didn't want to think about these things, but Kelsea could and did.

Who killed Jonathan Tear?

Kelsea frowned at the piece of loose sapphire in her lap. She wished she could speed up Katie's memory, skip over that mental film, but sapphires or no, that had never been within her power. She could only watch and wait. She wondered if she had the power to make Katie kill Row Finn before it was too late—for they were not always divided, Katie and Kelsea; sometimes they blended, in that wholly organic way that Kelsea remembered from those last desperate moments with Lily—but something in her balked at that solution. It seemed too easy. Row was riding a wave in the Town, a wave of discontent and fear, but was he really the cause? Kelsea didn't think so. A part of her wanted to kill Row anyway, just on principle, but she recognized that part very well: the Queen of Spades, forever circling in her mind, always looking for a way back in. Past, present, or future, it made no difference; that side of

Kelsea would be perfectly happy to run through the new world, grinning blackly, meting out justice with a scythe.

"No," Kelsea whispered.

"You've gone very quiet over there," Simon remarked. "Did I put you to sleep?"

"No," Kelsea replied slowly, in a louder voice. "Simon, let me ask you: if you had the chance to go back into history and correct a great evil, would you do so?"

"Ah, the old question."

"Is it?"

"Yes, with a clear answer. Physicists look at it in terms of the butterfly effect."

"What is that?" Kelsea didn't know why she was pursuing this; killing Row was no answer for the Town's troubles. According to history, the Tear assassination was the problem, but there was no guarantee that killing Row would prevent that. She wished she could see everything, know everything, all at once.

"I've only read one book on the subject," Simon told her. "The butterfly effect deals in the tendency of infinitesimal variations to amplify over time. You never play around with history, because the change you thought you were making for the better is likely to cause so many unforeseen ripples that it may well add up to a net loss. Too many variables to control the outcome."

Kelsea considered this for a moment. Simon had presented a scientific argument, but beneath it was a moral question: whether she had the *right* to gamble with the future. In the brief six months she had sat on her throne, she had made many decisions, some good and some disastrous. Two Kelseas warred inside her: the child raised by Barty and Carlin to believe in easy rights and wrongs, and the Queen of Spades, who had come to see everything in shades of dark grey. The Queen of Spades didn't care about moral questions.

"You didn't answer me, Simon. What would *you* do?"

"You mean, would I dice with the chance that something even worse would come along?"

"Yes. Is it a good gamble, or a poor one?"

"I think the outcome would be entirely a matter of chance, of circumstance. Neither a good gamble nor a poor one, but a great gamble, one in which you would stake all, seeking a vast reward that might not materialize even if you did succeed. I am a cautious man, not a gambler. I don't think I would chance it."

Kelsea sat back on her heels, nodding. She saw the argument. Even if she somehow succeeded in killing Row Finn, another Row might simply spring up in his place. Power was a double-edged sword; it didn't make Kelsea any more likely to do the right thing, and oh, the disastrous results when it led her wrong . . . She closed her eyes and there was Arlen Thorne again, his face scrubbed with blood.

"Strange turn of the conversation," said Simon. "Can I ask—"

A hollow boom echoed through the dungeon. Emily woke instantly, jumping to her feet; Kelsea sensed that she, like Mace, was embarrassed to be caught napping. She raised her knife to face the end of the corridor.

"It is them?" Kelsea asked. If, as Emily said, Mace was planning a rescue attempt, it would explain what Emily was doing down here in the middle of the night.

"No." Emily shook her head. "More than a day early."

A fusillade of clanging blows rang through the corridor. It sounded like a child banging pots together, but in the echo-prone environment of the dungeons, the noise was almost deafening, and Kelsea had to clap her hands to her ears until it stopped.

"Is it a mob?" asked Simon from his cell.

Kelsea raised her eyebrows at Emily, who shook her head. According to the page, the Palais was now surrounded by a mob, one selected and directed by Levieux. Mace and the Fetch, working together; Kelsea would have to see it to believe it. As the echoes faded, a woman appeared on the staircase and came sprinting down the corridor.

Mad, was Kelsea's first thought. The woman appeared to be wearing only a robe, and her hair was in disarray. She held a torch just above her head, and it seemed only blind luck that she had not set her own hair on fire. Her breath gasped from her throat, and her eyes were wide and desperate. The hem of her robe was stained with blood.

"Declare yourself!" Emily cried. But a moment later Emily was flung aside like a rag doll, straight into the wall, where she collapsed to the floor. As the woman skidded to a stop in front of her cell, Kelsea's mouth dropped open. No one would have recognized this deranged creature as the Queen of Mortmesne.

"No time," the Red Queen panted. "Right behind me."

She dropped to Emily's inert body and began digging through her pockets. "Key, key, key. Where is it?"

The squeal of wrenching steel echoed down the hall from the stairwell, and a low animal moan emerged from the Red Queen's throat. She took her hands from Emily's pockets, defeated, and sat back on her heels for a moment before moving on to the chain around the woman's neck.

"What is that?" Kelsea asked.

The Red Queen pushed herself to her feet, holding the silver key in her left hand.

"It looks like a child," she murmured, unlocking Kelsea's cell and throwing the door wide open. "But it's not."

She held out her right hand, and there were Kelsea's sapphires on her palm. Kelsea gaped at this offering. The Red Queen's face was calm, but her eyes were wide with panic.

"Help me," she whispered. "Help me, please."

A giggle echoed down the corridor, and the Red Queen jumped. Leaning out of her cell, Kelsea saw a small form, too small to be anything but a child, at the foot of the stairwell. But this child's chin was smeared with red, and it wore a bib of blood.

"You are good at hide-and-seek," the child lisped, her thin voice echoing down the hall. "But I have found you now."

"What is it?" Kelsea whispered.

"One of his. Please." The Red Queen grabbed Kelsea's hand and pressed the sapphires into her palm, and Kelsea realized, astonished, that she was speaking not in Mort, but in Tear.

"Please. They are yours. I give them back."

Kelsea stared at the sapphires in her hand. She had spent so many months longing for her jewels, longing for the ability to punish and retaliate. But now that she had them in hand, she felt exactly the same. All of the power she had drawn from the sapphires, all of that ability to channel her anger into force, it was gone. But there was something there, for now she realized that she could actually tell them apart. The two jewels might appear identical, but they were different, utterly different, two discrete voices inside her head . . .

She had no time to analyze the difference. The child—a little girl, Kelsea saw now—was coming down the corridor, loping on all fours like a wolf, her teeth bared and face twisted in a snarl.

The Red Queen ducked behind Kelsea, clutching her shoulder in an iron grip of terror. Kelsea wondered what she was supposed to do in the two seconds before the child reached them, how on earth she was supposed to have time to make a plan, let alone act . . .

And time slowed down.

Kelsea saw this quite clearly. The child, which had been coming along the corridor at great speed, was suddenly reduced to the lazy velocity of the mud turtles of the Reddick. She moved only by inches.

No hurry at all, Kelsea thought, marveling. *I have all the time in the world.*

She looked down at her sapphires. Different, yes, but connected, wed to each other somehow. One of them was William Tear's sapphire; it spoke to her clearly, not in words but in a flow of images, of ideas, speaking of the good and the light. Tear's sapphire, which had allowed him to master time, to bring them all safely across the Atlantic and God's Ocean. Carlin had always said that Tear's settlers were lucky to stumble on the new world, the equivalent of hitting a bull's-eye on a dartboard in the pitch-black. But that wasn't true at all. William Tear had known exactly where he was going. There was no luck involved, because—

"It came from here," Kelsea whispered, feeling the very rightness of the idea. A piece of Tear sapphire had somehow found its way into the old world, and Kelsea saw its journey clearly, like a story inside her head: passed down from Tear to Tear, hidden and smuggled, sometimes to the far corners of the earth, concealed from the powerful, guarded from the weak. Centuries of Tears, all of them fighting to hold back the darkness, to keep it at bay. Tear's sapphire dealt in time; it had allowed her to slow the ravening child before her, to lengthen the hallway until it was nearly infinite, to see into the past.

How could I ever have thought they were identical?

The difference was like a chasm in her mind. The other jewel's voice was low and hectoring, speaking of petty slights and jealousies and desires, of sneaking and spying, anger and violence. This sapphire had also been passed down through generations of Raleighs, but it had never really belonged to any of them, not even to Kelsea.

Row Finn?

She thought so. Once he saw what Tear's sapphire could do, he would surely have tried to make his own. But he had not succeeded, not entirely, because this jewel was not independent. Kelsea could feel the bond between the two; Tear's sapphire governed in some way that she couldn't fully understand. Kept separate, Row's jewel could do very little, but together . . .

"Carlin," Kelsea whispered. Somehow, Carlin had known, because Row's sapphire had lain around Kelsea's neck all through her childhood—she could almost see all the days of her youth reflected in its glassy surface—while Carlin had kept Tear's sapphire hidden away. And the Fetch had known, too, for he had deliberately withheld Tear's sapphire while Kelsea was being tested. Row's sapphire was capable of small things; in several quick blinks of memory, Kelsea saw the Caden assassin lying on the floor of her bathroom; the Mort camp spread out below her eyes; the woman in the Almont, screaming as her children were taken away. She had been able to see things far away, to defend her own life. These were useful bits of magic. But once the two were a pair again . . .

"Oh," Kelsea gasped, horrified. An entire phalanx of images marched in front of her eyes now: hundreds of soldiers in the Mort army, gone in a spray of blood and bone; the vast web of cuts and slices that had covered her; General Ducarte's face, twisted in agony; a set of open, bleeding cuts on the backs of Mace's hands; and worst of all, Arlen Thorne, who had suffered an even worse life than that of the Red Queen, but somehow deserved no mercy, because . . .

But Kelsea could not even remember what reason she had cobbled together for mutilating Thorne. She remembered doing the deed, remembered black wings opening inside her, a darkness so inviting that a newly crowned Kelsea Glynn, one who seemed years younger in hindsight, had longed to lose herself inside it. But only madness waited there, the same madness that Finn and his ilk had always wanted to inflict on the Tearling . . . greed and callousness, lack of empathy, a narrowing of mind until only one lonely voice was left, surrounded by a void into which it could howl only a single word: *Me.*

With a cry of disgust, Kelsea yanked Finn's sapphire away from Tear's and held it up before her eyes, thinking *I want none of this, I want no part of it, I want my own self back—*

Something enormous wrenched inside her, as though muscle were peeling away from bone, and she suddenly understood. The Red Queen couldn't use the sapphires, not because they belonged to Kelsea, but because there was nothing left to use. Kelsea had drained them dry. The two sides, Tear and Finn, had been warring inside her for months. For a moment Kelsea felt as though her own flesh were pulling apart, as though she would literally split down the middle with the force of that wish to have Row gone, to be Kelsea Glynn again . . .

And then it was done. The great divide inside Kelsea seemed to seal itself closed. She was still angry, yes, but it was *her* anger, the engine that had always powered her, not to punish but to fix, to right wrongs, and the relief of that was so great that Kelsea threw back her head and howled. The scream echoed up the corridor, but to Kelsea it seemed much more powerful than sound, as though it must shake the Palais to its stone foundations. For a moment, she expected the entire building to come crashing down around them.

When she opened her eyes, she found that the child had covered more than half of the distance. Row's sapphire still dangled in front of Kelsea, not dark now, but bright and sparkling, its many facets gleaming, as though asking whether she would like to put it on again, just to try, just to see—

She wrapped her fist around the jewel, blocking out that light, and shoved it back into the Red Queen's hand. An old memory occurred to her: speaking to the Fetch beside a campfire, back when she knew nothing and understood nothing, not even the real import of her own words.

"Keep it, Lady Crimson. I'd rather die clean."

She didn't know whether the Red Queen heard her; the woman remained frozen beside her, her eyes wide, almost mad. Only the faintest twitch of her fingers indicated that she registered the necklace, was beginning to close her hand into a fist.

Casting around, Kelsea found that the page, Emily, was still lying unconscious at their feet, a large blue bruise in bloom at her temple. She could be no help, but beside her limp, curled fingers lay a long dagger, beautifully made. Kelsea grabbed it and found that it was more length than she was used to; Barty's knife, confiscated from Kelsea long ago in the Almont, had been at least two inches shorter. But this was at least a weapon that she could wield.

"It's strong," the Red Queen told her, her words slow and distant. "Stronger than a man."

"Then you'll have to help me," Kelsea replied.

The Red Queen merely stared at her.

"Help me! Do you understand?"

"With this?" The Red Queen lifted Finn's sapphire.

"No. Put that away."

The Red Queen tucked the sapphire away, and Kelsea felt relieved when it was out of her sight.

"I have magic, but it's no match for this creature," the Red Queen admitted. "So what then?"

"Good old brute strength. You help me hold her down, and I shove this dagger in her heart."

The Red Queen shook her head. "These are not the monsters of the pre-Crossing fiction. They are something else."

"Do you have a better idea?"

The girl was only two feet away now, preparing to spring. Kelsea tightened her grip on the dagger, murmuring to herself, almost a prayer.

"I put my trust in fiction."

Then the girl was upon them, and Kelsea felt her pulse jump, time losing its elasticity and snapping back into itself. She had expected the girl to attack her first, since she was armed, but the child ignored Kelsea and sprang for the Red Queen, knocking her flat. The Red Queen forced her away, but Kelsea sensed that the blow was weak; the Red Queen was faltering. Kelsea grabbed the girl's hair, yanking her backward, but she was astounded at the strength of the child; she came, but her hands did not release the Red Queen's shoulders and the Red Queen came with her, all three of them tumbling on the hard stone. The dagger flew from Kelsea's hand, clattering to the floor behind her. She detached herself from the pile and scrambled after it, while behind her, the Red Queen continued to grapple with the girl, cursing in Mort.

The dagger had landed against the bars of Simon's cell. Kelsea grabbed it and looked up to see Simon in front of her, inches away, crouching behind his bars. She had never gotten a good look at him before, and now, despite everything behind her, she froze in shock.

He was General Hall.

But no, she had left Hall in New London, while this man had been imprisoned here for a long time. Hall's brother had gone in the shipment, long ago . . . but Kelsea got no further, for a shriek echoed behind her. The girl had dug her nails into the Red Queen's collarbone, and her mouth was less than an inch from the Red Queen's shoulder. The Red Queen was trying to beat her away, with no success. Her eyes rolled in desperation. Tucking her head low, Kelsea ran at the girl and tackled her, breaking her from the Red Queen and knocking her across the flagstones. The child recovered almost immediately, but Kelsea was ready; she jumped on the girl's left arm, pinning it down, and shoved an elbow up underneath the child's throat, holding her dangerous teeth away.

"Help me!" she shouted at the Red Queen. "Her other arm!"

The Red Queen crawled over. She was injured; Kelsea's mind registered the fact, but there was no time to do anything about it. The girl was writhing beneath her, trying to buck her off, and her strength was unbelievable. Even with the two of them pinning her arms, Kelsea nearly lost the dagger again.

"She's too strong!" she shouted. "*Hold* her, will you?"

The Red Queen nodded, and a moment later Kelsea felt some of the girl's wild strength diminish.

"I've got her," the Red Queen hissed. "But not for long. Hurry up!"

"Father!" the child screamed. "Father, help me!"

One of his, Kelsea's mind repeated, and again she wondered how on earth the boy Rowland Finn, charming and selfish, had traveled the long road to this place. Her hands shook, but she held fast to the dagger, planting one of her knees in the girl's rib cage to stop her wriggling.

"Stop, Majesty!" Simon shouted from his cell. "She's a child!"

"No child," Kelsea panted. She took a good grip on the dagger. Rogue thought—*What if Carlin could see me now?*—drifted through her head, but she ignored it and brought the dagger down. The blade slipped smoothly into the center of the girl's chest.

The child screamed, a terrible sound, both human agony and the wretched squealing of an animal caught in a trap. Her body bucked and spasmed, and both Kelsea and the Red Queen were hurled backward. Kelsea heard a hollow boom as her head hit the bars of Simon's cell, such a resounding impact that her teeth clattered together. There was no pain; Kelsea waited for it, but before it could come, she tumbled into the dark.

General Hall had always hated this plan. For one thing, they were relying on Levieux, the phantom of Mortmesne, and nothing that Hall had heard about Levieux was a comfort. He claimed to be able to guide them through the Palais to the dungeons, even to the Queen's cell, but would not tell them how he knew the way. There was nothing to even say whether this was the real Levieux, since no one ever saw the man. One of Levieux's people was a Cadarese, and though Hall had never met any Cadarese, he knew they were not to be trusted. Worst of all, this entire operation relied upon a mob, and despite Levieux's claim that he had given his people clear instructions, Hall knew that no one could truly direct a mob. The northern and western ends of Demesne were now on fire, more than ten city blocks burning out of control, and the local fire brigade was nowhere to be found. A force assailed the city's northern gate, drawing what little enforcement Demesne still had, but what this force was or where it came from, Levieux refused to say. Hall's operations were designed with certainty in mind, elimination of all variables achieved through repeated testing. This plan was madness, and they would only get one shot. It was too much to risk for one woman, even a Queen, but there was no talking to the Mace, who seemed to be in the grip of a fixed delusion that if they could only get the Queen out, all would somehow be well. No one could convince him otherwise, but Hall, who prided himself on realism, was prepared for disaster.

But so far, things had gone without a hitch. The Palais gates were open and unguarded, so the Mace's plant had at least done her job. There was no sign of any security, and this made Hall uneasy; surely the woman couldn't have suborned an entire Gate Guard? Levieux's mob had already flooded the Palais, and Hall could hear the sounds of wreckage echoing throughout the upper floors: breaking glass and wood. Their little band—Levieux and four of his people, Hall and Blaser, and eight of the Queen's Guard—had gone in the other direction, down several flights of stairs, following Levieux toward the dungeons. But they met no resistance, met no one of any kind. Their route was stunningly easy, and Hall didn't trust it.

Then there was the smell. Hall had been a soldier far too long to miss that copper tang in the air. Blood had been spilled here, plenty of it, and not long ago either. They didn't see a single body, but as they progressed down the stairs, they saw floors and hallways dappled with puddles of red.

The Mace's plant was supposed to be at the bottom of the stairs, ready to open the doors to the dungeons, but she was nowhere to be seen. Instead they met a pair of iron gates that looked as though they had been hit with a ram. The bars were warped, and one of the doors dangled by the barest grace from a single hinge.

"What in hell did that?" Blaser whispered.

"Ready for anything, now," the Mace said. He had pulled out his namesake weapon, and his face was pallid, almost ghastly, in the dim torchlight. If something had happened to the Queen, Hall wasn't sure what it would do to the Mace.

"Come on, let's get it done."

They crept down the staircase, the only sound the flicker and crack of their torches. Hall had been worried that Levieux and his people would be a nuisance, but he needn't have been; they were the quietest of the bunch. Hall didn't hear a single scrape or footstep.

"Sir," Kibb said quietly. "Got a blood trail here."

Hall looked down and saw it: every few risers, a small, dark sparkle of blood dotted the grey stone. In all of his worries over this venture, he had never thought that the Queen might be in real danger. She was a valuable prisoner, a bargaining chip; even if the Red Queen chose to have her beaten for spite—such things went on in the Mort dungeons all the time—the Queen would not face death or serious injury.

But at the sight of the blood, something seemed to tighten in Hall's heart. In the past few weeks, he had revisited his angry words to the Queen many times. He had called her a glory hound. He owed her an apology, but there had been no chance.

"Blood's running in her direction," Levieux muttered, and Hall thought that even he was unnerved. Levieux was a cool customer; Hall had met with him only twice, during meetings in the Keep, but he had never seen the man rattled until now. The sick feeling in Hall's midsection seemed to double. He had known that this plan was too easy, that something was bound to go wrong.

But please, he begged the universe, anyone, *not so wrong as this.*

The rumors Hall had heard about the Mort dungeons were not exaggerated. It was bone-cold down here, even to a soldier who had slept rough in the outdoor winter on several campaigns. Many of the cells they passed contained not even the standard pallet of the New London Jail. Most of the torches on the walls had long since burned out, and there were long stretches during which the torches carried by Levieux and Coryn provided the only light.

No guards, no jailors, Hall thought. *What in holy hell happened here?*

Whatever it was, it was clear that no one cared whether these prisoners lived or died. Only some of them appeared to have blankets, and many were coughing, hollow chesty coughs that Hall judged symptomatic of pneumonia. Some of them cried for water, displaying empty buckets through the bars as Hall went by.

"We'll find a key," the Mace told them, but even Hall heard the unease in his voice. They had expected to fight their way through the dungeons, to break the Queen out or die trying; a grueling bit of combat, to be sure, but at least it would be a known hazard. They had been prepared to lose some of their number, but none of them had anticipated this. In one cell, a heavily pregnant woman begged them to let her out. Behind Hall, one of the Queen's Guards uttered a low curse. All the combat in the world seemed preferable to Hall, and he was not alone. Several turns into the dungeon, Blaser silently began to retch.

"How much farther?" the Mace asked Levieux.

"Two turns right and down."

As they approached the second turn, all of them slowed, and Hall doubled his grip on his sword. A moment ago, he had been thinking that he would relish an open battle, but now his flesh had begun to crawl. Ahead of them, a staircase descended into darkness, and Hall could feel freezing air emanating from below. The blood trail led down the stairs.

"Quietly," Levieux cautioned them, and began to step silently down the staircase. They were forced to go single file now, and Hall took a position behind the great, bearlike form of one of Levieux's men. The staircase wedged them tight, and for a moment Hall was beset by claustrophobia, with the walls closing in and people ahead and behind. The walls reverberated with the thud of many feet above as Levieux's people tore the upper levels of the Palais apart.

At the bottom of the stairwell, the line halted. The entire corridor was dark, but the stench of blood seemed to have deepened and refined down here, almost precipitant, a low, sickening throb of rusting copper each time Hall took a breath.

"Torches up front," the Mace murmured, and Coryn passed his torch forward. It was enough to illuminate the corridor, but Hall could not see past the shoulder of the enormous man in front of him.

"What is that?" the Mace demanded.

"Don't move," said Levieux, but Hall, able to bear the wait no longer, pushed his way around the giant until he could see as well.

Far down at the end of the corridor, perhaps fifty feet away, lay a body in front of a cell. The cell door hung wide open. Hall could not identify the body, for there were two figures hunched over it, so small that at first he mistook them for vultures. But then one turned, and Hall saw that it was a child, a little boy.

"Get back!" Levieux shouted. "Morgan, Howell, Lear, up here now!"

But it was too tight in the corridor, Levieux's men pushing up toward the front while the rest tried to shove their way back toward the stairs. The Mace did not retreat, and so neither did Hall, shoving his way forward until he stood beside the Captain.

"What are they?" the Mace asked Levieux.

"The plague on the new world."

"They're only children!" Hall objected.

"Keep thinking that, General, right up until they bleed you dry." Levieux raised his sword, for now the little boy had clambered to his feet and begun moving forward.

"Who is that?" Pen demanded, his voice rising. "Who's dead down there?"

"It's her cell," Levieux replied quietly. "Stay here."

He and his four men headed down the corridor, leaving the Mace and Hall standing there. Blaser had moved forward to stand at Hall's shoulder, but the rest of the group still crouched near the stairwell.

"The plague," Hall repeated. "The attacks in the north?"

The Mace didn't answer, but Hall was already filling in the blanks for himself. He had heard of the destruction in the Reddick and northern Almont; had Hall still commanded an army, he might already have been sent to get the situation under control. As it was, the force that assailed the Tearling remained unchecked, moving steadily south. There were almost no survivors. The few rumors Hall had heard spoke of animals with incredible strength. But children?

The little boy lunged forward, with a hiss that made Hall's skin prickle, and knocked the Cadarese flying. The other child—a girl, Hall saw now—darted into the fray, wrapped herself around Levieux's leg, and sunk her teeth into his thigh.

"Five men might not be enough," the Mace said, and ran forward, Hall and Blaser on his heels.

"Stay back!" Levieux shouted. He yanked his leg free, cursing, and threw the girl toward the big man, Morgan, who held her struggling form long enough for Levieux to run her through with his sword. The girl shrieked, a sound like the peal of alarm bells.

"Christ," Blaser muttered. Hall turned to the Mace, to see if he would protest, but the Mace merely watched, stone-faced, as though well familiar with this sight.

The boy had jumped on top of the Cadarese, Lear, and somehow pinned him down. Now Howell grabbed the child and ran him into the bars, hard enough that the boy fell, stunned. Howell grabbed one arm, Alain the other, and Lear straddled the child with a knife. Hall could watch no more; he turned away, closing his eyes when the boy began to scream.

"Done," Levieux said, an unknown amount of time later. "Come on."

The Mace moved down the corridor, his Guard surrounding him, and Hall followed. He felt as though he were in some sort of waking nightmare, and the scene that met him was more terrible still: the two children lay on the ground, bleeding, but further down the hall was another child, a girl whom Hall had not noticed before, with a dagger buried in her chest. Just in front of the open cell lay a fourth body, a woman, tall and blonde, and now Hall finally understood why the children had reminded him of vultures: the woman's torso was pulped, her ribs poking cruelly through the leftover meat.

"Kibby?" the Mace demanded.

Kibb had already disappeared inside the Queen's cell, and now his voice echoed from inside. "Nothing. No one here."

Hall barely heard this conversation. He had frozen in front of the adjacent cell.

"No sign? No message?"

"No. Pallet, candles, matches, two buckets. That's all."

"Where is she?" Pen demanded.

Hall raised his hand and waved it in front of the bars. The prisoner before him did not wave back. The man's head was shaved and he could have done with a few good meals, but the face was Hall's own, staring back at him.

"Simon," he murmured.

"Neck's broken." Coryn's voice came from far away; he was leaning over the blonde woman. "Clean death, before these things."

"Ah, damn," the Mace muttered, kneeling beside the corpse. "She did her job."

Simon reached out through the bars, and Hall grasped his hand, resting his other palm on his brother's cheek. Hall had not seen his twin in nearly twenty years, had worked all that time not to think about him at all. Yet here Simon was, solid and real.

"But where's the Queen?" Elston asked. In other circumstances, Hall might have laughed at the plaintive note in the big guard's voice. Simon's lips formed words, but nothing came out. Hall leaned toward the bars.

"What?"

"The Red Queen. She took her."

"What's that you say?" The Mace shouldered Hall out of the way, but Hall clung to Simon's hand as he skidded to one side.

"The Queen hit her head on the bars. The Red Queen carried her away."

The Mace looked from Hall to Simon for a moment, then seemed to dismiss the resemblance as a problem for a later time.

"Where did she take her?"

Simon pointed in the opposite direction to that from which they had come.

"How long ago?"

"I don't know. Many hours, I think. There's no time here."

"FUCK!"

Hall jumped. Pen stood with his back to them, his shoulders heaving.

Hall turned back to Simon, noticing for the first time the cell walls behind him, covered with drawings and schematics. They used to sit for long hours, the two of them, designing contraptions, drawing the plans in the dirt with a stick. Engineers. Hall blinked tears from his eyes and, realizing that Simon was still locked in, began casting around for a key.

"Where would she go?" Dyer asked Levieux.

"I don't know."

"Gin Reach." The Mace's voice was little more than a croak, and Hall saw, alarmed, that the man's face had drained of all color. "She's in Gin Reach. Andalie told us so, and I didn't listen."

"None of us did," Elston reminded him. He put a hand on the Mace's shoulder, but the Mace shook him off, and suddenly Hall felt it coming, sensed that the boiling point inside the Captain had finally been reached. The Guard seemed to have the same idea, for they instinctively began to back away as a group, turning their heads. Hall turned back to Simon and kept his eyes resolutely on his brother's face as it erupted behind him: a long, wordless howl of rage and grief.

Chapter 10

Gin Reach

The malicious have a dark happiness.

—*Les Misérables*, VICTOR HUGO (PRE-CROSSING FR.)

M y Palais is on fire."

Kelsea jerked awake from a doze that had been deepening toward sleep. They had been riding for nearly a day, and her head was beginning to ache again, sharp throbs of knifing pain that pulsed outward from the enormous knot at the back of her skull. She drew rein and found the Red Queen staring behind them.

"Look."

Kelsea turned and found the silhouette of the Palais, jutting upward from the distant Demesne skyline. The upper windows belched fire, and the entire apex of the castle, including the balcony on which she and the Red Queen had stood on that long-ago day, was obscured by a dark nimbus of smoke.

"The immortal do not flee," the Red Queen murmured, words that sounded almost rote to Kelsea, as though the older woman had practiced them many times in her mind.

They had escaped Demesne by means of an underground stable that, according to the Red Queen, had been prepared for her long ago by Ducarte. The stable was well stocked with clothing, water, cured food, and coin, but the Red Queen's lost expression told Kelsea that she had never expected to need such a place and was astonished to find herself there. Kelsea was scarcely less astonished; the Red Queen, with an escape hatch? She wondered what would have happened if that knowledge had become public.

The Red Queen had torn their clothing and ratted Kelsea's hair into a nest. They hid the coins against their skin, and then the Red Queen dappled Kelsea's face with blood from the gash at her wrist. Kelsea didn't entirely understand the reason for these preparations until they emerged from the dim basement of an abandoned building, some distance from the Palais. They had been able to hear the roar of conflict from underground, but Kelsea was completely unprepared for what met her on the streets.

Demesne was in chaos. Uncontrolled fires raged at several points on the city's horizon. Mobs roamed free, shouting Levieux's name. The district around the Palais, clearly one of the city's wealthiest, was a battle zone of barricaded houses under assault by both citizens and Mort soldiers. They didn't want to be discovered as wealthy on these streets, but Kelsea couldn't seem to work up any fear, for it felt too extraordinary to be outside again. She had almost forgotten that there was anything but the fetid air of the dungeon, the dim light of torches. Even this wrecked city was a welcome landscape.

At several points on their journey through the city, Kelsea briefly considered simply breaking cover and turning the Red Queen in, then presenting herself as a Tear slave. The streets were full of Tear voices, escaped slaves now turned rebels, and surely the Mort would not be interested in a lone Tear when they got hold of the noble to end all nobles. Surely Kelsea was justified in leaving the Red Queen behind. She had spared the Red Queen's life, and the Red Queen had spared hers. There was no debt here.

And the Tearling beckoned, distant but suddenly close. Once she got out of the city, she could ride straight west and cross the border in little more than a day.

Home.

Of course the idea was foolish. Demesne was a vast city, and Kelsea had no idea where she was. She was forced to trust the Red Queen's navigation, and they had finally escaped Demesne by bribing five soldiers on the city's south gate. Once out, they had ignored the Mort Road and begun a steady journey southwest. Kelsea had no idea where the Red Queen meant to go, but as long as they were heading toward the Tearling, she felt no need to deviate. She was surprised to feel an odd sense of responsibility for the Red Queen. The woman was all alone now, cast adrift in a country that screamed for her blood. If the Red Queen were caught, what the Mort would do to her would be bad, very bad, but what the Tear would do would be even worse. She could not go unpunished, Kelsea's mind insisted, not forever. But Kelsea didn't want to see her brutalized either.

"The girl by my side," the Red Queen continued now, her voice distant as she stared at the flaming ruin far behind them. "The girl by my side, and the man in grey behind."

"Are you casting a spell?" Kelsea asked. "Or talking nonsense?"

The Red Queen turned to her, and Kelsea felt an involuntary shudder work its way up her spine. Whatever her relationship with Tear's sapphire—and Kelsea had no idea precisely what that was—it still allowed her to see, to catalog and analyze the small tics that other people tried to keep hidden. Over the course of this day, she had become more and more certain that the Red Queen was only holding herself together by the barest margin. *Un maniaque,* Thorne had named her . . . and how would such a person really do under the pressures of blind flight? Beneath the Red Queen's businesslike exterior, the exigencies of getting themselves out of Demesne, Kelsea sensed the first threads of madness.

"I am not immortal," said the Red Queen. The look she bent on Kelsea was a mixture of hatred and obsequiousness, and Kelsea was not sure which one made her more uncomfortable. "Are you happy, Glynn? You have brought me down."

"You brought yourself down!" Kelsea snapped. "All that power! You could have done anything with it, and look what you did."

"I did what I had to do to hold my throne."

"You're a liar. I know about your court, Lady Crimson. I know how you conducted yourself. Slaves tortured and raped—and the men too; don't think I haven't heard about your predilections. People enter your laboratories and never come out. That's not necessity. That's carte blanche."

The Red Queen's face darkened, and Kelsea felt something ruffle her hair, though the air was still.

"Be careful," she said softly. "You do not want to open this box."

The Red Queen stared at her for another long moment, then muttered a curse and turned back to the city.

"We've gained enough distance, Lady Crimson. Why don't we just go our separate ways?"

"Well, you may if you like, Glynn," the Red Queen replied. "But I would just as soon hold together until our paths diverge. Two women together are safer than one."

That was certainly true, but Kelsea sensed the falsity behind the statement. They were no ordinary women, and the man who tried to rob or assault either of them would certainly regret it. The Red Queen was afraid of something else. Finn's children, perhaps? They had seen no more of the horrible things since leaving the Palais, but Kelsea could think of nothing else that would frighten this woman, save perhaps for Finn himself. They had stopped several hours ago to rest and take some food and water, but the older woman had forbidden Kelsea to light a fire.

The Red Queen was rubbing her wrist again. In the stable, Kelsea had dressed the wound, washing it with water and wrapping a bandage. The two punctures were very deep, and they had already looked inflamed. Bite marks.

"What?"

The Red Queen had caught her staring. Kelsea turned away, looking across the landscape. They had finally left the broad, trimmed grass of the Champs Demesne behind. The ground beneath them had turned to high grassland, shot through with veins of silt. It was slightly better cover, but not the most comfortable place to spend the night.

"We should keep moving," Kelsea said. "Where is it you mean to go in the end?"

"To the Dry Lands. There is nowhere else I can hide."

"What about Cadare?"

"I can't go to Cadare," the Red Queen replied flatly.

"Well, I can stay with you until we cross the border. After that, I need to return to my city."

"That's fine," the Red Queen replied, her voice unconcerned, and again Kelsea had the strange sense that the woman didn't care where they went, so long as they went together.

What is she afraid of?

They rode southwest for the next several hours. When the sun touched the horizon, they stopped to rest within sight of the border hills. This far south, the land was not covered with pines, only grass and shrubs and occasional greenery. Boring landscape, but still Kelsea stared at her surroundings, fascinated. Less than fifty miles to the north, Hall had made his stand, and Ducarte had forced the Tear army off the hillside by setting the forest on fire. Even Kelsea, who would have liked to see Ducarte in a Tear prison for the rest of his life, had to admire the simplicity of the strategy: if your opponent would not be moved, you simply burned him down.

Dinner was another meal of cured meat and fruit. There was plenty of game around here, deer and rabbits, but the Red Queen had once again forbade Kelsea to light a fire.

"Did you ever try to kill him?" Kelsea asked. "Row Finn?"

"Yes. I failed. He's not quite mortal. No shape; I couldn't grab hold."

Kelsea didn't perfectly understand the Red Queen's words, but she thought she had some idea. When she killed Arlen Thorne, she had been able to see to the core of him: not solid, but solid enough, limned in poisonous light, and a younger and angrier Kelsea, desperate over all the things beyond her control, had had no trouble gaining hold.

"Do you know how he became what he is?"

"The dark thing? In some ways. He used to speak of it, after—" Here the Red Queen paused, casting a furtive glance in Kelsea's direction. "He used to say that he had forced his own survival. Almost bragging, I think. He used to teach me things."

"How long were you up in the Fairwitch?"

"Two years. Long enough for all who knew me to think me dead." Kelsea saw a brief flash of hatred in her eyes. "But you know this, Glynn. You know all about me."

"Not all. I don't see clearly. It's like skimming a book. Why did your mother send you into exile?"

"She didn't. I ran away."

"Why?"

"None of your fucking business."

Kelsea blinked, but persevered. "Did you learn magic from Finn?"

"Some. Enough that, when the time came, I was able to create my own. But not enough to ward off disaster." The Red Queen frowned, and Kelsea noticed that she was rubbing her bandaged wrist again, working at it with her fingers.

"Does it hurt?" Kelsea asked.

The Red Queen didn't answer.

They continued to travel southwest. The weather grew colder and soon the land began to dry. Streams and rivers vanished, and even watering holes and wells became scarce. In a small village in the lower flats, they stopped and Kelsea traded gold for water, bargaining in Mort while the Red Queen stood silent beside her. Often, Kelsea thought of how she could simply vanish, leave the Red Queen behind and make straight for New London. She was the better rider; in fact, she thought the Red Queen might even be secretly frightened of horses. How long had it been since the woman had left Demesne, or traveled anywhere without a driver? Out of the Palais, the Red Queen had begun to seem less substantial, not the witch-sorceress of Mortmesne but only an ordinary woman, lonely and lost. What were initially small things—scattered focus, tremors in her speech—became more pronounced the farther they traveled from Demesne. The Red Queen looked behind them constantly, and Kelsea could not tell whether she truly saw something, or whether the natural terminus of her paranoia had finally been reached.

"What is it?" she finally asked, when the Red Queen pulled her horse to a halt for a third time that afternoon.

"We're being followed," the Red Queen replied, and Kelsea was unnerved by the certainty in her tone. The Red Queen had begun to rub her wrist again.

"Let me take a look at that," Kelsea offered.

"Get away!" the Red Queen hissed, slapping her hand away, and Kelsea withdrew with a gasp. For a moment she could have sworn the Red Queen's eyes had gleamed a bright, burning red.

"Do I need to restrain you?" Kelsea asked flatly.

"No. I will beat it. I control my own body, even if I control nothing else."

Kelsea had her doubts, but she could think of no way to act on them. Even if she succeeded in subduing the Red Queen, where could she go with a bound woman? She felt, again, the urge to simply cut loose, flee north toward her own city, her Keep, her life. But again, something held her back.

What ties me to her? Kelsea wondered. *What binds us together?* She had gone through the woman's mind as one might search a dwelling, carelessly, with no regard for decency or privacy, and only now did Kelsea realize that there might have been cost attached to that invasion, a price she had never considered.

"Don't worry about me," the Red Queen said roughly. "Let's go on."

On the third day of their journey, they climbed the gentle slopes of the lower Border Hills, and Kelsea was finally able to look out over her kingdom, the vast plain of the Almont stretching before her as far as her eye could see. Instead of the pleasure she had expected, she felt almost sick. She had sacrificed much for this broad stretch of land, her imperfect country, but something told her she wasn't done yet. When she looked down, she found herself clutching William Tear's sapphire in a hand that was damp with sweat.

That afternoon they reached the beginning of the Dry Lands, more than a hundred miles of desert that stretched across the Cadarese border. They would need to stop and purchase cold-weather gear, furs, and tents; Carlin had once told Kelsea that the Dry Lands became nearly as cold as the Fairwitch in winter. In the distance, Kelsea could see several dark spots, scattered villages, but all around them stretched a vast landscape, parched and colorless and unforgiving. Kelsea sensed no end to it, even beyond the horizon.

Far to the west, she saw a stain in the sky, punctuated by lightning. The storms in the Dry Lands were legendary, fearsome and inexplicable ecological phenomena in which the water seemed to come from nowhere. Torrents of rain poured down, but the water did not alter the character of the landscape one whit; everything remained as parched as before. Technically, the Dry Lands were part of the Tearling, but to Kelsea, the desert seemed to be its own kingdom, lonely and cold.

"What do you mean to do?" she asked the Red Queen. "We'll die trying to cross that."

The Red Queen turned, a mad sort of desperation in her eyes. She was clutching her wrist again.

"He knows where I am," she said quietly. "I can feel it. He'll send more. I need to get away."

"Well, you can't hide in the desert."

"What's your point?"

"Why not come back to New London with me?" Kelsea asked. "I'll—"

She halted, unable to credit the words that had almost escaped her mouth. *I'll protect you . . .* but she couldn't do that. The Tear would treat the Red Queen as a war criminal, and they would be right to do so.

"One of those outposts is bound to have an inn," she finished lamely. "We have enough coin for a proper bed and bath, at least."

The Red Queen swallowed and nodded, putting on a good front of her old self-control. But to Kelsea's eye, it was only a shadow of the real thing.

Unraveling, she thought again. The Red Queen blinked, and this time, Kelsea couldn't deceive herself; the woman's pupils were tinged with red.

"Yes," the Red Queen replied. "A bath and bed. That would be nice."

The first village they came to was little more than a hamlet, a town as grim as the landscape surrounding. As they started down the narrow sand track that seemed to pass as the main road, Kelsea spotted a small weather-beaten sign driven into the sandy earth:

Gin Reach

The houses here were little more than functional piles of wood, and no one had taken any trouble to make them prettier. Only one building had glass windows and a bright, pleasant awning; Kelsea was hardly surprised to see that it was the town's pub. She thought she felt eyes staring down upon her, but when she looked up, she found that all of the second-story windows were shuttered. The wind had picked up, blowing sand against Kelsea's face. A storm was coming, and the entire town appeared to be battening down the hatches.

The town's inn turned out to be a large house boasting three guest rooms. The keeper assured them that he had only one guest; the two of them would have their privacy, a remark followed with a distinctly lecherous wink. The Red Queen didn't seem to care, dropping down coin for two hot baths to be brought to their room. After the luxury and callousness Kelsea had seen littering the Palais, she would have expected the Red Queen to do poorly at a small-town inn. But she seemed fine, giving an easy riposte when the innkeeper tried to flirt, and this made Kelsea wonder again at what she had missed inside the Red Queen's mind, the complex life she must have led.

When they undressed for their baths, the Red Queen removed her bandages and Kelsea saw that the marks on her wrist had disappeared. Kelsea's unease doubled; the punctures she had treated had been deep and nasty, and if this was no natural healing, then what was it? As they bathed, each lounging in her own steel tub, Kelsea watched the Red Queen from the corner of her eye. She showed few signs of fatigue; indeed, despite the cold weather they had been traveling under, the Red Queen looked physically strong, stronger than she had since they set out from Demesne.

What am I afraid of? Kelsea wondered, as they climbed into their beds. She couldn't say, but her skin was prickling, as though an invisible animal waited just behind her, ready to pounce. She felt eyes on her again, but when she glanced at the Red Queen, she found her turned away, resting comfortably on her side in the other bed. Kelsea tried to stay awake, but exhaustion overtook her, and she finally gave up trying to keep watch and blew out her candle. A terrible storm was upon the town, thunder that shook the building to its foundations, and Kelsea slipped easily into a dream of the Argive, the train of cages that had sat just on the border. If Kelsea and her Guard had come even a day later, the caravan would have gone, vanished into Mortmesne.

That was a moment, the dream-Kelsea thought, *a moment in time, just like the death of Jonathan Tear. If I had missed that moment, what would have happened? Where would we be now?*

But the dream of the Argive was gone, morphed seamlessly into another. Kelsea stood on the high scaffold, and before her was Arlen Thorne, driven to his knees. All around them, the mob raged, a cacophony of screaming voices. Thorne looked up, and Kelsea saw that he was in his final extremity, his face a mask of blood.

I'm sorry! Kelsea tried to scream, but before she could, a hand grabbed her ankle. She looked down and saw Mhurn at her feet, grinning wide, his face upturned, exposing the wide red smile she had cut into his neck. His hand began to work its way up her calf, and Kelsea did the only thing she could do: jumped off the scaffolding and into the sea of upturned, screaming faces awaiting her. At the last moment before she landed, she realized that they were all Mhurn and Thorne, waiting for her, and she gasped herself awake.

A woman stood over her in the dark.

Before Kelsea could even draw breath to scream, a hand jammed over her mouth. There was great strength in this woman; she held Kelsea's shoulders easily, pinning her to the bed.

I was wrong, Kelsea thought bitterly. Whatever the Red Queen had become, Kelsea should never have taken her eyes off her, just as Mace would never take his eyes off a known enemy. She had allowed herself to be lulled by companionship and mutual interest, lulled into forgetting that there was more than a century of hatred sitting between Mortmesne and the Tear, between red and black.

The Red Queen bent down, her face nearing Kelsea's, and Kelsea heard the whistle of the woman's breath at her ear, thought she could feel the bite of teeth against her throat.

"You will suffer, bitch," the Red Queen hissed in the darkness. "You will suffer for my master."

Kelsea froze in sudden recognition. The threat had been real, but she had mistaken the source. Not the Red Queen at all, but—

"Brenna," she whispered.

E wen was not good with new places. He had lived in New London all of his life, but several times he had gotten lost in strange sections of the city. Da said Ewen had no compass inside. But after two weeks in Gin Reach, Ewen thought that even Da would be satisfied. He knew every inch of the town's four streets, and could even recognize who lived in some of the houses.

He and Bradshaw had caused a stir when they arrived; Bradshaw said it was because they had money to spend. This confused Ewen, for Gin Reach held very little to spend money on. Once a week, a sour-looking man drove a covered wagon down the main track and stopped in front of the pub. While the publican and his assistant removed bottles and barrels from the wagon, the townspeople came out of their houses to bargain with the sour man for food, clothing, or a few novelties such as paper or fabric or medicine. The town had a small, grim farming patch out behind the southern stretch of houses, protected from the desert with fencing and canvas tarp, and most of what people seemed to barter was the food they grew: root vegetables, leeks, and potatoes, things that needed little light. But the only places to spend actual coin in Gin Reach were the pub and the inn.

When Ewen saw the witch, he almost didn't recognize her. The woman Ewen remembered had been white as bone, ageless, with eyes like daggers. She might have been twenty years old, or fifty.

But the woman he saw now was red-cheeked and looked to be in the prime of youth. Her hair, which had been the color of sunfaded straw when Ewen last saw her, was a rich, healthy gold. She was much changed, yes, but he still recognized the witch beneath, standing in the doorway of the inn. She didn't see him, for at the sight of her Ewen dove for cover into a narrow alley between two houses.

That night, he and Bradshaw had a long talk about what to do. Bradshaw said that Brenna's powers were well known, that she could control even strong men with a glance. Neither of them felt comfortable about trying to capture her, not even the two of them against one. But Bradshaw insisted that the Mace must be told, that one of them must stay in Gin Reach while the other took the message.

Ewen did not want to stay here. Every moment that day, trailing her from the inn, he had felt as though Brenna would turn around and spear him with her eyes. He had not dared to follow her as she wandered into the desert, for there was no cover out there, and anyway, even Ewen knew about the Dry Lands. Da used to say that the desert liked to show a man hidden pictures, things that weren't there, draw him away and get him lost. Men would die of thirst, simply chasing the pictures in their heads. Ewen waited in front of the inn until Brenna returned at sunset and disappeared inside, and then he fled back to the basement room he shared with Bradshaw, feeling like a mouse dismissed by a hawk. No, he did not want to stay here, keeping an eye on Brenna.

But the alternative was worse. They had been in Gin Reach for two weeks, and by now General Hall might have been forced to move. If the regiment was not where they had left it in the southern Almont, Bradshaw said, then the messenger would have to go all the way to Mortmesne and make contact with the Mace.

Mortmesne! The most terrible of all lands, a place of darkness and fire and cruelty. He did not want to stay alone in Gin Reach, but even less did he want to visit an evil kingdom. Bradshaw insisted that Mortmesne was not so bad as all that, but Ewen did not want to find out. Even the mention of the journey was enough to make him sick to his stomach.

"Well, one of us has to go," Bradshaw said firmly. "And if it has to be me, then you'll need to be very careful here, Ewen. The witch can't spot you, or you're cooked. Understand?"

Ewen nodded halfheartedly. Bradshaw left, and in the days since, Ewen had become a spy. This was not easy work, for each day he would have to come up with a new and creative way to watch the inn, not only so that Brenna did not notice but so that the townspeople didn't begin to talk. He often went to the pub, which was only a bit down the street from the inn and had a good view of its entrance. But this was not easy either, for Ewen didn't drink. Long ago, Da had cautioned him against ale, warning that it would only get him into trouble, and he had absolutely forbidden Ewen to drink any spirits. The latter was no hardship; Ewen had tasted whiskey at Christmas once, and thought it tasted like bad vinegar. But Da's strictures did present problems now, when Ewen was trying to spend all day in a pub. Even he knew that no one spent all day in a pub unless he was a drunk. He thought about getting an ale and sipping it slowly, but in the end he could not. Da was dead, yes, but that had made his rules more powerful, not less. Ewen could not break them.

He told the publican that he was waiting for a friend to arrive in town, and after some discussion, they agreed that Ewen would drink water and pay ale prices. Ewen worried that the man would talk about their strange arrangement, but his worries were needless; unless the discussion involved money or alcohol, the publican didn't seem to want to talk at all. He was content to have Ewen sit at the end of the bar, drinking glass after glass of water, only getting up occasionally to use the filthy toilet at the back of the pub. It was very boring, this spy work, and on the second day,

Ewen brought his lead and paper and began to sketch the people around the bar, the street outside. He knew his sketches were not very good, but the publican, at least, seemed to appreciate them; after several hours of apparent disinterest, he sidled over to watch Ewen draw. After several more hours, he asked Ewen if he might draw something as well. Ewen gave him a piece of paper and a short stub of lead. He wondered if anyone ever drew in Gin Reach. There wasn't much inspiration here; the surrounding landscape was as bleak as anything Ewen could have imagined. He drew the people, the buildings, the sky, but his eyes were never far from the door of the inn.

Twice more, Brenna left the inn and wandered up the main track, then continued out of town into the desert. Her steps were almost aimless, but not quite, and by the third day Ewen had begun to wonder just what she was doing here, why she didn't move along like most of the other travelers, who stopped in Gin Reach merely to outfit themselves before they attempted to cross the Dry Lands. Brenna did not visit the few shops that existed for this purpose, nor did she try to buy anything else, not even food. Indeed, except for her strange forays into the desert, she didn't leave the inn at all. This Ewen thought he understood; robbed of the white sickness that she had suffered before, Brenna was a fairly pretty woman, and when she walked down the street, men turned their heads. She still retained her forbidding aspect; no one tried to speak to her, and no one dared follow her out into the desert. But she certainly attracted attention, and Ewen sensed that this was not what she wanted. She was waiting for something, being careful. Ewen could only monitor her in the daytime, and he had no idea what she did while he slept.

On the fourth day after Bradshaw's departure, two more travelers arrived at the inn. They were heavily cloaked, but Ewen sensed no threat from that, for many travelers in Gin Reach seemed to want to keep their business to themselves. Brenna did not emerge to meet the newcomers, so he dismissed them from mind and returned to his drawing.

That night, there was no sleep for anyone. A storm had welled up above the desert, a storm unlike anything Ewen had ever seen before. Brilliant lightning cracked the sky from horizon to horizon, and the thunder was so strong that it shook every building on the street. Ewen, who was afraid of thunder, knew that he would never sleep through such a storm, certainly not alone in their basement room. He stayed late at the pub, and apparently the rest of the town had the same idea, for every table in the place was packed. The publican was so busy that, when Ewen ran out of water, he plopped a full pitcher on the bar and hurried away without even asking for coin.

The room was too noisy for Ewen to enjoy drawing, so he merely rested his head on the bar, keeping his eyes trained out the window. Every few seconds came a flash of lightning, long and brilliant moments that illuminated the entire street in bluewhite. Despite the thunder, Ewen's eyelids began to get heavy. It was nearing midnight, and he had only stayed up past midnight three times in his whole life, the three Christmases before he went to work in the Keep dungeon. He wondered if the publican would allow him to fall asleep with his head on the bar. The thunder sounded likely to crack the world in two, but even though he was afraid of thunderstorms, Ewen was not as frightened as he thought he would be. Who would ever have imagined that he would leave New London, travel halfway across the New World, and then be able to take care of himself in a strange town? He wished he could have told Da about it, but Da was—

Ewen sat up quickly. Lightning had flashed again, and though the flare of lamplight on the window glass made it difficult, he thought he had seen a cloaked figure carrying something out the door of the inn.

Ewen slid off the stool and went to stand before the glass. He could hardly see anything in the darkness outside, only the barest outline of the inn's facade. Then lightning splintered the sky, and he saw that a wagon stood before the inn, the clear shape of a bundle in the back.

Forgetting his paper and leads, which still sat on the bar, Ewen went outside and was immediately drenched. The storm was so loud that he could hear nothing from the pub behind him. He meant to take a closer look at the wagon, but no sooner had he crept out from under the pub's awning than the lightning flared again, illuminating the dark silhouette in front of the inn. Ewen scrambled backward, pressing himself into the shadows. For a moment there was only darkness, and then the lightning showed him the witch's profile beneath the cloak. Her head swiveled from side to side, reminding Ewen of a dog that had caught a scent. He pressed his back against the wall with all of his might, praying that he was hidden, that those pale eyes could not see him . . .

After an eternity, Brenna left the cover of the inn's doorway and proceeded down the steps. The next flash of lightning revealed a second bundle slung over her shoulder, and Ewen realized, with mounting horror, that the bundle was the size of a man. He had not seen what Brenna had done to Will in the Keep, but he had heard plenty of tales in the guard quarters. Elston said that when Brenna had finished with Will, he was nothing more than mince.

Brenna climbed into the seat of the wagon and took the reins. She was leaving, Ewen realized, and his first reaction was a vast relief. The witch was up to no good; she might even have killed someone. But she would drive away, out of Gin Reach, and then she would no longer be Ewen's problem. When Bradshaw returned, they could leave this awful town on the edge of nowhere and go back to New London, to Ewen's brothers, to the life he knew.

But then, his heart sinking, Ewen realized that that wasn't quite true. The Mace had told him to keep an eye out for anything unusual, and here was a witch, transporting what looked like people in the middle of the night. More, Brenna was an escaped prisoner, and before Ewen had ever spoken to the Mace, he had been, first and foremost, a jailor. Da had made him a jailor, chosen Ewen even though his brothers were smarter and braver, and he had never let a prisoner escape.

Ewen looked through the window of the pub behind him, but they were all talking and drinking. Perhaps he could ask the publican for help . . . but no, the publican would never leave his bar. If only Bradshaw were still here to tell him what to do! But there was no time. In another flash of lightning, Ewen saw that the wagon had already begun to roll. He groped at his waist and found that he still had his knife. No sword; the Mace had never allowed him to have one. Ewen wouldn't have known how to use it anyway, and even his knifework was very sloppy. Venner had said so.

Not a real Queen's Guard, he thought again. Even real Queen's Guards were afraid of Brenna, but there was no one else. No help would come in time.

"I'm going, Da," he whispered into the rain. "I'm going, all right?"

He slipped off the wall and began to work his way up the street, following the wagon.

When Kelsea woke, she was first aware that her hands were bound behind her, and next, that she was drenched. She was on the floor of a moving wagon, and for a moment she wondered, astonished, if she was still on her way to Mortmesne, if the past few months had been nothing but the deepest dream. She opened her eyes and saw nothing, but then lightning flashed and she found, relieved, that this was a different wagon, smaller. There was a large bundle beside her, and in the next flash of lightning Kelsea caught sight of a pair of dark eyes beneath a hood: the Red Queen.

Brenna.

Kelsea twisted around and found a cloaked figure driving the wagon. Kelsea remembered nothing after hearing Brenna's voice in the darkness. There was a smear of blood on the Red Queen's forehead; had they both been knocked out? Kelsea had taken too many head wounds lately, but it wasn't a concussion that frightened her now. She didn't know how Brenna had gotten free of the Keep, but the woman wasn't in Gin Reach by accident. She had come for Kelsea, just as she would have come for anyone who had harmed Arlen Thorne. Kelsea wriggled helplessly, trying to judge whether she still wore Tear's sapphire. She couldn't tell. Would the sapphire even do any good here? Brenna was rumored to be a witch, but her actual powers were an unknown.

The wagon halted and Kelsea closed her eyes, nudging the Red Queen to do the same. Whatever else Brenna might be, she had incredible strength; she pulled Kelsea from the wagon as though she weighed nothing, rolled her from the cloak, and dumped her on the ground. Kelsea slitted her eyes, trying to determine where they were, but even with the brilliant illumination of lightning, she could barely see anything through the driving rain. The soil beneath her cheek felt like sand. They must be in the desert.

Brenna grabbed her and carried her some distance from the wagon. Kelsea tried to stay limp, but Brenna tickled her ribs, and Kelsea could not keep herself from an involuntary twitch.

"Don't bother, True Queen," Brenna muttered. "I know you have been awake for some time now. Feigning unconsciousness will not serve you."

"What do you mean to do?" Kelsea asked.

Brenna did not reply, but the next flash of lightning revealed a wide, bestial grin. She looked different, younger, but Kelsea could not assess the change before the light faded again. A few more steps and the rain stopped pelting her face and body; they were in a shelter of some sort. Brenna dumped her without ceremony on a hard stone floor, and Kelsea yelped as she landed on her elbow.

"Wait here, little queen. I will not forget you."

Kelsea gritted her teeth and tried to pull herself upright. With her hands tied behind her back, the best she could do was to wriggle on the floor. In desperation, she looked down at her chest and found the sapphire peeking out from her shirt. But no, it was the wrong sapphire, not the one she needed. Tear's sapphire was not for inflicting wounds. Finn's sapphire would have helped her here, but she had given it back to the Red Queen. Why had she done that? She could barely remember, and her mind gave her nothing but a flash of Arlen Thorne's face.

After another minute Brenna returned, her grating footsteps tramping across the stone floor. With a thud and a sharp cry, the Red Queen landed beside Kelsea, and then Brenna moved away.

"Who is it?" the Red Queen whispered.

"Brenna. Arlen Thorne's witch."

"Witch indeed. I can't find her at all."

Kelsea nodded agreement. Brenna was like Row Finn; she had never existed clearly within Kelsea's mind, as other people seemed to. So many children born after the Crossing, born with oddities that had filtered down to the present-day Tearling in such unpredictable ways. Magic was all over the Tear, if one took the trouble to look, and so much of it seemed to trace back to that one moment, the ships gliding through the hole in the horizon. But was the Crossing really at root, or was it Tear's sapphire, the sapphire that ran underground all through the Tearling?

What has it done to us? Kelsea wondered, momentarily distracted. *What has it done to all of us?*

A match flared, and she saw Brenna's silhouette across the room, crouching over a pile of sticks. They were in some sort of stone building without windows. Kelsea could hear rain pounding on the wooden roof. The place itself seemed long abandoned;

a few chunks of wood in the corner were all that remained of furniture.

Brenna straightened, clapping her hands together to clear them of ash, and Kelsea saw that she'd been right: Brenna looked different. Her formerly white hair was honey-blonde, and her cheeks were bright with color.

"You're no longer albino?" Kelsea asked.

"I never was. People are quick to believe the first foolish glance of their eyes."

"What are you, then?" the Red Queen asked. Kelsea sensed her playing for time, but what good would that do them out here? Even if Mace and Pen had somehow managed to track them from Demesne, they would never find this place. Brenna had not stumbled upon an old abandoned house in the desert by accident. This place had been chosen.

"Mort Queen! My master spoke of you often." Brenna glanced at the fire, which had strengthened, casting flickering shadows on the walls. "We will wait for the fire to build a bit, so we can all see well. Otherwise, this will not be nearly such good fun."

"What are you?" Kelsea asked, following the Red Queen's lead. Delay was better than nothing.

"I am a tool. My master's useful tool."

"What sort of tool?"

"You will not distract me, bitch. But I will tell you, as it pertains to the show." Brenna said the final word with relish, and Kelsea shuddered. She smelled torture here, in one form or another. The woman's excitement was too pronounced for anything less.

"Before I could even walk, our handlers in the Creche realized that I had a curious talent," Brenna continued. "I absorb pain. Not physical pain, but pain of the mind, the heart. I could take a man's worst memories, the most terrible things he had done or had done to him, and absorb them into myself. For the hour they paid for, my clients could be free of care."

"I suppose people paid a high price for that."

"Oh, they did." Brenna squatted down and checked Kelsea's bonds. "But the relief was only temporary. At the end of the hour, they had to take their pain back."

"Ah," Kelsea murmured, seeing Brenna's strange value now. To certain parties, she would be worth a lifetime's supply of morphia. "And what about Thorne?"

Brenna slammed the side of Kelsea's face into the floor. Kelsea tasted blood in her mouth.

"You don't say his name. I saw what you did. I saw—" Brenna fell silent. In that moment, she seemed distracted, but Kelsea could make no use of her distraction. The Red Queen was struggling to sit up, but she was having no more success than Kelsea. Playing for time was all they had left.

"What did you do for your master?" Kelsea asked.

"I took his pain, and held it." Brenna's features were clear, almost beautiful. Her eyes were a deep, cold shade of blue. "I never gave his pain back. It leached the life from me, took my youth and turned me pale, but I held his pain so that he could do the things he needed to do. To keep us safe."

Kelsea closed her eyes. She had misjudged Thorne, categorized him as a pure sociopath, but he was not. He had felt pain when he was dying, great pain, far greater than the wounds Kelsea had inflicted. Brenna had no longer been able to help him.

"So you're a conduit, then?" the Red Queen asked in Tear. "To drain off pain?"

"Sometimes." Brenna grinned, a grin so savage that Kelsea shuddered again. "But I have other talents. My master rarely needed them, but I think we will make good use of them here."

She grabbed the Red Queen by the hair and dragged her into a sitting position. The Red Queen grunted with pain, but did not scream, as Kelsea was sure Brenna had intended.

"You, Mort bitch, my master spoke of many times. You tried to cheat him when you thought you could get away with it. You will make a good demonstration."

"Demonstration of what?"

Brenna squatted on her haunches and stared into the Red Queen's eyes. The Red Queen tried to turn away, but she could not, and gradually her head stilled, her gaze fixed and pinpointed on something Kelsea could not see, her mouth dropping open in horror.

"I own pain," Brenna remarked, almost casually, never breaking gaze with the Red Queen. "I manipulate it. I can draw pain out if I want. But I can also magnify it."

The Red Queen began to squeal, a high, animal squealing, a hog in a slaughtering pen. Kelsea closed her eyes, but could not block the sound.

"Think of the worst thing you've ever done, the worst that's ever happened to you," Brenna whispered. "I can make you live there."

The squealing stopped. The Red Queen's eyes had rolled up into her head. Her face gleamed with sweat, and a thin line of drool had begun to work its way from her mouth. Her entire body shuddered.

"Stop it!" Kelsea cried. "You have no reason to do this to her!"

"She cheated my master," Brenna replied steadily. "That's reason enough, but not all. I want you to see what's in store for you, Tear bitch. This show is for you."

"Motherrr!" the Red Queen howled.

"I think we can loose her now," Brenna remarked, straightening. She produced a knife, bent over, and began to cut the Red Queen's bonds. "She's not going anywhere. And it makes for a better show."

"Mother, I'm *sorry*!" the Red Queen screamed, and Kelsea saw that tears had begun to leak down her cheeks as words tumbled from her mouth. "Please don't! Don't, Mother! I'll be good, I promise! Don't sell me away." Her unbound hands went to her face, her nails drawing a long set of gashes down one cheek. Blood ran from the wound and began to drip down her neck. Kelsea rolled over and retched.

"Do you have bad memories, Kelsea Glynn?" Brenna asked softly. "Anything you regret? Anything you've been trying to run from?"

Kelsea wriggled away from the words, but Brenna was right on her, lifting her head by the hair.

"I will find it. Whatever it is, believe me, I will find it and it will happen to you again and again, until you know nothing else."

Kelsea shut her eyes, determined not to meet Brenna's gaze. Brenna tossed her on her back, and a moment later Kelsea felt the gentle prick of fingernails on her eyelids.

"Open them," Brenna whispered. "Open them or I will take them from you."

Several feet away, the Red Queen was still sobbing and pleading with her invisible mother. The sound was terrible, but the thought of being blind was worse. Kelsea opened her eyes and found Brenna's face right over hers.

"Where is it?" Brenna whispered, and Kelsea realized in horror that she could *feel* the woman inside her mind, searching, prying. "Where is that thing, that worst thing?"

Is this what I did? Kelsea wondered, appalled. Brenna was working through her mind with all the finesse of a thief tearing apart a drawer full of clothing; it was like being bludgeoned. Kelsea tried to break eye contact, but she could neither look away nor close her eyes.

Did I do this to others?

"Buried deep," Brenna muttered. And Kelsea realized, terrified, that Brenna was drawing nearer to a deep, dark pocket in her mind: Lily's memories, Lily's life before the Crossing, constant fear punctuated by staccato notes of violence and violation. Lily's terrible life, which Kelsea had been forced to live as well.

"Ah," Brenna murmured with relish. "I see you now."

Kelsea gave a tremendous heave, her body arching off the ground. But she still could not break the contact. Somewhere nearby, she heard the Red Queen choking.

"What do we have here?" Brenna asked, her voice teasing. Her fingers tickled Kelsea's ribs, making her writhe, but Kelsea still could not look away. She could feel Lily's memories climbing up from their dark hole in her mind, scrabbling for purchase, gaining traction. Greg Mayhew, Major Langer, the animal called Parker, soon they would all reach her, and then—

"You leave her alone."

Brenna jumped away. The contact in Kelsea's head broke, and she moaned at the mercy of that, the relief of Lily's memories falling back into the darkness of her mind, where they belonged. Her eyes were dry and aching; she had to blink a few times before she could focus on the figure in the doorway. There she found the last person she would ever have expected: Ewen, the Keep jailor.

"Ewen, run!" Kelsea shouted. Ewen had a knife, but his eyes were wide, the eyes of a child afraid of the dark. Kelsea could not have him die here, not Ewen, not when she had already killed so many others . . .

"Yes, get out of here, boy," Brenna snarled. "This is none of your business."

"That's the Queen of the Tearling," Ewen replied, his voice trembling, "and I am a Queen's Guard. The Queen is my business. You leave her alone."

"*Queen's Guard*," Brenna repeated, her voice dripping with mockery. "You're a plaything to them, a mascot. You don't even have a sword."

These words took a visible toll on Ewen; his white face paled even further and he took a great gulp of air. But still, he raised his knife and took another step forward into the room.

"Ewen, don't look at her!" Kelsea cried. The sound of gagging came from her left, and when she turned, she saw the Red Queen throttling herself. With a tremendous heave, Kelsea rolled onto her stomach and began wriggling toward her.

"Evelyn!"

Staring off into the distance, the Red Queen removed her hands from her throat and reached down, her fingers hooked into claws. Then, in a single swipe, she tore a wide gash open on her right thigh. Kelsea tried to kick her hands away, but could find no leverage.

"Evelyn, wake up!"

"Mother?" the Red Queen whispered, and with dawning horror, Kelsea realized that the Red Queen was reaching out for her. She scooted backward, but the Red Queen began to crawl toward her, continuing to reach out, her hands grasping at nothing.

"Mother," she croaked, weeping. "I'm sorry I ran."

Brenna had cornered Ewen, and she advanced on him now, slowly, the knife tucked behind her back, a smile stretching her mouth.

"Let us discuss this, boy. Come here, look at me."

"No!" Kelsea shouted, but she saw, despairing, that Ewen was already caught, staring at Brenna with wide eyes and open mouth. Kelsea felt a light pressure on her ankle, looked down, and screamed; the Red Queen was stroking her foot, her mouth upturned in a blood-dabbled smile.

"Mother?"

Sobbing, Kelsea scrambled away, crawling toward Ewen, desperate to break him away from Brenna. She pulled herself forward on her good elbow, one sliding foot at a time, shouting Ewen's name, but miserably aware that she was moving too slowly, that she would not reach them in time . . . and then she looked up, stunned, as Ewen's voice echoed throughout the stone room.

"I see that you have a knife behind your back."

Brenna's smile slipped. She stared at Ewen for a long moment, eyes wide and teeth gritted in concentration.

"You will drop your knife."

Brenna's face contorted with rage, so much anger that Kelsea could feel it across the room, like heat. Ewen moved forward, raising his knife, and Brenna's eyes rounded in shock.

"You can't," she whispered. "You can't be—"

"Drop your knife," Ewen demanded again, and Kelsea could only stare at him, wondering if she was dreaming. He was nearly twice Brenna's size—though until a few moments before, Kelsea had been sure that Brenna was the larger of the two—and she retreated before him, backing toward the fire. She stabbed out wildly with her knife, but Ewen remained just out of her range.

"Put it down."

"No!"

"Put it down," Ewen repeated. His face was like a wall, both stubborn and patient, and Kelsea suddenly got an inkling of what was going on here: Brenna had picked a bad target. There was nothing inside Ewen for Brenna's particular brand of suffering to latch on to, because Ewen was different.

Good.

"Where is it?" Brenna shouted, her eyes locked on Ewen's face. She stabbed at him again, but this time she swung beyond her reach and lost her balance, falling forward. Ewen made to grab her, and she sliced at his arm, then scrambled backward, right into the fire.

"Grab her!" Kelsea shouted, wriggling wildly. Ewen was trying to pull Brenna from the fire; he let out a cry as the flames seared his hand. Brenna's shrieks echoed through the tiny stone building until Ewen finally succeeded in hauling her free, but her thick dress was flaming and there was nothing to tamp the fire. Brenna screamed in agony as Ewen hovered over her, helpless. A stomach-churning smell had begun to fill the air, one that Kelsea remembered well from the Argive.

"Roll her!" she shouted at Ewen. "Roll her on the ground!"

Ewen gulped and began rolling Brenna with his feet, trying to damp the fire. But Kelsea knew it was already too late. Brenna had stopped screaming.

"Glynn."

She looked down and found the Red Queen lying beside her. Her eyes were only half open, but Kelsea could see a red gleam between the lids. Something awakened inside Kelsea, an atavistic instinct that spoke of danger, but she asked, "Are you all right?"

"No." The Red Queen gestured toward her body, which was a bloody mess. "But I am back, at least."

"Majesty?" Ewen asked in a broken voice. "Majesty, I tried my best, she ... I think she ..."

"Ewen, come here."

"Majesty—"

"I need you to cut my bonds."

Ewen scrambled to his feet and hurried over with his knife. Kelsea wriggled to one side as he began to cut, then her wrists were suddenly free and she clasped them in front of her and stretched, feeling her shoulders sing in relief.

"You listen to me, Ewen," she ordered. "She would have killed me. She would have tortured me for pleasure, and then she would have killed me. And she would have killed *you* if she could have caught you. But you didn't kill her. You asked a prisoner to surrender her weapon, and she refused."

Ewen nodded, but a shadow had fallen across his face, and Kelsea did not think it would be an easy shadow to dispel.

"How did you come to be here, Ewen?"

"The Captain, Majesty. He sent me here. Me and Bradshaw."

"The magician? Is he here?"

"No, Lady. He went to fetch the Captain, days ago. It's just me."

Kelsea pushed herself to her feet and crossed the room to stand over Brenna. Her body was a blackened ruin, and Kelsea felt a stab of grief. She had despised this woman, but in the end, Brenna's grudge had been legitimate. The truth had been staring Kelsea in the face for weeks: executing Thorne had been a terrible mistake, and what she had done to him in the process had been even worse.

"Ewen," she muttered. "There are cloaks in the wagon outside. Bring them here."

Ewen hurried away, his face betraying relief at being given an easy task. Kelsea drew a deep breath and regretted it immediately; the air stank of charred flesh.

"Glynn," the Red Queen whispered again, and Kelsea returned to squat beside her, picking up Brenna's knife along the way.

"When we get back to town," she told the Red Queen, "we'll tend to your wounds."

"No need. Look."

Kelsea looked down and found that the gashes in the Red Queen's thighs were already healing somehow, flesh reassembling itself from nowhere.

Ewen returned, almost running, with the cloaks, and Kelsea directed him to throw them over Brenna's corpse. She planned to cremate the remains, but that was nothing Ewen would need to see.

"Glynn," the Red Queen croaked again. "Send the boy outside."

Kelsea nodded to Ewen, who hesitated for only a moment before he left the tiny house, closing the door behind him. Kelsea turned back to the Red Queen and caught another flash of red in her eyes.

"I am changing," the Red Queen said steadily. "Changing into something else. I am no longer master of myself. Something in my blood tells me to kill you, and I want to listen to it."

Kelsea drew back.

"I could stand feeding on flesh. In some ways, I have done nothing else, all the years of my reign." The Red Queen smiled, her eyes deep red flares. "But to be controlled by another, never directing my own fate . . . I lived that life long ago. I cannot face it again."

"What happened to you?"

The Red Queen offered a hand, and Kelsea saw Finn's sapphire sitting on the Red Queen's palm.

"Would you see, Glynn? If you would, you must do me a kindness in return."

Do me a kindness. The words echoed inside Kelsea's head, and she saw Mhurn, his upturned face smiling as she cut his throat. She was suddenly frightened, even more frightened than she had been when she had woken and found Brenna standing over her in the dark.

"I wouldn't kill you before. What makes you think I'll do it now?"

"It is different, Glynn. Now I am begging you."

Kelsea shut her eyes. Something pawed at her hand, and she looked down to see the Red Queen prying open her fist, depositing Finn's sapphire into her palm, and then squeezing her hand closed again.

"I know what you fear," the Red Queen whispered. Her eyes glinted red. "You fear to become me."

That was wrong. Kelsea did not want to become the Red Queen, no, but this wasn't what kept her awake at night. What she feared, more than anything, was becoming her mother.

"You should fear it. But death is fluid. There is all the difference in the world between cold-blooded murder and the prevention of agony. And Glynn, I am begging you."

Kelsea looked down at Finn's sapphire. She did not want it, could not wear it, but she could not simply cast it away either. Powerful things had to be guarded. If she was a Tear, as Finn and the Fetch had claimed, then her family had been guarding such things for a very long time.

"I can't kill myself, Glynn. I don't have it in me. But you could, I think, and take no injury from the act. You make yourself into whatever you wish to be."

Kelsea almost winced at these words. Again she saw Mhurn, smiling as Coryn slid the needle into his arm. At the time, Kelsea had thought it was mercy, but was it really? The Red Queen lay before her, not the clumsy mangled body, but the woman beneath, outlined in red light. Yet the Red Queen was fading, being overtaken by something else . . .

"I don't have long, Glynn. Look and see."

Kelsea looked, and almost drew back in terror. The woman's mind, which had fought her so hard before, was now wide open, a vast, roaring metropolis of thoughts and ideas and memories and regrets. Sound, sight, feeling, all of it swept over Kelsea like a tide, so strong that she thought she might drown.

At the bottom of it all was the mother, trapped in a vast web of contradictory feelings: love, hatred, jealousy, longing, regret, sorrow. The Beautiful Queen had viewed young Evelyn as a pawn, just as Evelyn herself now viewed others, a cycle that seemed to Kelsea almost inevitable, and the sadness of that idea nearly made her stop and withdraw from the Red Queen's mind. But she didn't, for, as always, the story was the compelling thing, worth all of its sufferings to find out the ending.

When Evelyn was fourteen, the Cadarese king offered the Tearling an alliance, a complicated trade involving horses and lumber, gems and gold. The negotiations had been long and complex, dragging on for months. By the end, both ambassadors were exhausted and the Tear court was utterly tired of entertaining the Cadarese delegation, which expected elaborate courtesies and consisted almost entirely of men who didn't know how to keep their hands to themselves. The entire Keep breathed a sigh of relief when the two delegations reached a tenuous agreement, and in order to seal the deal with goodwill, the Beautiful

Queen threw in Evelyn, the court bastard, as a gift to the Cadarese king.

Evelyn was used to being treated differently. She had lived with the snide remarks, the praise that others heaped on Elaine—her beautiful sister, the purebred—while in Evelyn they only seemed to find fault. She was even used to her mother's neglect, which vacillated between indifference and irritation. But this final betrayal . . . Evelyn had not been ready for it. There was a scene there—an image that would not come clear to Kelsea, perhaps because it existed in a haze for Evelyn as well—a scene of screaming and recrimination and tears and, finally, begging, fruitless begging that Evelyn remembered only dimly, through a dark veil of humiliation. Her mother had not been moved, and in the end Evelyn had been bundled off with the Cadarese. Her last view of the Keep was almost identical to Kelsea's own: standing at the far end of the New London Bridge, rent with sorrow, surrounded by men she couldn't trust, her eyes drawn helplessly back to her city. But by the time the delegation had traveled out of sight of New London, the sorrow had turned to rage.

The Cadarese delegation never made it home. On the third night out, the ambassadors, drunk on a complimentary keg of Tear ale and grandiose dreams of the rewards they would receive from the King for completion of their mission, went to sleep without securing the strange, ugly child they were hauling home. She had been so curiously withdrawn throughout the journey that they had forgotten all about her. They had gone through the bulk of the keg, and most of them barely put up a struggle when the child Evelyn tiptoed up, knife in hand, and began cutting throats.

A hand grasped Kelsea's.

"I don't have long," Evelyn whispered. "Please. Everything is cold. And my heart . . ."

Kelsea listened for a moment, and found that the woman was right; her heart was beating, but oddly, sluggishly, as though it were a clock winding down, so many ticks and then a pause. But there was so much more story to see! Only one man had woken completely, and at the sight of the blood-drenched child, her teeth drawn back like an animal's and her eyes glittering with death, he had fled south into the Dry Lands, never to be heard from again. The incident had wrecked the Cadarese alliance, although it was hushed up and very few people knew what had really happened; the popular story was that negotiations had simply failed. Even now, Kelsea could stop and marvel at how well Evelyn had unwittingly served her own future, for if the Tear and Cadare had built a lasting alliance, Mortmesne could never have risen to the dominance it had enjoyed. Instead, the murder of the ambassadors—a murder that the Cadarese king believed, until the end, had been committed by the Tear—had soured the relationship between the two countries for years to come. When a young sorceress emerged from nowhere and began to wreak havoc on what was then New Europe, there was no unity, and thus no concerted effort to stop her. But that was years in the future. After killing the Cadarese ambassadors, Evelyn had fled north and—

"Please," the Red Queen repeated.

"Can you not end yourself?" Kelsea asked in desperation.

"I have tried already. The giving in, it goes too much against my grain. My body will not accept that there is no future."

Kelsea believed it; the anguish in Evelyn's eyes was too real. Given the choice, this woman would want to end her own life, to control her death as she had mastered everything else. Even dimly, Kelsea could see the agony it would cost her to put her death in the hands of a stranger.

"I don't want to do this," she said, and was surprised to find that the words were true.

Evelyn smiled grimly. "There's a thing my mother used to say: have is the hell of want. This is where we've ended up. Please."

Help me, Kelsea begged, not knowing to whom she spoke.

Barty? Carlin? Mace? Tear? The Queen of Spades, the thing that had been inside her when she murdered Arlen Thorne—for she understood, now, that it had been murder—that thing was gone. But there was nothing to replace it. There was only Kelsea. She had wanted to be herself again, but only now did she understand how much that wish would cost. She could feel Evelyn's heart before her, as vulnerable as though it lay in her hands.

"Soon it will stop on its own," Evelyn whispered. "And I am afraid, so terribly afraid, that it will begin to beat for someone else."

Kelsea hesitated, a rogue part of her still desperate to see the end of the Red Queen's story. Row Finn was there, waiting, and there was so much more that Kelsea needed to know . . .

"Please," Evelyn repeated. "I am at the end."

And she was. Kelsea felt the woman's heartbeat unraveling. The ghosts of Mhurn and Thorne seemed to wander in and out of her field of vision, but strangely, Kelsea did not fear them. Katie, too, was there, demanding a share of Kelsea's mind. Kelsea sensed time growing short, and she raised the knife over Evelyn's chest, gripping it in both hands so that it would not slip. As with Mhurn, she had no courage for a repeat.

"He fears you, you know," Evelyn whispered. She gestured to Finn's sapphire, now dangling from Kelsea's hand, its dark facets glittering in the firelight. "Take that, and get it done."

Kelsea stared at her, but Evelyn had already closed her eyes.

"I'm ready, child. Don't lose your nerve now."

Kelsea took a deep breath. Their faces were before her again—Mhurn and Thorne—but Evelyn was right; there were many different kinds of death.

"A kindness," she whispered, blinking back tears.

"Yes." Evelyn's lips lifted in what might have been a smile. "A kindness."

Summoning everything she had, Kelsea brought down the knife.

Book III

Chapter 11

The Tear Land

The resurgence of fundamentalist Christianity in William Tear's town was a great blow, one that Jonathan Tear clearly recognized but could not counteract. Few things are more dangerous to an egalitarian ideal than the concept of a chosen people, and the divide drawn by the early iteration of God's Church helped to exacerbate the many ideological faults that already underlay the landscape. When the chips were down, Tear's people were ready to turn on each other, and the fall of the Town was very quick, so quick that this historian wonders whether all such communities are not destined to fail. Our species is capable of altruism, certainly, but it is not a game we play willingly, let alone well.

—*The Crossing in Hindsight,* ELLEN ALCOTT

In the two years following William Tear's death, Katie Rice had learned many things. She was with Jonathan constantly, and Jonathan sometimes simply knew things. But there was more to it than that. Sometimes Katie felt as though she existed at the hidden heart of the Town, a hub where all of the Town's secrets were buried, and by now she knew many things, even some she wished she did not.

She knew, for instance, that when Lily Tear was in the final extremity of her childbirth, Jonathan and Mrs. Johnson, the midwife, had tried to perform a caesarean section. The results were ghastly, and Lily had died screaming. Katie would hear those screams to the end of her days, but that was not the worst of it. In the last moment, a thought had come arrowing out of Jonathan, the thought limned with despair, and yet so clear and sharp that Katie could almost read it, as though he had written it down:

We are failing.

Katie didn't understand this. Lily's death was not Jonathan's fault; if anything, it was his father's fault, for failing to return with doctors, or even to bring the White Ship safely in the original Crossing—though Katie could not truly believe this, not with the memory of Tear's anguished face upon her. He had already punished himself. No fault could be laid at Jonathan's door, but Katie knew that he blamed himself for his mother's death. No man was an island, perhaps, but Jonathan was at least an isthmus, and Katie did not try to talk him out of his guilt. He would not be comforted, could only work his way out of it in time. Katie knew him well enough to understand that.

She knew that two more children had disappeared: Annie Bellam, while walking up from the dairy, and Jill McIntyre, who had been playing hide-and-seek down by the schoolyard, both of them gone without trace. These disappearances were bad, but because of Jonathan, Katie also knew that the depredations in the graveyard had begun again, that fifteen graves had been dug up over the past fourteen months, all of them belonging to children. The Town at large did not know about the graveyard—Katie herself had filled in several of the graves, tamping them down with extra dirt to hide the settling and covering them with leaves—but after the McIntyre girl's disappearance, the Christers had gotten much worse. Paul Annescott, or Brother Paul, as he now styled himself, claimed that the disappearances were a judgment on the Town, a punishment for weak faith. This did not surprise Katie; what floored her was the number of people who listened. It was just as she'd feared: with William Tear gone, there was no voice strong enough to counteract the increasingly hysterical flow of religious rhetoric. Mum and Jonathan were working on it; Jonathan did not quite have his father's ability to sway a crowd, but he could talk a good game when he needed to, his voice quiet and logical, the voice of a man who only wanted what was best for everyone. But it wasn't enough. Eight months earlier, some hundred people had begun construction of a church, a small white clapboard building on the southern end of town, and now that the church was finished, Annescott held sermons there every morning. He had given up his day job of beekeeping, but no one dared remonstrate with him, not even Jonathan. Katie knew many things now, but she didn't know how to fix what was wrong with the Town. She hoped Jonathan did, but couldn't be sure of that either, and she had an uncomfortable feeling that the rest of Jonathan's guard was riddled with doubt as well.

Gavin was the worst. He complained constantly about the shifts Katie assigned him, how they interfered with his duties to the church. If she had known he would turn out so devout, she would never have chosen him, but she couldn't let him go now. He was still the best knifeman in the group, and Morgan and Lear looked up to him almost as much as they did Jonathan. (*More, perhaps,* Katie's mind often remarked, and she shuddered, feeling that nothing good could come of that.) This in turn swayed Alain and Howell, who followed wherever the majority led. Virginia remained Katie's staunch ally, but even this felt like a failure to Katie, that she had been able to retain the loyalty of the one woman in the group, but not the men. She didn't know whether it was sexism or not, but either way, she thought that William Tear would have been disappointed. Sooner or later, she knew, Gavin was going to challenge her for leadership of Jonathan's guard, and Katie had no idea how she would fight off such a challenge. Jonathan himself would back her, but Katie shouldn't need Jonathan to intercede; that would only confirm her lack of authority. The problem went round and round in her head, but she could see no answer that didn't include throwing Gavin out of the guard.

Of course, all of these disagreements had to be hushed up outside their circle. To the Town, the seven of them were merely Jonathan's friends, and one of them was with him at all times. At night, a member of the guard slept on the spare bed they had moved into Jonathan's living room. There was much grumbling about night duty, and Katie knew that most of them—Gavin and his people, at least—thought she was being alarmist. Katie didn't care. There was still no sign of the violence that William Tear had foreseen, but she didn't doubt that it was coming, and she was determined to spot it far in the distance. She had made Tear a promise, and that promise seemed to mean infinitely more now that he was dead. Some days she still felt as though she and the others were children, merely playing at adult business, but they had no alternative. There was no one else.

She knew that Row Finn had completed two expeditions with Jen Devlin's team of mountaineers and that, a month ago, he had left on a third. As Row's friend, she also knew that he was no more interested in exploring than she was. But it was only from Jonathan that she learned what Row was seeking up there in the mountains: sapphire, the same sapphire that lay around Jonathan's neck. Everyone had found small chunks of the stuff from time to time; it seemed to underlie the bedrock of the Town. But in the mountains, the sapphire was much easier to get to, much easier to chip out in large, unbroken pieces. Jonathan knew this, and so Katie knew it as well, but she didn't understand precisely what Row would want with that sapphire, or what he meant to do with it if he could bring some back. She did know Row well enough to know that if there was something of value in the world, he would certainly want it for himself, and so in the past two years she had found herself looking at her old friend with something worse than regret: suspicion.

When Row was not off exploring mountains, he went to church every day. He was popular there, so popular that sometimes Paul Annescott let him give sermons. Katie had listened in a couple of times, though she was forced to do so from a stand of oaks across the road; Row's sermons were so popular that people spilled out the back door and onto the porch. Katie would listen, biting her nails, while Row's voice boomed through the packed doorway, talking about chosen people, people who were better and more deserving. He did have an excellent voice for a preacher, even Katie had to admit, deep and imbued with emotion that Katie suspected was wholly ersatz. There was an undertone of ruthlessness in Row's sermons that Katie was not sure others would catch; after all, she had once known him better than anyone. He had always been a consummate actor; the question was how much of the boy had filtered into the man. From Gavin, Katie knew that the church accepted Row's trips to the mountains as a pilgrimage, forty days' wandering in the wilderness or some such thing, and this, too, made her uneasy. Row would enjoy the parallel with Christ; always, he had felt cheated by his lack of status in town. If Row wanted to gull his church, Katie would shed no tears for them, but the idea of so many gullible people at any one man's beck and call seemed inherently dangerous.

To Jonathan?

She didn't know. In some ways, Jonathan was the biggest mystery of all. Katie often wondered why he should need a guard, when he knew so much more, saw so much more, than the rest of them. Sometimes it felt as though their guard was entirely for show, but Katie didn't know who they were trying to fool. Sometimes she even wondered whether William Tear had had any plan at all, or whether he had assembled them and trained them simply on a whim. Katie had the ability to kill a man with her bare hands, but how did that benefit anyone, when she couldn't even see the enemy she was fighting?

"What's wrong with this place?" she demanded of Jonathan one day, on their way to the library. People waved and smiled at them, but even Katie could feel the great vacancy behind these greetings, sensed the smiles melting the moment they turned away. Something in the Town had become twisted, and until Katie could find the end of the thread, there was no way to unravel it.

"They forgot," Jonathan replied. "They forgot the very first lesson of the Crossing."

"Which is what?" Katie hated when Jonathan talked about the Crossing. He knew plenty about it, more than anyone else their ages, but he would only parcel out the information in tiny nuggets.

"We take care of each other." Jonathan shook his head. "Even the original members of the Blue Horizon seem to have forgotten."

"Not Mum!" Katie snapped. "She knows."

"Much good it does."

"What does that mean?"

Unexpectedly, Jonathan took her hand. Katie thought about pulling away, but didn't. Jonathan's hand was warm, not unpleasant, and after all, what did she care if people saw them holding hands? Half the Town thought they were sleeping together anyway; it was a source of great amusement to the rest of the guard.

"Your mum is broken, Katie," he told her. "I'm sorry to say it, but her life was wrapped up in my father, and without him, she has nothing to keep her running."

Katie began to protest, but something silenced her, a voice inside that no longer allowed her to argue with the unpalatable truth. Every year that voice became stronger; Katie resented it sometimes, but it was often useful, particularly in a town where so much now depended upon the politics of pragmatism. Mum wasn't right, hadn't been right since William Tear had left. She went through the motions of her everyday life, but Katie almost never saw her smile anymore, and it had been months since she had heard Mum laugh. Mum *was* broken, and she wasn't alone. Tear's departure had torn the guts from the Town, and the longer he failed to return, the more Katie saw her community as a pack of wolves, fighting over the carcass. At the last meeting, Todd Perry had called for a vote to allow people to carry knives in town. Jonathan, Katie, and Virginia had weighed in heavily on the other side, and the motion was defeated by a narrow margin. But they couldn't deceive themselves about which way the wind was blowing.

"I hate them sometimes," Jonathan remarked quietly. "It's not how my father would have felt, but I do. Sometimes I think: if they want to walk around armed and build fences and let a church tell them what to do, let them wallow in it. They can build their own town of closed thinking, and live there, and find out later what a shitty place it really is. It's not my problem."

For a moment, Katie was too shocked to reply, for Jonathan had never expressed such ideas before. With his guard, he was the eternal optimist; there was nothing that couldn't be fixed, and now she was alarmed by the hopeless tenor of his words. She had promised William Tear that she would protect Jonathan, and she had always assumed that such protection, if it came to that, would be an act of knives. But now she wondered whether Tear might not have meant this moment, right here. Memory overtook her: sitting with William Tear in the backyard, five years ago now, the sapphire clutched in her fist. Had Tear known, even then?

"You're right," she said. "It's not how your father would have felt."

"I'm not my father."

"That doesn't matter, Jonathan. You're all we have left."

"I don't want it!" he snapped, dropping her hand. They were in front of the library now, and at the sharpness in Jonathan's voice, several children on the bench looked up, their eyes keen at the prospect of an argument.

"Too bad," Katie replied. She felt for Jonathan, she truly did—and, some nights, lying in her narrow bed, she thought that she might feel for him quite a bit—but this wasn't the time for sympathy. A guard was like a stone wall, and good stone didn't yield. Good stone cracked right down the middle before it would give an inch. She lowered her voice, mindful of the children listening in: perfect little receivers, ready to carry the conversation back to their parents.

"No one ever wants the fight, Jonathan. But if it comes to you, and it's a righteous fight, you don't walk away."

"What if we're destined to lose?"

"You don't know that."

"Don't I?" he demanded. His hand had crept up toward his chest, and Katie knew that he was clutching the sapphire that lay just beneath. The desperation in the gesture, the dependency it revealed, made Katie suddenly furious, and she snatched his hand away, feeling like a hypocrite as she did so, for she understood Jonathan's hatred, his contempt for these people who were too stupid to know that their future danced on the edge of a knife, a future of rich and poor, of violence and swords, of people bought and sold—

How do you know that?

I don't know, but I do.

This was true. It was as though someone else were inside her head, knowing it for her. The knowledge made her sick, but she thrust it away, focusing on Jonathan.

"You don't *know* anything," she hissed. "I don't give a fuck about magic, or visions. The future isn't set. We can change it at any time."

Jonathan stared at her for a long moment, and then, unexpectedly, he smiled.

"Are you laughing at me?" she demanded.

"No," he replied. "Just remembering something my father said before he left."

"What?"

"He said that I had picked the right guard. That you were the one to carry us through."

For a moment, Katie couldn't reply. Her anger vanished and she was suddenly moved, moved beyond description, to discover that after all these years she had not been found wanting in William Tear's eyes. He had chosen her to guard his son.

"Crisis over," Jonathan muttered, and shook his head ruefully. "But not for long. You might not believe in my visions, but I know when trouble's on the way, and there's bad trouble coming down the pike."

He did know, Katie admitted reluctantly to herself, but she shrugged it off and took his hand again, tugging him toward the library. "Not this afternoon, sibyl. Now hurry up."

Three days later, Row Finn walked back into town, alone. He must have been thirty pounds lighter, his clothing torn and ruined and his carrying pack barely in one piece. His steps were stumbling, and he appeared to be delirious. When he saw Ben Markham and Elisa Wu, who were fishing on the banks of the Caddell, he collapsed.

The story passed like quicksilver through the Town. According to Mrs. Finn, who jealously guarded her son from visitors, the expedition had become lost in the high mountains and they had succumbed, one by one, to exposure and starvation. Row had lasted the longest, and it was only by barest chance that he had found a narrow natural trail that led him down a pass. He had survived the journey home by eating such roots and berries as he was able to forage in the great forest.

The Town believed this story. Katie did not.

She had not seen Row yet, but she had heard plenty. His church flocked to him, determined to fatten him up. Virginia, who had gone over to see Row two days before, said the house was full of food, baked goods and soups.

"Women too," Virginia told Katie grimly. "Awful lot of women in that church like seeing Row Finn bedridden, I can tell you that."

For the rest of the mountain expedition, the Town had a rare united moment of genuine mourning. Jen Devlin in particular was an enormous loss. They held a single service for the eleven dead, a service through which Katie stood dry-eyed, watching not the various people who spoke in memory of the dead, but the Finn house, clearly visible two streets down the hill. She was desperate to question Row, but she didn't want an audience when she did so. The conversation would not be a good one. She didn't want to suspect her old friend, but she couldn't help it.

In the end, it took her more than a week to find him alone. Row's church was off on some sort of prayer retreat in the plains for two days, and his mother had gone to a card party. Row's tale had made Mrs. Finn a much sought-after guest, and Katie liked the woman even less for the grasping and desperate embrace of her fleeting popularity. The sight of her happily following a group of women, women who'd wanted nothing to do with her until now, made Katie want to shake the woman awake.

Katie didn't bother to knock before entering the Finns' house. When she reached Row's room, she found him on his side in bed, his eyes closed, his face that of an angel in repose. The weight he had lost only made him better-looking, his cheekbones like carved marble. Katie couldn't help wondering who Row would have been if he'd been born without that face.

"I know you're shamming, Row."

His eyes popped open, and he smiled. "You always know, don't you, Katie?"

"About you, I do." She dragged up a chair; there were several spread around the bed. "Hiding from all your guests?"

"They do wear me out."

She looked around the room, taking in the homemade bouquets and boxes of baked goods, and gave a derisive snort. "I suppose that's the price of being the new messiah, isn't it?"

"I'm not the messiah," Row replied, smiling pleasantly, but his eyes held their same old devilry. "Just a devout man."

"Why don't you tell me what happened to you out there?"

"That story is all over town by now."

"It is." She smiled, but her smile wasn't as genuine as Row's; it felt like winter on her mouth. "But I'd like to hear *your* story."

"Don't you trust me, Katie?"

"Don't play with me, Row. What happened?"

He told her substantially the same story she had already heard: lost in the mountains, the expedition dying slowly of starvation and cold. He had outlasted them by rationing his food carefully, and by huddling for warmth with the two horses until they too succumbed. There were only two points where Katie sensed Row fiddling with the truth: the food rationing, and the trail he had found down the mountain. But Katie couldn't make him shake his story, and finally she gave up and leaned back in the chair, unsatisfied.

"Didn't you miss me, Katie?"

Katie blinked. She *had* missed him, though she hadn't realized it until this moment. Things were more interesting with Row around; that hadn't changed, even if everything else had. But at the same time, the Town felt safer with Row gone.

"I missed you, Katie."

"Why?"

"Because you know me. It's useful to have everyone think I'm good, I suppose, but it's tiring too."

"I knew your church nonsense was a lie."

"Brother Paul is dying."

Katie blinked at the abrupt change of subject. "Of what?"

"Cancer, Mr. Miller thinks. Brother Paul should live out the rest of the year, but not much longer, and the pain may force him to end his own life long before that."

"Is he allowed to end his own life? I thought that was a sin."

"Maybe, but for most people, faith is a pretty flexible business."

"I've noticed."

Row grinned. "It doesn't have to be a bad thing, Katie. The faithful are *easy*. Easy to convince, easy to direct, easy to discard. When Brother Paul dies, he'll hand the church off to me."

"What do I care?" Katie asked, but inside, she felt a chill. She thought of the packed church she had seen at Row's last few sermons, the glut of people pouring out onto the porch.

How many? she wondered. *Three hundred? Four?*

"You could help me, Katie."

"No."

"Think about it. God has made these people malleable. They'll believe any damned thing that comes out of Brother Paul's mouth."

"Or yours."

"Or mine. We could make so much use of that!"

"To do what, Row?"

He grabbed her hand. If she had been talking to the new Row, charming and false, a few moments ago, she saw now that he was sincere. That made it worse, somehow. She would rather hear this from her enemy than from her old friend. She wanted to yank her hand back, but then she stilled as Row pulled a silver chain from beneath his shirt. Sapphire glimmered in the afternoon light.

"Where did you get that?" she demanded. "It's Jonathan's!"

"No, it's mine. I made my own."

"How?"

"You always thought William Tear was perfect," Row said with a chuckle. "But he's not."

That was no answer, but Katie's brow furrowed all the same, for she sensed an artful mixture of truth and lies in Row's statement, sensed that there *was* an answer there, if only she could riddle out what he meant.

"It works for me," Row told her. "Just like it works for Jonathan. I see things. I *know* things. I know that the great saint is dead."

Katie jumped up, knocking over her chair, and leaned over to grab his shoulders, slamming him back against the headboard.

"You'll keep your mouth shut, Row."

"Think about it, Katie," he repeated, ignoring her. "Tear is gone. The Town we always talked about, the Town where smart people like us would lead, and the rest would follow. We could make it ourselves."

Katie wanted to protest that she had never thought any such thing, but she had, she remembered now. She had thought so many awful things when she was young. It hurt to remember them. Row dislodged her hands from his shoulders, and belatedly, Katie realized that, starved or not, he was much stronger now. Katie saw devilment in his eyes . . . but not the harmless sort she remembered from when they were young. He tucked the silver necklace and its sapphire back underneath his shirt.

"What about all the nonbelievers, people who don't belong to your church? You think they'll sit happily by?"

"They'll be gone."

The flat certainty of this answer made her cold, for she sensed violence in it, a vast, nascent shadow whose contours she could barely glimpse.

"And what about me, Row?"

"Ah, Rapunzel. I wouldn't let anything happen to you." He grinned crookedly, just like the old Row, and for a moment Katie's guard wavered, all of her suspicion suddenly buried under nostalgia. They had been so *close* once, the two of them!

"What do you say, Katie?"

Despite everything, for a moment she was tempted to say yes, for even now, Row's vision still had the power to sway her: the place they had talked about for years, a true meritocracy, with none of Tear's ambiguous ideas to get in the way. She and Row had planned it together, built it like a castle inside their heads.

But I'm a different person now, Katie realized. *All the resentment I used to feel, it doesn't bind me now. I can let it go.*

But could she? All the contempt she felt for the people in the Town—fools with so little sense of self that they needed to believe in an invisible God who would peek inside people's bedrooms—that contempt suddenly overwhelmed her, and she could see Row's vision spread out before her: a town where such people were relegated to disenfranchisement, where their own foolishness was quarantined so that it could hurt no one. How wonderful it would be to live in a town where weak minds were punished, where people like Row and Jonathan—

Now who's being a fool? her mind demanded. *Jonathan? You really think there's room for Jonathan Tear in Row's paradise?*

That brought reality back with a thud. Katie might not know how Row meant to implement his grand plan, but she knew Row. He had always hated the Tears, hated the idea of them even more than the people themselves. Jonathan was not William Tear, perhaps, but he was far too dangerous to be allowed in Row's kingdom.

Katie stood up from her chair, feeling long-buried sorrow twist her insides. All those years ago, she had known that one day she would have to choose. But she hadn't known that it would have to be today.

"I can't go with you, Row," she told him. "I serve Jonathan Tear."

Row's face tightened, but only for a moment, and then that spurious good humor reappeared.

"Ah, yes, the infamous fighting force."

Katie's mouth dropped open.

"Did you really think I wouldn't find out, Katie? There are no secrets in this town. I've always known Tear was a fraud, but you didn't, did you?"

"He wasn't a fraud!" she shouted, outraged. "It's for Jonathan! It's to guard Jonathan!"

Row smiled indulgently, as though she were a child. "That's what Tear told you, certainly. But think about it, Katie. It may look like a guard, but what Tear was really training up is a police force. A *secret* police force, answerable only to his son. What sort of utopia needs secret police?"

"You think I don't know that you're jealous of Jonathan?" she demanded, and had the pleasure of watching Row's face darken. "You've always been jealous of him! You've always wanted what he has!"

"And what about you?"

"I serve the Tears," Katie repeated stubbornly. "I serve Jonathan."

Row threw back his head and laughed. "See, Katie? You're one of the faithful too!"

Katie grabbed him again, meaning to yank him from the bed. In that moment she hated Row, hated him utterly, because she could already feel his words digging into her mind, making her think twice, making her *doubt*. But after another moment she released him and backed away. Jonathan was there, always, and it would not serve Jonathan if she picked a fight with the Christers' favorite son now.

Row stretched again, but this time he swung his legs out of bed and got up. He was wearing nothing beneath his sheet; Katie did her best to look away before it dropped, but she failed, and the brief glimpse she got made her feel like she was burning inside. Then she was ashamed. This was her oldest friend; what had happened to the two of them? When had everything changed?

"How's that messiah working out for you, Katie? Spotted any feet of clay yet?"

"You stay away from Jonathan. Don't even come near him."

"I won't need to, Katie," Row replied, grinning . . . but now the grin seemed not appealing, but reptilian. She turned away, but a moment later her entire body spasmed as Row slid a hand between her legs.

"You look all you want, Katie."

"I don't want to."

"It must be exhausting, devoting all your time to a second-rate William Tear. Why not trade up?"

Katie's fists clenched. Beneath the excitement that had gathered in her belly, she felt a titanic wave of anger building, that he should think her such a fool, that he should treat her like one of the hundreds of other women in town who had already succumbed. They might not be friends anymore, but surely she deserved better than that?

"Tear's paradise will collapse beneath Jonathan's feet, Katie, just as I knew it would. And who will people turn to in the wreck, if not God?"

She fled then, ducking clumsily out of Row's room, banging her shoulder on the frame as she went.

"Think about it, Katie!" Row called after her. "You're on a sinking ship! Come over to mine, and just see how far we sail!"

Katie stumbled down the hallway, her eyes full of tears. On her way down the steps, she bumped into Mrs. Finn and several other women, but she could not even bring herself to exchange pleasantries, could only shoulder past the women with a muttered apology, moving faster with each step. By the time she reached the bottom of the porch, she had broken into a run.

L ady."
 Mace's voice. That was good, for even here, at the end of the world, she would have liked to see Mace one last time.

"I know you hear me, Lady. Will you wake up?"

Kelsea didn't want to wake up. She could feel William Tear's sapphire at her chest, almost like a companion that had accompanied her on strange journeys, but she was beginning to think that she had never needed the jewel to see into the past, for they were all with her now: Tear, Jonathan, Lily, Katie, Dorian . . . even Row Finn.

"Lady, if you don't wake up, I'm going to have you baptized."

Her eyes popped open, and she saw Mace sitting beside her bed, holding a candle. Around him was a darkened room. She sat up quickly.

"Lazarus? Is it you?"

"Of course it's him." Coryn appeared out of the gloom. "As though you could mistake that set of shoulders for anyone else."

Kelsea reached out to Mace, but he did not take her hand. They stared at each other for a long moment.

"I'll see myself out," Coryn muttered. "Glad you're well, Lady."

When he opened the door, Kelsea saw a piece of hallway lit by torchlight. Then the door closed, and she and Mace were once again staring at each other. Kelsea was reminded, suddenly and painfully, of that day on the bridge. The chasm between them had been vast, but it felt even larger now. She read distrust in his eyes, and it hurt far more than anger.

"Where are we?"

"In the house of a woman who was loyal to your mother. Lady Chilton."

"We're not in Gin Reach."

"No, Lady. About a day's ride north, in the southern Almont. You've been in fugue since we found you, three days ago."

"Three days!"

"It was a long one, Lady, and worrisome for the Guard. We should let Pen in here soon, lest he begin to chew on the furniture." Mace smiled, but the smile did not meet his eyes.

"You haven't forgiven me, Lazarus."

He remained silent.

"What did you expect me to do?"

"Tell us, dammit! I would have gone with you."

"Of course you would have, Lazarus. But I thought I was going to die. Why would I ask anyone to follow me there?"

"Because it's my job!" he roared, and his voice seemed to shake the timbers of the tiny space. "It's what I signed on for! The choice was mine, not yours!"

"I needed you to stay behind, Lazarus. I needed you to run the kingdom. Who else would I have trusted to get it done?"

At this, Mace's anger seemed to fade. He looked down at the floor, his cheeks coloring.

"You chose wrong, Lady. I failed."

"What do you mean?"

"The Keep is under siege."

"By whom?"

"The Arvath, with a legion of Mort. Our people are holed up inside, but they won't hold out forever. New London is under the rule of the mob, but the mob, too, is directed by the Arvath."

Kelsea's hands tightened on the covers. Her knuckles were white, but she hoped that Mace wouldn't notice. The thought of the Holy Father in her Keep—*sitting on my throne!*—was like a dark hole inside her. The entire city, the entire kingdom, at the mercy of Anders's poisonous god . . . the thought made her insides seethe, but in this moment, Mace's doubt seemed even more pressing.

"It was as much my fault as yours, Lazarus," she said softly. "Some days I wonder whether I shouldn't have let the cages roll."

"You were trying to do the right thing, Lady. It's not your fault that it went so wrong."

That made her think of Simon, of their long conversation in the dungeons. Whether the topic was physics or history, it made no difference; trying to do the right thing so often ended in wrong.

Kelsea shrank from the idea, for she felt it as the first step on the road to paralysis, an inability to make any decision at all for fear of unforeseen consequence.

"But me," Mace continued, "I left. We all left to get you out. We left the kingdom wide open, so the Holy Father could steal it."

"You can't have it both ways, Lazarus. Either the grey cloak stays on always, or it comes off for greater exigency. It was my fault, perhaps, for asking you to be both Queen's Guard and Regent. I'd imagine the two would often be at cross-purposes."

"Do not coddle me, Lady."

"Done is done, Lazarus. We both fell down, but you once told me there was nothing to be gained by dwelling on the past. The future, now, that's everything."

She extended her hand again.

"So what say we forgive each other, so we can keep moving forward?"

For a long moment, Mace merely stared at her hand, and Kelsea waited, feeling, again, as though she stood before a precipice. The Red Queen's face surfaced briefly in her mind, then disappeared. It had been a long journey from that edge to this, but something told Kelsea that the journey wasn't done, and how could she go anywhere without Mace? Guard, voice of doubt, voice of conscience . . . she needed all of these things. Her throat constricted as Mace reached out and took her hand.

"Wide as God's ocean," she whispered. "You remember?"

"I remember, Lady." He looked away, blinking, and Kelsea took the opportunity to stretch her arms and shoulders, which were still sore from Brenna's bonds. The news about the Holy Father roiled in her chest. She would have liked to go back and fix her own mistakes, but the roots of this problem went far deeper, all the way back to the fledgling settlement, the beginnings of the Tearling, where everything had begun to go wrong.

Tear was able to shuttle through time, she thought defiantly.

And there had been times, deep in her fugues, when Kelsea felt as though she were almost doing the same, not just seeing but traveling, as though she were actually there, in Lily's world, in Katie's. But she did not control it. Something was still missing.

"Lazarus, there was a man in the cell beside me, an engineer."

"Simon, Lady. We have him."

Kelsea smiled, relieved to hear some good news. God only knew what good a printing press would do the Tearling now, but still she was glad that Simon had gotten out.

"Where is he?"

"Downstairs. We can barely get Hall to concentrate on anything lately."

"Twins," Kelsea replied, nodding. "I see now."

"Why did you want him, anyway?"

She explained about the printing press, expecting Mace to make a scathing remark about books or reading. But he listened quietly, and when she was done, he remarked, "That's valuable, Lady."

"It is?"

"Yes."

"And where is the real Lazarus?"

His mouth twitched. "I have been . . . reading."

"Reading what?"

"Your books, Lady. I've read nine of them now."

Kelsea stared at him, genuinely surprised.

"They're good, these stories," Mace continued, his cheeks stained with light color. "They teach the pain of others."

"Empathy. Carlin always said it was the great value of fiction, to put us inside the minds of strangers. Lazarus, what of my library?"

"Still in the Queen's Wing, Lady, and under siege as well."

Kelsea's hands balled into fists. The idea of the Holy Father touching her books—for a moment, she thought that she would be sick all over the bedspread.

"Anyway," Mace continued, clearing his throat, "I see the value of such a press. If we ever get past this, Arliss and I will help Simon acquire his parts."

Kelsea smiled, moved. "I missed you, Lazarus. More than I missed the sunlight, even."

"Did they harm you, Lady?"

She grimaced, thinking of the jailor, the beating. Then she was ashamed. There had been plenty of other people in that dungeon. As a queen with something to trade, Kelsea had enjoyed a privileged position. Those others had had nothing.

My suffering was real, she insisted.

Perhaps. But do not let it blind you to those who suffer worse.

"No permanent harm, Lazarus," she finally replied. "I will put it behind me."

She looked around the room, at the candlelit shadows that flickered on the wall. Somewhere, very distant, she heard people talking.

"Lady Chilton's house, you said? I don't know her."

Mace sighed, and Kelsea saw that he was framing his words very carefully. "She is not . . . well, Lady. It will not be a risk-free accommodation."

"What's wrong with her? Is she mentally unstable?"

"That would be a kind word for it, Lady."

"Then why are we here?"

"Because we needed a place to wait out your fugue, and Lady Chilton was willing to take us in. We couldn't stay in that damned border town; too much attention. This house is large enough to house the people we brought with us, and there are plenty of supplies. Lady Chilton was well prepared for siege when the Mort came through. Mostly, though, we're here because she owes me a great debt."

"What sort of debt?"

"I saved her life once. She still remembers it."

"What's wrong with her?"

"Her malady is not our business, Lady. She has promised to stay in the upper floors, away from you. I hope to be out of here by tomorrow."

Kelsea was still uneasy at this, but she had no options to offer. She looked down at herself and saw that she was still wearing the filthy clothes she had worn out in the desert.

"I need some clothes."

Mace gestured toward the dresser. "Lady Chilton has loaned you a dress."

Thinking of the desert reminded Kelsea of the rest of that strange night as well, and she asked, "Is Ewen here?"

"Yes, Lady. We met up with him in Gin Reach, and a very strange tale he told us too."

"Strange, but true."

"Ewen torments himself with the idea that he's not a real Queen's Guard; 'mascot' was the word he used. I sent him to Gin Reach only as a precaution. Never thought anything would happen to him there."

"He saved my life, Lazarus. More, perhaps." Kelsea closed her eyes and saw Brenna's face, an inch from her own, her gaze digging into Kelsea's mind, into Lily's mind beneath.

We were both there, Kelsea realized suddenly. *Both there at once, Lily and I. How can that be?*

"Well, I will tell the rest of the Guard, Lady. If Ewen played the part of a hero, they will honor him for it."

"He did." She pushed back the covers. "Toss me that dress."

A few minutes later, Mace led her out into a long hallway lit by torches. The walls were constructed not of the light grey stone that held up the Keep but of deep, sand-colored blocks that appeared to have been etched by wind and time. A draft whipped down the hallway, ruffling Kelsea's hair and causing her to shiver.

"Poor insulation," Mace commented. "This place should have

been upgraded at least ten years ago, but Lady Chilton has let it go to ruin."

"Did she come to my coronation? Why do I—"

But she got no further, for Elston and Kibb suddenly came skidding around the corner, half the Guard behind them. Before Kelsea could even greet them, her hand was crushed in Elston's massive grip.

"Are you well, Lady?" he asked.

"Fine, El."

"I prayed for you, Lady," Dyer told her, and grinned as she slapped him lightly on the cheek. The sight of them made Kelsea smile, but at the same time, she felt uneasy. Mace, Elston, Kibb, Coryn, Galen, Dyer, Cae . . . all around her were glad faces, beloved faces, people she had missed, but beneath her joy at seeing them again lay a feeling of doom, delayed and distant but real all the same. If the Keep was truly under siege, they were all exiles now, people without a home.

"Are you in pain, Lady?" Coryn asked. "I have my kit."

"I'm fine," she replied, accepting handshakes from Kibb and Galen. Looking around, she found one face conspicuously absent.

"Where's Pen?"

"I sent him off to ride the perimeter, Lady," Elston replied. "There's no danger out here; we're on the plain, and any threat can be seen from miles away. But he was driving us all mad, poor lovesick—"

"Remember yourself!" Mace barked, and Kelsea felt a blush color her cheeks.

"Sorry, Lady," Elston murmured, but his eyes glinted with such good humor that Kelsea shook her head and swatted him on the shoulder.

"Who else is here?" she asked.

"Hall and his people are downstairs. Levieux, too, and he has requested a word with you when you have a moment."

"Levieux?'

"He was useful, Lady, helping us break into the Palais," Mace replied quickly, tipping her a look that said they would talk about it later. Kelsea nodded, but when she thought of the Fetch, she could not picture the man, only the boy, Gavin. What did that mean? She looked past Elston and jumped; for a moment she was sure that someone was standing down at the end of the corridor, watching her. But when she blinked, the figure was gone.

"Lady?"

She turned to Mace. "I thought I saw someone, down there at the bend."

"You're still not well, Lady."

Kelsea nodded, but the more she thought about it, the more she was certain that the figure had been there: a woman, in a long black dress and dark veil.

Mentally unstable, she thought, and a thread of unease wormed its way inside her.

"We'll leave in the morning," she told them.

"Lady?"

"You said that the Keep was under siege, Lazarus. We can't simply stay here, hiding, while the kingdom burns. What sort of queen would I be?"

"Ha!" Dyer turned to Coryn. "That's ten pounds!"

Mace shook his head. "We knew you were going to say that, Lady. My only question was how long it would take to come out."

"Well, it's true."

"You have no army, Lady. The Holy Father has an entire battalion of Mort mercenaries. The only thing you can accomplish by returning to New London is to get yourself killed."

Kelsea nodded, trying to take this advice to heart, to be the smart queen that she should have become. But she couldn't wait out here, in the middle of nowhere, away from everything. What could be fixed that way?

"Lady."

She turned, and there was Pen, coming from the other end of the hallway.

"Pen!"

She began to run down the corridor, but Mace grabbed her wrist. "Hold, Lady."

"What?"

"Things are no longer the same." Mace turned to the rest of the Guard. "All of you, back to your posts! You will see the Queen at dinner!"

Her guards moved along, and Kelsea couldn't help noticing that they seemed suddenly anxious to be away. Within a few seconds, they had all disappeared around various corners.

"Lady." Pen reached them, bowed. "It's a pleasure to see you well."

She stared at him, confused. This cold man was not the Pen she knew. Then she remembered the scene on the bridge, and understood. Pen was angry with her, of course he was, just like Mace. She had fled from all of them, from her Guard, straight into the arms of the enemy. She had tried not to think of Pen while she was in prison, but of course he had still been here, stewing in that betrayal. Well, she would make it up to him. She would—

"Pen will no longer be your close guard, Lady," Mace said flatly.

"What?"

"Starting tonight, Elston will take over Pen's duties."

Kelsea turned to stare at Pen, who in turn stared at the floor.

"What's happened?" she demanded.

"I will give you two a few minutes, but only a few," Mace replied, speaking to Pen. "After that, you will not be alone together again."

Pen nodded, but Kelsea turned on Mace. "You don't make changes to my Guard behind my back, Lazarus! I didn't ask for a new close guard. This isn't your decision."

"No, Lady," Pen said. "It's mine."

She turned back to him, her mouth falling open. They had been sleeping together, yes, but they could end that! It was no reason to change the Guard.

"Pen? What is this?"

"A few minutes," Mace repeated. Then he retreated down the hall toward Kelsea's room. Pen waited until Mace disappeared inside before raising his eyes to Kelsea, and she almost flinched at what she saw there: utter professionalism, nothing more.

"You don't want me anymore, Pen?"

"I am a guard, Lady. It's all I've ever wanted to be, ever since the Captain found me." He shrugged, smiling, and for a moment the ice broke and he was the old Pen, the Pen she knew. "I love you, Lady. I think I've loved you ever since you asked if you could help put up that damned tent. But while you were gone, I discovered that I cannot love you and be a Queen's Guard, all at once."

Kelsea nodded, but the nod was reflexive. She didn't love Pen, did she? She no longer knew. Sex had welded them, made them something far more than they were intended to be at the outset. Something moved over Pen's shoulder, and Kelsea thought she saw, again, a dark figure standing down at the end of the hall. Another blink and it was gone.

She returned her attention to Pen. Her pride was wounded; of course it was. But if she gave in to that impulse, she would lose not just a bed partner but a friend as well. She firmed her jaw, doing her best to conceal her disappointment.

"Do you mean to remain on the Guard?" she asked.

"Yes, Lady. But I will not be your close guard. And you will have to treat me as you treat the rest, or I can't stay."

She nodded slowly, feeling something like sorrow break inside her. They had not had many nights, the two of them, but they had been good nights, somewhere halfway between love and friendship, an oasis of sweetness in the harsh desert that comprised Kelsea's life since leaving the cottage. She would miss that side of Pen, but deep within the pain was a kernel of respect for him, growing larger every second.

We're alike, she thought, staring at Pen's face. Behind her eyes, she suddenly saw her city, its rolling hillsides aflame, and she realized that this work, the great work of her life, outweighed anything that she would ever want for herself. There might be more men, many of them, but none of them would ever get in the way of the work. She would not allow it.

Taking a deep breath, she reached out, offering her hand for Pen to shake. Pen smiled, his eyes bright and unguarded, and Kelsea realized that she would never see him this way again. They would talk, and laugh, and give each other hell, just as Kelsea did with the rest of her guards . . . but it would never again be like this. They shook hands, and Pen held on to her hand for a moment before he dropped it, swallowing. When he looked up again, Pen the man was gone, and he was now Pen the guard, his eyes flicking over her, distant and analytical.

"You don't look well, Lady."

"I just woke up." But he was right. She had been awakened by Mace. Katie's voice beat insistently against her mind, refusing to leave her alone.

"Levieux is here, yes? I need to speak to him." She needed to speak to him, all right, grab his shirt and shake him until he coughed up some answers about what had happened to Jonathan Tear. There was no need to wait for the slow pace of Katie's vision, not when she could demand the whole story from someone who had actually been there.

"You'll have to wait, Lady." Mace had reappeared behind her, with Elston in tow. Kelsea could not get her bearings in this place; there was something odd about the corridors, some proportion that was off. "Levieux left several hours ago, and said he won't be back until late. But there's dinner downstairs. Pen, go."

Pen left. Kelsea watched him go, feeling one last pang of sorrow, and then she turned back to Mace and Elston, her mouth hardening.

The work!

"This corridor moves, sir," Elston muttered. "I keep catching things around corners."

Mace looked over his shoulder, his face tightening. "I don't trust the mistress of the house. The sooner we're out of here, the better."

"Is this agreeable to you, Lady?" Elston asked. "Me as your close guard?"

She nodded, smiling up at him, though her heart ached.

"Let's get some dinner, then."

She followed them down the hall.

Kelsea came awake in darkness. For a moment, she didn't know where she was—it seemed every night was a new place to sleep these days—but then a torch snapped in its bracket and she remembered: she was in Lady Chilton's house, in the chamber Mace had assigned her. Elston was just outside the door.

Something was in the room.

Kelsea had heard the softest of movements behind her, little more than a whisper of air, somewhere near the door. She debated rolling over, but when she tried, she found her muscles frozen. She didn't want to see. Unbidden, her mind conjured up an image of the little girl in the dungeon, and Kelsea felt her entire body break out in gooseflesh. She could shout for help; Elston was just outside. But the child in the dungeon had been very quick.

Another soft sound, closer now, the soft rasp of leather against the floor. A footstep, perhaps, but Kelsea's imagination said differently. She pictured the child two feet from her, poised to leap.

Not like Brenna, her mind whispered, and Kelsea felt her nerves suddenly galvanized. No, she would not be taken as she had been by Brenna, overpowered, lying helpless. Keeping still, she flexed all of her muscles, preparing them for motion. Her knife was beneath her head, tucked into its scabbard under the pillow; there was no way to grab it without giving warning. But she thought she could have it out half a second after she began to move.

One last step, right beside Kelsea now. She whipped into motion, rolling toward the sound, and connected solidly, tumbling out of bed to land on top of her attacker. For a moment she saw a dark silhouette beneath her, and then the figure emitted a low, ratlike squeal as it fell backward. Kelsea jerked her knife from its scabbard and scrambled on top of the thing, looking for its neck. Then she drew back, horrified.

The creature had no face.

But a moment later, Kelsea realized how ridiculous that was. She had been fooled by the firelight, by her own overstimulated imagination. This was no monster, only a woman, wearing a long black dress and a lacy veil that covered her entire head. The woman tried to scramble backward, but Kelsea straddled her, pinning her down.

"Lady Chilton, I presume," she panted, exploring the veil with her hands. "And what do you want with me, that you stalk me around the house?"

Finding the edge of the veil, she jerked hard, tearing the lace away and revealing the woman's face to the light. But now it was Kelsea's turn to scramble backward as fast as she could, her breath tearing from her throat in a single harsh rasp.

The face beneath the veil belonged to her mother.

Chapter 12

The Mistress of the House

Hell? Hell is a fairy tale for the gullible, for what punishment could be worse than that we inflict upon ourselves? We burn so badly in this life that there can be nothing left.

—*Father Tyler's Collected Sermons*, FROM THE ARVATH ARCHIVE

"It was Mace's idea," the woman said, as though that explained everything.

They were sitting in two high-backed armchairs, facing the chamber's empty fireplace. It was cold, but Kelsea had taken the Red Queen's superstitions to heart, and refused to light a fire. She didn't understand Row Finn's long game—not yet—but if he was truly free, Kelsea could only be a threat to him now.

The torchlight was very dim, but Kelsea could not stop staring at her mother, hoping to find a flaw in her appearance, something that would indicate that the entire thing was a trick. But she found no such reassurance. The woman before her was older than the portrait Kelsea had seen in the Keep, fine lines bracketing her mouth and eyes. The black dress and veil, indicative of mourning, aged her further. But she was unmistakably Elyssa Raleigh.

"What was Mace's idea?"

"Why, to get me out." Elyssa gave a tinkling laugh. "So many people trying to kill me. It was almost exciting."

Kelsea looked to the door, almost in desperation. She had ordered Elston to fetch Mace on the double, but she had done so through a closed door, and now she worried that Elston might have misunderstood her words. When Mace got here, she thought she might throttle him. All of the guilt Mace had dispensed when Kelsea kept things to herself, and here he had been holding the biggest secret of all in his hands.

"Carroll and Mace were the best of my guards, the smartest, you know–" Elyssa paused, her doll's mouth turning down at the corners. "Mace told me Carroll is dead."

"Yes," Kelsea replied automatically, but a moment later she realized that she had never seen *his* body, either. Was he still out there somewhere too? Were Barty and Carlin? How could she take Mace's word about anything now? For years, Kelsea had wanted so many things from the woman sitting before her, love and approval and vindication and, later, a chance to scream into her face. But now that the moment was here, Kelsea didn't know what she wanted, except to wish that she were not in this room. She had gotten used to hating her mother, had grown comfortable with it. She didn't need the status quo shaken up now.

"They both had the idea, but Mace was the one who snuck me from the Keep. All those hiding places he has, you know. He moved me here." Elyssa frowned again. "It's a dull life, so far from the capital. Mace visits whenever he can, and I have my business–"

"What business?" Kelsea asked sharply.

"Dresses," Elyssa replied proudly. "I'm one of the most sought-after designers in the Tear. But I have to work from here, send someone to take measurements and orders." Her mouth drooped. "I can't go anywhere."

Kelsea grimaced. Any number of harsh phrases came to her lips, but she held them in. She would give this woman her full, undiluted opinion, but only after she got the whole story.

"But I am so pleased to see you!" Elyssa exclaimed, putting a hand on her arm. Kelsea tensed, but Elyssa seemed not to notice, too busy examining her, eyes roving over her face.

"And so pretty too!"

Kelsea recoiled, almost as though she'd been slapped. All of those days in the cottage when she had stood by the window, looking out and waiting for her mother to come . . . she had been so sure that her mother would be wise and kind and good, that she would praise Kelsea, as Carlin did not, praise her for all the things she had learned, all the work she had done. Even if Kelsea had been pretty, that was not the praise she waited for, because even in her youngest years, she had already known how little it truly meant. For a moment, she hesitated on the point of telling Elyssa that this beauty wasn't her own, then swallowed the words.

"I thought there was a body," she croaked. "When you died, there was a body."

"So there was," Mace replied behind her, making Kelsea jump. He had slipped silently into the room while they spoke, and now his large form emerged from the shadows to rest a hand on Elyssa's shoulder.

"How did you get in here?" he asked.

"This place is full of secret passages. A trick I learned from you."

"The body," Kelsea demanded. "You said there was a body."

"The Queen's dead body," Mace agreed, "lying in bed with a cut throat."

"How?" Kelsea demanded.

Mace merely looked at her for a long moment.

"Ah, Lazarus, no. A double?"

"A perfect double, close enough to fool even the rest of the Guard."

"Where did you find her?"

"Carroll found her. In the Gut, plying her trade."

Kelsea stared at him, as though seeing a stranger.

"It was very clever of them, really," Elyssa put in. "To think of it, and then find someone who looked so much like me. It was a shame she had to die, even if she was only a whore."

Kelsea's hand curled into a fist, but she held it back. The creature in the other armchair wasn't worth it. But Mace . . .

"You did this, Lazarus?"

"I'm a Queen's Guard, Lady. My first job is to protect the Queen."

She glared at him, for his words had opened a wide gulf inside her. For the first time, she understood that there were two sides to that statement, one good and one dreadful. Mace, too, had a job to do, just as Kelsea did. Sometimes she thought she would do anything to bring her crumbling country back together, but there was a low beneath which she wouldn't sink . . . wasn't there?

"We had a new assassination attempt every day, Lady. Some of them astonishingly clever too, probably originating in Demesne. Carroll and I knew that sooner or later, someone would get past us. We couldn't just sit and wait for it to happen."

"And this was your solution?"

"Yes. That, or let the Queen die."

"What about the kingdom you left behind? And to my uncle, of all people? What about them?"

"The safety of the Queen, Lady," Mace replied inexorably. "All else is secondary."

"Did you find a double for me too?"

"No, Lady. I knew you wouldn't allow it."

"Damn right, I wouldn't!" she snapped. "I don't know what kind of moral carnival you think we're running, but—"

"You know me now, Lady. You didn't know me twenty years ago. I was a different man then, not so far removed from the Creche."

"Oh, he was!" Elyssa broke in, patting Kelsea's hand before Kelsea could snatch it away. "Shouting and fighting and then sulking in the corner when he didn't get his way. Carroll used to call him half wild, and he wasn't wrong."

Kelsea removed her hand from the arm of the chair, feeling sick. Despite the difference in age, her mother seemed younger than Kelsea, almost like a child . . . but Kelsea would not allow her to escape that way. Child or not, she owed answers.

"Why did you give me away?"

"I had no choice." Elyssa's eyes darted toward Mace, then away, a furtive movement. "You were in danger."

"You're lying."

"Why do you want to talk about the past?" her mother pleaded. "The past was so ugly!"

"Ugly," Kelsea murmured. Mace shot her a pleading glance, but she ignored him, disgusted. Was he really going to run interference for this woman, even now?

"Lazarus, leave us alone."

"Lady—"

"Close the door behind you and wait outside."

He stared at her for another long, anguished moment, and then left.

Kelsea turned back to her mother. Some part of her displeasure seemed to have finally broken through to Elyssa, who had begun to fidget in her chair and would not meet Kelsea's eyes.

"You made all of them promise to keep the shipment from me."

"Yes."

"Why?" Kelsea heard her own voice rising in anger. "What possible purpose could that serve?"

"I thought I would be able to fix it," her mother said quietly. "I thought it was a temporary solution, and soon we would think of something else, long before you came home. Mace is so smart, I thought surely he and Thorne—"

"Thorne, fix the shipment? What in holy hell are you talking about?"

"I wish you wouldn't swear. It's so ugly."

That word again. If her mother had set out deliberately to anger Kelsea, she could not have chosen a better. What good was anything, after all, if not beautiful? Her mother's mind seemed to Kelsea like a still, frozen pond; ideas might skate across it, but nothing would ever penetrate. Kelsea wanted accountability, wanted her mother to answer for her selfishness, her poor decisions, her crimes. But how did one demand accountability from such a frozen waste?

"I hoped you would never need to know," her mother continued. "And it didn't turn out so badly! We kept the peace for seventeen years!"

"You didn't keep peace." Kelsea's temper was here now; she sensed it stalking just around the edges of her mind, waiting for any chance to present itself. "You *bought* peace, by trafficking the people you were supposed to protect."

"They were poor!" Elyssa insisted indignantly. "The kingdom couldn't feed them anyway! At least in Mortmesne they would be fed and taken care of, that's what Thorne said—"

"And why would you ever question the words of Arlen Thorne?" The urge to smack her mother across the face was so strong that Kelsea was forced to shove her hands beneath her thighs, sitting on them until it passed.

This is my mother, she thought. The idea was unbearable. How she wished that she were Carlin's daughter, anyone else's. This woman had given her half of what she was . . . but only half. The thought struck Kelsea like a life rope, and she leaned forward, suddenly forgetting her anger.

"Who is my father?"

Elyssa's eyes dropped, her expression once more anxious. "Surely it can no longer matter."

"I know you worked your way through your entire Guard. I couldn't care less. But I want a name."

"Perhaps I don't know."

"You do. So does Lazarus."

"He wouldn't say?" Elyssa smiled. "My faithful guard."

Kelsea grimaced. "Lazarus doesn't belong to anyone."

"He did, once, to me." Elyssa's eyes were distant now. "I threw him away."

"I don't want to hear about it."

"Why do we speak of the past?" Elyssa asked again. "It's long gone. I hear the Red Queen is finally dead. Is it so?"

Kelsea closed her eyes, opened them again. "You won't distract me. My father. I want a name."

"It doesn't matter! He's dead!"

"Then there's no reason not to tell me."

Elyssa's eyes darted away again, and an awful suspicion suddenly crossed Kelsea's mind. In all of her ruminations on who had fathered her, there was one option she had never considered, because she couldn't. Mace would have told her.

No, he wouldn't, her mind reminded her, almost smugly. *He's a Queen's Guard, through and through.*

"One of my guards," Elyssa finally replied. "I took up with him for only a few weeks. He didn't *matter*!"

"The name."

"He was so sad when he came to us!" Elyssa was babbling now, her words running together. "He was a good swordsman, even though he came from farm country. Carroll wanted him for the Guard and I only thought to make him feel better, didn't mean to—"

"Who?"

"Mhurn. I don't know if you ever met him—"

"I met him." Kelsea heard her own voice, flat and almost suspiciously calm, but her mother wasn't one to notice such things.

"Did he know?" she demanded. "Did he know he was my father?"

"I don't think so. He never asked."

Kelsea felt a wave of relief, but only a small one. There seemed to be two halves of her mind now, running parallel tracks. One functioned well enough, but the other was transfixed by memory: blood spurting over her hand and Mhurn's smiling face, eyes hazy with morphia.

I killed my father.

"Carroll brought Mhurn into the Guard. He had lost a wife and daughter to the Mort and oh, he was a wreck!" Elyssa looked up now, and Kelsea saw a rare hint of rueful honesty in her eyes. "I've never been able to resist a wreck."

Kelsea nodded, keeping the pleasant smile on her face with an effort. "It's not my weakness—"

I killed my father.

"—but I have read of it. Please, go on."

"When Mace found out, he was just furious, but you know he didn't have any right to be, we were long done by then. Sometimes I do wonder, though, if he took you away merely to punish me—"

"Lazarus took me away?"

"He and Carroll. They did it behind my back!" The trace of a pout crossed Elyssa's lips. "I would never have given you away."

Kelsea sat back in her chair, Mhurn pushed mercifully into the background. Finally, an answer to the question that had tormented her since that day on the Keep Lawn: why would a woman as selfish as this one give her child away for safekeeping? Kelsea had conjectured all manner of reasons, and yet had missed the simplest answer of all: her mother hadn't given her away. Others had made the decision for her.

But why?

"I missed you a great deal at first." Elyssa's voice was musing, as though she were describing something that had happened to someone else. "You were a sweet baby, and oh—how you used to smile at me! But it turned out to be a good choice. Else we would have had to find a double for you too!"

She giggled, and at the sound, something in Kelsea finally broke open. She sprang from the chair, knocking it over, grabbed the smiling woman, and began to shake her. But that wasn't enough. She wanted to slap her mother, demand that she account for her failings, that she make amends somehow.

"Lady," Mace murmured, and Kelsea paused. He had stolen back into the room, and now he stood several feet away, his hands raised to halt her.

"What, Lazarus?" Her hands were only inches from her mother's throat and she wanted, oh she wanted . . . Her mother was not true evil, perhaps, any more than Thorne, or the jailor, or even the young Row Finn. But all the same, she wanted so *badly* . . .

"Don't do it, Lady."

"You couldn't stop me."

"Perhaps not, but I would have to try. And she is . . ." Mace took a deep breath. "She is not worth it."

Kelsea looked down at her mother, who had shrunken into her chair and was staring up at her with wide, surprised eyes. Worse than surprised—bewildered, as though she could not imagine what she had done wrong. Kelsea wondered if a much younger Elyssa had looked just this way as the assassination attempts began, shipments rolling beneath her windows each month, a woman unable to understand why she wasn't loved by all the world . . .

"Don't do it, Lady," Mace repeated, his voice pleading, and now Kelsea saw that he was right, though not for the reasons he believed. No matter what Kelsea did here, she would not have what she wanted. She longed for revenge, but the woman she wanted to unleash her fury upon was not this one. This woman-child could never comprehend the magnitude of her mistakes. There would be no explanation, no accountability. There would be no catharsis.

No one for me to hate.

In a book, the thought would perhaps have been liberating, would have healed something deep inside Kelsea. In reality, it was the loneliest idea she could have imagined. All of the strength faded from her arms, and she backed away.

"There, that's sorted," said Elyssa, her face brightening. "Are we all done with the past now?"

"All done," Kelsea replied, though her voice sounded ghastly to her own ears. They would never be done with the past, but her mother wasn't one to understand that. Elyssa stood up from her own chair, her arms outstretched, and Kelsea saw, horrified, that her mother meant to embrace her. She scooted backward, stumbling over the uneven stones.

"What is it?" her mother asked, her voice bewildered again and, worse, a little hurt. "There are no more secrets now. We can finally get to know each other."

"No."

"What? Why not?" Elyssa stared at her, that faint hint of a pout back at the corners of her mouth. "You're my daughter. I wasn't a perfect mother, certainly, but you're grown now. Surely we can put the past behind us."

"No, we can't." Kelsea paused, choosing her words very carefully, for she never planned to speak to this woman again. "You are a selfish woman, and careless, and stupid. You should never have had the fate of others in your hands. I believe that I am a better person for having been raised by Barty and Carlin, for never having known you. I want no part of you at all."

Her mother's mouth fell open. She began to protest, but Kelsea turned away. Elyssa tried to follow, but Mace moved to block her way.

"Where is your door?" he demanded.

"What door?"

"Your door," Mace repeated patiently. "How did you get in here?"

"It's here." Elyssa tapped the wall, and a door opened to reveal a black rectangle in the stone. Another secret passage; was no building in this kingdom just as it appeared?

"Go."

"But she doesn't understand! She–"

"The Queen has spoken."

Elyssa's lips rounded in outrage. "I'm the Queen!"

"No. You traded your crown for safety, long ago."

"But–"

"Will you go? Or must I escort you?"

"You used to be my best guard, Mace!" Her mother sounded as though she were on the verge of tears. "What happened?"

Mace's jaw tightened. Without another word, he guided her through the doorway and yanked the door shut behind her. For a long minute, fists slammed against the other side, and then there was silence.

"Does the Guard know?" Kelsea asked Mace. "The rest of them?"

"Only Carroll. He always used me for the jobs no one else would do. I often think it's why he recruited me."

"She could always come back," said Kelsea. "She could just come right down the hall, and show herself to the whole guard."

"She won't."

"Why?"

"Because I told her I would kill her if she did."

"Did you mean it?"

"I don't know."

Kelsea sat on her bed. She wanted to lie down, go back to sleep and forget all of this. But she sensed that if she and Mace didn't have this conversation now, they never would. Kelsea would lose her nerve, and they would fall back into their easy, sometimes acerbic friendship, a still pond that both of them would want to leave undisturbed.

"I killed my father," she told Mace. "I didn't know, but I did it, all the same."

"Yes, Lady."

"Why didn't you tell me?"

"If you hadn't put Mhurn out of his misery, Lady, we would have. It was the right thing to do. He was broken, and at the time, it seemed unlikely that you would ever find out who he was. Certainly none of us would ever have told you, not after that."

"You should have told me."

"To what end?"

Kelsea couldn't answer that. She had killed many people; was this so different? And what was so important about blood anyway? She had just cut ties with the woman who'd borne her, and it had been the right decision. She might have many feelings about that scene down the line, some of them tinged with regret, but not nearly as much regret as if she'd made a different decision. Blood did not make Elyssa a better mother, nor had it made Mhurn a father; he had knifed her in the back. Kelsea felt far closer to Barty and Carlin, even to Mace, than she ever had to her own parents.

"Only as strong as I want it to be," she whispered. Someone had said that to her once. Mace? The Red Queen? She couldn't remember. Animals cared about bloodlines, but humans should have evolved to do better.

The circumstances of your birth don't matter. Kindness and humanity are everything.

This voice she recognized: William Tear, speaking to Lily on one of the worst nights of her life. If it was true, if that was the Tear test, then both of Kelsea's parents had failed.

"Where do we go from here, Lazarus?" she asked. "Do I stay in exile, just like she does, hiding out here in the middle of nowhere while things get worse and worse?"

"I don't know, Lady. We can't stay here, not for long, but I don't know where we go. New London is under the Holy Father and the Mort, but you have only seventy-five soldiers downstairs. It would be suicide to go back."

Kelsea nodded. She was no stranger to charging into the lion's mouth; indeed, reckless action had been the foundation of much of her queenship, even when all she could do was get herself killed. But it felt equally reckless, somehow, to simply sit here, guaranteeing her own safety while her kingdom burned. That was her mother's way.

"We came so far, Lazarus. Did we really come all this way only to fail?"

"Sometimes that's just how it turns out, Lady."

But Kelsea didn't believe that. Perhaps it was simply her long life of reading books, where plot was carefully scripted and every action taken was supposed to mean something. They had fought through too much together to fail now. There must be some option, even if she couldn't see it. Her restless mind searched the past, the many-layered history of the Tear through which she had suffered. Jonathan Tear's death was approaching rapidly, a terrible tragedy . . . but could it have been averted? And would that really have saved the Tear? Katie might have been able to kill Row Finn—maybe—but the Town's problems were deeper than a single man, and killing a would-be dictator only left an empty throne. Kelsea sensed a solution somewhere in the past, but it would not come clear, not yet.

How did Jonathan Tear die?

Katie had not shown her yet, but she could no longer wait for Katie's memories to unfold. She looked up at Mace, who still watched her with worried eyes.

"Where's the Fetch?"

They found him out on the second-floor balcony with Hall and several of his soldiers. The sun was about to break the eastern horizon, but the morning air was crisp and cold; winter had truly come. Lady Chilton's—*my mother's*, Kelsea thought, *my mother's*—house was surrounded by scrubby patches of grass that glittered with ice crystals in the ivory morning.

As Kelsea and her guards emerged onto the balcony, Hall and Blaser bowed. She was glad to see both of them, though she had to cut off something from Hall that sounded horribly like the beginnings of an apology. On her way through the house, they had passed through a gallery that overlooked the entryway, a vast stone floor where soldiers slept, fewer than a hundred, all that remained of Hall's army. The idea of him apologizing to her was intolerable.

The Fetch and his four men stood on the balcony, all of them peering eastward through spyglasses. For a moment, Kelsea was transfixed by the sight of them: Howell, Morgan, Alain, Lear, and Gavin, five boys of the Town, now grown up and apparently damned.

Kelsea turned to her Guard. "Leave us alone for a moment."

"Not a chance!" Elston snapped.

"Great God, El, do not make me go through this with every man in the Guard."

"Elston," Mace said quietly. "Come on."

Elston cast a murderous look at the Fetch, but followed Mace back through the glassed-in doors that gave egress to the balcony. Pen and Dyer went with them. Pen showed no reluctance at all, and Kelsea felt a slight twinge, then shelved it. She would learn to live with Pen's indifference. There were more important matters to hand. At a signal from the Fetch, his four men followed, Morgan tipping an imaginary hat to Kelsea as he went.

As the doors closed, she turned back to the Fetch. She had not seen him for a very long time—or so it seemed—and he was as handsome as ever, but even so, she was surprised to find that his hold on her had diminished. She might be looking at the man, but she couldn't help seeing the boy, Gavin: arrogant and careless, an easy mark for Row Finn. Seeing the foolish boy that he had been was a lessening of the man, and though Kelsea's first reaction was disappointment, she found it followed quickly by relief.

"You look well, Tear Queen," he remarked. "Very well, for a girl who's been in prison."

"I am well."

"And what became of the Mort Queen?"

"I killed her."

The Fetch made a sound of amusement.

"You don't believe me."

"I believe you. I'm laughing at myself."

"Why?"

"Once, I thought that was what you were here for: to rid us of the Mort Queen once and for all. Now you've done it, and we're no better off than we ever were. The Tear still fails."

"You had a hand in that failure, Gavin."

His breath caught, but a moment later he said, "I knew that you would eventually find me out. Row knew it too."

"What does he want?"

"What he always wanted. A crown."

"What crown?"

"The Tear crown. Row made it, silver and sapphire, but it was no ordinary piece of jewelry. Row said it would allow him to fix the past."

"Fix the past," Kelsea repeated, wide awake now. She had spent months trying to figure out how to fix the past. "How?"

"I don't know. He always thought he had been robbed, that

chance had stolen something from him. He was too smart to merely be Sarah Finn's son."

"Where is this crown?"

"Somewhere in New London. I've been hunting it for months, with no luck. The priest stole it from the Arvath when he fled—"

"Father Tyler?"

"Yes, but we can't find him. I traced him as far as the Creche, but then lost the scent."

Kelsea nodded, though her heart ached at the idea of the old priest down there. Mace might be able to find him, but she couldn't ask Mace to go back into that hellhole. He had told her of his Creche project over dinner the night before, and though she was pleased that he had taken her words to heart, she had wondered why he would hire the Caden for such a job. Now she knew, and how bad would such a place have to be, to frighten Mace off? He would surely scoff at all of this, crowns and magic; Kelsea could almost hear the dry skepticism in his voice. But the siren song of that idea—*fix the past, fix the past*—echoed in her head. She turned back to the Fetch.

"Did you kill Jonathan Tear?"

"No."

"You and Row were friends."

He blinked, startled by the question, and then replied, "Yes. We were. I thought we were."

"Why did he hate the Tears so much?"

"Row always said that his birth was a great error."

"What does that mean?"

"I don't know. But he said the crown would correct the error." The Fetch turned away, his voice cracking. "We only wanted to rebuild a decent society, like they had before the Crossing—"

"What are you talking about?" Kelsea hissed. "The world before the Crossing was even worse than ours!"

"But we didn't know that!" The Fetch looked at her, his face almost pleading. "They never told us. We only knew what Row said. He said it was a better world, where smart people who worked hard were rewarded with a better life. Better houses, more food, a brighter future . . . that's what he offered us."

Kelsea clenched her fists. Once upon a time, she had thought herself in love with this man, but now it seemed like an episode from someone else's life. The boy, Gavin, overshadowed everything. If the Fetch had declared undying love for her in that moment, she would have spat in his face.

"Why in God's name didn't you tell me all of this before?" she demanded. "What did you hope to gain by keeping so much from me?"

"You credit me with more purpose than I had, Tear Queen. The answer is much simpler: I was ashamed. Would you find it so easy, to lay your worst moments bare before a stranger?"

"No," she replied after a moment. "But nor would I put my pride before the good of the kingdom."

"What good? All of that is done, three hundred years done. What can it possibly matter now?"

"The past always matters, you fool," Kelsea snarled. "Once and for all, who killed Jonathan Tear?"

"Oh, Row killed him," the Fetch replied wearily. "He killed all of them, Dorian and Virginia and Evan Alcott, anyone who would have been a problem. He even killed Ms. Ziv, the librarian, but that was too late; she had already sent most of the books from the library into hiding."

"He didn't kill all of those people alone."

The Fetch looked up at her, his gaze stony. "Are you trying to shame me further, Tear Queen? I was a fool, but done is done. I have shed my tears for the past."

"What happened after Jonathan died?"

"I helped Katie get away. It was the only good thing I ever did, because Row meant to get rid of her too. But she was pregnant, she told me so, and I couldn't get past that; it would have been too great a sin . . ."

"Forget that!" Katie replied shortly; the word *sin* never failed to irritate her, and she was sickened by the idea that he had not found Katie worth saving until she was carrying a child. "Who was the father? Jonathan?"

"She wouldn't tell me." The Fetch turned away, but not before Kelsea saw a hint of old hurt in his eyes, and she suddenly remembered that he had once asked Katie to a festival. He had admired her, perhaps more, enough to help her flee . . . but not enough to help Jonathan. "She vanished, and took Row's crown with her. When Row found out, he went mad, and I thought he would kill us all, but by then he had already started to fade. Katie had cursed us, but it took months for us to notice that something was wrong."

"She didn't punish you enough."

The Fetch's face went red with anger, and for a moment Kelsea thought he might try to strike her. But after another moment his fist dropped, and he leaned weakly on the balcony railing, defeated. "Say what you like, Tear Queen. But when you have lived centuries, when everyone you love has died around you and the world is full of strangers, you might know better."

But Kelsea was in no mood to feel empathy now. She turned to survey the land beyond the balcony, squinting northward in a futile wish to see New London. But which New London? Katie's, or her own? Both were now under siege, and Kelsea felt a sudden stab of grief for the failed dreams of William Tear. He had worked so hard for his better world . . . all of them had, Lily and Dorian and Jonathan, all of those people who had boarded the ships. They had fought and starved and even died in pursuit of mankind's oldest dream, but they hadn't known that Tear's vision was flawed. Too easy. Utopia was not the clean slate Tear had imagined, but an evolution. Humanity would have to work for that society, and work hard, dedicating themselves to an unending vigilance against the mistakes of the past. It would take generations, countless generations perhaps, but—

"We could get there," Kelsea murmured. "And even if not, we should always be growing closer."

"What was that, Tear Queen?"

Kelsea looked up, not seeing him, suddenly sure of what she had to do. She didn't know whether the past could be changed, whether William Tear's mistakes could ever be repaired. But to not even try seemed the most reckless course of all, and now Kelsea saw that she, too, had been caught by Tear's vision, just like Lily, just like the rest of them. Mankind's oldest dream . . . even the possibility was worth dying for. She reached beneath her shirt to clutch Tear's sapphire, sensed his better world, hundreds of years away, yet so close she could almost touch it. And who was to say which was more real: the present, or the past? In the moment before she turned and shouted for Mace, Kelsea realized that it didn't matter.

She lived in both.

Two hours later, Kelsea sat astride a horse, surrounded by her Guard, as well as Hall and his soldiers. Mace sat in front of her, and Kelsea's arms were tied around him with thick ropes. It had been Mace's idea, and a good one; a fugue might come upon Kelsea at any time now. If her Guard thought her bonds odd, they gave no sign of it; Coryn had bound her up and Kibb had tied his artful knots. The very act of being bound had been useful, for now it seemed too late to change her mind about going back. Kelsea wasn't a perfect atheist, not really; she took far too much comfort in the idea of the inevitable.

"How fast can we ride?" she asked Mace.

"Faster now that you're not slowing us down, Lady," Mace had replied, and the remark had silenced Kelsea, just as he had intended.

Nearby sat General Hall on his grey stallion, his brother Simon beside him, and behind them the sad remnants of the Tear army. The Fetch and his people were there too; Hall and the Fetch seemed to have an affinity of sorts, for Kelsea had seen them talking during the preparations for this ride. Kelsea felt the ultimate fraud; she knew that the only reason Hall and most of the Guard had agreed to this course of action was that they believed she would take care of it somehow, equalize the odds.

Can I do that? Kelsea wondered. *How?*

She didn't know. Tear's sapphire was around her neck, Row's sapphire tucked deep inside her saddlebag, nestled beside the chunk of rock she had taken from the past. But what good had these things ever done? Mace had once told her that she would have been better off without her sapphires, and Kelsea wondered if he wasn't right. Somewhere in New London was a crown, a crown that might help her, but that might only be a fool's hope. Chances were good that she was leading them all into a slaughter.

But I can't stay here, she thought, feeling resolve strengthen inside her. She looked up at the windows of her mother's house, sparkling panes that reflected the bright desert and revealed nothing. At the idea of leaving the black-clad woman behind, Kelsea felt only relief. She would not stay here while New London burned. It was, after all, better to die clean.

"Let's go then," Mace said abruptly, and turned his horse. Kelsea swayed with him, her stomach dropping; with no control of the horse and her hands tied, she sensed the journey would be extremely unpleasant. But there was no help for it. Katie was there again, her mind doubling Kelsea's, almost overshadowing it. Kelsea remembered this from that last night in the Keep, when Lily's mind had pulled her back constantly, beyond her control. She and Katie had moved toward each other gradually, like two spheres approaching each other in orbit, but now Kelsea felt as though the eclipse was almost upon them.

"We ride for New London!" Mace shouted over the assembled crowd of soldiers. "We will not stop except on the Queen's or my command! If all goes well, we should be there tomorrow evening!"

If all goes well, Kelsea thought sickly. They turned toward the northwest, and even at this great distance, Kelsea fancied that she could hear screams.

Please, Tear, help us, she begged silently. She even held her breath for a moment, hoping for an answer, but none came. William Tear could not help them. They were alone.

Chapter 13

The Tearland

'Tis here, but yet confus'd:
Knavery's plain face is never seen till us'd.
—*Othello*, WILLIAM SHAKESPEARE (PRE-CROSSING ANGL.)

T he Town had changed.

Katie could not adequately describe the change, even to herself. But she sensed it every time she walked through the commons. The streets were different than they had been in her youth, empty and cold. Neighbors had fenced themselves in, and dilapidation had begun to set in here and there among the houses, as those who could not maintain their own dwellings were left without aid. The Town had begun to smell of blight.

One night, forty families had simply up and left. By the time anyone realized they were gone, the group was already far out on the plain, working its way steadily south. Jonathan had wanted to go after them, but Katie had talked him out of it. None of these families were part of Row's church, and at least half of them had reported grievances over the past year. Even if Jonathan convinced them to return, they would be met with the same persecution they had faced before: rocks thrown through windows and pets slaughtered in the dead of night. Two weeks ago, a mob had cornered Ms. Ziv and battered her with sticks, forcing her to close the library.

Katie might have chosen to leave town as well, had her responsibility not been so great. But since Jonathan was here, she wasn't going anywhere. All the same, the loss of those forty families had taken a toll; among them had been two of the Town's best carpenters, several dairy farmers, and—most painful to Katie—Mr. Lynn, who ran the sheep farm. Without him, the quality of the Town's wool was sure to go down.

There was more than one culprit here—small-mindedness fed off religion just as surely as the other way around—but Katie couldn't help turning her eyes north, toward the steeple of the little white church at the edge of town. In the year since Row had taken over the congregation, his sermons had steadily darkened, and the church had darkened as well. Row's God was an avid policeman of personal behavior, and the idea that such policing was anathema to the very idea of the Town no longer seemed to disturb anyone but Katie and Jonathan. Those who weren't working seemed to be constantly at the church, which rocked and rolled all day long, whether Row was speaking or not. Katie would have liked to blame religion itself, but even she could not deceive herself that fully. A church was only as good or bad as the philosophy that emanated from the pulpit. All of her rage now focused on the people who followed Row, people who should have known better. They must have known better once, or William Tear wouldn't have brought them on the Crossing. He had chosen his people carefully; Mum always said so. But things had shifted now, so profoundly that Katie could not predict what anyone in the Town would do, except Jonathan and, oddly enough, Row.

She had begun to follow Row almost idly, as a sort of exercise. He was up to no good and she knew it, but that didn't make him any easier to catch. He went to the church every day, where he gave sermons in the morning and evening to anyone who wanted to listen. Whenever he left the church, women thronged him, and there was a different woman at his house each night, though he was very circumspect; the women never arrived until midnight or one, long after most of the Town was asleep. Katie briefly considered bringing these affairs into the light, but in the end she held her hand, slightly disgusted with herself. She was attracted to Row—that day in his bedroom had never left her mind, not really—and she did not deceive herself that no envy colored her feelings, but private behavior was private behavior, and hypocrisy made it no less so. If she wanted to catch Row at something, it would have to be public, an issue that affected the whole Town. Nothing less would do.

In between sermons, Row went to Jenna Carver's metal shop, and as the days went on, this devotion to duty began to puzzle Katie more and more. She had asked around and found that Row's church took care of him: the congregation maintained his house, and the women had once degenerated into an actual scratching catfight over who got to bring Row his dinner. He had no need of a day job anymore. But every day, without fail, he went to Jenna's shop and stayed for five or six hours. One afternoon, when Katie had found an opportunity to sneak up to the shop and peer in the windows, she found the glass papered over, the window blocked up.

Up to no good, she thought on the way home. She still remembered that night, long ago, when Row had taken her down to the metal shop and showed her Tear's necklace. But years had passed, and now he might be making anything in there. Katie decided that she had to know.

The next day, she waited outside the shop, concealed behind Ellen Wycroft's mill. Row had left the shop to give his evening sermon, but Katie had to wait another hour, until dinnertime, before Jenna Carver left the shop as well. The sun had already set; the year was rapidly moving from autumn to winter. On Friday night, the Town would hold the autumn festival, the last party they enjoyed before it came time to seal everything up and buckle down for the snow that was surely coming. Katie had loved the festival when she was younger, but each year since William Tear's death it seemed more grim, all gaiety forced and everyone in Town watching each other narrowly, looking for signs of weakness. But Jonathan couldn't skip the festival, so she had to go. These days, Katie rarely let him out of her sight. Virginia and Gavin were with him now, having dinner, but even that arrangement wasn't perfectly comfortable. Katie liked to guarantee Jonathan's safety with her own eyes.

Jenna's front door was locked. Looking around the street, Katie saw no one. In the years since she and Row had come down here, a few people had built houses on the Lower Bend, but now those people were inside for dinner, their doors shut. Half of the lamps on the street hadn't even been lit. A few streets over, Katie heard a dog barking, short, staccato yaps that repeated over and over. No one bothered to quiet the dog; all of the consideration that had marked Katie's childhood was long gone.

Seeing that the street was empty, she pulled her knife and bent down to the lock. Her mind remarked that William Tear wouldn't like what she was doing, picking a lock in a town that had been built on the right to privacy. Then she realized that was nonsense; Tear was the one who had taught them to pick locks in the first place. Picking locks, constructing barricades, knifework, hand-to-hand combat, resisting interrogation . . . Tear had taught them all of these skills. Once, the only locked building in town had been the library, at night after Ms. Ziv went home. But since Tear's death, people had begun to lock their doors, and even to install additional locks. Most of them were crude, homemade deadbolts and chains, but the lock on Jenna's shop was real, fashioned of metal and designed to take a key.

Secret police, Row's voice whispered in her head. *Secret police, answerable only to Jonathan.*

The knife slipped in her hand. Katie swore, pushing a sweaty lock of hair out of her eyes, and started over again. It took only five more minutes of jimmying before the door clicked open. Jenna was an excellent metalworker, but no locksmith; Tear would have been disgusted.

Katie crept into the darkened workshop and shut the door behind her. Striking a match from the box in her pocket, she spotted a lamp on a nearby workbench and lit it. The glow was thin and sickly, but enough to see by. Casting over the workbench, she found a small wedge of wood and jammed it under the door. If Jenna—or worse, Row—came back unexpectedly, she could break the back window and make a run for it.

She hadn't been in here since that night five years before, but a quick glance showed that very little had changed. The workbench and tables were still crammed with work in progress. Jenna would make jewelry from scratch, but she also did a healthy business repairing pieces that had come over in the Crossing. Katie held the lamp high as she moved down the long table that was Row's workbench. She saw several waste pieces of silver, but no sapphire. The drawer where Tear's sapphire had been, so long ago, was now empty but for a small scraper.

I should have had him watched years ago, Katie thought angrily. *How much did he get away with in the dark? How much, while we sat around playing with knives?*

But another voice asked her if that was the town she wanted to live in: a community that kept its citizenry under constant surveillance in the name of safety. Tear had said something about that once, hadn't he? Yes, he had, long ago, when Lear had asked a question about the duty of government to keep its citizens safe. Katie closed her eyes and was suddenly back there: in the Tears' living room, fifteen or sixteen, with the fire burning and Lear's question hanging in the air.

"In such cases, Lear, safety is an illusion," Tear told them. "A discontented population will erode even the most secure state. But even if safety were somehow achievable by force, Lear, ask yourself this: how important is safety? Is it worth steadily undermining every principle on which a free nation was founded? What sort of nation will you have then?"

Katie's breath halted. She had been running her hand over the surface of Row's worktable, almost halfheartedly, already aware that whatever was here, she had failed to find it. But her fingertips had just encountered a subtle set of bumps, not rough but sanded down, too symmetrical to be splinters. She brought the lamp closer and stared at what was there: an edge of some kind. She tried to get her fingernails under it, then dug at it with her knife, but nothing doing; the edge was too fine. Katie thought for a moment, then placed her fingers on the raised bumps and pushed down. With a soft, metallic *ping*, a section of the table popped up, revealing a hidden compartment. Inside was a brightly polished box of deep red wood.

Cherry, Katie thought. There were no cherry trees in town, but Martin Karczmar had found at least a few in his explorations across the river; the cherries he brought back were highly prized in the Town, and even the twigs were highly valued by woodworkers. But to get this much solid wood, one would have had to chop down an entire tree. Who would go to that much trouble?

She lifted the box from the hidden compartment. It had been polished so hard that the surface was almost as smooth as iron. The box had a latch, but thankfully, no lock. Katie thumbed the latch and opened the lid, then gasped.

Nestled inside the box was a crown. It appeared to be solid silver, set here and there with bright blue stones that looked remarkably similar to William Tear's sapphire. It was a beautiful piece of workmanship; Katie held it up to the light, admiring the thing, but her mind was also working, running far outside Jenna's shop.

Why would Row make this thing, and in secret? What would he need a crown for?

Don't be daft, her mind whispered. *There's only one answer to that question.*

The door latch rattled. Katie nearly dropped the box, then hugged it to her chest. The knob turned, but the wedge she had stuck beneath the door held easily.

Someone knocked.

Silently, Katie set the box on the worktable and tiptoed toward the door, pulling her knife from its sheath. There was a chance that light would leak around the doorframe, but that was all right; Jenna could have left a lamp burning while she went home to dinner. Katie leaned against the door, putting her ear to the wood. She could hear nothing, but she sensed that the person had not gone away.

Is it you? she asked silently. Row always seemed to know every other damned thing; did he know that someone was in here, playing with his new toy?

Taking a good grip on her knife, she bent down and began to silently wiggle the wedge from beneath the door. Her heart was hammering, blurring her vision, and her palm oozed sweat around her knife.

How our bodies betray us, she thought ruefully. It was nothing like the practice ring. She got the wedge loose and stood up slowly, feeling one of her knees pop. She put a hand on the doorknob, meaning to throw the door open, but in the end she hesitated, unable to take the final step. If someone was standing there, what did she mean to do? Stab them? Could she really kill a person? What if it was Row? Could she kill him? She didn't know, and for a long moment, she stood frozen, unable to move an inch.

The footsteps retreated, and then came the clomp of boots going down Jenna's steps. Katie sagged against the door, her heart thudding in relief. She wiped a palm across her forehead and it came away wet. She waited a few more seconds, to see if they would come back, and then darted back to the worktable. She had stayed too long already; Row's sermon would be ending soon. He might come back at any time.

Katie put the crown back into its box and slid the latch closed, then stared at the gleaming surface, her mind moving restlessly. It was only a crown, not a weapon; even if Row held secret dreams of being King of the Town—and he did; she knew he did—the crown would not help him achieve them. She could leave it here, put it back into its compartment, and no one would be the wiser. But something inside her cautioned against reading the crown at face value. Why was the thing so elaborate, set with so many sapphires? What did Row hope to achieve?

Stealing was one of the worst things someone could do, the antithesis of what the Town stood for, for there was no more unequivocal statement that something would not be given freely than the fact that one had to take it. Katie had never stolen anything in her life, and she sensed that the act would open a door inside her, a dark door not easily closed.

We thought Tear was perfect, but he wasn't, she thought grimly, staring down at the polished surface of the box. *He deserted us, right when we needed him the most. And if Tear's words can't be trusted, then who do we listen to?*

Yourself.

The idea seemed dangerously heretical, even worse than stealing. But no other answers were forthcoming. Katie scooped up the box and slipped it under her loose sweater, where she tucked the end inside the waist of her pants and pulled the drawstring snug. Then she doused the lamp and crept outside. She kept a careful eye out for Row, but saw no one, and when she turned the corner of the next street, she wrapped her arm around the box and broke into a jog. She was still frightened, badly so, but she felt like laughing, and several peals escaped her as she disappeared into the woods, heading for the heart of town.

This year's autumn festival looked just as always: streamers festooned the trees around the center of town, the many paths surrounding lit with paper lanterns. The artisans set up stalls in the square, displaying the wares for which they were willing to barter. But here, again, things were different. The cheer that usually marked this occasion was absent. Customers wandered between stalls, and the ale flowed freely, but everywhere there seemed to be knots of people, talking furtively and looking over their shoulders. The artisans, who usually brought tiny pieces of craftwork that they gave away to small children, now drove a hard bargain on everything.

Katie found that she was unable to relax. She seemed to hear whispering everywhere. She and Gavin and Virginia moved around the stalls, an instinctive triangle of which Jonathan was always the center, and she felt eyes upon them, eyes that moved the very instant she turned to look around. She felt as though she were steadily working down some sort of checklist for paranoia, but could not convince herself that it was all her imagination. People smiled at Jonathan, but all of the smiles seemed false.

Someone pressed a mug of ale into her hand, but Katie left it sitting on a table. Mum was there, watching, but that was only part of it. Katie sensed something building, hovering over them, almost like the static charge in the air before a vast storm came rolling out of the south. Everywhere she looked she saw bright eyes, glistening teeth, gleaming skin. She felt as though she had a fever. Music had started up now and people were dancing in a broad, cleared space in the center of the common, but the dancers looked wrong to Katie, as though they were trying too hard to force a jovial atmosphere, to cover up something rotten, ward off the Red Death.

"Katie!"

She jumped as someone grabbed her around the waist. Her hand was already going for the knife beneath her shirt when she realized it was only Brian Lord.

"Come have a dance with me, Katie!"

"No!" she replied, removing his hands. She felt as though everyone was staring at her, but when she turned, their eyes were somewhere else. Brian disappeared and she continued to move around the crowd, looking for a place to sit.

"Katie."

She turned and found Row, standing behind her. His eyes flicked over Jonathan in quick assessment, seemed to dismiss him, then turned back to Katie.

"What do you want, Row?"

"A dance, what else?"

Katie snuck a look at Jonathan, but he and Gavin and Virginia had turned away to a nearby stall hung with leatherwork: boots and belts.

"He's fine," Row murmured into her ear. "He always was fine, Katie. He doesn't need you. Why not have a moment for yourself? No one has to know."

He tugged on her hand again, and Katie followed him, past Mrs. Harris's gingerbread stall and into the trees behind. The trees closed in around them, and Katie felt a moment's alarm—*so much dark here!*—before she remembered her knife. Row was trying to tug her deeper into the woods, but she halted, pulling free of his hand.

"What do you want?" she repeated.

"You stole something, Katie."

"And what would that be?"

He put a hand on her waist, and she jumped.

"Where is it?"

"I don't know what you're talking about," she replied, trying to keep her thoughts veiled. She had buried the crown in the woods behind the town park, several feet beneath the roots of an old, dry oak. No one would ever find it unless they were looking for it, but Row had been able to peer inside her mind before. A twig snapped as he stepped closer, looming over her in the dark. She thought of that other night, so long ago, and a chill went down her spine. How had they gone from two children sneaking through the woods to this? Where had the rot sunk in? His hand was still on her waist, and Katie removed it, pushing his fingers away.

"Don't play with me, Row. I'm not one of your church fools."

"No, you're not, but you have been conned. We all have, by Tear."

"Not this again."

"Think about it, Katie. Why keep everything such a secret? Why hide the past?" He grasped her arm, moving out of a patch of shadow, and Katie saw that his face was pale, his eyes wide and febrile, almost red in the moonlight. For a terrifying moment he reminded her of the thing she had seen in the woods that night, and she stumbled away, nearly falling against a nearby tree. But when she looked up, he was only Row again.

"I know why he hid the past, Katie. He didn't want us to know that there was another way it could be. Each according to their gifts . . . the smart and hardworking rewarded, and the lazy and stupid punished."

"That may play with your congregation, Row, but not with me. I don't need to take your word for history. I *read*, Row. Your paradise is a nightmare."

"Only for the weak, Katie," Row replied, a smile in his voice. "The weak were pawns. But you and I could be anything."

He pushed her up against one of the trunks, his hands groping roughly at her clothes, and Katie found that she didn't want to stop him. She was drunk, but the culprit wasn't alcohol. It was oblivion. She remembered that night, years ago, Row standing at her window, beckoning her out into the night world. She hadn't known why she went then and didn't know now ... except perhaps that she wasn't supposed to. Maybe it was just that. She didn't love Row, thought she might even hate him, deep in some dark place where love and hate were closer than kin. But hate was its own aphrodisiac, vastly more powerful, and she hooked her fingers into claws and tore her way down Row's back.

He shoved inside her and Katie came, not even expecting it. Bark dug into her back, but she didn't mind; the pain seemed to fit everything else. Row was fucking her now, fucking her the way she'd read about in books, and the pleasure of it was so unbeliev-able that Katie jammed her palm across her mouth to keep from screaming. Only a hundred feet away, the festival went on, peo-ple talking and laughing. She tried to think of Jonathan, but he was far away, in the light-filled universe beyond the trees. Row's mouth was on her neck, her breasts, biting at her nipples until she thought they must bleed, but the pain fed the thing inside her. Part of her wished that this could go on forever, that they would never have to go back to town, where they were only enemies now. She was working on her third orgasm when Row stiffened, shoved deep inside her and held for a long moment, then collapsed, pant-ing, against her shoulder.

"It's not too late, Katie," he whispered. "We could be kings."

She stared at him, feeling the break inside her seal back up, returning her to herself. She was twenty years old, Jonathan was nearly twenty-one, Row was twenty-two. She couldn't make ex-cuses for any of them anymore, including herself.

"Kings," she repeated, pushing him off, wincing as he with-drew. "I notice you only made one crown, Row. Was it for me?"

"Katie—"

"Of course not. You're not built to share, so don't bullshit me. But this isn't your town. It belongs to the Tears."

Row laughed. Katie felt as though she were missing some vital piece of information. For perhaps the hundredth time, she wondered why William Tear hadn't killed Row long ago. Surely he had seen this coming.

"I'm giving you a last chance, Katie. Come on board with me."

"Or what?"

Row said nothing, but it didn't matter, for a moment later a scream split the air. Katie whirled, but she could see nothing through the trees, only the glow of lights from the festival. Several more screams came in quick progression, echoing through the trees from the brightly lit common. Katie began to run, but it felt like moving through mud. Row giggled behind her, a cold sound, the sound that Katie imagined worms would make as they squirmed eagerly through the gap in a coffin. She caught sight of moving clothing through the trees as people ran from the festival, shrieking, and she pulled her knife as she ran, thinking that it didn't matter any longer if people saw her with it, people should know that there was some force in this town beyond Row and his sorry band of sycophants, even if Jonathan paid for it later.

She came around the corner of Mrs. Harris's tent and halted. The common was deserted, but bright lamplight illuminated the tents, their edges waving in the breeze, and the ground, a carpet of shattered crockery. She stared at the shards for a few moments before she understood: beer mugs, dropped in flight, their remains littering the cobbles. She looked to her right and felt her breath stop.

Two bodies lay together on the ground in the center of the common, the street beneath them soaked with blood. Katie crept closer, reached down, and turned one of the bodies over, jumping back with a low, horrified cry as she saw Virginia's face, eyes wide and mouth slack. Her throat had been cut. A thin trickle of blood ran down her chin. Without thought, guided by a feeling of terrible inevitability, Katie reached out and turned over the second body.

It was Mum.

Katie's first thought was to be grateful that Mum's eyes were closed. There was blood on her neck and soaked into her shirt, but with her eyes closed, she looked oddly peaceful, the way Katie had always seen her in sleep. But Katie's paralysis lasted only a moment before she stumbled away, clutching her arms around herself, her eyes wide and wounded, breath gasping from her throat.

Jonathan!

She stared wildly around, but she saw no sign of him, and none of Gavin either . . . Gavin, who had been on guard duty while Katie took a bit of rest and relaxation out in the woods. There was a tinkle of broken crockery behind her and Katie whirled around, certain that it was Row, coming for her. This was Row's work, his people, and they couldn't kill Mum and let Katie live, because she would kill them all—

But it wasn't Row, only a fox, one of the tiny kits who lived in the woods, come to investigate the bonanza of leftover food on the ground.

Katie turned back to the two corpses before her, feeling oddly numb, almost analytical. Someone had knifed Virginia and Mum, but it hadn't been Row. Who had it been? Virginia had been guarding Jonathan. She and Gavin . . . where was Gavin? No one could get past him with a knife. Katie stared around the common, feeling the pressure of eyes upon her. Row was still here somewhere, he must be. Out in the woods, perhaps, watching her, gloating over how easy it had been to distract her, to get her out of the way, make her a fool . . .

"Where are you?" Katie shrieked.

But there was no sign of anyone, only the deserted common, the bright lamps swinging in the late autumn wind.

⋙ ⋘

She kicked down the door of Row's house easily; it was an old house, built just after the Crossing, and the door fell into the front hall with a crash. Katie darted inside, her knife held out before her.

A large painting of Row, done by his mother, dominated the front hall. He was eight or nine in the picture, and it wasn't very good, but his mother had decorated the frame to a ridiculous extent, embellishing it with flowers and glued-on sprigs of holly. Katie had walked past this portrait hundreds of times, barely noticing it, let alone taking account of what it might mean, all of those flowers dripping down the border, still emitting a saccharine, rotten scent.

She found Mrs. Finn in the living room, sitting in her rocking chair, staring into the fireplace. The house was cold, but there was no fire in the grate, and this fact bothered Katie for no reason that she could understand. Mrs. Finn barely even looked up as Katie entered the room.

"Get out, Tear whore."

Katie halted, dumbfounded. She had never liked Row's mother, but they had always gotten along fine; in fact, Katie had hidden her contempt for the woman much better than Row had. But Mrs. Finn's tone held as much vitriol as her words.

"Where is he?"

"He's in charge now," Mrs. Finn replied. "We don't have to put up with your lot anymore."

"What lot would that be?" Katie asked, peering around the room. Row certainly wasn't here, and she saw no clues. Katie wondered whether she was going to have to beat the information out of his mother. Could she even do that? Perhaps not, but every word out of the woman's mouth made the idea seem easier. Mum was dead—Katie's mind shied away from the thought, closing it off—but this horrible woman lived on, still making excuses for her son, even now.

"All of you," Mrs. Finn snarled, "thinking you're so much better than us. Ignoring my smart, brave boy for that weak nancy over there. All those books, they haven't helped you, have they? *My* boy wields the weight in this town."

"So you're jealous of Jonathan as well," Katie remarked, fingering her knife. "Just like Row."

"Jonathan Tear is a fraud!" Mrs. Finn snapped. "He's not his father, and why should he be? His cunt of a mother ruined everything!"

Katie drew a wounded breath. Of all of her memories of Jonathan's mother, in that moment she could only think of the portrait that hung on the Tears' living room wall: Lily, bow in hand, beatific smile on her face, and her flower-strewn hair streaming out behind her. Though she knew it from books, Katie had never heard the word *cunt* spoken aloud in her life, and the hate in that single syllable stopped her cold.

"You used to be Row's friend, girl. I remember, and he remembers too. They just had to crook their fingers, and you dropped him cold."

"Where is Jonathan?" Katie demanded. It occurred to her then to wonder why she hadn't been taken *with* Jonathan, but that answer came easily: Row wanted his crown back, and hoped Katie would lead him to it. She didn't understand the world that Row and the Tears lived in, jewels and magic and things unseen, but she could recognize that the crown meant nothing but trouble, and in that moment she resolved never to go near it again. It could rot in the soil forever.

Mrs. Finn smiled, spiteful. "My boy doesn't need you anymore. He has his own gifts. William Tear can't hurt him any longer."

Katie narrowed her eyes, trying to make sense of the last statement. So far as she knew, Tear had never paid the slightest bit of attention to Row; indeed, that lack of distinction, the sense that Row had never been valued according to his worth, was the fundamental problem. Row had always thought that he deserved better. But William Tear had neither culled Row nor praised him, not even when it was warranted, not even when he should have, given Row's intelligence and resourcefulness. Tear had ignored him so successfully that it must have been deliberate ... and now a horrid suspicion grew in Katie's mind. She stared at Mrs. Finn, already trying to reverse her thoughts, because she didn't want an answer to this question, didn't want to know—

"I have been reading all morning," Mrs. Finn announced. She reached for the table and Katie jumped forward, so keyed up that she was sure that Mrs. Finn must have a knife of her own. But Mrs. Finn raised nothing more than a book, leather-bound, with a gilt cross on the cover.

"Do you know the story of Cain, child?"

"Cain?" Katie asked blankly. She had read the Bible, of course she had, to make sure she understood what was flowing from Row's pulpit. But in that moment the name meant nothing to her.

"Cain. Unfavored son, ignored and passed over through no fault of his own. God's will." Mrs. Finn smiled again, and the smile was no longer spiteful now, but ghastly, as though she were peering through an aperture toward her own death. "I've read Cain and Abel many times. We had a god in this town, unjust and corrupt, but he's gone now. My son will have his rightful place."

"Your husband—"

"My husband died four years before the Crossing!" Mrs. Finn snapped. "We were coming here to make a better world, and how does he start? By choosing her! Even before the first boat ran aground, everyone knew!" Mrs. Finn clutched the arms of her rocker, her voice lifting into a scream. "I was four months pregnant and he left me for an American!"

Katie backed away, narrowly resisting the impulse to clap her hands to her ears. Mrs. Finn would never give Row up. But if Katie stayed here, Mrs. Finn would keep talking, and Katie didn't want to hear any more. She thought of her younger self, sitting on a bench with William Tear in the fading sun. If she had known everything then, would she still have said yes?

"I know my Bible," Mrs. Finn muttered with grim satisfaction. "We're godly people in this house. Cain rose up."

Katie opened her mouth to say something, she wasn't sure what—possibly that Cain and all of his descendants had been cursed forever for that one irredeemable act—but before she could speak, she felt the hairs stir on the back of her neck. She whirled and saw Gavin behind her, his raised fist coming at her. The blow drove her sideways, slamming her head into the wall. And then she didn't care about any of them . . . not William Tear, not Mum, not Jonathan, no one.

When Katie woke, she was freezing. She seemed to be in a room of vast darkness, one that admitted neither light nor anything else. Her nostrils stung, and after a moment, she realized that she could smell mold: decay and damp earth, all around her. She reached out and found warm flesh beside her.

"Katie."

"Jonathan," she breathed, and for a moment she was so overwhelmed with relief that imprisonment seemed a very small thing. Jonathan was not one for embracing, but Katie didn't care; she pulled him to her, wrapping her arms around him in the dark. Mum was dead, she remembered now, and Virginia. They were all dead: Tear, Lily, Aunt Maddy. She and Jonathan were the only two left.

"Are you injured?" she asked.

"Not yet."

The answer chilled her, but Katie did not pursue it. She released him and began to feel around her. Stone floors, stone walls, all of it covered with a thin layer of slimy damp that felt like moss. Some sort of basement. Everyone had a basement, but the Town's houses were made of wood, not stone. Above her head, far in the distance, Katie heard something that she at first took for a high wind, but a moment later she realized that it was too musical for that.

"Singing," she murmured, and then, a moment later: "We're under the church."

"Yes."

She cocked her head, listening again. The music had the thick sound of a choir, but it was distant, so distant. They were deep underground, too deep for anyone to hear them, even if they screamed in unison, and this realization, too, made gooseflesh prickle on her arms. Row had built this room, he must have. But for what?

"There must be a door."

"Don't bother," said Jonathan. "It's padlocked."

"I can pick a padlock."

"Not this one." Jonathan sighed, and Katie heard grim humor in his voice. "Your friend is quite the locksmith."

"He's not my friend," Katie snarled, moving down the wall. Her hand finally encountered wood, the doorframe, and then a door, so thick that even when she pounded on it, hurting her fist, she was rewarded only with a heavy, dead *thuck*.

She retreated, stepping over Jonathan, and dropped to sit against the wall again.

"Are they dead?" Jonathan asked. "Virginia and your mother?"

"Yes," Katie replied. Tears were in her throat but she fought them, biting her lip until she drew blood. If she started crying in this dark place, she would never stop.

"Gavin," Jonathan replied, wonderingly. "Row I knew about, but Gavin . . . I just never thought—"

Why not? Katie wanted to scream at him. *Why didn't you know?*

You know about every other goddamned thing, so why didn't you know about this?

She took a deep breath, trying to settle herself. *No percentage in panic,* William Tear had always told them, and even an imaginary Tear was a calming presence. Gavin was a traitor, and Katie could only assume that the rest of the guard had turned as well. No one was coming for the two of them. If there was a way out, they would have to find it inside this room. Above their heads, the singing spiraled upward, reaching a crescendo on a high note and then dying away.

"What does Row want with us?" she asked.

"He wants my father's sapphire."

"Well, why doesn't he just take it?"

"He can't," Jonathan replied. He paused, and Katie sensed that he was framing his response very carefully. Her temper cycled into life again—did he have to keep secrets even now?—but the spurt was short-lived. The Tears were what they were. She had known what she was signing on for, ever since that day in the clearing when Jonathan had grabbed her hand and spoken nonsense. She had no right to complain now about where they'd ended up.

"I don't understand everything about my sapphire," Jonathan continued. "Neither did my father, though he certainly knew more about it than I did. Row's always wanted it for himself, but it can't be taken. I have to give it away, and he knows that too."

"What happens if he tries to take it?"

"Punishment."

"What does that mean?"

"Give me your hand."

Katie reached out and Jonathan took her hand, then wrapped it around something cold. She had not held Tear's sapphire for many years, but she still remembered the feel of it perfectly: cold, yes, but alive, almost breathing beneath her fingers.

"They're all in there," Jonathan murmured, wrapping his fingers around hers. "Tears and Tears. I don't even know how far back they go; I've barely scratched the surface. This jewel has a mind of its own, but it's their minds, all of them. My father's in there, and someday I will be too . . . all of us together."

Katie closed her eyes, and for a moment she held her breath, wishing she could see the thing as Jonathan saw it, know what he knew, move through that secretive, unseen world. But she wasn't a Tear, never had been. She would never see further than what Jonathan told her, and while there was sorrow in that thought, there was also relief. Jonathan had spent his life tormented by visions; there was a price attached to Tear's magic, though few knew of it. Lily had, Katie felt certain, and perhaps Mum. But she sensed that Row might not know. A ghost of an idea flitted through her mind, then danced away.

What can we do? she wondered. She could take Row in a fight, perhaps. But could she kill him? She thought of the thing that had chased her through the woods, white limbs and staring red eyes, a creature that Row had undoubtedly created, operating in the dark while the rest of the Town slept. Could she kill that? She had no knife; someone had taken it off her while she was unconscious. But would it even have mattered? This tangle was too deep for knives.

"Row is powerful," Jonathan continued. "But not infallible. He's been playing with things he doesn't understand, and though he doesn't know it, that makes him weak."

Katie nodded, understanding this statement in intent if not in specifics. Row was careful, but not cautious. His reach had always exceeded his grasp, and one of the earliest lessons Katie had learned on Tear's practice floor was that overreach left you wide open, even if you couldn't see the vulnerability yourself. It was always easier to see such things from outside the circle; if only she could have stood outside *this* circle, somehow, assessing the situation as dispassionately as she had then.

Katie.

She jumped. Something had moved in her mind, deliberate but alien, a voice that was not her own.

"What?" Jonathan asked.

She shook her head. The singing had started again upstairs. Her brain felt as though it were splitting in two. Did Jonathan know who Row's father was? If not, she couldn't tell him. She had never understood what she felt for this odd young man, but whatever it was, she didn't have to tell him about William Tear, to undermine everything Jonathan thought he knew. That had never been her role.

The chain outside the door rattled, and Katie heard the snap of the padlock opening. Torchlight flooded the room, and Katie saw that they were in a long, narrow chamber, perhaps twenty feet by ten. The stone walls were slicked with moisture, trickling down from the ceiling.

Who built this? Katie wondered. *And when?*

Gavin came in, followed by four more men: Lear, Morgan, Howell, and Alain. Katie watched them stonily, wishing she could have her knife back for even five seconds. She couldn't take Gavin, but the other four would be easy pickings.

"We've brought water," Gavin announced shortly, as Lear and Howell placed a bucket on the ground. Gavin seemed to have read her thoughts, for he had his knife in hand, and his eyes were never far from Katie as he moved across the room.

"How long will we be down here?" she demanded.

"Not much longer, I think. Row's busy now, but he'll deal with you when he's done."

"Was I not nice enough to you, Gav?" Jonathan asked, and Katie couldn't restrain a smile at the mockery in his voice. "Did my father not make you feel special enough?"

"It's not about that!" Gavin snapped back. "It's about the town we want!"

Jonathan shook his head, an expression of disgust crossing his face, and Katie saw Gavin flinch. He needed so badly to be liked, Gavin did, even by the people he had fucked over. It was a deep weakness of character, and Katie stared at him with so much contempt that he flinched again.

"What sort of town is that?" she demanded. "A town where Row tells you all what to do, and you do it? He's certainly managed you well enough here."

"I make my own choices!" Gavin hissed. "And none of us can do that in a town of Tears!"

"So that's what he told you," Jonathan mused. "We're in the way of democracy?"

"You are!"

Katie wanted to contradict Gavin, tell him to shut up, but she could not. For a single, odd moment, she saw Jonathan through Gavin's eyes, Row's eyes, and honesty bubbled inside her, a truth as unpalatable as it was undeniable. They were wrong, all of them, but in this one thing, they were right. How could you tell everyone they were equal, when the Tears stood there, bright and shining, different from everyone else? How could anyone build a fair society in William Tear's town?

But a moment later she shoved the thought away, horrified.

"And what about you four?" she asked, turning to Howell and the others. None of them would meet her eyes except Lear.

"We promised to protect the Town," he told her. "We have to have a clear direction. We have to cut dead weight."

"Dead weight. And what does Row plan to do with us?"

Lear looked miserably at the other four, and Katie saw, alarmed, that none of them knew.

"I see. You're all helpful advisers, until you're not."

"Shut up, Katie!" Gavin roared. He kicked at the bucket on the floor, coming dangerously close to spilling it; water slopped over the side to land on Jonathan's feet.

"This is why I didn't pick you, Gavin," Jonathan murmured. "You have a hole inside, and you'll fill it with anything. Quality not required."

Gavin raised his knife, but Lear grabbed his arm, speaking quickly. "We were only supposed to bring the water."

Gavin stared at the two of them, Jonathan and Katie, for another long, furious moment, then pocketed his knife and headed for the door. "Come on. They're not our problem anymore."

Katie bared her teeth. Only a moment ago, she had been thinking that Gavin was too stupid to merit anger. But at his words, the dismissal in them, the idea that he might wash his hands of the situation simply because that was what he chose to believe, Katie felt several small explosions fire in her brain.

"I will be your problem, Gavin Murphy!" she shouted after him, as the group of men exited through the door. "You're a traitor, and when I get out of here, I will treat you like one! Even Row can't protect you from me!"

The door slammed behind them, but not before Katie caught a glimpse of Gavin's face, pale and suddenly terrified. She grinned at him, showing every tooth, and then the padlock snapped shut and the light disappeared.

"I admire bravado," Jonathan remarked drily. "But that's a tough threat to make good on."

"I don't care. He's scared of Row; he can be scared of me too."

"He's scared of everything, Gavin. It makes him incredibly easy to manipulate. That fear ruled the pre-Crossing; my father used to talk about it. Entire countries would close their borders and build walls to keep out phantom threats. Can you imagine?"

"Yes," Katie said shortly. It had taken only twenty short years to take Tear's good town and turn it into a wreck. All Row had needed was a church and, perversely, a lack of faith. She could believe anything now. She tipped her head back against the wall, closing her eyes. Somehow it was easier to bear the darkness that way. "How did your father beat them?"

"He didn't. He tried, but in the end he had no choice but to run away. They called it the Crossing, but in reality, it was nothing but a retreat. And now that's failed too."

His voice was bleak, so bleak that it arrowed straight down to Katie's core and seemed to slice her open. She groped for his hand in the dark, twining his fingers with hers.

"Don't be a prat."

"I'm not." Jonathan's voice suddenly strengthened, as though he had resolved something. "I need you to do something for me."

"What?"

There was a clink of metal in the darkness, and then Katie jumped as she felt something slither against her neck, a heavy chunk of stone tumbling down her breastbone.

"What are you doing?"

"I'm giving it to you."

"Why?"

"Because you're tougher than I was. You always were." Jonathan's voice was bitter in the darkness. "You'll take much longer to break."

"Neither of us will break."

"I will." Jonathan's hand clasped hers. "We're out of options. It's better than nothing."

Katie made a face. The Tears were pragmatists; they always had been. But she couldn't help longing for something better: not a compromise but a silver bullet, the holy grail of government. Where was it, that one perfect thing? She felt that if she could only find it, she would be willing to spend her life working to make it fire.

Fine words in a dungeon, Jonathan's voice mocked her.

Katie frowned, then leaned her head back again. It was time to wait, to clear her head, to prepare for the moment when her oldest and closest friend would come through the door, carrying a knife meant for her.

Time drifted. Hours, days perhaps, Katie couldn't see. Sometimes she slept on Jonathan's shoulder, sometimes he on hers. Sometimes she woke in the dark with no memory of where she was, and then she would feel Jonathan's hand in hers and realize that it hardly mattered whether they were in a dungeon or in a clearing, in the Town or outside it. They were together, the two of them, united in purpose, and that brought them a thousand times closer than they had ever been, so close that when Jonathan's hand slipped beneath her shirt and Katie climbed into his lap, it seemed almost an afterthought, natural outgrowth of a place they had already been, not love but something a thousand times more powerful, and when Jonathan entered her, yanking her hair back to expose her throat, Katie almost shrieked with pleasure, and when the sapphire at her throat began to glow, illuminating both Jonathan's face and her own, she saw that he was not entirely himself, that he too was in the hands of something else, and then she forgot as her mind stuttered and then fired, thinking over and over *Now we are together now we are one—*

When it was over, they dozed. Jonathan said nothing, and neither did Katie, but she didn't think either of them were really sleeping. They were each waiting ... preparing, in their own ways, for that ultimate moment: the click of the lock, and the opening of the door.

Chapter 14

The Great Gamble

When the invasion of New London finally came, it was very different from what anyone had imagined. More than one thousand Mort soldiers entered the defenseless city, looting and burning as they came, and of these, five hundred went on to lay siege to the Keep. The Holy Father had hired these troops—and, as later evidence revealed, had gone to great expense to transport them in secret—but as is so often the case in the hiring of mercenaries, the outcome reached was not the outcome sought. The Mort felt badly used, and they came not only for wealth, but for blood and revenge. The carnage can only be estimated, for few were left alive to chronicle it, and none of these able to write . . .

—*The Tearling as a Military Nation*, CALLOW THE MARTYR

Staring up at her city, Kelsea felt a curious sense of doubling. She was looking at New London, a place she knew well. The cluster of houses on hills, the grey fortress of the Keep, the white tower of the Arvath, all of these things were familiar. But at the same time, she couldn't help seeing the city through Katie's eyes, as a vast cancer of ruined potential. Knowing what New London had been meant to be made it much worse to see what it had become.

The western side of the city was aflame. Even from here, at the base of the southwestern slope, Kelsea could hear the screams as people fled the fire, but she didn't deceive herself that the fire was the only problem. The Mort were loose in her city. There was no wall on the western side, and it was an easy climb up the hill to the base neighborhood, the Lower Bend. But Kelsea didn't know where to begin. She was surrounded by armed men: Hall and the remainder of his army, as well as her Guard. But they weren't enough. She couldn't retake her city by force.

"Majesty," Mace muttered urgently.

She turned south, toward the vast dust cloud that had been following them for the last day. At first it had been small, little more than a slight disturbance of air on the horizon, but in the past few hours it had resolved itself into a wide, dusty haze spread across the Lower Almont. Her Guard had kept an uneasy eye behind them, but there had been no time to stop. Kelsea turned to the Fetch and found him watching her, his eyes wide and hopeless.

"Is he coming for you?" she asked.

"No, Tear Queen. For you."

"What are you jabbering about?" Elston asked. "Speak sense. What is that?"

"The Orphan."

"The Orphan is a children's fable," Dyer protested.

"Hush, Dyer." She paused, suddenly struck by a thought, and moved over to crouch beside the Fetch.

"What really happened to Row? After Jonathan died?"

"Cursed. We didn't know Katie had Jonathan's magic until after Jonathan was dead, and once we found out, even Row didn't dare touch her. She fled, but first she cursed us all." The Fetch gestured to the four men around him, who nodded unhappily, then turned his doomed eyes back to the dust cloud behind him. "She cursed us as traitors, and we still pay and pay."

"What about Row?"

"I don't know what Katie did to him. Row began to fade, and then he simply disappeared. The Town fell into warring factions, tore itself apart. Half of the population struck out eastward across the plains. It was only years later that we found out Row wasn't dead, but in the Fairwitch."

"And I let him loose," Kelsea murmured. She needed no spyglass to see them now: a horde of small, dark forms, running on all fours, advancing north across the plains. Had she led them to her city, or had they been coming here all along? She didn't know, but it hardly seemed to matter any longer. She had no answer for the tide below . . . no answer in the present, anyway. She didn't understand what Row Finn had become, but she didn't believe he could be beaten here. This problem, like so many, began in the past, and it was too late to fix.

"Lady," Mace repeated. "We must move. Now."

Kelsea nodded, then looked back up the hill. The immediate problem was up there. She needed to get into her Keep, but pandemonium reigned. Her city was overtaken with violence . . . which left Kelsea back where she had been all along.

She dug into her pocket and brought out Row's sapphire. The blue facets sparkled in the dying light, and again Kelsea had the uncomfortable feeling that the jewel was winking at her, almost daring her to put it on.

What choice did I ever have? she wondered. *Carlin raised me to eschew force, but this world is ruled by force. It's too late for anything else.*

She turned to her Guard, who were clustered around her on the hillside. General Hall and his twin brother were there, too, though Hall's sorry band of soldiers waited several hundred feet down the slope. Even Ewen was here, having doggedly insisted on following them to the city. Kelsea thought that Bradshaw had taken Ewen on his horse, but she could not be sure of anything about that journey. Too many miles had been spent in the twilight of Katie's mind. But now she could regret, at the end, that Ewen was with them. She wished he would have stayed behind, stayed safe. She wished she could have kept them all safe, her Guard, her country, wished she could have wrapped them away and hidden them in the past, or perhaps the future. Anywhere but the present. She dangled the necklace from her fingers, watching the light play across the chain.

Force, she thought. *Force is what's left when all other options are exhausted. Even Carlin must have known that.*

"We're going up there," she told them. "To the Keep. Your first instinct will be to protect me, I know—"

"Here it comes," Dyer muttered.

"But do me a favor and protect each other. Understand, Dyer?"

"Yes, Lady, yes! Because that's what I signed up for: to guard other guards while I leave the Queen to her own devices."

She glared at him for a moment, but found that she could not maintain it; after a moment, she shook her head and continued.

"Smart mouths aside, I mean what I say. I don't know what will happen when I put this on," she held up the sapphire, "but it can't be the safest thing in the world. I may not be myself; I may be—"

The Queen of Spades.

She swallowed. "I want you all to stay out of my way. Agreed?"

None of her Guard would meet her eye, except for Mace, who raised his eyebrow expressively.

"I mean it."

"Are we going to go?" Elston asked. "Or are we going to wait for those things out there to come up and kiss us on the mouth?"

Kelsea glanced behind her and saw that the tide of children had nearly reached the base of the hill. Taking a deep breath, she put on the second necklace, and as it settled between her breasts, she felt a horrible comfort there, the comfort of coming back to a house that had long since been wrecked but which was, nevertheless, home.

"Come on," she told them, and scrambled up the hill, not waiting to see whether they would follow.

N ow," Aisa breathed, and Father Tyler nodded.
Together, they shoved at the grating over their heads. It was heavy, solid iron, but Aisa could feel some give. If they had been strong men, there would have been no problem. But Father Tyler was as frail as ever, and Aisa's body was racked with fever. Her wounded arm felt as though it had been shot through with veins of molten iron. They pushed until Aisa's entire back ached, but still only revealed a quarter-crescent of deep evening-blue sky.

"That's something, anyway," Aisa muttered. "A few minutes and we'll try—"

She fell silent, listening.

"Is it them?" Father Tyler whispered, but Aisa put a hand on his wrist to keep him quiet. She thought she had heard something in the tunnel below, the scrape of a boot on stone.

"Again," she panted. "Quick."

The two of them grasped the edge of the cover and shoved. Bright lights danced before Aisa's eyes, but the cover was halfway off now. Starlight illuminated the edges of the ladder upon which they perched, and for a moment Aisa felt her balance waver, felt as though she would simply fall, not into the tunnel she had just climbed out of but into a darkness deeper than any she had ever known.

"I can squeeze out," Father Tyler murmured. He clambered a few more feet up the ladder, snaking his thin body through the half-moon opening, then boosted himself up and out. The beaten leather satchel he carried with him gonged against the top of the ladder, and Aisa winced. No one in the tunnels below could fail to hear that sound.

Aisa had given the Caden the slip several days ago, vanishing into a deep crevice in the main tunnel while they walked ahead. It had not been an easy decision, for she felt a great deal of loyalty to these four men. But her loyalty to the Queen was stronger, and she knew that the Queen would have wanted Father Tyler back safe in the Keep. She had thought it would be a relatively quick and simple business: fetch Father Tyler from his hidden alcove, smuggle him up to the Keep, and then come back down with no one the wiser. She could claim that she had gotten lost in the tunnels for a day or so. Very neat, very easy.

She had forgotten that the Caden were not fools.

In hindsight, she realized that they must have known something was up from the very moment she had discovered Father Tyler. She had felt uneasy, leaving him down there, and her worry must have showed. When she slipped them, they had not gone on up the tunnel as she had thought, but had waited, hiding, to see where she would go and what she would do. It was only this morning that she began to suspect that she and Father Tyler were being tracked through the tunnels, and by that point, it was too late to make an alternate plan. They were on the southern edge of the Gut, an area of the labyrinth that Aisa did not know well and could not navigate with any skill. It seemed their best hope to get up and outside, but this, too, presented dangers, and they had been forced to wait until dark.

As soon as Father Tyler was up and out, he resumed shoving the manhole cover. His leverage was better now, and even on his own, he was able to move the iron disc well out of the way. He reached down into the hole.

"Come, child. Boost yourself up."

Aisa did. She usually resented being called a child, but somehow, coming from the old priest, it didn't irk. She took his hands and bent her knees, preparing to spring upward, then shrieked as a hand clutched her ankle.

"Where do you think you're going, girl?"

Kicking frantically, she peered downward and saw the dim white circle of Daniel's face. Her kicks were ineffective; his hand on her ankle was like iron. Again she thought of simply letting go. She was close to death, had been so for days. Only concern for the priest kept her fighting that grim spectre off.

"We gave you a clean shot, girl," Daniel hissed. "And how do you reward us? That's a ten-thousand-pound bounty you're trying to hold for yourself."

"I'm not after a bounty," she panted.

Daniel's face moved closer, and she realized, alarmed, that he was climbing the ladder beneath her. His other hand encircled her calf, squeezing until she squealed.

"We're a guild, you little cheat. No one holds back money from the guild."

"That's a lie!" she gasped. "You did! They told me! Lady Cross! You let her go and kept the money and they threw you out!"

Daniel gaped at her, and in that moment Father Tyler leaned over the edge of the hole and swung his satchel in a short, sharp arc. The business end of the bag thumped Daniel in the face and he fell, howling, from the ladder.

"Come, child!" Father Tyler cried. "Now!"

Aisa took his hands and let him pull her up from the hole. She saw immediately that she had misjudged their position; they were not in the Gut any longer, but on the edge of the Lower Bend. She could find her bearings here easily, but they were at least a mile from the Keep Lawn. It was too far. She could barely walk, let alone run. Her arm was a dangling web of agony.

From the hole at her feet came a string of curses, then the deep gonging sound of boots climbing the ladder.

"Child, we must go!" Father Tyler grabbed her good arm and pulled her along. Aisa blinked, half blind with pain and fever, seeing little, hearing a deep voice inside her head, long ago. A father's voice, but not Da's.

"Pain," she whispered to the priest, covering her eyes as the brightly lit windows passed by them, an endless panoply. "Pain only . . ."

Her legs tangled and she began to collapse. A moment later, though she barely felt it, the priest had picked her up and begun to run with her in his arms. Each step made Aisa feel as though her head would split open, but she thought Father Tyler must know where he was going, for he darted down a nearby alley, then another, wending his way carefully around the edge of the Gut, heading for the center of the city.

Javel was hungry. He could feel the hunger, like a rock, deep inside his stomach, a gnawing, cloying sort of pain, so closely aligned with nausea that sometimes he could not tell the difference. For a while the pain went away and he forgot it completely, but all it took was one whiff of food, and hunger came surging back. They had already begun to ration the provisions, and now, no matter how hard the Gate Guard worked, they were down to two small meals a day. The Keep was still relatively well stocked from the Mort invasion, and if needed, the food would last for a long time. But siege was siege.

After a long fight, they had finally succeeded in getting the Keep Gate closed, bolstering it with wooden bars. In a brave move, Vil had led a small force down the wall and onto the drawbridge, laying a wall of bricks on the bridge while the Mort slept, so that by the time they woke, the mortar had hardened into a real obstacle. But yesterday, the Mort had broken the wall and gone to work on the Gate. The wood reinforcements were gradually weakening, but Vil did not seem perturbed. He was acting true to form, as a hero, not thinking of himself but of the people upstairs, the women and children trapped in the Keep. Vil might be a hero, but Javel was frightened.

From time to time, Vil would take two or three Gate Guards up to the balconies on the higher floors, where they could look out over the city. There was nothing good to see. As many Mort as swarmed below on the lawn and the drawbridge, there seemed to be twice as many out in the city proper, setting fires, carrying off goods, and much, much worse. Javel didn't want to watch, but he seemed unable to help himself. The vantage was too good, and the sound of screaming carried easily across the lawn. But today the view was mercifully hazy, obscured by smoke from the fire that burned across the western skyline of the city.

"If only that fire would travel over this way," Martin remarked. "They've got oil down there, and nowhere to dump it."

"Fire would be just as bad for us," said Vil. "Too much wood in here. The bridge is wood."

Javel kept silent. The idea of being trapped in here, fire ringing them all around, was too terrible to contemplate. He wondered, for perhaps the hundredth time, why he couldn't have been born brave like the men around him. What good had his cowardice ever done anyone? Allie's face, set with contempt, flashed before him, and he closed his eyes, as though he could somehow retreat from her gaze.

"Has the Holy Father shown up today?" Vil asked.

"Not yet," Martin replied. "But he'll be here. These are his troops. The Queen should charge him with treason."

"What Queen? Is there a Queen here?"

"I only meant—"

"I know what you meant," Vil replied tiredly. "Enough. Let's go down. We need some sleep."

But when they reached the ground floor, they found not quiet, but a raging argument in front of the Gate, the entire Gate Guard toe-to-toe with a group of Queen's Guards and a woman Javel recognized easily: Andalie, the Queen's witch. At her side, holding her hand, was the same tiny girl who had spoken to Javel before. He shivered at the sight of them.

"What is this?" Vil demanded. "Why aren't you at your posts?"

"The woman, sir," Ethan replied. "She insists that we open the Gate."

Vil turned to Andalie, his gaze uneasy. "Nonsense."

"The Queen is coming," she replied. "Open the gate."

One of the Queen's Guards moved forward, the same archer that Javel had noticed before. He was little more than a boy, but his posture was so combative that Vil actually moved back a step.

"The Mace left Andalie in charge!" the archer snapped. "Open the gate!"

He shoved Vil, and Vil fell backward. Marco and Jeremy drew swords, but they found themselves facing more than twenty Queen's Guards, all of them armed to the teeth. Javel considered the men before them for a long moment, but he was not seeing them; instead, he saw a tall woman sitting astride a horse, a woman of many sorrows, with a crown on her head. In his mind he heard the shrieks of women and children.

It would take a brave man to open the door, Dyer's voice whispered.

Are you brave, Javel? Allie, her voice neither cruel nor kind, honestly doubtful. And last of all, the Queen's voice, long ago in the Keep:

Don't you want to find out?

Javel did.

A moment later, he had turned to the doors behind him and begun to attack the bolsters in a frenzy, dragging down one wooden plank at a time. Hands were on his shoulders, pulling him backward, but eventually they stopped and he realized, gratefully, that other hands were helping him, many hands, dragging down the enormous planks of wood from the stack, slowly revealing the thick oak of the Keep Gate.

T he Arvath was the first building to fall.

It fell quickly, so quickly that Kelsea almost felt cheated. She had wanted to see the Holy Father's house drop piece by piece, the white stone first cracking, then peeling, then dropping in great chunks, the way snow fell from trees during the first good spring melt. She wanted to see the thing crumble. But the fall was very quick; she had no more than turned her mind to that rising white spire than wide cracks traveled its circumference, cracks so thick that Kelsea could even see them from here. The gleaming cross at the top went first, plummeting from the pinnacle, and within ten seconds, the entire building had gone down in a tornado of dust.

Cheat or not, it was still very good. Only now did Kelsea realize how much of herself she had given away during the past few months, how much of her personality had been dead, dampened beneath the rigid control she had imposed upon herself in order to survive in the dungeon. Everything had been painted in shades of grey down there, and there had been no percentage in letting her temper out, letting it romp. She wondered whether she had nearly gone mad, whether she would even have noticed if she had crossed the border and sunk into insanity. Maybe it would only have seemed like the next phase.

It didn't matter. Now she was free.

Dimly, she sensed her Guard around her, following her lead as she led them through the city. They were running, all of them, for Row Finn's creatures were right behind them, and now Kelsea could also sense the man himself, not far back, all of his attention focused upon her. Sometimes she thought she could even feel his eyes. Several times her guards stopped to loose arrows into the street behind them, but Kelsea knew they would hit nothing. Row's children were too quick.

They crossed the Circus and Kelsea sensed, rather than saw, people scattering from her path. They didn't seem to matter, all of these people. Their problems were so small; Kelsea sensed them as she flew by: problems with spouses, with money, with drink.

They should scatter, she thought grimly, as though this journey were an argument in which she had been somehow vindicated. *They should scatter. I'm the Queen of Spades.*

They circled around the outside of the Gut, where the houses and buildings descended into a valley, the cup between two hills. Once upon a time this depression had held an amphitheater, where William Tear's utopians would meet and decide things by popular vote. Democracy in action, but not really. Behind everything had been Tear, always Tear, and when that driving force was gone, the Town had nothing, left open to the lowest common denominator. Leadership was all that stood between democracy and the mob. As they crossed the Gut, Kelsea sensed the Creche beneath, a great anthill of chambers and tunnels, built God knew when. Thinking of that deep dungeon sunk in the earth, Kelsea wondered if the Creche had been built by Row himself. Who knew what he might have accomplished in the dark?

If only I could stop it, she thought, the thought now so familiar that it seemed to run a set course, a well-worn groove in her mind. If only anyone could have stopped it! As they began to leave the Gut behind, Kelsea sent a massive crack running through the earth, just as she had done when she cracked the New London Bridge all those months ago. The street beneath her trembled, but she didn't stay to watch the effects of her handiwork. She knew how it would go, could predict it as surely as Simon could predict the operation of one of his many machines. The crack would travel deep, all the way down through that warren of tunnels where the dark heart of New London lived. Struts would collapse, foundations would sink, even the streets themselves would begin to tumble into the fissure she had made. It might take hours, or days, but eventually the Gut, the Creche, these would be nothing more than an archaeology site, infinite layers of wood and stone for someone to excavate in the distant future.

"Lady, no!" Mace shouted. "The girl! Aisa!"

Kelsea shrugged that off, annoyed at his interference. What possible value could one life hold against the vast expanse of pain that had gone on beneath these streets? Perhaps, given enough time, the entire city would fall through a hole in the earth, settling into so much detritus. That outcome seemed entirely right. How could you rebuild on a broken foundation? They would have to wipe it clean and start over.

That's Row talking.

The voice was Katie's, but Kelsea shrugged it off as well. Rebuilding could come later. Now, she wanted only to punish. Down the Great Boulevard, where people scattered before her approach. She made eye contact with a woman standing in front of a milliner's, and the woman began to scream.

What do they see? Kelsea wondered. She turned, meaning to ask Mace, but he was nowhere to be seen. Twenty feet behind her, Elston was struggling with several men in the black uniforms of the Mort army.

Mort? she thought bemusedly. *Here?*

She turned her attention to the Mort soldiers and they dropped to the ground, the chests of their uniforms darkening with blood. The rest of her Guard was still with her, but Kelsea couldn't help noticing that they did not look at her, that they worked hard to keep their eyes elsewhere. No one had ever liked the Queen of Spades . . . not Mace, not her guards, not anyone. The sapphire throbbed against her skin, and now she could feel Row Finn inside her head, his long life, a seemingly endless accumulation of experiences, no time to linger on a single one, but she saw

Her own pudgy fingers playing with jacks on wooden floorboards

Her worthless mother sitting at the table, weeping by candlelight, and Kelsea stared up at the woman and felt something that was almost hatred, contempt coursing through her heart

William Tear standing across the road, staring at her from a distance, his face betraying both suspicion and sorrow

Following Jonathan Tear up the road, both of them young, no more than ten or eleven, but Kelsea's heart burned with hunger, the hunger to be someone special, a golden child in the eyes of the Town

Jen Devlin's face beneath her, eyes bulging and cheeks turning purple as Kelsea throttled the woman, neither liking nor disliking the agonized confusion in Jen's eyes, only thinking that it was Jen's own fault for trusting, for thin..ing she meant well

Staring down at the pile of rough-cut sapphires in her hand, not sure what to do with them, not sure what she had accomplished, only that here at last was something that was *hers*

They crested the rise of the boulevard and here was the Keep Lawn, but not as she had left it. There were more Mort here, scattered across the lawn and circling the Keep. The drawbridge was down and the gate appeared to have already fallen, but the bulk of the Mort were busily at work with a ram, all the same. Several of them were trying to climb the Keep's stone outer wall, aiming for the balconies on the third floor.

"Where's the Captain?" Coryn shouted behind her.

"Gone!" Elston shouted back. "He was with us on the boulevard, and then I don't know!"

Kelsea shook her head. She could not be bothered with Mace right now, or with any of them. She had business to tend to, for she had spotted something on the lawn below: a white tent, topped with a cross. If His Holiness had escaped the Arvath, so much the better. Her mind reached out to Row Finn, looking for fire, the fire he had always controlled, and when she found it she gasped in joy, watching the white tent go up, men's shrieks echoing through the fabric. The men on the walls were next; they toppled into the moat and disappeared, leaving only a widening pool of blood on top of the water. The men at the gate had oil, she saw now, and had been preparing to set fires themselves, across the wide front expanse of her Keep. She grabbed at the men's insides and yanked, smiling as blood sprayed across the lawn and their bodies fell where they stood.

"Lady! The Captain!"

Elston's voice. Annoyed again, Kelsea turned and saw that he was pointing up the hill toward the entrance to the boulevard. The view struck a chord of memory in her, so clear that it was almost déjà vu, and she shivered, coming back to herself a bit; when

—People of the Tearling!—

had that been?

At the entrance to the lawn, Mace was battling with four men in red cloaks. It was a day for memories; for a moment, Kelsea wondered whether they were back on the shores of the Caddell, battling for their lives. A small form was beside Mace, tiny really, next to his bulk, battling as well. The tiny warrior's hood dropped, and she saw Andalie's daughter, Aisa, trying to hold off two Caden with her knife. Her face was bright with fever, and her left arm dangled limply at her side. It was no contest; as Kelsea watched, one of the Caden grabbed her and broke her neck over his arm.

Behind her, Kelsea heard a long shriek from the Keep: Andalie, but Kelsea could not trouble about her now either. A third form was fleeing down the hill toward Kelsea and her Guard, and the tide of violence inside Kelsea was momentarily muted as she recognized Father Tyler. Unreality washed over her again, the same sense of being half in a dream that she had experienced, on and off, ever since she had woken in her mother's house.

Father Tyler had the look of a scarecrow; his filthy clothing hung off him like a sail. Mace covered his retreat, holding the four Caden off. Dyer and Kibb had gone to help him, but there was no need for that; Kelsea could take care of the four cloaked men easily. She no longer feared the Caden, or anyone else.

"Get her inside!" Mace shouted. He left Dyer and Kibb to it and came running down the hill, shepherding them all onward.

Inside where? Kelsea wondered, but when she turned back to the Keep she saw that, by some miracle, the gate was open. Dead Mort lay strewn around the drawbridge and the lower lawn, and Kelsea could only marvel at the sight; had she done that? No, of course not. It had been the Queen of Spades.

"Lady, run!" Elston shouted, grabbing her arm, pointing to the top of the hill. Following his gaze, Kelsea felt real fear overtake her for the first time that day. The entrance to the Great Boulevard was crammed with children, a horde so vast that they were shoving and squeezing past each other to gain access. Like the little girl in the dungeon, they loped on all fours, and this made it easy to distinguish the tall figure on two legs who stood in their midst: Row Finn, with pale white skin and glaring eyes. He had finally dispensed with his handsome face, and Kelsea had no power to stop him. She sensed a wall there, surrounding him and the children, the same sort of shield the Red Queen had thrown up to defend her army below the New London walls.

"Come on, Lady!" Elston shouted again, and Kelsea allowed him to tug her down the lawn. Now she was running with a solid bloc of guards around her, and she did not see what became of Dyer or Kibb, or of the Caden.

"Majesty," Father Tyler panted beside her. Never in her life had she seen a man so ill-used, so close to collapse. He held out a thick strap, and Kelsea saw that he was still carrying his old satchel, though it looked considerably the worse for wear. Did he expect her to carry it for him? Now?

The old Kelsea would have carried it for him, Carlin's voice mocked in her head, and Kelsea took the satchel, frowning.

"Thank God," Father Tyler said, tears pouring down his cheeks. "Thank God."

She stared at him, confused, but they were pounding across the drawbridge now and through the gate. Mace caught up to them as they ran and as soon as they were through, he began shouting orders, leading Kelsea around several piles of broken brick. She saw many faces: Andalie, white with horror as she clutched Glee in her arms; Devin; even Javel, in the uniform of a Gate Guard. But there was no time to speak to anyone, for the Guard was already hustling her down the hallway. Behind them, Kelsea could hear Row's children still coming, a high-pitched screaming that seemed to be inside her head as well as without. Glancing backward, she saw that the corridor was covered with them; they swarmed over the Gate Guard, climbing the walls and ceiling, their movements sickening and insectile. Father Tyler's satchel bounced against Kelsea's leg, hurting her knee, but she couldn't give it back to him; the priest had been left behind.

"Here," Mace said, throwing open one of the many doors on the main hallway. "Seal us inside."

He pushed Kelsea through, and she was relieved to see Pen, Elston, Ewen, Coryn, and Galen follow them inside. Mace slammed the door behind them.

"Bar the door!" he shouted.

Elston and Coryn put their shoulders to the door just as it began to shudder. Pen stood in front of Kelsea, sword in hand. She sank to the floor, blinking, and Father Tyler's satchel thudded to the ground beside her.

"Ah, God, Lazarus," she murmured. "How I failed."

"That's not you talking, Lady," Mace grunted, shoving his shoulder against the pile of men holding the door closed. "Don't you get maudlin on me now."

What else am I supposed to do? she wanted to ask. Mace had chosen this room well; the door was thick oak, but it would not hold forever. The Queen of Spades was gone, and all that remained was Kelsea, who was not nearly so resilient. A great blow shook the door, and the room echoed with a moan of wounded wood. With nothing else to do, Kelsea opened Father Tyler's satchel and found two items: an old, battered Bible and a large red box.

"Push, boys!" Mace shouted. "Push for the Queen!"

Another blow echoed off the door, but Kelsea barely heard it. She stared down at the polished cherrywood surface. She had seen this box before, in Katie's hands. It was nearly as old as the Tearling, but here it was. Flicking the latch, she opened it and stared down at the crown inside, perfect in every detail, just as Katie had seen it.

He wanted to be a king, she thought. *That's all he ever wanted, and wouldn't I love to introduce him to the Queen of Spades? Oh, how I would love that—*

BOOM!

Another great blow shook the doorframe, and several of her guard cried out at the impact. Coryn flew backward.

Brought back to herself, Kelsea picked up the crown, ignoring a weakly hectoring voice that seemed to travel through her fingers all the way to her brain—

Don't you dare!

—and placed it on her head. Beyond the stone walls, she heard Row Finn scream with rage.

She had expected the crown to be heavy—it had felt so in the box—but it was light as air on her head; she felt its power travel through her, a line of current directly down to her chest, a pleasure so great that it was agonizing, making her close her eyes. She opened them and

Found herself in the cottage.

But it was empty. She had always been able to tell, even upon waking, whether Barty and Carlin were home. Now she could sense their absence. Nothing moved in the rooms around her. Even the dust motes dancing in the light seemed lethargic, undisturbed.

She was standing in the middle of Carlin's library. She felt years younger, seven or eight perhaps, as on those mornings when she used to come in here and curl up in Kelsea's Patch and feel that all was right with the world. But Kelsea's Patch was not here; in fact, the room held no furniture at all, apart from the bookshelves. Carlin's books surrounded her on all sides . . . but not old and beaten, as so many of them had been in Kelsea's youth. These books looked brand-new. Instinctively, Kelsea reached for one—she had not held a book in so long!—and found that she had taken down *The Bluest Eye*. But when she opened the cover, the pages were blank.

Alarmed, she pulled down another book—*Something Wicked This Way Comes*—and flipped through it. Nothing, only a collection of empty pages.

"Carlin!" she called. But there was no answer, only the sleepiness of the empty cottage on a Sunday afternoon in her childhood. She used to love the times when Carlin was gone, when it was just her and Barty and neither of them needed to look over his shoulder, anticipating disapproval. But at the sight of the blank books, she felt the cottage's familiar quiet tilting into nightmare.

She took down Carlin's Shakespeare—surely that bulwark of language was too indelible ever to be erased—but it was blank as well. In a panic now, Kelsea pulled down book after book, but they were all empty. It was only the semblance of a library, nothing more. Without words, the paper held no value.

"Carlin!" she screamed.

"She's not here."

Kelsea turned and found William Tear standing behind her. His presence seemed quite reasonable, as things always did in dreams. Only the empty books were too awful to be true.

"Why are they blank?" she asked.

"I would guess because the future is undecided." Tear picked up two of the discarded books and placed them gently back on the shelves. "But I'm not sure. I never tried to dabble in the past."

"Why not?" Kelsea demanded. "The pre-Crossing . . . you could have gone back and changed it, couldn't you? Frewell, the Emergency Powers Act . . ."

"It seemed easier to control the future by changing the present. The past is an unwieldy thing."

His words tugged at Kelsea's memory. Someone else had told her almost the same thing, hadn't they? Something about butter-flies . . . it seemed decades ago.

"You think I have no right to meddle with the past?" she asked.

"I didn't say that. But you should be prepared for the decision to cost you."

"I am prepared," Kelsea replied, not sure whether it was true. "There's no other option. The Tearling is wrecked."

"The Tearling," he murmured, his voice musing. "I told them not to name things after me."

"They didn't listen." Kelsea looked around at the library, the empty cottage. "Why are we here?"

"To speak, child. I used to talk to my ancestors as well, though not in this place. We would go to Southport, to the promenade where I grew up. It used to scare me, seeing the prom so empty . . . but then, I was younger than you."

"Do you know who I am?" Kelsea asked.

"I know you're my blood, else I wouldn't be here. But are you Tear, or Finn?"

Kelsea considered this question for a long moment, then admitted reluctantly, "I don't know. I don't think anyone does. Why did you cast Row off?"

"We didn't tell him. His mother was supposed to keep it a secret."

"Why didn't you tell him?"

"I didn't know Sarah was pregnant until after the Landing. I couldn't stay with her, not once I knew that Lily was more than a vision. Sarah demanded that I choose. I chose Lily, and so lost my son."

"But Row knew."

"Yes. She was a weak woman, Sarah, and Row a consummate manipulator. She never kept anything from him for long."

"You were proud of him."

Tear frowned, troubled. "I was proud of his potential. But I foresaw ruin."

"Ruin is upon us," Kelsea pressed. "Can you not help?"

"What is your name, child?"

"Kelsea Glynn."

"Glynn . . . I don't know that name. I see that you have many stories to tell, and I would like to know what became of our town. But I sense that your time is short. Come."

He led her out of the library and down the cottage's tiny front hallway. Everywhere Kelsea saw items she remembered: Carlin's silver candlesticks; the vase that Kelsea had chipped when she was twelve; the shoe stand that Barty had carved to hold their boots. But there were no candles in the sticks, no boots in the rack, and the vase was brand-new.

Tear opened the front door and beckoned her on. Following him, Kelsea expected to see the same raked patch of dirt that had always fronted the cottage, but when she stepped outside, she gasped and clapped her hands to her ears.

They were in a howling tunnel, Kelsea's skin buffeted by wind that seemed to blow in all directions. She was reminded of the tunnels from Lily's memory, fast cars and deafening sound, but this tunnel was empty, no cars or people. Instead of the concrete walls of Lily's time, Kelsea saw the tunnel as a broad vista, people and places, all of them constantly in motion. Her vision seemed to stretch for miles.

"What is this?"

"Time," said Tear beside her. "Past, present, future."

"Which is which?" Kelsea asked, looking right and left. She could not distinguish the scenes before her.

"It is all one," Tear replied. "The past controls the future; is that not why you're here?"

Kelsea's gaze fixed on one scene, and she walked down the empty tunnel to have a look at it: a small room with wooden floors and stone walls. A group of men were holding the door closed with all of their might, and behind them, on the floor, a woman sat cross-legged, her eyes closed, her bowed head circled with a crown. As Kelsea watched, a crack appeared in the door, and the wood began to split.

"Very little time," Tear repeated. "You could go back there. Or you could choose something else."

But Kelsea was already searching, reading the scenes in front of her, faster than she had ever read any book.

So much time here!

And there was, but it was Kelsea's time, for in the seemingly infinite number of scenes before her, there was nothing she did not recognize. She saw the shipment rolling through the Almont, nine long cages snaking their way toward Mortmesne. She saw the White Ship going down in its terrible storm—Great God, if she could only have prevented that!—saw President Frewell standing behind a podium; saw a much younger William Tear jumping from an airplane; saw Lily watching in tears as her younger sister was marched down the hall by four men in black uniforms . . . on and on it went. And now Kelsea saw scenes even more distant, further and further back, to a time without cars or electricity or even books. It frightened her, the howling emptiness of that world, most of humanity locked into a bare struggle for survival. She didn't want to go back there.

She turned her attention to the future, but what she found there was even more terrifying. She would die in the Keep, torn apart by Row's creatures. They would be a constant torment to humanity, but one day they would be eradicated when someone invented an inoculation; Kelsea's vision broadened, and she saw the Tearling, hundreds of years along, a despotic kingdom that had built on Kelsea's legacy and extended its dominance into empire, the entire new world under Tear control. This new Tearling was no better than Mortmesne, bloated with its own power and driven by a sense of superiority so well-honed that it bordered on manifest destiny. And that made perfect sense. The danger of empire, after all, lay in the character of emperors.

"Choose quickly," Tear said, his voice dispassionate.

Kelsea looked back and found that Row's children were on her Guard, moving faster than their blades could follow. One of them finally succeeded in toppling Mace, biting into his shoulder. Kelsea felt a crack open inside her, wide and deep, and she clamped her mouth shut to keep from wailing in grief. Pen went next, his sword no use against the creatures that swarmed his ankles and pulled him down. Within a few seconds, the woman with the bowed head was left unguarded, and they swarmed toward her.

"Even here, time doesn't hold forever," Tear told her. "Choose."

Kelsea turned numbly back to the panorama before her, skipping through the scenes, her mind moving faster than it had ever moved, until she found what she was looking for: Katie and Jonathan, sitting in a dank room. The room was lightless, but Kelsea could see them, both asleep, Jonathan with his head on Katie's shoulder.

"This," Kelsea told Tear. "I choose this."

She held up Finn's sapphire. The Queen of Spades was there, hovering, but Kelsea did not fear her any longer. The things Kelsea could not do, the things that needed to be done, these were her province. Both of them had been born in anger.

Coming home.

"You're sure?" Tear asked.

"Yes."

"Then luck to you, child." He patted her shoulder. "One day, perhaps, when your time is done, we will meet again. I see you have a story to tell, and I would like to hear it."

Kelsea's eyes filled with tears. She turned to thank him, but Tear was gone.

Chapter 15

The Tearling

—*The Early History of the Tearling*, AS TOLD BY

In the dark of the cell, Katie woke with a start from the strangest dream of her life.

She had been talking to Jonathan's mother, the two of them wrapped in mist, not the white mist that covered the Town when autumn crept down from the mountains, but a thick curtain of dark grey. You could stare into that mist for a hundred years, in a hundred directions, and not be able to find your way out.

"I need your help," Lily told her, and Katie nodded; it was only a dream, after all. She should have been afraid, for Lily was long dead, three years. But Katie was not afraid. She had always loved Lily in life, and she could not believe that Lily's ghost meant to harm her now.

This was not to say that this version of Lily was not frightening. From time to time, Lily would blink and Katie would glimpse something else beneath the surface, something terrible. This Lily was not kind, not understanding, but vengeful . . . but Katie did not think it was revenge against her that Lily sought. She hoped not. She felt as though, at any moment, Lily might shed her skin and reveal something entirely other, a black and slumped shape that wore Lily as a mask.

"What kind of help?" she asked, but she was only partly listening. The other half of her mind was tuned back in to the cell, waiting for the click of a key in the lock, the sign that Row had come for them. She thought she would promise Lily anything, if only it would get her out of this place and back to Jonathan. Katie stared at Lily's face, seeking clues, but she saw only a deadly sort of patience. And now she noticed something else: Lily was wearing a crown, a silver circle studded with blue jewels. Row's crown! And Katie suddenly relaxed, because this seemed the most indisputable proof that this was a harmless dream. Row's crown could not be here, on Lily's head. Katie had buried the thing in the woods, and it would remain there forever, unable to harm anyone.

"I need to be here," Lily said. "I need you to allow me to be here."

Katie's brow furrowed, but she nodded, almost in a trance, allowing Lily's voice to drift over her. For a few moments she became confused, thought she was speaking not to Lily but to William Tear; then the world locked solidly back into place and she blinked stupidly as light flared above her head. She had spent hours waiting for the click of the lock, and she had missed it. Gavin and his four flunkies stood above them, all of them holding torches in one hand and knives in the other. Too many for Katie to take, even if she'd had her own knife.

"Get up," Gavin ordered tonelessly. "He wants to see you."

He bent down to take her arm, but Katie shook him off.

"Don't touch me, traitor."

"I'm no traitor. I'm helping to save this town."

She gritted her teeth, wondering how he could be so blind, so stupid. Katie wasn't sure of what the Town needed either, but she knew that whatever it might be, it would not come from Row, who only wanted all things for himself. But Gavin's face was smug and certain. Katie longed to punch him; she clenched her hand into a fist, then froze, puzzled, as her hand unclenched of its own volition. Something shifted, restless, inside her mind, and then was still.

Did I dream? Katie wondered. *Did I dream all of that?*

"Come on," Gavin said. "Follow Lear."

Katie did, wondering why they didn't bind her hands. There *had* been a dream, she remembered now, but she was damned if she could remember what it had been. As she tromped up the staircase—a long staircase, many more stairs than any similar structure she had ever seen in the Town—she felt a thud as something heavy bounced off her breastbone. Tear's sapphire; of course, still tucked beneath her shirt. Jonathan had given it to her, during that long, dreamlike interlude in the dark. Katie wondered whether she was dreaming now. If only she could wake up in her own narrow bed, her book next to her on the bedside table and Mum in the next room. If only that were how this ended.

She glanced at Jonathan and found him pale, but composed. The torchlight flickered and for a moment, every line of his cheekbones was limned in grey, his face a skull. Katie nearly gasped, but remained quiet as she felt his hand twine with hers in the dark.

"We tried, Katie," he whispered, the words nearly inaudible. "We did our best."

She turned to stare at him, but Jonathan was looking straight ahead, focused on the future, hardly noticing that his words had stabbed her in the heart, put her right back in the clearing, fifteen years old, that day when she and Jonathan had been the only ones left behind. If only she could go back there! There was so much they could have done differently, starting with Row. Katie could have strangled him in the woods, buried his body with no one to know.

Tear wouldn't have wanted that.

Tear is dead. Why should he bind us any longer?

There was no answer, only that sense of movement, deep in her mind, a slither of thoughts that were not her own. For a moment the tangle loosened, and a single thought came through

—spades—

and then it was gone.

They reached the top and found themselves in a long, cramped hallway, lit by torches. Katie glanced behind them but saw only the beginning of the staircase, a wide mouth that yawned downward into darkness.

How many people? Katie wondered suddenly. *Row didn't build that dungeon for Jonathan and me. Christ, how many people has he kept down there?*

As they neared the end of the hallway, a long, narrow shadow fell through the doorway and Katie tensed, preparing to go for Alain's knife. He had always been the weakest fighter among them. Even though Gavin would likely knife her in seconds, perhaps she would have the time to put a blade through Row's heart. It would be worth dying herself.

But it wasn't Row. Katie had been deceived by the shadow. The form that came through the doorway was a little boy, less than four feet tall, but Katie had to squint at him for a long moment before she recognized Yusuf Mansour.

"What the *fuck*?" she spat at Gavin. "What have you done to him?"

Gavin looked away, and Katie realized, disgusted, that he didn't even know. The Yusuf Katie knew had been a sweet boy, bright with numbers and eager to please. The creature before her now had Yusuf's face, but that was where the resemblance ended. He was pale, so pale that his skin almost appeared white, and his eyes were dark, fathomless hollows. He did not smile or show any other sign of recognition, only stared at the group, and as they moved toward the door, Katie saw with alarm that Yusuf's eyes were fixed on Jonathan.

The last thing she remembered was walking through the doorway.

R owland Finn had pictured this moment in his head so many times that when it came, he almost expected it to be disappointing. Here was Jonathan Tear, the favored son—oh, and his heart still burned at the unfairness of that; Tear had given the Town nothing—and here was Katie, her head bowed, and that was right too, because Katie of all people should have been penitent—

Katie looked up, and Row felt his equilibrium vanish. The lightest touch of fear seemed to breathe on the back of his neck.

Katie was supposed to be sorry. For years, whenever he had imagined this moment, he had known that first: Katie would be sorry that she hadn't come with him. Her posture was right, cringing and defeated, but her face was all wrong. She stared at him with no expression, her face almost blank, as if with shock. She didn't seem to know where she was.

Row turned to Gavin, who stood nearby with a pathetically eager look on his face. Unlike Katie, Gavin performed perfectly, like a puppet; only shake a string, and he would do as he was told.

"What's the matter with her? Is she drugged? Beaten?"

"No," Gavin replied. "We didn't touch her."

Row dismissed that, turning to Jonathan. "You! Where's William Tear's sapphire?"

Tear raised his eyes, and Row recoiled at the pity on his face. Jonathan Tear did not get to feel sorry for him, not now, not when Row had won.

"You will give it to me," he told Jonathan. "No one is beyond the reach of pain, not even a Tear."

At that, Katie stirred slightly, and Row saw something, a ripple beneath that drugged expression on her face. Then she was still. A distant alarm seemed to go off inside him. It was almost as though she were in a trance . . . but Katie didn't have trances. She had never had any gifts. Row turned back to Tear.

"Give it to me."

"No," Tear replied, almost wearily. "If you're going to kill me, may as well do it now. You won't have it."

Row frowned. He didn't dare actually *take* the jewel; that was the hell of it. His own sapphire worked, but only sporadically, inconsistently, nothing like the power he had felt when he held Tear's jewel. And yet it had never occurred to him to simply kill Jonathan and take the thing. He knew it could not be that easy—nothing ever was—but beneath the knowledge was a deeper certainty: any magic that could be seized by force was hardly worth having. Row had earned his power, had been honing it for years. No one could simply walk in and take it away.

He snapped his fingers at Yusuf, who darted forward, his face twisting in a bestial grin. That grin chilled Row, yet he couldn't help but feel an almost paternal pride. This child, who was no longer a child at all, was his own creation. He had two more under construction, deep in the catacombs he had dug beneath the church, but even these three were nothing compared to what he could make. There would be so many more.

He had hoped that the sight of Yusuf would wipe the pity from Tear's face, but here again, he was disappointed. Jonathan merely stared at the child for a long moment, then said, "So this is what you've been doing in the dark. Even my father didn't think you would stoop this low."

Row clenched his fists. Even now, after all these years, he hated this idea, that William Tear would have talked about him, behind his back, talked about him in the very bosom of that family from which Row had always been excluded. Tear, Lily, Jonathan,

Katie, the Rice bitch, all of them had been on the inside, and he had been out.

He turned back to Katie, who continued to appear almost catatonic. She had stolen his crown; she knew where it was, but Row knew he would not get that information without a fight. Jonathan's pain would be doubly useful here, but now, staring into Katie's muddled eyes, he wondered if she was even capable of understanding that Jonathan was being tortured. Would she even notice?

It wasn't supposed to work this way, damn it! he thought again. *She was supposed to cry! Both of them were supposed to be afraid!*

He snapped his fingers in front of Katie's face, but she ignored him. Instead, she turned to Jonathan, extending her hand, and Jonathan took it. Jealousy, kitten-clawed, scratched its way down Row's spine. He didn't like the way Katie and Jonathan were looking at each other, communicating without talking. Once, that had been the two of them, Row and Katie. In a town that had forgotten him, only Katie had seen him clearly. The longer she and Jonathan kept looking at each other that way, the more uneasy he became, until he finally told Lear, "Break them apart."

Lear grabbed Katie and tugged her away. Katie looked up, and Row took a step backward. Her face was a wild bloom of color, and her eyes had narrowed to bright green slits. In the next moment she leapt across the room and attacked Jonathan.

Row stared at this development, too shocked to respond; he had ordered Gavin to keep an extra close watch on her, assuming that if she went for anyone, it would be himself. But now she was grappling with Tear, climbing his back. Lear and Gavin and the others stood frozen, their mouths gaping, as Katie gritted her teeth and wrapped her arms around Tear's neck. Tear didn't even fight her off, only stood there, gasping for breath, and at the last minute Row realized what was happening and jumped forward, but it was too late. The snap of Tear's neck was almost deafening in the high, hollow emptiness of the church. Katie dropped him, and the body slumped to the ground, eyes wide open and staring.

"God help us!" Gavin shouted, and Row wanted to tell him to shut up—only a fool like Gavin would still believe in God, at this of all moments—but he bit his tongue. He might need Gavin now. Katie stared down at Tear's body, her shoulders heaving, and Row watched her, feeling as though he had never seen her before.

"Katie?" he asked.

She looked up, and Alain began to shriek.

Katie's mouth was open wide, so wide that she appeared to be screaming herself. As Row watched, the hole opened wider and wider, growing in circumference until it seemed that her mouth must swallow her head. Her eyes and nose tipped backward until they seemed to be first on top of her head, then behind it. The open mouth grew into a black hole, and Row watched, frozen in horror, as first a hand emerged, then an arm.

Alain bolted from the room, still screaming, Howell and Morgan right behind him. Gavin and Lear stayed put, but Gavin had drawn into the corner of the pulpit, wrapping his arms around himself, his eyes wide and bruised as he watched Katie transform. Now a shoulder had emerged, and while Row watched, the edges of the hole rippled and a head pushed its way through, and as he glimpsed the face, Row screamed himself. The dead didn't frighten him. He had been dealing with corpses for years. The dead didn't frighten him, but this was no corpse.

This was a ghost.

Lily Freeman had emerged from Katie's form, shedding it as easily as a snake sheds its skin, leaving Katie's behind, a small heap discarded on the floor. Lily was naked, her body streaked with black, like smears of earth, her long dark hair unbound, not the woman Row had known but someone much younger. He had seen this Lily before, in the portrait that hung in the Tears' front room. Several times, Row had snuck in to explore the Tear house when no one was home, and the portrait of Lily had always struck him, though he couldn't say why. However little use Row had for his mother, he had always been able to feel her anger when he looked at that picture, at the wildly happy Lily who had ruined everything, taken everything that the Finns should have had.

Lily was wearing his crown. Row stared at its glinting blue and silver, horrified; he had been ready to commit murder to get it back, even to torture Katie, if it came to that, but he could no more snatch the thing off a ghost's head than he could have taken the jewel from around Jonathan Tear's neck. It might as well have been on the moon.

She turned to look at him, and Row screamed again. The face was Lily's, but the eyes were gaping ebon pupils. Her mouth was hard, a black-edged grimace, as though the lips were lined with soot.

"You were right, Row," she whispered, and that was the worst of all, for the words were Katie's, Katie's voice echoing from the mouth of this filthy apparition. "We don't have room for special people here."

She lurched forward, and Row scrambled away, stumbling behind one of the ten pews that lined the right side of the church.

"No saved people," Lily rasped. "No chosen people. Only everyone, all together."

A shadow darted forward into the light: Yusuf, snarling, his hands up and hooked into claws, and Row felt a wild burst of relief, because even though he didn't understand everything about the child, he knew what it was capable of—

Lily turned on Yusuf and snarled, a sound with no more humanity than the grunt of a pig. Yusuf flinched, as if struck, and fell to the ground, twitching. In the corner, Gavin gave a low moan and wrapped his arms around his head, covering his eyes. Lear was nowhere to be seen; he had collapsed in one of the pews.

"We were such good friends," the apparition whispered, its voice sibilant, the sound of an animal carcass being dragged across stone. "Why do you run away?"

Row turned and dashed down the row of pews, but when he glanced behind him, there she was, at the end of his row, even closer than she had been before. She smiled at him, and he saw that her teeth were needles.

"Katie?" he asked, and then, his mouth full of dark horror, "Lily?"

"Katie? Lily? Ah, Row." It giggled, raising its arm, and Row saw that it was holding a spade, not one of the small gardening tools the Town used at harvest but a broad, flat spade, tall as a man, its head dripping blood.

He fled then, toward the doorway, where blessed sunlight poured in, thinking *God, get me out of this, please, and I'll be the man they think I am, Brother Row, Father Row, anything, only—*

He was no more than five feet away when the doors slammed shut, and he ran into them full speed, bouncing off and falling to the ground with blood seeping into his left eye, a swirl of blackness over the vision in his right.

How can this be? his mind demanded, wild and hectoring. *We planned it so well! They performed so well! How can this be?*

Nearby, he heard the dragging crunch of feet coming closer, and squeezed his eyes shut. When he was a child—he hadn't thought of this in so long—he had been afraid of monsters in his room at night, but if he closed his eyes long enough, they always went away. What he wouldn't give to be back there, curled up in his bed, five years old!

Fingers grabbed his shoulders, their tips like claws, and Row was jerked to his feet. He opened his good eye and found those deep black pupils staring directly into his. When it spoke, its breath wafted through those needle teeth, and it was the smell of the crypts that a thirteen-year-old Row had pried open, looking for treasure, not sure yet what he meant to do but he knew he had the will to get it done, even then—

"I defend this land, Rowland Finn. No one wants to know how I do it, but I do."

Row began to scream.

Katie woke up gradually, with the sense of having slowly broken free of an unfathomable dream.

She was lying on the floor in the middle of the church, just in front of the pulpit where Row had given so many of his sermons over the years. Something cold lay against her chest, and after a moment she realized that it was the silver chain, Jonathan's sapphire around her neck.

Raising her head, she saw a body lying several feet away. It looked like Jonathan, but it couldn't be; the two of them had just come up the staircase. She dragged herself to her knees and crawled over to him, turned him over.

Jonathan's dead eyes stared up at her.

Katie barely felt surprised. A dim corner of her mind murmured that she had always known it ended this way, of course she had, William Tear had told her . . . but lack of surprise did not mute her grief.

A choking sound came from the far side of the church. Katie looked around wildly and saw Gavin, crouched in the corner, his wide eyes upon her.

"What did you do?" she demanded, though the venom in her voice was buried beneath tears. "What did you do to him?"

Gavin shook his head, his face whitening with panic. "Not me! I swear!"

She pushed herself to her feet and strode over to him; as she came, Gavin wrapped his arms around himself and drew into a tiny ball in the corner, his voice breaking with panic.

"Please, Katie, I'm sorry, *I'm sorry!*"

For a moment she hesitated over him, thinking how good it would feel to kill him, how easy and pleasurable and fair—but the thought of Jonathan's corpse, lying behind her, held her back.

She turned and found that the church doors were wide open, a beautiful summer day pouring into the aisle. Outside, she could hear the distant shouts of children at the park. None of it seemed to connect to what she saw in here: Jonathan's body, Gavin cowering in the corner.

We were coming up the stairs, she thought, *and then?*

At the far end of the aisle, near the doors, she saw a wide, dark pool that looked like oil. But when she ventured closer, the smell hit her like a slap, and she saw the lift and buzz of innumerable insects around the puddle, flies and gnats. Near the puddle lay a glimmering object; when Katie drew closer, she saw that it was a blue jewel on a silver necklace.

She turned back to Gavin and asked, "Where's Row?"

Gavin began to sob, and this made her so angry that she strode over and slapped him in the face.

"It's all well and good to cry now, you little shit. What are we supposed to do?"

"I don't know."

Disgusted, she left him and picked up Row's necklace. The chain was sticky with blood, but she wiped it clean with her shirtsleeve, her movements almost absent, clutching the sapphire in her hand. Row should never have had it anyway; it wasn't his to begin with. He had cheated to get it. Her eyes fell on Jonathan's corpse again, and she felt tears leak down her cheeks, not only for Jonathan but for all of it, the Town's ruined potential, so far sunk as to allow whatever had happened here. She bent to Jonathan's body, stroking his hair from his forehead. All those years of keeping him from harm, and this was how it ended. And yet deep down she was confused, for beneath the clear outcome she saw here—Row vanished, Jonathan in a heap on the floor—she sensed that nothing was right. This was not how it ended. Just beneath this, almost seen, was a different ending: Jonathan dead, yes, but she had never seen his body. She had fled, fled and gone, leaving Row and Gavin to whatever hell might await traitors to the Town . . . but even as she tried to make it come clear, this second vision vanished, dissipated in smoke. She had not fled; she was still here, and in the thought Katie felt responsibility descend upon her like a mantle.

"Gavin. Get up."

He looked up at her, his eyes wide and fearful. He was only twenty, Katie thought, and it baffled her that an age that had once seemed so ancient now stood revealed as almost unbearably young. In that moment, Katie thought that she could even have pitied Row, who, after all, had been nearly as young and stupid as the rest of them.

"Get *up*."

Gavin bolted to his feet, and Katie saw that he was afraid of her. Well and good.

"You helped break this town, Gavin."

He gulped, his eyes flicking involuntarily to Jonathan's body, and Katie nodded as she read his unspoken thought.

"No room for Tears, you said. But I'm not a Tear, and neither are you. Neither is Lear, or Howell, or Morgan, or Alain. You helped Row break this place. Now you're going to help me fix it. Do you understand?"

Gavin nodded wildly. His fingers crept up toward his forehead, as though he meant to cross himself. But at the last moment, his hand dropped away, and he stood bewildered.

Waiting for instructions, Katie thought contemptuously. Well, Gavin had always needed someone to tell him what to do. She finished cleaning blood from Row's necklace, using her spit where it had begun to cake, polishing until the sapphire looked good as new. She considered putting the chain over her head, but at the last moment she paused, not sure why; some long-buried fear that demanded caution, that spoke of ghosts . . .

After another moment's thought, she slipped the sapphire into her pocket. In the long years afterward, Caitlyn Tear would think often on this necklace, and sometimes she would draw it out and stare at it. Once or twice, she even considered putting it on.

But she never did.

K elsea woke to a bright, sunlit room.

Not her room in the Keep; she had never seen this place before. It was a room of white-painted walls, small, but neat, with a desk and chair and two bookshelves filled with books. The light came from a large glass window over the desk. A small, exploratory wriggle told Kelsea that she was lying in a narrow single bed.

My room.

The thought came from nowhere, from a distant corner of her brain that seemed to still be half asleep.

Kelsea sat up, pulled the covers back, and swung her feet onto the floor. Sheets, pillows, floors . . . everything in this room seemed incredibly clean. She was so used to the Keep, where boots tracked mud and everyone was too busy to be bothered about it. But someone clearly cleaned this room.

I do, Kelsea thought. Again the thought was odd, alien, accompanied by a flash of memory: sweeping the floor with an old, serviceable broom.

What happened? she wondered. *How did it end?*

"Kelsea! Breakfast!"

The voice made her jump. It was a woman

—*Mum*—

but the sound was muffled, as though she were calling from a floor down.

Kelsea pushed herself up from the bed, and as she did so, she felt the familiarity of this place solidify in her mind. This was her room, ever since she was little. Over there was the door to her closet, which was filled with the sort of clothing she favored: a few dresses for fancy occasions, but mostly comfortable pants and sweaters. This was her desk, these were her books. She lingered beside the bookshelf, looking over the titles. Some of these books she knew, and she pulled them down and opened them, relieved to find words on each page—here was Tolkien, here was Faulkner, here was Christie, Morrison, Atwood, Wolfe—but she did not recognize the editions. They were in good condition, clearly well cared for. She knew these books, even their spines. Some of them she had loved since childhood.

"Kelsea!"

The voice sounded closer, and she cast an almost panicked look at the doorway. Her mind drew a blank.

My name is Kelsea, she told herself. *At least I know that much. My name hasn't changed.*

She hurried over to the closet and pulled out pants and a blue sweater. The floor of her closet was littered with empty boxes, and Kelsea stared at these for a moment before she remembered: of course! She was getting ready to move out, but to where? Her mind felt as though it were filled with mineshafts, tunnels that hid this life from her gaze. She was supposed to be packing up her room, but she had been dawdling for the past couple of weeks, not wanting her belongings to be boxed away where she couldn't get to them.

When she was dressed, Kelsea opened her bedroom door, cautiously, as though expecting to find dragons on the other side. She saw a short hallway with several closed doors, and, ahead of her, a descending staircase. On the wall near the top of the stairs hung a floor-length mirror, simply constructed of glass and wood. She smelled eggs cooking.

"Kelsea Raleigh, get down here this minute! You'll be late for work!"

"Raleigh," she murmured to herself. That was right. There was no Glynn here, no Barty or Carlin, because she had never been fostered; she had grown up her entire life right here in this house, and now she was tired of it, tired of having Mum wake her up in the mornings, tired of having Mum know all of her business. She loved Mum, but Mum drove her crazy. Kelsea wanted a place of her own. That was why she was moving out.

She moved toward the stairs, still half in a dream, but a glance in the mirror brought her to another halt.

Her own face stared back at her.

She put a hand on the smooth surface of the mirror, her eyes searching hungrily. Here was a girl of nineteen, with a round, good-natured face and bright green eyes. A step backward showed that she had a solid, well-fed figure. Not Lily, this woman, her appearance neither pretty nor remarkable . . . and yet Kelsea could have stared at her forever.

My own face.

"Kelsea!"

After a last look, she went on down the stairs.

At the bottom, she found an open doorway leading into a dining area. There were plates on the table, not bulky stoneware but fine ceramic work, blue on white. She touched the edge of one plate and found it smooth.

"There you are!"

She turned and saw Elyssa Raleigh standing in a tiny kitchen that opened off the dining room. She had a spatula in one hand and a plate in the other. She looked frazzled.

"Here, have breakfast!" She shoved the plate into Kelsea's hand. "I've no time this morning. I have to be over at Mrs. Clement's;

her daughter's getting married and she wants the most *ridiculous* dress . . ."

Kelsea took the plate, feeling this lock into her mind, another solid piece of information: her mother was a dressmaker.

"Go, go! You're going to be late as well!"

Her mother pushed her toward the table, and Kelsea sat down. She felt herself drifting, almost becoming untethered. No one would have recognized Queen Elyssa . . . because there was no Queen Elyssa, never had been. Kelsea had never felt less like eating; she could only watch her mother bustle around the kitchen, putting things away, occasionally vanishing through an open door that, Kelsea knew, led to the cold pantry.

A dressmaker, her mind whispered. Kelsea could accept that, but she felt the rest of it, the world beyond this house, looming over her, a vast unknown. Who was her father?

"Time for me to run," her mother said. "Give me a hug."

Kelsea looked up at her, stunned and angry. As though she would embrace this woman, this woman who had done so many selfish things . . . or had she? Kelsea felt suddenly lost, wandering the vast gap inside herself, the chasm between the world she had always known and this kitchen. Queen Elyssa had wrecked the Tearling, but this was not Queen Elyssa. The woman before her was vain, perhaps; Kelsea sensed that this had been a point of contention between them for a long time. But she was no destroyer of kingdoms.

"Kelsea?" her mother asked, frowning, and Kelsea knew that some of what she'd been feeling must have shown on her face.

"I know you're anxious to move out, Kel. I was at your age too. But I will miss you. Can I have a hug?"

Kelsea stared at her for a long moment, trying to push the past away, or at least make some peace with it. She had never been a forgiving person; it was too easy a journey from anger to resentment. But her mind demanded a basic level of fairness, and that fairness said that her mother was no danger to anyone. Could Kelsea really hold her responsible for that other life, when this mother made no decisions, only clothing?

Moving stiffly, as though she were manipulating someone else's limbs, Kelsea stood up and put her arms around her mother, her mother whom she knew so well . . . and yet not at all. As they hugged, she was inundated with a bright scent, something like lemons.

"Have a good day, love," her mother told her, and then she dashed from the kitchen, leaving Kelsea staring at her full plate. A clock hanging over the sink chimed, telling her that it was nine o'clock. She had to be at work at nine thirty.

"But where do I work?" she asked the empty space.

She couldn't remember, but she knew the way to go.

O n the street outside, Kelsea had to pause.

The houses, for one thing. They were so . . . neat. Clean, new-painted wooden houses, set close together, a forest not of trees but of white cupolas and gables, climbing the hillside above. No fences bounded them; many of the yards boasted oak trees, and several had been laid with flowerbeds, but otherwise they shared space. And here, *here* was something Kelsea had only seen through Lily's eyes, in the falsely cheerful neighborhoods of pre-Crossing New Canaan: mailboxes, one in front of each house.

Stunned, almost dazed, Kelsea wandered down their front path to the street. She noted their mailbox, bright yellow, with the number 413 painted on it in red. The street was busy; horse-drawn wagons passed every few seconds, and people hurried by, clearly on their way to work as well. Everything seemed tidy and prosperous, but that made Kelsea think, again, of New Canaan. She saw many good things here, but were they *real*?

Without thinking, she turned right and hurried up the street along with the rest of them, the same route she took to work every morning, but her eyes searched everywhere, looking for answers. She felt as though something had eluded her, something so elementary that her mind refused to acknowledge . . .

She had walked more than half a mile before it hit her. She had passed many people on this street: laborers, dressed in stained clothes and dragging their tools; well-dressed men and women who seemed to be heading for some sort of office; haulers, transporting all manner of goods covered with canvas in their wagons . . . but nowhere did she catch a glint of armor, not even the telltale bulkiness of a cloak that told of armor concealed beneath. And on the back of this realization came another: she had seen no *steel*. No swords, no knives . . . Kelsea peered at the people who passed her, looking for the hint of a hilt, of a scabbard. But there were none.

What did we do?

Obeying the habit of her feet, Kelsea followed the road to its end, then turned left onto a broad road that she recognized as the Great Boulevard. There were the same rows of shops with their cheerful awnings: milliners, chemists, shodders, grocers . . . but something was different, and again, the difference was so fundamental that at first Kelsea could not identify it, could only move forward, footsteps wandering, mind far away. She glanced to her right and came to a dead halt.

The window in front of her was full of books.

Someone ran into her, and for a moment Kelsea lost her balance, before a man grabbed her arm, holding her up.

"I'm sorry," he called over his shoulder, hurrying away. "Late for work!"

Kelsea nodded numbly, then turned back to the window.

The books were arranged in an artful display, several risers ascending in a pyramid shape. Kelsea saw books she recognized— *Filth, The Great Gatsby, We Have Always Lived in the Castle*—but many more she had never heard of: *In This Burning World*, by Matthew Lynne; *Legerdemain*, by Marina Ellis; a host of other books that had never sat on Carlin's shelves. The hand-lettered poster above the display simply read: "Classics."

Kelsea backed up a few feet, being more careful now to avoid the oncoming rush of people heading to work, and was rewarded with another hand-painted sign, this one hanging beneath the awning that covered the shop.

"Copperfield's Books," the sign read.

The shop was closed; the room behind the display was still dark. Kelsea walked up to the door and tried to peer inside, but she could see very little; the door was made of some sort of tempered glass, designed to block light. She had seen such glass in Mortmesne, in the Red Queen's chambers, but nothing like it had ever made its way into the Tearling before. Kelsea backed away and returned to staring at the display. It was a bookshop. Her favorite bookshop. Most of the books on her shelves at home had been purchased right here. It was her favorite place to come on a Saturday afternoon.

A clock chimed somewhere, several streets over, startling her. It was already nine thirty. She would be late for work, and despite her wonder, longtime instinct kicked in and got her moving again; she was never late for work. She hurried up the boulevard, keeping hold of her bag so that it would not bounce against her hip, just as she had done every day since she had graduated school at the age of seventeen . . . and yet something was different here, something so different that—

"Great God," she whispered.

She was standing in the middle of the Great Boulevard, staring down more than a mile of road. She had been here once before, in this very spot, on the day she and Mace first came to the city, and she remembered how the Keep had loomed over them as they approached, titanic, casting its long shadow down the boulevard.

But now there was no Keep.

Kelsea stared down the road for a long moment before she could fully confirm this fact for herself. Where the shadow of the Keep should have been, there was nothing, only the distant silhouette of more buildings where the boulevard rolled over the hilltop. Seeing this, Kelsea turned her head to the right, searching automatically for that other bulwark of the New London horizon ... and found no Arvath.

Kelsea stared at the empty horizon for a long time.

"Carlin, do you see this?" she whispered. And somehow, she thought that Carlin did.

She began walking again, trying to work out what this meant. No Keep, no Arvath ... what did these people have? Who was running this city? She dug in her mind, hoping that it would come up with this answer as well, but nothing came. She would have to fill the blanks in as she went.

"Fine," she muttered. "I will."

Her steps took her to the right now, off the boulevard and onto a narrow street that should have led to the outskirts of the Gut. But even a glance was enough to tell Kelsea that the Gut had changed as well. The warren of run-down, leaning houses and smoking chimneys now appeared to be a thriving commercial district. Neat copper plaques hung outside each door, advertising professional services: an accountant, a dentist, a doctor, an attorney.

What did we do? her mind asked again, and now the voice was Katie's, demanding answers, demanding assessment. But Kelsea felt as though she needed to be very careful here. Demesne, after all, had also looked like a pleasant, prosperous city from the outside.

She was at work.

Kelsea looked up at the structure in front of her, a brick building several stories tall. Each floor had many windows–Kelsea couldn't get used to the sight of all this glass–and the front door was accessed by broad steps, made for many people to climb. Kelsea looked down and found another sign, this one bolted to the ground.

New London Public Library

She stared at this sign for a long time, until the clock chimed another quarter hour and she realized that she had to get moving, that she really was late for work. She went up the stone steps, opened a glass door, and found herself in a cool, cavernous room. These windows must be tempered as well, she realized, to keep out the heat. Everywhere she looked she saw high, stacked shelves of books . . . she could not even begin to guess how many there were. Dimly, Kelsea realized that this was the most extraordinary thing she'd seen today, but she could not wonder at it. It seemed that her capacity for astonishment had been exhausted. She loved this library, but it was her workplace.

She passed behind the checkout desk, which was unmanned—the library didn't open until ten—and went downstairs into the labyrinth of offices on the basement floor. Her coworkers waved to her as she passed, and Kelsea waved back, knowing each of their names, but she did not want to talk to them. She only wanted to sit down at her desk. She was in the m ddle of an enormous project, she remembered now; a wealthy man had died, leaving the library all of his books, and they needed to be cleaned and categorized. It was soothing work.

"Kelsea!"

She turned, and there was Carlin, standing behind her. For a moment, Kelsea thought it was simply another phase of a dream—with some bemusement, she saw that Carlin was wearing the exact same pair of reading glasses that she had always worn in the cottage—but the disapproval on Carlin's face was too familiar, too sharp.

"You're late," Carlin said. Her tone implied that it would have been preferable for Kelsea to be dead.

"I'm sorry."

"Well, it's only the first time. But you don't want to have a second. Understand?"

"Yes."

Carlin disappeared back into the nearest office, closing the door behind her, and Kelsea was not at all surprised to see another plaque on this door: "Carlin Glynn, Head Librarian." After a moment, she continued down the hallway with uncertain steps. She wondered whether she had gone mad. Perhaps this was simply another fugue, another reality that lived somewhere on the far borders of the Tearling she knew.

What if it isn't?

She halted in the middle of the hallway, arrested by this thought. Was it possible? What if the three of them—Kelsea, Lily, Katie—had actually done it, taken past, present, and future and somehow welded them into this place?

Mankind's oldest dream, Kelsea thought, and deep in her mind she heard Tear's voice, William Tear who had seen this place in visions, long before anyone else even knew that the Tearling might be real.

No guns, no surveillance, no drugs, no debt, and greed holds no sway at all.

But was that this place? The idea seemed impossible to Kelsea, to whom even small victories had always come with a price. Even if the world before her eyes was not a dream but solid, surely there would be a downside, something to undercut everything she had seen. Surely there would be a cost?

She reached her office—"Kelsea Raleigh, Junior Librarian"—and when she opened the door she found the far wall piled floor-to-ceiling with books. Old, new, all kinds of books, and at the sight of them something in Kelsea loosened for the first time. She had seen more books today than in her entire lifetime in the Tearling, and surely a world with so many easily accessible books could not be so terrible. But still, something inside Kelsea, that dark twinge of warning, made her grab a battered volume from one of the piles and open it wide. Finding the pages covered with words, she breathed a sigh of relief. Everything she had seen around her today said that she had done it, achieved more for her small kingdom than she could ever have hoped for. Even Carlin would have been proud, if she had only known, but Kelsea did not need Carlin's praise any longer. The Tearling was safe, and Kelsea could be content with that.

And for a while, she was.

The more Kelsea saw of the new Tearling, the better it looked to her eyes. Perhaps it was not William Tear's unattainable dream come to life—there were still subtle gradations of wealth, and human nature made personal conflicts inevitable—but the community was extraordinarily open, with seemingly none of the corruption that had marked the Tearling or its neighbors. There was no traffic, not in drugs or people or anything else. If a man wanted to carry a weapon, there was no law against it, but Kelsea did not see so much as a single knife, except at the butcher shops, and violence appeared to be limited to the occasional fist-fight brought on by too much ale.

Books were indeed everywhere, and the city boasted six different newspapers. There were no homeless; though some were wealthier than others—doctors in particular commanded a good living—everyone in the city was housed, fed, clothed, tended, and Kelsea heard none of the grumbling that had characterized the later years of the Town. This baseline of care had been the true heart of William Tear's dream, the engine that had driven them all to board the ships, and it hummed merrily along here, unquestioned, enshrined in the community.

Nor was New London the only such city; replicas of William Tear's prototype now stretched across the new world, loosely governed by a parliament that seldom convened. There was no Mortmesne, no Cadare. Even if Evelyn Raleigh had once existed, she could never have become the Red Queen.

In the days that followed, Kelsea visited the parliamentary building, which was seated not far from the old site of the Arvath; the University of New London—from which she herself had graduated, not so long ago; and, last and most strange, the Tear Museum, a two-room exhibit, open to the public, which was housed near the old warehouse district. There Kelsea listened to an overenthusiastic tour guide tell the story of the Crossing; of William Tear, who had led them across the ocean; of Jonathan Tear, who had been murdered by a traitorous adviser, Row Finn. This adviser had been subsequently hacked to death by Jonathan Tear's guards, putting a quick end to his rebellion.

Kelsea was only half listening. On the wall of the first room hung a row of portraits, many of which she recognized: William Tear, looking as though he would rather be anywhere else; Lily in the field with her bow, looking backward even though the future was still ahead of her, wide open; and Jonathan Tear, his face impassive, dark eyes dim with worry. Only the last portrait was new to Kelsea, and she hung back from the group, staring at the picture for a long while, as the tour guide's bright, merry voice poured over her.

"Caitlyn Tear, first and only Queen of the Tearling! She ruled for a very long time, until the age of seventy-seven."

The portrait was not the same one Kelsea had seen in the Keep, not even close. This Caitlyn Tear was older, her face prematurely lined, her mouth taut. Her hair was still as long and lustrous as ever, hanging loose down her back, but she wore no crown. A forbidding woman, Kelsea thought, one who laughed very seldom, if ever.

"Queen Caitlyn helped to write the Tear Constitution, and many of our current laws come from the time of her reign. It took her more than fifty years to design and build the Tear Parliament, but when she was seventy-seven, she finally handed over her government to Parliament and stepped down from the throne. The Tearling hasn't had a monarch since!"

Kelsea absorbed this information quietly; it was not the ending she might have foreseen, but in hindsight it made perfect sense. A constitution and a parliament . . . it seemed a marriage of the best of pre-Crossing England and America. Katie might not have known that, but Lear would have, Lear who was a student of history. Katie would have needed all five of them, Gavin and Howell, Lear and Alain and Morgan, all of them with their different gifts. Kelsea found that she liked that, liked the thought of the five of them spending the next sixty years atoning for their crimes. Not many lifetimes, only one. It seemed fair.

"Her jewels are still right here!" the tour guide said breathily, indicating a display case that ran the length of the room. Kelsea peeked over her shoulder and saw them there: two sapphire necklaces, lying on a field of blue velvet. Unreality washed over her, and she had to clutch the edge of the glass case for a moment before she backed away.

When the tour ended, Kelsea followed the tour guide from the room, glancing uneasily back at the glimmer of sapphire in the sunlight, but it was already too late. Somewhere inside her, an alarm had gone off, the same alarm she had felt that first morning in the library. In her long history with these two jewels, they had always been double-edged, and though they no longer belonged to her—might never have belonged to her—they remained an uneasy reminder that nothing was easy. There was always a cost, and for the first time in many days Kelsea thought of Mace, of her Guard. Were they out there, somewhere? Some of them might never have been born; she had absorbed enough of Simon's talk on the butterfly effect to understand that. But if Carlin was alive, perhaps some of her Guard might be too. Mace and Pen, Elston, Coryn and Kibb . . . she would give anything to see them again.

But could she find them? As she emerged, blinking, into the sunlight, and surveyed the broad horizon of the city before her, Kelsea felt daunted. It was a bigger world, this New London, and there was nothing comparable to the Queen's Guard. Swordcraft was not valued. Her guards might not stand out at all.

But how could she not try? Something extraordinary had happened, a schism in the timeline of the world, and Kelsea suddenly realized that, more than anything, she had been longing for someone to talk to, someone who had been there with her. She still remembered the past, and if she remembered, surely others would as well. Even if they didn't believe her about Katie and Row and the rest of it, they could at least talk about the Keep, about old times, about the world they all knew.

Two days later, she saw Pen.

She was at the grocer, looking for grapes—though it was early for them to be in season—when she caught sight of him, walking past just outside the window. Her heart gave a great leap and she dashed out of the grocer, shouting his name.

He did not turn around. He had a leather rucksack slung over his shoulder, and Kelsea followed the rucksack through the crowd, calling after him. He did not seem to hear her, and this made Kelsea wonder all over again if she were crazy, if this was only the most extensive and vivid dream anyone had ever had. Finally, she caught up with him and grabbed his shoulder.

"Pen!"

He turned and looked at her with no recognition at all. "I'm sorry?"

"Pen?" she asked uncertainly. "Isn't it you?"

"I'm sorry," he repeated, "but I think you've mistaken me for someone else. My name is Andrew."

Kelsea stared at him for a long moment. It *was* Pen, in every detail . . . but he had a different name.

"I wish you a good day," he told her, patting her shoulder, and then turned and walked away.

Kelsea followed. She was not foolish enough to approach him again—the lack of recognition in his face seemed to have frozen her heart—but she could not just let him disappear, not once she had found him. Keeping well back, she followed him through several streets, until he turned in at a small stone cottage, set well back from the road. As he headed up the front steps, a door opened, and Kelsea saw a woman standing there, a pretty blonde woman with a baby balanced on one hip. Pen kissed her, and they went inside and shut the door.

Kelsea stood for a long time, staring at Pen's house. She had never felt so alone in her life, not even in the cottage with Barty and Carlin. Barty, at least, had loved her. Perhaps Carlin had too, in her own way. But Pen did not know her. He had never known her. And now a truly horrible thought struck her: what if all of her Guard were this way? What if all the people who had loved her, fought with her, taken care of her, would think of her as a stranger now? She had always told Mace that she would be willing to sacrifice anything for her kingdom, but here was a price she had never considered: being alone.

Eventually, she turned her steps from Pen's cottage and forced herself to walk away, back toward home. She had been busy lately, preparing to move out of her mother's house and into a tiny flat closer to the library. It would be the first home she had ever had to herself, and the idea had thrilled her . . . but now all of her bright pleasure in having a place of her own seemed as ersatz and meaningless as a rainbow. For a rogue moment, she wished she had died in the Keep; at least then she would have had all of them around her. They would have been together.

Twice more she went back to the Tear museum, to stare at the glittering sapphires in their case. Even through glass, Kelsea's fingers itched to lay hold of them, to take the jewels and reset everything, even wreck the kingdom, if it came to that, if only she could have her life back again, her family around her—

She had not returned to the museum for a fourth visit, but it didn't matter. The damage was already done.

Over the next few weeks, without even meaning to, Kelsea began to ask her colleagues at work if they had ever met a man named Christian. She had thought it would be a common enough name, but it turned out not to be; there were few churches in New London, and at any rate the name seemed to have fallen out of favor, even among the devout. Kelsea didn't know why she was looking for Mace; even if she found him, it could only mean a repeat of the same terrible scene she'd had with Pen. But she felt that she had to know. Some of her Guard had never been born, perhaps, but some of them might still be out there, and knowing that, Kelsea could not leave it alone.

It turned out that even in this New London, Mace cut a recognizable figure. It took Kelsea only a few inquiries to discover that a man named Christian McAvoy was the head of the city constabulary. This Christian McAvoy was a big man, well over six feet tall, and he was generally considered an excellent police officer, hard but fair. You didn't want to lie to the man, for he would always know.

For two weeks, Kelsea dithered. She wanted to see him, but did not want see him. She was drawn to the idea, yet terrified. But in the end she went.

She went on her lunch break from the library, taking a taxi wagon across town. She would not bother Mace, she told herself; she only wanted to see him. It would do her good to see him, to know that he truly existed, that he, like Pen, was happy in this new place. That Kelsea had done him some good. She did not want to disrupt his life. She only wanted to see him.

But when the time finally came, when the tall man with Mace's face emerged from the police station and looked straight through Kelsea, as though she didn't exist, she knew that she had made a terrible mistake. All of the strength left her limbs. She was standing just across the street, on the stairs of the building opposite the station, and as Mace hurried down the street, she collapsed onto the stairs, burying her head in her hands.

I remember them all. I remember them all, but they don't remember me. They never will.

The idea was so hopeless that Kelsea began to weep. She had bargained for this, she told herself; she had done a great thing, an important thing, more important than any one life. Her kingdom was now a thriving economy, with open trade and a free flow of information. The Tearling had laws, codified laws, and a judiciary to enforce them. Church had been cleaved from state. The kingdom was dotted not only with bookstores but with schools and universities. Every worker earned a living wage. People raised their children without fear of violence. It was good, this country, and all Kelsea had been forced to trade for it was everything. She suddenly remembered yelling at the Fetch, telling him that he had deserved his fate: to watch all of those he knew and loved die around him. She hadn't known, hadn't understood. She sobbed harder, so lost that at first, she didn't feel the gentle hand on her back.

"Are you all right, my child?"

Kelsea wiped her eyes, looked up, and saw Father Tyler.

"It's all right for you to be here," he assured her, mistaking her look of alarm. "God's house is open to all, especially the grieving."

"God's house," Kelsea murmured. She hadn't even noticed the tiny cross on the roof of the building behind her. Father Tyler's face was pale, but not the thin, starved pallor that Kelsea remembered; she would wager that this Father Tyler was no longer an ascetic. He bore little resemblance to the timid, frightened creature of the Arvath.

"Would you like to come inside?" he asked. "Even for a few minutes, to get out of the sun?"

Kelsea did want to, but she knew that she could not. Father Tyler treating her as a stranger as well . . . it would be more than she could bear.

"God's house is not for me, Father," she said heavily. "I am not a believer."

"And I'm not a Father," he replied, smiling. "I'm just a Brother. Brother Tyler. This is my church."

"What is your church called?"

"It has no name," Father Tyler—she could not think of him as Brother—replied. "Parishioners come whenever they want. I give sermons on Sundays. Sometimes we go out and do good works."

"Bully for you," Kelsea muttered uncharitably. She would have given her entire world to see Father Tyler, but all she was left with was Brother Tyler, a smiling man of God who didn't know her from Adam.

"Who do you grieve for?" he asked.

"It doesn't matter."

"Of course it does." He sat down beside her, wrapping his arms around his knees. Kelsea would have wagered house and lot that he no longer suffered from his terrible arthritis, and wondered how that miracle had been achieved. But of course, the Tearling was now full of doctors. Central New London even had a hospital.

"Have you lost a loved one?"

Kelsea hiccupped laughter, for it was somehow worse than loss. Everyone around her continued, oblivious, happy in this new world. She had not been left alone so much as left behind, and she could not imagine a loneliness more vast.

"Tell me, Father," she asked, "have you ever met someone who lost their entire life?"

"Yes, but never someone so young as you. And that makes it a tragedy."

"What do you mean?"

"How old are you, child? Eighteen, nineteen?"

"Nineteen."

"Well, there it is. You're a healthy young woman—you are healthy, aren't you?"

Kelsea nodded.

"You're a healthy young woman, with your whole life ahead of you, and yet you sit here weeping for the past."

I've already lived my life. But Kelsea did not say it. She had not burdened Pen or Mace with the past they could not know; she would not burden Father Tyler either.

"The past colors everything," she told him. "Surely a man of God and history knows that."

"How do you know I'm a man of history?"

"A guess," Kelsea replied wearily. She was in no mood for this, for tiptoeing around a man she had once known well, pretending not to know him at all. She lifted her bag onto her shoulder.

"I have to go, Father."

"A moment more, child." His keen gaze swept over her. "You've lost everything, you say."

"Yes."

"Then look around you." He swept an arm before him. "All these people. Surely you should be able to find something new to care about."

Kelsea blinked, alarmed at the optimism in his words. How could anyone possibly be that resilient?

"Your advice is good, Father," she finally replied. "But it's advice for someone else. I thank you for the place to rest."

"Of course, child." He waved toward the building behind him. "You are welcome at any time, to come back and talk."

"Thank you."

But Kelsea knew she wouldn't return, and she didn't look back as she descended the church steps. She still felt slightly dizzy, as though the ground had been yanked from under her.

All of these things that are gone now . . . where did they go? Are they still out there somewhere?

She wished she had not come to the police station. Only pain had awaited her there, just as she had known it would. Even Mace was lost to her now.

Surely you must be able to find something new to care about.

But what could that be? She had already achieved her life's great work. She had saved the Tearling, and now she was no longer a queen, only an ordinary young woman. There were no more heroics to be done. What could she possibly do as Kelsea Raleigh? She liked her job at the library; she loved her little flat. Was that everything? How could it not be an empty life, after watching kingdoms rise and fall?

There are upsides, too, her mind remarked, in a flat, dry voice that Kelsea recognized as Andalie's. *No one wants to murder you now, do they? You haven't killed anyone yourself. You've been cruel to no one.*

True. The Queen of Spades, the shadow of vengeance that had fallen over Kelsea almost from the moment she had taken her throne . . . she was gone, buried in the distant past. Kelsea could feel her absence, like a splinter that had been withdrawn, and she felt certain—as certain as she could be of anything in this new world—that the Queen of Spades would never trouble her again.

There was gain there, great gain, perhaps . . . but Kelsea did not trust herself to see it clearly. The past stood in the way.

At the junction of the Great Boulevard—now called Queen Caitlyn's Road—Kelsea climbed down from the wagon and began the slow walk back to work. Checking her watch, she was relieved to see that she had plenty of time. She had not been late again since that first morning, and Carlin had stopped checking her watch when Kelsea walked in the door, which was a relief. Carlin had not changed in the slightest; Kelsea wanted her approval badly, but Carlin was going to make her earn every inch. Just like old times. Kelsea felt tears threatening again, and walked faster. But beneath the tears, Father Tyler's words beat against her brain.

Your whole life ahead of you.

She wished this idea would simply go away. To let go of the unrecoverable past and attempt to grasp a future . . . that would take courage, far more than she possessed. The past was too much a part of her.

You've got guts, Queenie, Arliss whispered in her head.

That was true; she had always had guts. But what she needed now was a concussion. How could she forget everything and start again, here, in this normal life?

She turned up the library walk, miserably aware that she was crying again. She dug in her bag, but she hadn't even been smart enough to remember a handkerchief.

There was worse to come: Carlin was on the library porch, sitting in one of the chairs. She liked to eat her lunch outside when the weather was cool, and so the rest of the staff generally avoided the porch on principle. Kelsea tried to walk past as quickly as possible.

"Kelsea?"

Murmuring a curse inside her head, Kelsea turned back.

"What's happened to you?" Carlin asked.

"Nothing," Kelsea replied, ducking her head, and in that moment she realized that it could almost be true. Nothing had happened, nothing real outside her head . . . but could she ever accept that? She wiped her streaming eyes, then jumped as she felt Carlin's hand on her shoulder.

Of all of the odd moments Kelsea had experienced in the past weeks, this was perhaps the most unsettling. There was no tenderness in Carlin, never had been; she never touched anyone, except to discipline. But now, the hand on Kelsea's shoulder did not pinch, and when she looked up, she found that Carlin's stern, lined face was kind. Astonished, Kelsea suddenly realized that in this new Tearling, anything could be different. Even Carlin Glynn could change, become someone else.

"Kelsea?"

Swallowing her tears, Kelsea took a deep breath and squared her shoulders. She was not a queen but a normal girl, a good citizen of the Tearling . . . her kingdom, which no longer needed saving, which had been made whole.

"Kelsea, where have you been?"

Acknowledgments

Anyone who doubts the need for editors in publishing has never had a good editor. This book was by far the most difficult and demanding writing I've ever done, and at several points I would have been quite happy to destroy it and never write anything again. My good friend and editor Maya Ziv hung with me through the long, messy process of turning an ugly first draft into a book I can be proud of, and any failings that remain in the final draft are those of my own imagination. Maya only made me cut a few of the dirty words too!

I am doubly fortunate to have not only a great editor but a great agent. Thank you, Dorian Karchmar, for always believing the Tearling was worth a lot of work, and no small amount of trouble on the side. There's more than one Mace here; I appreciate the fact that you kept me safe, both personally and professionally, while I wrote these books. Everyone else at William Morris Endeavor has been unbelievably good to me as well; thank you to Jamie Carr, Laura Bonner, Simone Blaser, Ashley Fox, Michelle Feehan, and Cathryn Summerhayes.

Thank you to everyone at HarperCollins, but particularly Jonathan Burnham, for giving me the extra time I needed to finish this book right. Thank you also to Emily Griffin, continuity wizard Miranda Ottewell, Heather Drucker, Amanda Ainsworth, Katie O'Callaghan, Virginia Stanley, and Erin Wicks, for all of your help over the years, as well as plenty of tolerance for my, ahem, troublesome idiosyncrasies.

Thank you to the many kind people at Transworld Publishers, particularly Simon Taylor, Sophie Christopher, and Leanne Oliver. Good people all, very nice to the uncouth American in their midst.

Both family and friends have been supremely understanding about the Mr. Hyde I reveal under deadline. Thank you to my husband, Shane, for helping me keep my sanity—and not losing your own!—while I was under tremendous pressure. Thank you, Dad, for never telling me to settle down and quit studying the humanities. And most of all, thank you, Christian and Katie, for being you.

As always, I am deeply grateful to all libraries and independent bookstores out there for their great love and support for these books, but I would like to give a particular shout-out to Copperfield's Books in Petaluma, and to fantastic employees Amber Reed and Ray Lawrason, who steer me toward good books.

M y final word is for the readers.

The Tearling is not an easy world, I know. Contrarian that I am, I am determined to make this kingdom echo life, where answers to our questions are not delivered neatly in a beautiful expositional package, but must be *earned*, through experience and frustration, sometimes even tears (and believe me, not all of those tears are Kelsea's). Sometimes answers never come at all. To all of the readers who stuck with this story, understanding and sometimes even enjoying the fact that the Tearling is a gradually unfolding world, full of lost and often confounding history, thank you for your faith in the concept. I hope you feel that your patience was rewarded in the end.

Now let's all go and make the better world.

About the Author

ERIKA JOHANSEN grew up in the San Francisco Bay area. She went to Swarthmore College, earned an MFA from the Iowa Writers' Workshop, and eventually became an attorney, but she never stopped writing.

THE FIRST TWO VOLUMES OF THE
THE QUEEN OF THE TEARLING TRILOGY

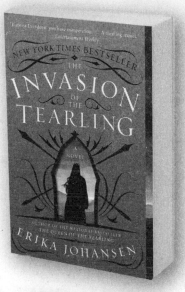

THE QUEEN OF THE TEARLING
A Novel
Volume I

THE INVASION OF THE TEARLING
A Novel
Volume II

"Magic and madness, sacrifice and greed, hope and resignation, so many gripping themes are explored in one of the most original and well-written series in recent memory."
— *USA Today*

"A fantastic trilogy."
— *Booklist*

"Katniss Everdeen, you have competition."
— *Entertainment Weekly*

For more details, visit: www.facebook.com/QueenoftheTearling
www.queenofthetearlingtrilogy.tumblr.com

Available in Paperback and eBook wherever books are sold.